The Infinite Passion of Life

Stories of Love, Life, and Passion in Northern Italy

THE ROCK & THE ROSE BOOK 1

D.J. PAOLINI

KDP ISBN: 978-1-7361195-0-1
IngramSpark ISBN: 978-1-7361195-1-8
Mobi ISBN: 978-1-7361195-2-5
ePub ISBN: 978-1-7361195-3-2

Library of Congress Control Number: 2020922569

Cover and interior design: AuthorPackages.com

First printing edition 2020.

Rock & Rose Press
29 Windham Drive
Eastampton, NJ 08060 USA

www.theRockandtheRose.com

ACKNOWLEDGMENTS

Who knew writing a book could be so hard? Or so rewarding? Or even a tonic for the times? I do not know if many people decide on their sixty-fifth birthday that they should write their first novel, but I wholeheartedly recommend it. Especially if you have the kind of inspiration and assistance that I had available to me. I needed it; in March 2020, I had finished the first draft of a novel set in June 2020—and then the world turned upside down. I commenced a mad scramble to reset the timeline to June 2017. Thankfully, I had substantial timeline metadata to ease the work—techniques I leveraged from my data modeling background.

I must thank two data-modeling (yes, data-modeling) colleagues for getting me into this. I always thought writing novels was something that, you know, authors did. I wasn't an author; I just wrote stuff. That was until I read Graeme Simsion's wonderful book, *The Rosie Project.* It was not so much "if he could do it, so could I"—I could only hope to write as well—it was that the idea became palpable. Then another data modeler extraordinaire, Steve Hoberman, he of the self-made technical publishing empire, provided me encouragement and guidance for navigating the fascinating world of "I wrote it; now what?"

What you see before you would be just as terrible as the dozen drafts that came before—were it not for the assistance of my editors. If you ever have an idea for a book and want to make sure you are headed in the right direction, I encourage you to work with my development editor, Julie Mianecki. Julie provided invaluable assistance in scoping the first book and framing the series concept. She understood the characters, sometimes better than I did. Julie helped make it a story. But the story would have been buried in typos, errors, and clunky prose if not for the efforts of my copy editor, Tiffany Tyer. Not only did she clean up my cluttered mess, she found ways to describe actions and present dialogue that made the story readable. Anything worth reading in this book is due to their efforts; any mistakes or tongue-trippers that remain are mine.

I was also fortunate to have a dedicated corps of beta readers. Their many contributions are interwoven throughout the book. I am forever grateful to the core of the corps: Tina Pastor, Deborah Phillips, Barbara Bunkle, and Jessica Costanzo—who provided substantial feedback about the characters and the tone and caught numerous continuity errors; Kevin May and Nate Hirschman, who provided significant assistance with Italian idioms and language; and, Andy Rowan, who helped develop the concept for the map in the front matter.

One of the tenets of The Rock & the Rose series is that historical events are accurately described. Another is that real locations are accurately portrayed. A third is that language and idioms are accurate and representative of Northern Italy. Besides the usual sources, I was fortunate to have access to the good people at *Italy Magazine* and *The Local*, as well as Gabrielle Euvino's incredibly useful and entertaining book, *What They Didn't Teach You in Italian Class*. If you would like to learn more about the twentieth-century Italian feminist movement, I urge you to read Luci Chiavola Birnbaum's well-researched book, *liberazione della donna: feminism in Italy*. But my best research source was our walks around Rimini. I extend my deepest appreciation to the citizens of Rimini for their hospitality during our visit in 2019.

I was most fortunate to have support and feedback from my family—a half-dozen who served as beta readers. In addition, my daughter Kelsey put her Italian skills to work early in the project. But this book would not have been possible without the love, support, and inspiration I received from my wife Patty. She is my soulmate, *the* alpha reader, and a world-class traveling companion. Not only did she encourage me when I wondered—often—just what had I gotten myself into, *lei è il mio angelo divino.*

"A different language is a different vision of life."

—Federico Fellini—

For Patty, ovviamente.

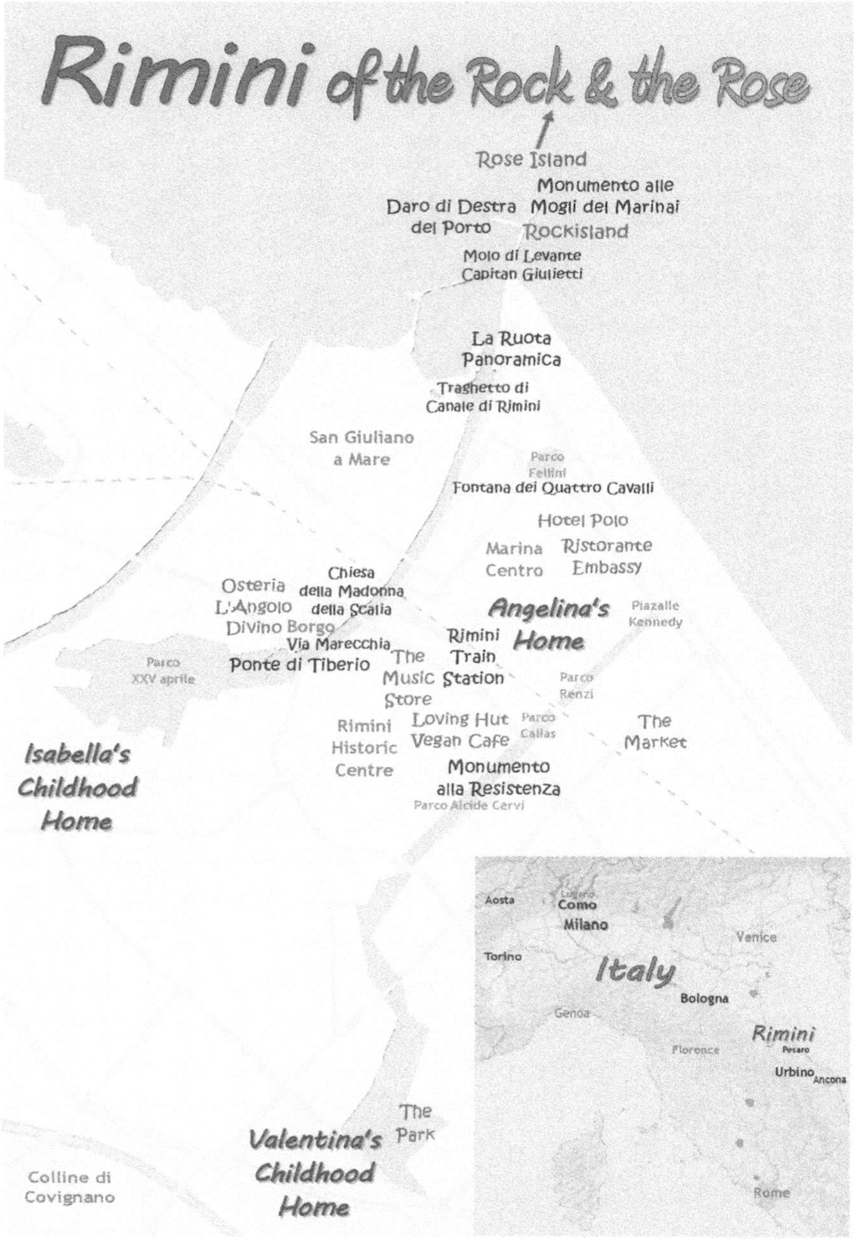

Rimini of the Rock & the Rose

Rose Island
Monumento alle Mogli dei Marinai
Daro di Destra del Porto
Rockisland
Molo di Levante Capitan Giulietti
La Ruota Panoramica
Traghetto di Canale di Rimini
San Giuliano a Mare
Parco Fellini
Fontana dei Quattro Cavalli
Hotel Polo
Marina Centro
Ristorante Embassy
Chiesa della Madonna della Scalia
Osteria L'Angolo Divino Borgo
Angelina's Home
Piazalle Kennedy
Via Marecchia
Rimini Train Station
Parco XXV aprile
Ponte di Tiberio
The Music Store
Parco Renzi
Rimini Historic Centre
Loving Hut Vegan Cafe
Parco Callas
The Market
Isabella's Childhood Home
Monumento alla Resistenza
Parco Alcide Cervi

Aosta
Lugano
Como
Milano
Venice
Torino
Italy
Bologna
Genoa
Rimini
Pesaro
Florence
Urbino
Ancona
Rome

The Park
Valentina's Childhood Home
Colline di Covignano

PROLOGUE

The Lovers

"I do not insist," answered Don Quixote, "that this is a full adventure, but it is the beginning of one, for this is the way adventures begin."
— Miguel de Cervantes Saavedra —

If Valentina had realized how the next five minutes would change her life, she'd have been anywhere but where she was: under the sheets with her best friend and lover, Isabella. The two teenagers were kissing and giggling, sharing terms of affection in their native Italian.

"*Ti amo, mia principessa.*" As Valentina gazed at her princess, the object of her love, she'd never been more certain of anything.

"I wish I could be as strong as you, my knight"—Isabella caressed Valentina's face—"my protector."

"And I as sweet as you, little princess."

***

On the ground floor, the older couple unlocked the front door to their Rimini home and trudged in with their bags. They were home several days early from their holiday visit with family in Bologna. Their premature return had been provoked by yet another in their never-ending series of pointless arguments the previous day—New Year's Day 1982. As they hung up their winter coats, the woman suggested that her husband tell their daughter they had returned.

"*Siamo tornati a casa.*" He spoke to the ceiling—it did not answer.

"Maybe she is out with her friends," said his wife.

Before he could reply, the man heard muffled talking and laughing coming from an upstairs bedroom. He'd been dreading this moment since his daughter Isabella turned thirteen five years ago. He had done everything he could to discourage her interest in boys, and theirs in her. Seeing the anger in his eyes as he turned toward the staircase, his wife put a hand on his forearm. He shrugged it off. As he climbed the stairs, the giggling and talking became louder. When he heard the two distinct voices engaged in intimate conversation, it confirmed his efforts had been unsuccessful.

This is what happens when I do not watch my daughter like a cat, he thought. He entered her room as she glanced up.

"*Papà!*" was all she could manage.

"What are you doing to her?" He spoke to the man's back. Unlike his daughter, he was not at a loss for words.

He said to his daughter, "I trust you to be home alone, and you repay me by fornicating with this—" He stopped mid-sentence as the man stood up and turned… into a woman!

"*Che schifo!*" He need not have said it—disgust etched his face. "This is sinful—it is unnatural!" He first pointed at his daughter, then waved his arms to the side as if he wished it would all go away. He pointed at the intruder and said, "You are evil. Leave my house!"

As her father pointed at the doorway, Isabella sat up and leaned forward, supporting herself on her balled fists, dread and anguish on her face as if she feared she would die. "Papà, no, we are in love. We want to be together—we need to be together!"

"You are women; you cannot be in love. This must be the devil's work. I will not permit it. Leave!" His rapid-fire cadence was like a machine gun, with a similar effect on his daughter. His hands had moved as if he was conducting an opera.

He turned and stared at this strange woman, still nude, who even barefoot was taller than him. She had blue eyes, like Isabella. Her dark-blonde hair was darker than his daughter's. The woman offended him—not her appearance, but what she was, and what she'd done to his daughter. She also intimidated him, which only made him angrier. He wondered if she might attack him. Instead, she donned her blouse then pulled up her panties.

"I am sorry, signore. I love your daughter, and I did not mean to upset you. You and your wife should discuss this with your daughter." The woman finished dressing with a calmness that matched the explanation she had just provided.

"*Basta!*" he yelled. "I need not talk about this with my wife or with her," he said, gesturing at his daughter as he emphasized the last word. "Now, for the final time, get out!"

"I will leave as you request, signore."

The man folded his arms, jerking his head in a see-that-you-do manner he hoped displayed his authority, but waiting until the stranger had turned away and was halfway down the stairs.

Isabella sat whimpering during his rant, but her lover's concession was too much. "*No, protettrice mia!*" She cried out again, "My protector!"

With the stranger gone, the man unfolded his arms and began waving at his daughter. "Go bathe, now! And when you are clean, pray for God's forgiveness and go to bed. We will speak again in the morning."

On the ground floor, he heard the stranger leave through the front door. As he walked down the stairs, he saw his wife wearing her ever present expression of concern. He had not realized until that moment just how much it annoyed him.

"Pour me some Nocino—we need to talk. We have a problem, but I have a solution."

***

"So, it is true?" Valentina asked. They had not seen each other in almost four months, but she'd heard from a mutual acquaintance that Isabella was being married off to a man over twenty years her senior, arranged by her father. She was both grateful and relieved when Isabella reached out to her for this meeting at a sidewalk table in front of the Ristorante Embassy.

"Yes, I am so sorry. Papà has forbidden me to see you, but Mamma told me I needed to say goodbye in person," said Isabella.

"But we love each other, and you do not love him. I doubt very much that he loves you."

"All true… but it does not change matters. I have humiliated my family."

"How does love ever humiliate anything?" Valentina asked.

They sat for a few moments, their eyes doing the only speaking, Valentina wanting to do more, but afraid to say more.

As Isabella sighed, Valentina said, "Come! Leave with me! Live with me! We will move to Roma! Milano! Venezia! We can be safe, accepted in a city. We do not need your family. I will take care of you." She watched as Isabella's eyes grew wide and she shifted in her seat.

"Oh, my protector, a part of my heart—the largest part—wants to go with you, the same part that will become a dark void because I cannot." Isabella shook her head as she spoke, but then brought her hands to the sides of her chin as if to make it stop. "I do not mean to hurt you. If it means anything, I will be in pain forever." She forced the words past her fingers.

Valentina said, "Then why live in pain? Come with me!"

"Oh, Val… for you, it would be easy. You have no family, no ties. I cannot just leave everything and everyone I know. You do not need my family, but I need my family." Isabella sighed, turned away, then returned her gaze. "If I thought my family would accept it, I would live with you in sin for the rest of my life. But they do not… they will not."

"*Mia dolce principessa,*" Valentina replied, "your family might surprise you. Just as love cannot humiliate anything, it cannot be a sin." Valentina raised her palm, open to the sky. "Surely God sees the love in people's hearts, not their genitalia. Come with me, my princess. I love you—we can live as if we were married." Isabella's eyes responded, growing wider than before.

Valentina dropped to one knee. "I promise that I will love you with all of my heart for the rest of my life." Isabella's eyes were now as wide as saucers as she stifled a gasp. She turned away from Valentina and scanned the sky as if looking for permission from God. Valentina had surprised herself with her spontaneous decision to propose; she could not imagine what Isabella was feeling. Neither noticed the stares of bemused passersby.

Isabella returned her gaze to Valentina. "Oh, how I wish!" She buried her face in her hands, weeping for a minute as Valentina returned to her seat. When Isabella lifted her head, she opened her arms wide, shaking her head vigorously from side to side, until she lifted her hands to the sides of her head as if to keep it from shaking off. "If I could accept your wonderful proposal, I would, but it is impossible!"

Rather than console her, Valentina argued her case. "Princess, you know how much I love Cervantes. We have read him together. Do you not remember what he wrote? 'In order to attain the impossible, one must attempt the absurd.'"

Isabella sobbed again, then stopped crying and sat up straight, her jaw set. She inhaled, then sighed. She returned her gaze to her soulmate. "Please stop… Do not make this more difficult." Isabella brought her hands together to plead her case. "I have already accepted a proposal—one as cold, calculated, and dispassionate as yours is warm, heartfelt… and… and passionate beyond measure." Valentina felt her world slipping away.

Isabella said, "Please know I will never forget you, my protector. We cannot be together, but I will love you for the rest of my life." She inhaled and stood. "I am sorry, I must go before my father sees us."

They walked out to the street and embraced. Valentina did not want it to end, knowing that if she let Isabella go, she'd lose her forever. Accepting the inevitable, she surrendered. As they separated, Isabella repeated, "I must go."

"Then I, too, must go. I cannot stay here and survive this."

Valentina stole one last glance at her princess as she turned to leave, struggling with her thoughts. *Some protector I am. But I just made a promise, and I will keep it.*

Valentina could not escape the self-contempt burning her soul as she hurried away, nor the regret for the pain she must have caused her soulmate with her cowardly retreat.

***

Before Isabella could respond, the love of her life turned the corner. Isabella stared at the now vacant sidewalk with a heart just as empty. She feared her blunt refusal had hurt and angered Valentina, but Isabella could see no other choice. Had Valentina known how Isabella truly felt, her protector would never have let go, never have given up. Isabella feared a confrontation between Valentina and her family would only hurt Valentina, and Isabella imagined herself paralyzed in response, unable to help, just as she'd been on that painful night they were discovered.

I am not brave like Valentina. She sighed. Isabella wondered if her lack of courage was a curse, or a blessing.

The day before her wedding, a mutual friend told Isabella that her soulmate had joined the Polizia di Stato and had left for training in Rome. Isabella wept herself to sleep that night, as she would on many of the nights that followed.

ONE

Angelina

It was out of sight—she wished it were out of mind.

Angelina Regina Roselli Fabrizzi awoke before the alarm. She glanced around the bedroom of the cottage—what her family had always called the large house—and took comfort in its familiarity. So many things were changing—she appreciated the simple stability of her surroundings. The home was one of the few detached houses in Brunate, and it had been in her family for six generations. Her mother, Isabella, had gifted it to Angelina as a wedding present, just as Isabella had received it from her mother. With few exceptions, Angelina had vacationed here every summer for the past thirty years. She loved the Lago di Como area, especially Brunate—the balcony of the Alps—as much as her hometown of Rimini.

Her earliest memory was of a summer here when she was three. She loved the water; she loved the trees blanketing the mountains. She loved watching the celebrities from afar—and she loved that everyone wore sunglasses.

At first, the memories brought a smile to her face, but then her mood darkened. She was thirty-three but felt older. The significant tragedy, drama, and financial pressures she had endured the past year—while they'd not yet taken a toll on her physical appearance—were draining the energy from her spirit.

Yesterday was another painful and stress-inducing day. She was in Como to close on the sale of two terrace houses. She'd only learned of her dead husband's complicated financial dealings, debts, and shady arrangements after he died. The first few meetings with an accountant last year were equal parts humiliation and pain. As he unraveled Giovanni's tangled and tortuous finances, the accountant had told her she must sell the two houses. The proceeds would pay off most of his debts and help her get above water. She didn't know how she would replace their income. Financial insecurity was a new and unwelcome state.

She possessed a *laurea* degree in business. Her mother and godmother had insisted on it, against the wishes of her husband and father. She had the degree, but no experience to market, nor any experience "living at the green," as her less-well-off schoolmates had called being broke.

Yesterday at dinner following the closings, her attorney had advised her of a plan that would involve renting her summer home. Not wanting to discuss details at dinner, he'd asked to meet with her again today before she returned home to Rimini.

She showered and dressed. She wore her all-black "widow's uniform," as Valentina had labeled the ensemble. Valentina was her godmother, her housekeeper, and her friend—*my only friend,* she thought as she sighed, acknowledging it was as much her choice as a conspiracy of the universe. She glanced around the house one last time before leaving for her appointment.

Her attorney was also her godfather, Angelo Spallini. He'd been the attorney for the Marvelli family, her mother's parents, for most of his professional career. He had started with the largest firm in Como, and when he'd left to launch his own practice, her grandparents had followed him to become his first clients. The Marvellis were distant relations of the Blessed Alberto Marvelli—still revered in Rimini—and were active in several Catholic lay organizations, both in Rimini and here in Como.

She tucked her long deep-auburn hair under her hat and exited the house. She locked the door, remembering a time when it was unnecessary. As she grasped the handle on her bag and turned, her real estate caretaker and manager approached with his ever-present smile.

"Buongiorno, Signora Fabrizzi*!"* he greeted her, practically singing. "*Mi fa piacere vederti. Come stai?*"

"*Così così,* Carmelo." Angelina smiled, before adding, "And I am happy to see you." Carmelo was always cheerful and interested in her well-being. He was one of life's blessings.

"I am so sorry you must sell your terrace houses. But I feel better knowing you are keeping this house and will still visit us. I will always have it ready for you, I promise."

"I know you will. I just wish I could pay you what I did." Angelina paid Carmelo to take care of the three properties, and he earned commissions on the rentals. "My godfather said I will need to rent this one, so perhaps that will help."

"Signora, please do not tell my wife, but I would take care of your house for free. Your grandfather helped my family when I was a boy, and he gave me my first job. I will never forget."

"And I am forever grateful, Carmelo." *Perhaps I have two friends, she thought.*

As she strode toward the funicular, the brief respite created by Carmelo's greeting evaporated, his last comment triggering conflicting thoughts.

How could my grandparents be beloved by people like Carmelo, yet treat my mother as they did? How could they shower me with affection over the years yet allow my father and my husband to treat me as they had? Her anxiety for this morning's meeting returned.

Her boots clicked on the cobblestones of the narrow street, and the wheels of her small rolling carry-on generated a deeper, more irregular tapping, almost musical. The street was empty of traffic, not even a bicyclist or dogwalker. With the high terraced wall on the uphill side, the trees and shrubbery on the other, and the street still asleep in the morning shade—her boots, her bag, and the birds the only sounds—Angelina took comfort in the solitude. Not that she enjoyed being alone, it was just… easier. And safer. People were so difficult… and mean. She would like to be loved, but she'd never again abide being hurt.

She boarded the bright red-and-yellow funicular carriage. As the tram began its descent, she couldn't shake the symbolism.

I truly am going from the stars to the stable.

The first third of the trip down the mountain was impressive, but the view exploded into a stunning panorama of the lake and town as the carriage passed the first request stop. Angelina gazed at the lake, trying to imprint the vision into her memory, trying to quell the nagging fear that she might not see it again. As the train entered the tunnel leading to the Como terminus, the vision vanished—but not her anxiety.

With the early June sun and the funicular behind her, she set off on the fifteen-block walk to the office for her nine-thirty appointment. She was in no hurry. It was not even eight forty-five, and it was only a twenty-minute walk. And besides, no one in Como was ever on time for anything. When visitors pointed out that all the clocks displayed different times, natives replied, "Why does it matter? We are all going to be late anyway."

She smiled as she approached the piazza Giacomo Matteotti. It always reminded her of Matteo. It also reminded her of Grandfather Giacomo. The voice of her ever-present conscience intruded. *But that was a long time ago, Angelina, in a life far removed from this one.*

Her smile dissipated when she glimpsed the imposing Cattedrale di Santa Maria Assunta, Duomo di Como behind the Como Lago train station, its green dome glowing in the bright morning sun. Historians acknowledged it as the last gothic cathedral built in Italy. Construction had taken almost four hundred years, and like many Catholic churches in Italy, it displayed an impressive collection of art: sculptures, stained glass, paintings, tapestries, and frescos.

The cathedral, with its imposing beauty and wealth, reminded Angelina of her family, of the summers spent here with her grandparents and her parents, Tàmmaro and Isabella. As a child, the story of *La Porto della Rana* had fascinated her. She'd often touch the vandalized carving of the frog at the Door of the Frog for good luck; by the time she was fourteen, she had concluded that the frog ignored her. Perhaps it required its missing head to dispense good fortune. Or maybe without its head, it only dispensed bad luck.

That would explain a lot, she thought mirthlessly.

Voltaire was correct: "God is a comedian playing to an audience too afraid to laugh."

On each visit since her husband's death, she imagined her mother's parents, Giacomo and Francesca, staring down at her with disapproval from the west wall of the church alongside the statues of Pliny the Elder and Pliny the Younger. She continued further along the lake to avoid the church. It was out of sight—she wished it were out of mind.

After turning off the lakefront, she stopped for a few minutes at the Bliss Café for a *pasticceria vegana* and *caffè doppio*. You could not walk through this part of town without tripping over a café. She preferred Bliss for its vegan pastry. Today she wanted extra sugar and caffeine, but what she needed was extra strength and courage. After finishing her breakfast, resolute and refortified, she walked the remaining six blocks to her godfather's office near the government buildings on Via Alessandro Volta.

INTERMEZZO

The Birth of Angelina

"Every man is the child of his own deeds."
— Miguel de Cervantes Saavedra —

Isabella's world was in ruins after her father discovered her with Valentina and banished Valentina from her life. The experience ripped a hole in her heart she knew would never heal. She went through the motions each day—going to school, attending Mass, going to sleep—but often not eating. It was more pain than anyone should have to bear. To make it worse, if that were possible, her father was forcing her to marry Tàmmaro Roselli, the son of one of his business partners.

While she made clear her objections, it never occurred to her to defy her father. Isabella did not have any affection for him, but she'd never disobeyed him. Her final meeting with Valentina to say goodbye was the closest she had ever come to defiance.

I was only following my mother's directive to say goodbye in person.

At least he did not force her to become a nun, like her sister. Ilaria had told Isabella several times the choice had been hers, but Isabella found it difficult to believe their father had not manipulated it. When her younger brother, Santino, had entered the seminary three years earlier, her father could not have been prouder. His pride turned to regret when Salvatore, her older brother, died two years later, leaving behind a daughter—Cristiana—but no sons.

I would have been packed off to a nunnery if Salvatore had provided him with grandsons. Of that, she had no doubt.

Much later, there were days when she looked back and wished that it were so.

***

Born in Rimini in 1940, Tàmmaro Roselli—known by everyone as Maro—grew up in nearby Vergiano during World War II. His family and thousands of other Rimini residents had evacuated to escape the incessant bombing inflicted on the city from all sides and by all sides in the conflict. He claimed to have met the Blessed Alberto Marvelli when he was six, but no one had ever corroborated his account. That did not deter him. He persisted with the story throughout his life until people accepted it as gospel, as is the way with most gospels. Without question, it impressed her father, who was a distant relative of the beatified Alberto.

Maro enjoyed the status his story offered. It did not just influence his approach to life, it became his cornerstone philosophy. He realized it was more important what you told people you did than what you actually did. Maro took direction from the fourteenth-century Florentine poet, Giovanni Boccaccio: "In this world, you only get what you grab for." Maro appreciated Boccaccio's outlook, although it puzzled him why the man had written a book about famous women. What woman could be famous except through the relationship with her husband?

He embellished his life story, creating imagined vignettes describing his family's activities in the resistance during the war and how connected his relatives were with the Cardinal of Bologna. His efforts succeeded because he was a creative storyteller, and because most of the people in his stories were dead. By the time he met Isabella's father, Maro was a minor celebrity in the province.

Maro's first wife had given him a son, now older than Isabella. His son, trying to escape his father's influence, had moved to São Paulo, Brazil, after the death of his mother and never returned. She died in childbirth with their second child, who also had not survived. In the ten years since, Maro had enjoyed the attention of many women: single, widowed, and even married—if the rumors were true.

***

Isabella hated being told of her good fortune for having secured such a famous husband. Rather than sincere congratulations, Isabella knew the comments were equal parts jealousy, envy, and scorn. She understood the only part that fortune played was the fortune of her family and how it was used to entice Maro. Her parents called it a dowry—she called it a bribe. While the Marvelli family was well-off, her mother's mother was a second cousin to one of the richest families in Bologna.

Her husband, like her father, claimed to be a God-fearing man. As much as he professed to love God, he loved more the rites and the rituals, the pomp and the pageantry, and the traditions and the trappings of the Catholic Church. He trumpeted his religiosity to anyone who would listen, and to anyone who did not. Maro made sure his pompous piety was on display whenever he was in the presence of church royalty. She believed her husband would have been much happier had he lived four hundred years ago during the time of the House of Medici.

As I would have been, she thought, then scoffed. *Four hundred years between us would have been perfect.*

Superstitions ruled the lives of both men, so much so that they were almost caricatures. If they had been women, Isabella imagined them marching around giving people *il malocchio*. Instead of giving people the evil eye, both wore large golden *cornetti* to protect from it. She found their practices distasteful and irrational. They cared more for symbolism, such as genuflecting and holy water, than they cared for people. In their code, you might go to hell for not lighting a candle, but it was okay to mistreat your family. Isabella thought herself a woman of faith, but religion played no role in her life. As expected, she attended Mass twice a week—sometimes more often—but out of obligation, not obsession.

Her marriage was disappointing on many levels. She found no joy in the act of sex, but that was of no concern to Maro. He was not her first man, but the two boys who had come before and convinced her of their commitment left as fast as they came. The second led to her meeting Valentina. Besides being her only female lover, Valentina was the only lover with whom she'd enjoyed sex, and the only partner from whom she had received love.

While ten years older than she, her husband shared the same worldview as her father. Her husband reminded her so much of her father that she sometimes imagined it was her father's voice complaining about the most recent meal, the unfinished laundry, or any of a multitude of other faults he either found or imagined. Both shared the same opinion of a woman's place in the world, one espoused by the Church. Each would dismiss them with "It is God's will" whenever she or her mother challenged either in even the slightest way.

Isabella sometimes distracted herself by thinking of the two advantages to Maro's age. The first was that after a few weeks of passion—his, not hers—following the wedding, he seldom bothered her, having lost interest or ability or both. She was fine with that. On the rare occasions interest and ability returned, she thought about her Valentina. She tried not to dwell on the second advantage—that he was likely to die before she did. It embarrassed her each time the thought surfaced, and—to her chagrin—it surfaced often.

Isabella had convinced Maro they should wait to have children until they were financially established, so they practiced birth control—just not effective birth control. They followed the rhythm method approved by the Catholic Church, advocated by supposedly celibate priests who failed to counsel husbands who came home intoxicated that they should not force themselves on their wives during their fertile time. Sadly, priests never told men it was wrong any other time either.

As a result, Isabella became pregnant despite her wishes, and on a mid-September day, less than two years after Giacomo's fateful discovery of Isabella with Valentina, Isabella's daughter, Angelina Regina Roselli, came into the world.

TWO

Angelina

That was the drop that made the vase overflow.

When Angelina arrived, she was greeted by her godfather's longtime assistant, Vittoria. Angelina removed her hat, jacket, and sunglasses, and placed them in the coat closet with her bag. Vittoria ushered her into her godfather's office. The attorney rose from behind his desk and stepped around it to hug her.

"*Angelina, mia figlioccia, come stai?*" he inquired. She knew his enthusiasm was genuine.

"*È una lotta, Avvocato Spallini,*" she replied as she took off her jacket and settled into a chair across the desk from him.

"Of course, it is a struggle. But you are strong and will prevail. And what is with this '*Avvocato Spallini*'? I have known you your entire life. Mother of God, I am your godfather! Have I not told you to call me Angelo? You are my namesake."

He delivered the comment with a smile. She knew it was not a reproach, just a game they played where she displayed respect for his age and stature, and he reminded her they were family. Her godfather projected maturity and dispensed wisdom like an ancient philosopher.

"*Sì, Padrino Angelo.*" She knew he'd accept the compromise as he always did, just as she knew he took great pride in being her godfather.

Okay, three friends, she scolded herself.

His warm smile faded as he spoke. "Angelina, Giovanni had his hands in the dough everywhere." Angelina nodded.

"We finished cleaning up most of his mess, but you still must make several painful decisions. You had to sell the two terrace houses. Of that, there was no question. Knowing its significance, I did not recommend selling your wedding gift." He folded his hands. "But I would not be doing my job as both your advocate and your godfather if I did not advise there is more to be done."

Angelina sighed. She knew what was coming. As she considered it, she imagined herself adrift in the sea—no rescue in sight, and no energy to swim.

Should I let the water win?

She'd always considered the cottage hers, to use whenever she needed to get away—which was more often now. Not that she never rented it, but only as an occasional Airbnb listing, not all season. She listed it at peak demand times when Carmelo had booked the other two properties, and it was always for a short duration when she was not planning to visit.

"Angelina, you must rent your Brunate house regularly, not sporadically. You can no longer think of it as your second home."

Stupid frog! Will this terrible luck ever end?

Angelina was tired of it raining on the wet. She wanted to throw something—preferably the frog.

"But, Godfather, you know how much I love it here. I need someplace to get away."

"*Cara mia.*" Her godfather sighed.

He sounds sadder than me.

"You know you can always come and stay with me and Antonietta. She loves you as much as I do." It was true—Antonietta had told her often that she wished Angelina were their daughter, rather than their own shiftless Marcella.

"I appreciate your love, your generosity. It is such a relief and comfort to know you are there if I need you, but it is not the same. Please do not be offended." She'd never knowingly said or done anything to offend him, but Angelina always worried that she might.

"Angelina…" He unfolded his hands and took a deep breath. "I have a solution. I know it is not what you want, but it avoids the worst case."

He laid out the terms of a rental contract he had drafted between her and Carmelo, or another listing firm should she wish. Her use of the house would be restricted. From May 1 through October 31 of each year, the broker would take priority. Angelina could reserve the house for six weeks the rest of the year, with a few other conditions.

I have a time-share, Angelina realized.

Unable to suppress her whining tone, she lifted her arms, palms up, and asked, "*Stai dicendo che ho una multiproprietà?*"

"Yes, much like a time-share, except you still own it, and you will receive the income after commissions and maintenance. This first contract is through October of next year and then is renewable each year. Either party can cancel it with sixty days' notice, subject to honoring any commitments for the current period."

"Is this forever?" One palm moved to the side of her face. "Will I ever get it back?"

"Under current circumstances, you need to plan for this indefinitely. Even with the sale of the terrace houses, you needed loans to close out Giovanni's 'deals.' We secured the loans with your vacation house—I did not want your home in Rimini at risk." Angelo rubbed his chin with one hand before continuing. "And because of your expenses there, I also recommend you rent out your ground floor room in Rimini, at least during the prime season. Please believe me, this is the best outcome given what you faced. Angelina…"

She expected him to continue, until she realized he was instead expecting her response.

Angelina sighed as she considered the proposal. Summer at Lago di Como was a wonderful time, not so easy to let go. Maybe she'd take her godfather up on his offer to visit. But late autumn and early spring were still exhilarating here. She knew she was unlikely to visit more often than six weeks a year. She decided her advocate had done well by her.

Fuck the water! I am alive.

"Okay, make it happen," she told him.

Angelo appeared surprised, as if he'd prepared for more discussion or pushback, but regained his composure. "Good, I will see to it. You can sign the agreement before you leave, and I will reach out to Carmelo—unless you would care to use someone else?"

"Carmelo, per favore!"

Angelo called to his assistant to print out the rental agreement. While they waited, he shifted into his godfather role.

"Angelina, there is something I must say, so please indulge me. I expected an argument from you about your house—"

"No, Godfather, it is an excellent plan. Thank you for your help." She felt uncomfortable interrupting, but more uncomfortable at his obvious concern and worry.

"That is what I mean. You are strong and decisive. You are a woman on her feet."

Angelina knew he meant her emotional stability, obviously not her financial stability.

"You must feel overwhelmed by the events in your life; these past few days have been especially difficult. Someone with less fortitude would have closed their shop and surrendered, but you did not. You have met every challenge, every drama, every problem." He shook his head. "Yes, even every trauma, with strength and courage."

Angelo leaned on his elbows and placed his chin on the backs of his hands. "I know you question why God has given you these burdens. I do not know why. Perhaps only He does." He lifted his head, and his eyes met hers. "But what I do know is that I am as proud of you as I could be of anyone."

Angelina smiled and said, "*Grazie*—"

"Please let me finish." She nodded, surprised by his misty eyes.

"I believe your bad luck, as you call it, must end. It is time someone broke a lance in your favor. I want you to enjoy life again. Have you been socializing… you know, with men?"Angelina shook her head this time.

"God knows the world could use more romance. You should do your part." He tried to make it a joke. Then, as his tight-lipped smile faded, he added, "Would you ever consider getting married again?"

Why is he asking me this?

She still mourned a man she did not love—and who did not love her. It brought to mind Marianne Dashwood's line from *Sense and Sensibility*—Austen was Angelina's favorite author: "The more I know of the world, the more I am convinced that I shall never see a man whom I can really love. I require so much!"

She—no, her inner Austen—answered him, "No, Godfather Angelo. I could not survive another marriage. The world will need to find its romance somewhere else. But thank you for your support. It means more to me than I can describe."

Angelo inhaled, as if to say more. Instead, he nodded in understanding.

***

Angelina signed the agreement, and after a few more pleasantries, she gave her godfather a long goodbye hug, thanked Vittoria, and walked down to the street. It was not quite eleven thirty. The meeting had taken less time than she planned. Her return ticket was for the 2:10 EuroCity train to Milano. The connection had her home just after six. If she skipped lunch and hurried, she might catch the 12:10 train and get home earlier.

It was only a fifteen-minute walk to San Giovanni station. With the claustrophobic canyon of Via Volta her other choice, she headed toward the broad, tree-lined Viale Varese. Besides trees, the avenue was home to dozens of parked cars, as far as she could see in both directions, many more than her last visit. She'd been on the street in the evening, the deserted parking spaces reminding her of an empty shoe rack after a sale.

Where do all these cars sleep in the evening?

She turned toward the station, Monte Croce rising behind it, her carry-on bag beating a tempo behind her. As she crossed Via Innocenzo XI, the Le Mani sculpture reached out to her. A monument celebrating public service, it was a favorite of tourists and residents alike, which she could not fathom.

She remembered the impression it made when she'd first seen it as a teenager—how could she forget? It was as if the town was trying to grab people with these giant hands to keep them from leaving. She tried to think of her memory as a joke. With Jane Austen still echoing in her mind, she remembered a line from *Pride and Prejudice*: "Follies and nonsense, whims and inconsistencies do divert me, I own, and I laugh at them whenever I can."

She avoided the grasp of the hands, collapsed the handle on her rolling bag, and carried it up the five dozen steps to the station.

San Giovanni. Obviously, they were not thinking about my Giovanni. While it was more concession than joke, a slight smile traced her lips.

After getting the attention of the agent at the ticket window, she determined she could exchange her ticket for the earlier 12:10 EuroCity train. There was one seat still unreserved in first class, and it was facing forward! She accepted it without another thought.

For the second leg, she had a choice: take two regionals, connecting in Bologna, and be home by four, or take the high-speed train to Lecce that should get her home by five. There was an hour layover in Milano for the Lecce train, which, although faster, did not get to exercise its speed until well south of Rimini. But she had no wish to ride the cattle cars, and she could use the layover to get lunch. She completed the ticket exchange and hurried to the platform.

She used the few minutes while she waited to call Valentina. There was no answer, so Angelina left a message telling her of the earlier train and that she'd be home about five. While on the phone, she heard the Brunate cannon reverberate across the lake, announcing to everyone that it was noon, more or less. Her train approached as she disconnected. She moved to the first-class section of the platform and dropped the handle on her bag as the carriages groaned to a halt.

She entered the designated carriage and scanned for her seat. It was mid-car, on the right side of the train as expected—but it was facing backward! She glanced at her ticket, and then at the digital readout above the seat, and realized the empty seat was not hers. Hers was the seat across, occupied by a middle-aged man, not unattractive. She considered the intruder. He was not a tourist, but despite his distinctive Italian shoes, she decided he was not a native either. More like a traveling businessman. *But they are nice shoes.*

She stared at him, projecting the universal signal—*you are in my seat*—but he did not move. When he smiled at her—likely preparing to give her a slick or sleazy pickup line—that was the drop that made the vase overflow. She waved her ticket at him, and the many frustrations of the last few days came spewing out in rapid-fire Italian.

THREE

Benjamin

Not all Americans are obnoxiously self-centered.

Ben LaRocca was upbeat as he entered the first-class car on the 9:10 EuroCity train in Zurich. He enjoyed traveling, which is both how and why he'd ended up living in Europe these past three years. And he never tired of using the European rail network, marveling at its efficiency and quality.

But this trip wasn't just any trip—he was moving to Rimini, a history-laden city on the Adriatic coast of Italy. It had seduced him after he'd spent two working holidays there, the first in the summer of 2015 while writing an article describing the city for an international travel magazine. For his second visit in the fall of last year, he wrote reviews for a travel guide. He was smitten on his first visit and homesick for it after his second.

Last month, his editor at the guide asked if he wanted to develop material for a feature covering the entire Emilia-Romagna region. She did not have to ask him twice. He set the wheels in motion for his relocation.

Ben had moved to Europe from New Jersey as part of a midlife career change, or, as his sister had described it, to start a new chapter. His parents had worried instead that he was running away. If he was honest with himself, there was truth to their concern: he was in pursuit of a personal clean slate. After spending time in Amsterdam, Ben took a position in Milano to reconnect with his Italian heritage and to broaden his writing opportunities.

He was a columnist for a Milano-based English-language news website but kept himself busy with multiple projects. Ben wrote technical documentation, magazine articles, and several short stories. He contributed to multiple travel publications and had finished his first novel. His agent was hawking the completed novel to publishing houses back in New York.

Once in Italy, he'd refined his passable Italian conversation skills while he helped his Italian colleagues hone their English. He liked the urbane Milano and felt a connection to it—a few relatives on his mother's side had emigrated from nearby Cernusco sul Naviglio, a northeastern suburb.

When coworkers asked why he was leaving Milano for Rimini, he provided a plausible explanation—he was seeking a more relaxed atmosphere. He chose not to share that part of the reason for the move was his love for Rimini—the history, the beaches, the nearby hills, and the people. He was uncomfortable being perceived as a romantic. Instead, he explained that in addition to the work for the travel guide, he was doing an in-depth article on the Republic of Rose Island. It satisfied their curiosity.

He wasn't lying—he intended to write the article. Ben believed himself to be truthful always, though it was sometimes difficult to stay "true" to that principle. He'd paraphrase Marlon Brando's character in *The Freshman*: "Every word I say, by definition, is the truth." Most people who knew him agreed. They also agreed that his impression of Brando left much to be desired.

On the trip from Amsterdam, Ben had stopped in Zurich over the weekend to see a friend and wrap up two articles for an expat travel magazine. He'd brought enough clothing and personal items to hold him over for a couple of weeks in Rimini until he could find an apartment and send for his belongings. To be safe, he brought all three pairs of shoes he owned. Today, he wore his dress shoes rather than his running shoes or English walking shoes—he did not expect to be walking much. Ben appreciated the Enzo Bonafè Blakes—they were lighter, more supple, and more comfortable in warm weather.

Besides, they make me feel more Italian.

He located his seat in the second first-class car—*Not the first second-class car*, he joked to himself. As with his impressions, not everyone appreciated his sense of humor, but it amused him. The reservation had him sitting backward on the single-seat side of the car. He liked his personal space, so he appreciated not sitting in a double. Realizing the seat opposite, facing forward, provided a better view, he glanced at the seat reservation display. Seeing it unreserved, he switched places.

He was traveling with a roller carry-on bag, a small duffle, and a backpack. Ben stowed the two bags in the overhead rack as the train began pulling away from the station. He kept his backpack at his feet, but unlike most of his contemporaries, he seldom used his laptop on the train, preferring instead to study people, enjoy the landscape, and take photos with his iPhone. If he thought of something he wanted to preserve for future use, he'd jot a note or record a voice memo on the phone.

The route through the Swiss Alps was one of his favorite journeys. The scenery and vistas were always magnificent, but the mountainsides and meadows in early June seemed to explode in more shades of green than one could name. With just an occasional wisp of clouds in the bright blue sky, the morning sun painted every new valley or peak in succession with a unique combination of light and shadow.

As the train approached Lugano, he gazed at the lake out the opposite side of the car. With the sun overhead, Lake Lugano was a magnificent, sparkling sapphire. On other trips, with cloudy skies, it had reminded him of a somewhat less magnificent emerald. On the far side was the Italian commune of Campione d'Italia. One of the many useless facts rattling if not prattling around in his head was that the town, although part of Italy, sat surrounded by Switzerland, unconnected to the rest of Italy.

That was how he felt sometimes—only it was Italy surrounding him. Having worked hard to develop his Italian-language skills, Ben was totally unprepared for the dozens of regional dialects throughout the nation—let alone the hundreds of micro-dialects. At times moving from one Italian town to the next felt—and sounded—like changing countries.

Ben's lone visit to Lugano had been ahead of his first visit to Rimini, attending the Lugano Jazz Festival with several friends. He'd hoped to glimpse the singer, Caterina Valente, who had retired there, but never even found out where she lived. Ben had grown up listening to her records played by his grandfather and father. When he was in fifth grade, because he'd kept requesting her records, his mother had announced that her Bennie had a crush on Caterina.

After exchanging train crews and crossing the border at Chiasso, the train continued the three kilometers to Como, pulling in on schedule just after noon. As a small group of passengers boarded, Ben gazed out the carriage window at the houses on the hillside opposite the station. A minute later, a tall woman, dressed in black, drew his attention as she strode toward him, scanning seat numbers. She wore a large-brimmed black hat, large black sunglasses, and a short black jacket over an ankle-length black dress with black boots. He remembered the old Hollies song, "Long Cool Woman in a Black Dress."

Thanks to the influence of his father and grandfather, Ben stored in his head an eclectic collection of popular music that went as far back as the swing bands of the 1930s. His mental jukebox began playing the song as the woman approached. Except for the chorus, he recalled no lyrics—just the melody. The singing in the song—in his opinion—was unintelligible, right up there with the golden oldie "Louie Louie." But that was not the reason.

His inability to remember song lyrics was a source of personal embarrassment and frustration. While he knew the music for thousands of songs, he'd never learned the lyrics for most of them. Every so often, a specific lyric created an intense emotional connection within him, but it was the melodies and arrangements of the music that fascinated him. He found it ironic that he could remember the dialogue of scenes from hundreds of movies—many of them obscure—yet he could not remember lyrics that most people knew by heart.

As the woman approached, Ben took her for a Milanese fashionista. With the oversized Dolce & Gabbana sunglasses, for a moment he wondered if she was their "face," Bianca Balti. She stopped and stood next to him. With her sunglasses, it was hard to tell, but he thought she was looking at him. He smiled back just as she began scolding—no, berating—him in Italian. Waving her ticket, she gestured at the digital reservation indicator above his seat. Ben didn't catch every word of her torrent, but she made it clear he was sitting in her seat. And it was just as clear that she wasn't the model.

"I'm s-sorry," Ben half stuttered, embarrassed by the attention as other passengers turned to gawk. He bolted from his seat, stumbling to get into the aisle and out of her way. The woman took possession of the seat with purpose and authority. He glanced around but found no other open seats in sight, so he moved with both reluctance and trepidation to the seat opposite the woman.

She commented to herself, yet loud enough for him to hear, which he assumed was her intent, "*Un Americano, ovviamente. Che palle.*" She continued in Italian, sotto voce. "Americans always think they can do whatever they want, sit wherever they please. They have no respect for our customs or even our language. Could they be any more self-centered?"

Ben listened to her, distracted by a tangential thought—her voice had a melodic quality. Her rhetorical question broke the spell, so he responded. "*Uh… Per favore, mi scusi, signorina,*" he said in Italian, his heavy American accent unmistakable. "I love your language. Please accept my apology. I understand about seat… uh"—he struggled to remember "*prenotazioni,*" but then continued—"reservations. When I boarded this train in Zurich, I checked, and the indicator was clear. I've always loved this trip through the Alps, and I chose this seat to enjoy the view." He waved a hand toward the window.

With the other hand, he pointed to the digital display above her seat. "I see now the reservation, but I assure you it was—um—blank this morning." He'd drawn a blank—literally—on the words for "available." He added in English, "I mean, available, sorry." Ben inhaled as he tapped his temple with his fingers. Then remembering, he said, "*a disposizione.*"

Unable to resist, he added one last remark. "And I also assure you that not all Americans are obnoxiously self-centered… any more than all Italian women are rudely judgmental."

She just stared at him—at least he thought she was staring. He could not tell with her oversized, over-dark sunglasses. Ben did not know what response he should expect—but expect one he did. She merely turned toward the window. Ben surrendered his expectation and turned away, taking her shaded stare and her stony silence for disagreement.

FOUR

Angelina

Any more than all Italian women are rudely judgmental.

The American finished his speech with "Any more than all Italian women are rudely judgmental." It was as if he'd slapped her. Angelina considered this American through her sunglasses. Some of his grammar was wrong, making it more difficult to sift through his mangled accent, but she understood what he meant. He was right. Rather than take offense, she instead thought that his response had been quite appropriate. It made her angry. Not at him—at herself.

I can imagine Godfather Angelo's surprise at how well I am socializing.

Her sarcastic thought was followed by the voice of her godmother.

You are not this woman. You are better than this. He deserves an apology.

Her godfather had told her often how proud he was that she kept her dignity and decorum in the face of challenges. Her godmother had been coaching her for years to be proper, polite, and, most importantly, respectful always, under all circumstances. Her behavior would have disappointed both godparents. It disappointed *her*.

If my godmother were here, she would be lecturing me. "Non scusarti, risolvilo, Angelina!"

Yes, she needed to stop feeling sorry and fix it. She turned to face the American.

She was rattled when he turned away. She cleared her throat to get his attention. Taking off her sunglasses, she met his gaze, then she gulped and looked away. She stared instead at the table between their seats and started speaking in English, with only the lightest trace of an accent.

"Signor, thank you for your apology, but it is I who must apologize. I purchased my ticket only thirty minutes ago. Obviously you could not have known I would reserve the seat when you sat down." She lifted her gaze back to his. This time she held it; he remained silent.

"You did not even question why I did not do the reasonable thing and sit in the empty seat"—she pointed at his seat with her open palm—"rather than make, as you Americans might say, 'a scene.' Please let me explain."

As he lifted his hand to stop her, she raised hers, tilted her head, and closed her eyes. "When I travel by train, I get..." She opened her eyes as she searched for the right words—her tongue experiencing what she could not describe. She asked, "*Come si dice cinetosi?* A sickness in?" Her arms made rocking motions out to her sides.

"Motion sickness?"

"*Sì*, motion sickness. I get motion sickness when I face to the rear. That is why I always try to reserve a seat facing forward." She paused as she composed herself. "I have much on my mind, but that is no excuse for my being, how you said, 'rudely judgmental.' Please accept my apology." Angelina sighed. *She wondered if she'd said too much.* She restored her sunglass shield to its original position and turned to gaze out the window through the darkened glasses that matched her mood.

FIVE

Benjamin

Wait—where did that thought come from?

Ben found her accented English enchanting. Her voice was melodious, and her English was British influenced with only a suggestion of an Italian accent. But her gaze met his and he froze, speechless. She had the most amazing eyes he'd ever seen—bright amber, glowing like a fire on its last log.

"No apology necessary. Is there anything I can do?"

The woman shrugged, mumbled, "*No, figurati*," and returned to staring out the window until their arrival in Milano.

The train arrived at Stazione Centrale Milano just before one o'clock. He watched the long cool woman—he couldn't shake the song—rise first to leave. He daydreamed for a moment but returned to reality when a fellow traveler moving toward the exit rapped Ben's right arm with a shoulder bag.

As he stepped onto the platform, Ben wished he'd grabbed something to eat on the train. He could sense his falling blood sugar. As its cauliflower sushi was sold out, he grabbed a prepared salad and a pineapple juice for lunch at the Juicebar on the ground level by the Burger King. Not his first choice, but it served its purpose.

***

The Lecce train that he was taking as far as Rimini was scheduled to depart at two o'clock. When he finished his lunch, he reentered the station and scanned the display board for his platform number, but it was too early. He waited near the wall, avoiding the hundreds of bustling purposeful travelers as they tried—occasionally without success—to avoid each other. The arrivals and departures board sat above and behind him, so he stepped away from the wall at intervals to search for his train. When at last train 8813 appeared with its platform, Ben grabbed his rolling luggage stack and made his way to *binario* sixteen.

There was only one first-class car. He found his seat, stowed his bags, and settled in. He had another single seat, facing the rear of the train. It was only two-and-a-half hours to Rimini, and he was unconcerned with the view. In his opinion, the trip across the Po Valley to Bologna was just this side of monotonous, and south of Bologna the farm country held little appeal. While he loved traveling everywhere, this was one of the few trips for which Ben considered the destination much more appealing than the journey.

Emerson never made this journey. He smiled at his observation.

He saw the woman in black enter the train car, still wearing the oversized sunglasses. She moved toward him, reading seat numbers, until she reached hers—opposite him again!

I may as well make the best of it.

"*Ciao di nuovo, signorina.*" He was aware that he was focused on pronouncing the words correctly, but not of why it suddenly mattered to him.

The woman said, "*Signora,*" pointing to the ring on her finger. "*Buon pomeriggio, signore.*" After she said good afternoon, a smile appeared on her lips, and she said, "This is quite the coincidence," in English.

Smile or not, Ben took the pointing at her ring as a reproach—don't mess with the married woman.

Oh, well, at least she didn't yell at me—and I got to hear her voice again. He smiled. *Wait—where did that thought come from?*

In the meantime, the woman settled into her seat and into her now familiar pose, staring out the window.

Ben watched the station recede as the train pulled away, every seat in the first-class car occupied. After several minutes, the train jolted to a stop. There was an announcement on the intercom. Because of track work, there would be a delay of twenty minutes between Parma and Bologna. The train began moving in the opposite direction. As he gazed out the window, Ben realized it would stay this way for the trip to Rimini. He turned toward the woman in black just as she closed her eyes and asked a question in Italian.

SIX

Angelina

There are not so many out there.

Angelina continued to stare out the window even after the train halted. She accepted the announcement of a delay with neither surprise nor concern. One did not ride Trenitalia regularly without expecting track or equipment issues. The train lurched and began moving in the opposite direction, so she was now facing backward. She slumped back into her seat when she realized this was how she'd travel back home. Angelina shook her head, unaware of her tight-lipped smile that wasn't a smile.

Now I know why someone knocked off the head of that damn frog.

She exhaled, more a release than a sigh. "What else is God going to throw at me?" she thought—no, wait, she said it! She did not mean to say that aloud. Without thinking, she moved her hand to cover her mouth.

Even before she finished the comment, the man across from her stood up and offered her his seat with a smile, without a hint of irony in his expression or voice. As she prepared to respond with a polite refusal, he told her, "*Insisto, per favore, signora.*"

As she accepted the invitation and they exchanged seats, she peered across at the American.

Chi è quest'uomo di fronte a me? she wondered.

When they first met, she'd yelled at him. She'd followed that with an inappropriate remark she still could not believe she'd made. When he'd asked if he could help, she'd declined ungraciously. And when they met again a few moments ago, she could not have been more impersonal or aloof.

Despite her crass behavior, he'd just made this noble gesture that had saved her from having to find a seat in second class—and likely from further humiliation. If she had needed to move, she was not sure she could have held it together. She worked to erase the vision of herself standing in the vestibule between the cars, sobbing as people smirked in contempt.

"*Grazie mille, signor?*" She hoped he interpreted the questioning tone as both a request for his name and a peace offering.

"Prego, signora. Sono il Signor Benjamin LaRocca, ma puoi chiamarmi Ben."

She liked the sound of his voice when he said "Benjamin." It was not the Italian pronunciation. She'd met several men named Beniamino. "Benjamin" was different—she liked the way it sounded. Out of respect, but also because his accent was grating, she shifted to English. "My name is Angelina Fabrizzi."

"I am pleased to meet you, Signora Fabrizzi."

Angelina noted his polite emphasis on "signora" and found it charming. Unsure why, she wanted to tell him she was no longer married. Instead, she replied, "My friends call me Angelina, please. I thank you again for your gallantry. What is your destination… if I might ask?"

After he told her, she replied, "Another coincidence! Rimini is my home. Are you on holiday?"

"I am writing an article about the micro-nation of The Republic of Rose Island which had been built off the coast of Rimini. I am also researching material for a travel guide. We are producing a feature on the Emilia-Romagna region. I have visited twice before, and I fell in love with the city."

"*Allora,* you are a writer." He nodded in agreement with her conclusion. "So, Benjamin, how long will you be in our city?" She was not comfortable shortening it and using his nickname. Besides, she liked the sound of "Benjamin."

Benjamin replied, "Forever, perhaps. I am relocating. I meant it when I said I love it. The last time I visited, I was homesick when I left."

Nobile e romantico. There were not many of them out there. She asked, "What do you write?"

"At first, travel pieces for several American and European travel magazines and guides. But I have been expanding my efforts since I came to Italy. I write for a news website in Milano. I have also published a couple short stories, and I just completed my first novel—as yet unpublished," he said.

"Is there anything I may have read?"

"Do you read many travel magazines?" he asked.

"No, sorry. Anything else? I subscribe to several American and British magazines."

After a moment, Benjamin said, "Well, last year, I wrote an article for an American fashion magazine on the state of women's satisfaction. I based it on several recent research studies. I doubt you'd have seen it."

When he told her the name of the magazine, Angelina knew it. In fact, she subscribed to it. Her godmother insisted she read a variety of publications to improve her English reading comprehension. She remembered the article, and it had resonated with her. The topic was sexual satisfaction—she assumed he was too polite to say it. But the author's name was not Benjamin. Wait, he had said to call him Ben. Ben LaRocca was the author. *He* was that author.

I am sitting across from the author Ben LaRocca… and I yelled at him!

"You are Ben LaRocca! I have read your article! You discussed the sexual satisfaction of women, and how society, for all the progress of the sexual revolution, still places men's satisfaction ahead of women's. It was fascinating. I was amazed that a man wrote it." Her words came spilling out.

Ben blushed, then rubbed the back of his head. He said, "Thank you. I am flattered, but most of the researchers were women. I merely wrote an article summarizing their work. It was my sister's idea."

She removed her sunglasses and examined this man—noble, romantic, and modest. Today has been one coincidence after another. She almost giggled when he had blushed but was glad that she hadn't. That would have been so disrespectful. But now he was staring—again.

"Forgive me, but were you crying before? Is everything okay?" he asked.

She took off her hat and shook out her hair. His gaze was now more intense, if that were possible. She knew why, but she had hoped he might be different. Perhaps he was different, only not as she'd hoped. She had always ignored the staring—worse, the comments—from others, choosing instead to withdraw and avoid confrontation. But not today—this time, she objected.

"I am ugly—*sfigurato*—yes? But I ask you not to stare at me. It is rude." She delivered her comments without anger, which surprised her.

Benjamin averted his gaze, but then returned it after only a moment.

"What do you mean?" he asked.

"You stare at me because I am strange. My eyes, my hair—they are wrong, different."

"I am sorry. I did not mean to stare. That was rude." He leaned forward in his seat. "You should think of me as a jerk, but not a mean one. More than one woman has called me clueless."

"A jerk?" Angelina understood what a jerk was but not why he admitted it, or why she should care.

"Look, I think you are captivating, that's all. I wasn't staring—I was gawking… gawking like a teenager. Do you know that word, 'gawking'?" When she nodded, he continued. "Like a nice, awkward, gawking, jerky teenager—but not a mean one. Even so, it was rude; it was wrong. Please forgive me. It won't happen again." He brought a palm to his chest.

Should I believe him?

She rubbed an eye absentmindedly. She was made uncomfortable by her skepticism—aware that her expression and body language showed her disbelief. She shifted to what she hoped was a more neutral pose. At least he was polite. That was different.

He did not mock me or pretend he was not staring.

She tried to change the subject. "Tell me more about your novel, please."

Instead of answering her question, Benjamin took a deep breath. "I meant what I said. I always mean what I say. I was staring at you, and, yes, that was rude. Forgive me. But I meant what I said." He held out his upturned palms and took another forlorn breath.

He surprised Angelina when he repeated his apology. It—and he—sounded most genuine and earnest. Did he not think she was disfigured?

As she gazed at him, with his dark, yet soft eyes, a brief image of a puppy came to mind.

I like puppies. She smiled. *Why am I thinking about puppies?*

She tried to sort out the multiple thoughts that were arriving like a spring avalanche.

Her mother had told Angelina almost daily that she was beautiful. Angelina had believed her mother but knew it had been the product of a mother's love. Her godmother admired the writings of Cervantes, and one of Cervantes's aphorisms was "No fathers or mothers think their own children ugly."

Cervantes never met my father. Angelina shook her head at the wry thought.

Perhaps Benjamin was being truthful and was just a poor judge of beauty.

Besides, he said I was captivating, not beautiful—it might not be a compliment.

She knew many American expressions and idioms, but certainly not all. Yet it had sounded like a compliment.

Angelina blurted, "I am a widow."

Why did I say that?

Before she could answer herself, she began describing her parents, her marriage to Giovanni, and his death. She did not offer many details, but enough that Benjamin acknowledged why today must be so overwhelming for her.

As she shared more of her life story, Angelina relaxed. Her breathing slowed. Her anxiety evaporated, a choking cloud of worry floating away, and she was not sure why. She had become more confident as they conversed, that much she felt. Angelina did not find many opportunities to engage in prolonged English conversations, so she'd forced her brain to shift gears when their conversation began. But this was something more... something different. She was never comfortable or confident speaking about herself—now she could not stop. As their conversation continued, Benjamin asked a few probing questions.

Is it the writer in him? she wondered.

"Was he *un mafioso*?" the writer asked at one point.

In reflexive response to his Italian, she replied, "*No, solo un furbone, un truffatore, non un malvivente.*" Catching herself, she repeated in English,

"He was a lowlife, a con man, not a gangster."

I hate even the thought of that man. I should change the subject.

For whatever reason, Benjamin stopped asking questions. Perhaps he sensed her discomfort. He instead simply listened or made reassuring statements, which helped nurture her newfound confidence.

"Please tell me more about your novel." When he hesitated, she added another "Please?"

He did not go into many details. Was he shy? Perhaps he was superstitious until it was published. He spoke little of his novel, more of his time in Italy. She spoke little of anything but much of herself.

The train returned to the main line after Bologna, but they were unaware, engaged as they were in revealing random layers of their respective lives.

It is not like we are peeling an onion, more like coaxing a sunflower to bloom, each petal contributing to the whole.

Despite her unspoken simile, neither she nor Benjamin took notice of the sunflower farms as the train pulled away from Cesena.

Was that the announcement for Rimini? I thought we just left Bologna.

Benjamin appeared surprised as well. "Wow! If the PA had not repeated it in English, I might have missed my station. We might have missed *our* station." She liked the silly grin that accompanied his correction.

They'd immersed themselves in conversation as though they were long-lost friends sharing intervening life stories. Angelina was not sure what was more amazing—that she'd lost track of time with him, or he with her.

I do not want to stop—I want to continue our conversation.

She wished they were going instead to Lecce, and the thought made her feel a little silly. She stood up and retrieved her bag. She smiled at Benjamin as he gathered his luggage.

Angelina stepped out first, carrying her small bag. Wearing his backpack, Benjamin followed her and set his two larger bags on the platform. Before she could speak to him, he returned to the train vestibule.

Angelina could not hide her surprise as Benjamin assisted a short woman down the steps to the platform. The woman must have been seventy-five years old, maybe older. He then returned and helped a man, just as short and at least as old, to the platform. Benjamin climbed back into the vestibule a third and fourth time and returned with first one and then a second enormous rolling suitcase. While resembling airline carry-ons, the bags were at least three times as voluminous.

Do they sleep in those bags? Angelina chuckled. The bags were that large—the couple was that tiny.

Still unsure what was happening, Angelina watched the woman whisper into the man's ear, after which he fumbled with his wallet. Benjamin shook his head and said something. The couple gave Benjamin a collective hug, and then the woman turned to Angelina.

"*Cara figlia,*" she said, "he reminds me of my Umberto when we met, so gallant! Hold on to him. There are not so many out there."

Angelina could feel the blush climbing up her neck. When she noticed Benjamin was blushing too, she turned away so he would not see her reaction—or that she had noticed his. She did not hear Benjamin's response over the noise of the departing train, but the old man half turned toward her and said, "How do you know you are not?"

Angelina looked at the woman, who smiled back before turning. *She was right—there were not so many out there.* She watched as the couple trudged into the station, pulling their bags behind them with what Angelina regarded as almost superhuman effort.

Benjamin said, "Sorry 'bout that. I'm not sure why she jumped to that conclusion."

Angelina did not understand every word, but she grasped the meaning. She noted Benjamin's sensitivity.

"Did you know that couple?" His response—that no, he did not—surprised, then warmed her. He gathered his bags, and her warmth changed to worry.

I do not want this conversation to end!

Before she considered a course of action or even the impact of her despondent desire, the voice of her godmother intruded.

You just met him. You must not be too forward, it warned.

After a round of mental arm wrestling, Angelina decided she'd share her contact information with Benjamin.

I am not being too forward. I am only doing this so he will know someone in town, she told herself, rationalizing, but the voice in her head was unconvinced.

SEVEN

Benjamin

It just wasn't the whole truth.

Ben watched Angelina disembark, convinced he'd never met such an enchanting woman. With her glasses off, he'd felt he needed to catch himself from falling into her amber eyes. When she'd removed her hat, long, thick hair had cascaded across her shoulders. It was the deepest auburn he'd ever seen, reminding him of fine mahogany. Where the sun touched it, highlights of red, copper, and even gold flashed, as if electric. From the top of her forehead, a streak of ash-blonde hair fell to frame the right side of her face. He could not remember seeing anything like it—*she must color it.* While he noted her distinctive appearance, it was her poise and self-assurance that he found most memorable. And her voice—how could he forget her voice?

As he followed Angelina, he observed a tiny older couple speaking in Italian and struggling with two large pieces of luggage in the train's vestibule. Neither traveler was over five feet tall, and both appeared to be well into their seventies. He had noticed them when they boarded in Milano, where they'd received help from someone. They were now alone.

"*Posso fornirti assistenza?*" They nodded their appreciation at his offer to help.

Ben first helped the older woman descend the steps as she smiled at him, patting him on the arm while thanking him. He returned her smile and acknowledged her thank-you.

"*Prego, nonna,*" Ben said.

Next, he followed with her male companion, who struggled with the higher of the two steps. Ben returned and exited twice more with their respective bags, grunting with each. How did they travel with them?

The woman whispered something in the man's ear, and he took out his wallet.

Is he going to offer me money? Italians don't tip. Maybe because I am an American...

Ben shook his head, and then explained slowly in Italian. "My thanks will be to live as long as you have with as much love as you share."

The man replied, "*Cent'anni,*" raising his arms as if offering a blessing.

Ben gave the traditional response, "*E anche tu.*"

A hundred years would be great; I'd settle for fifty.

His warm feeling transformed into embarrassment when the woman turned to Angelina and encouraged her to hang on to him, presuming she and Ben were more than just fellow travelers.

"We just met; we are not a couple," Ben said.

"How do you know you are not?" the man answered loud enough for Angelina to hear, then winked at Ben. The couple said goodbye with a joint hug—damn, they were strong—and headed into the station, lugging their sizeable bags.

Ben removed his backpack and stacked it with his rolling bag and small duffel. He turned to Angelina and apologized for the woman's comment.

"Did you know that couple?" Angelina asked.

"I'd never met them before. When they boarded in Milano, someone helped them. I just assumed it was someone in their party, but I guess not."

He wasn't sure what to make of her widened eyes as he explained.

She is embarrassed that the woman assumed that we were together.

"What did you tell them?" she asked.

Ben hesitated for a moment.

This will sound corny, he thought before answering.

"I told them I only hoped to live as long and be as in love as them one day."

Angelina smiled, nodded her head once, and said, "Well—"

Ben, thinking she was about to say goodbye, interrupted her. "Please forgive me if I am being too forward, but what are you doing for dinner?"

She said nothing, and with her sunglasses on, he could not read her expression. Was that the start of a smile, or a smirk? Her silence convinced him that he was too forward.

Think quick! he thought, poor grammar and all. The best he could do was rationalize.

"It would be great to get some advice from a native about where to look for apartments in town."

Well, it was the truth; it just wasn't the whole truth.

EIGHT

Angelina

So, tell me about your godmother.

Noble and romantic, gallant and sweet. Angelina found herself daydreaming. When she had first read his article, she'd recognized that her fantasizing was just an escape. The author and researchers were from North America; she had never traveled outside Italy. But now, Signor Fantasy was standing next to her—in Italy—and very real. And nothing he had said or done gave lie to her fantasy.

I should grab the ball on the bounce and give him my number.

But when Benjamin surprised her—again—with a dinner invitation, the words representing her intended offer to exchange contact information had piled up in a jumble in her mouth and were now sliding dangerously close to the tip of her tongue. She pursed her lips to stop them from spilling out.

And he worries that he is being forward? I wanted to give him my phone number and ask him to call me!

It took a moment, but Angelina collected her thoughts.

"I would enjoy that very much, and I would be happy to help you in your apartment search… but there is a complication." Angelina shook her head and raised her hands, palms up. "I am a vegan, and I do not eat out often. I do not know if there are any restaurants nearby where I could eat." She worried he might change his mind, but she wanted to give him a graceful exit.

Maybe I should invite him to my home for dinner.

"Me too! I eat vegan," he said, as he shook his head and raised one arm to mirror her.

He is just saying that.

Benjamin said, "One reason I love Rimini is that there are so many options. I know of a couple places nearby. If you are up to it, there's a nice vegan café a few blocks from here."

Another coincidence? This cannot be real.

"You have all that luggage, but if you do not mind, I would love to stretch my legs." She hoped she had not misused the expression.

Benjamin pointed to her five-inch platform boots. "Are they Gucci? Will you be okay to walk?"

She chuckled. "No, they are Sam Edelman synthetics—not real leather. They are quite comfortable."

She worked to hide her surprise, and the questioning thought prompted by his thoughtful question—*Someone who worries about my comfort?*

***

They strolled southwest for ten minutes through the central historic district to the café on Via Quintino Sella, wandering past dozens of Vespas and bicycles parked along the streets. The neighborhood, with a distinct college-town vibe, boasted several university buildings. Angelina had not walked this part of town in many years. It had changed since she attended university.

Just like me.

Once inside, Angelina removed her hat, and she felt safe enough to take off her sunglasses.

Wow, what an impressive vegan menu, she thought. *I need to go out more.*

They sat at a table for four in the near-empty restaurant. After they ordered, Benjamin asked her if she had any advice for his apartment hunting. She provided several options, and several places to avoid, and then he again surprised her with a question.

"Forgive me for asking, but what did you mean on the train by 'disfigured'?"

Angelina coughed, took a sip of mineral water, then coughed again, trying to think.

Should I tell him he is being too presumptuous, that I do not want to discuss it?

She waited for her conscience to answer her as she expected, but this time the line was dead. The server bailed her out when she arrived with their salads and asked if they needed anything, but the interruption was short-lived.

"I'm sorry. I don't mean to pry, but it makes no sense to me," he said.

He stared across the table with the same puppy eyes she'd observed on the train.

I like those puppy eyes—perhaps they are a sign. I will tell him and hope for the best.

"You have seen my eyes. Who has such eyes? No one I have ever met. As a child, other children taunted me, or worse. They called me *occhi da cagna* or *occhi da lupa.*" At his confused expression, she confirmed, "Yes, dog eyes or wolf eyes. When they wanted to be nasty, they yelled *occhi da cagna*—bitch eyes." She sighed and turned toward the window before turning back.

"The comments about my eyes made me feel like a *mostro*—not a monster, I think you say 'freak.' Those were bad enough, but when my hair darkened to this color and this streak"—she grimaced as she flicked her hair—"appeared, it convinced everyone an imp of Satan had possessed me."

Benjamin protested. "But Italians love red hair!"

She scoffed. "If my hair were red, and only red—if I were a true *rossa*—perhaps they would have accepted me. But not with this color, these eyes, this *streak*," she said, flicking it again as she emphasized the word. "Instead, they called me *pelliccia malvagia* or even *malpelo*, saying I had evil fur." She could feel her quickened pulse, aware that her tone had sharpened.

Benjamin replied, "Children can be mean and insecure about differences. Your family and friends must have told you how beautiful you were. Right?"

She understood that his question was intended to be comforting. Their entrees arrived, and neither of them had yet started their salads. The server placed the plates on their table with the tact not to ask about the untouched salads.

As an answer, Angelina said they should eat, and they did, eating in silence, which she appreciated. Between bites, she glanced at Benjamin, and a puppy dog gazed back at her.

Benjamin broke the awkward silence and asked if she liked the food.

"It is delicious." She hoped her smile indicated her sincerity.

How did I not know of this place?

They ordered *caffè* when the server cleared their plates. Angelina took the conversation in another direction and asked Benjamin to talk more about his book.

"My novel is based on my experience as a volunteer firefighter back in New Jersey, my home."

Volunteer firefighter? She thought she knew what the words meant, but the concept was unfamiliar. "What is a volunteer firefighter?"

After describing it, Benjamin added, "I know there are many such volunteers in France and Switzerland, but I am not sure about Italy."

The concept amazed Angelina—people risking their lives in such dangerous work when not their job, their career. As he spoke, Angelina looked at Benjamin as if she were studying a new species. *Someone who helps people, rather than hurts them—how refreshing.*

As he described first his experience as a volunteer and then his approach to writing about life, she realized he was the man she'd daydreamed—no, to be honest, fantasized—about when she'd first read the piece. *Another coincidence?*

Her godmother had smiled when Angelina first described the article and the author, but Angelina knew Valentina had been showing condescension, not concordance. She had told Angelina that she was just romanticizing. *What does she know about romance?*

They sipped their *caffè*, the silence less awkward than earlier. Perhaps it was the jolt of caffeine, or her conscience missing in action, but Angelina returned to Ben's question and decided, *I need to stop being a rabbit and answer his question.* She coughed to clear her throat.

"You asked about my friends and family. Well, my father told me all the time that I was ugly—a curse placed on him by God for some unidentified past transgression. My mother was only nineteen when my grandfather forced her to marry my father, who was forty-two." Angelina was unaware that her hands had taken on a life of their own.

At seeing his wide eyes, she confirmed, "Yes, forty-two. They both died in the same week when I was twenty. My grandparents had all died by then." Angelina sighed and raised a hand near her cheek. "They never called me ugly, but they also never called me beautiful. In fact, they rarely called me at all." She turned up her palm before retrieving it and sighed again.

"My uncle was a priest, and my aunt was a nun. Each said I had a beautiful soul but never spoke about my appearance. They both died a few years ago." Angelina watched Benjamin shake his head.

"There are only four people who have ever called me beautiful: my mother; my godfather, Angelo; my godmother, Valentina; and Matteo." Her fingers counted along with her list.

"My mother said what she believed, of course, because every mother thinks her child is beautiful." Angelina and Benjamin both nodded their heads.

"My godfather is also our family attorney. He has always been there for me, and he is just like family. My godmother, Valentina, was my mother's best friend, and she has watched over me ever since my parents died. She is also my housekeeper and my dearest friend. She *is* family." When she mentioned Valentina, it stirred up memories Angelina suppressed.

Angelina brought her hands together as if in prayer and began rocking them in time with her words. "I met a boy, Matteo, in my second year of university. We began dating around the time of my mother's illness. He was sweet, and when he called me beautiful, he was the only one—" She sighed. "The only one outside my family circle who had ever said that to me—and I believed him!" Her palms exploded from their prayer pose, as wide now as her moist eyes, but she was not crying. And she was no longer angry.

Benjamin stared at her. He had also brought his hands together to mirror hers. As she spoke, he rested his elbows on the table and his chin on his thumbs, his index fingers touching his nose. When she finished, he crossed his arms against his chest before sitting back.

Did I say too much?

But puppy eyes returned her gaze; she saw no judgment.

Is that compassion, empathy, or sympathy?

She decided she did not care. She was just relieved it was neither contempt nor disgust.

"Did you want to marry Matteo?" His question did not feel impertinent.

Angelina sniffled. "No. I did not love Matteo, but I really liked him. He said he loved me—and that, too, I believed. I was twenty. He was a year older, and my first sexual experience. He was sweet. I know I said that before, but he was. For a few months, even though my mother was sick, I was happy—safe. We might have married—eventually."

"What happened?"

"My father caught us. *Cogliere in castagna.*"

"What?" Benjamin appeared confused. "Picking a chestnut?"

"Oh, yes, he caught us red-handed. Well, it was more than our hands." She smiled as she looked at her hands waving in front of her. "He was livid, calling me a *puttana*—a whore. He said I would never have a proper husband, leaving him with the burden of supporting me." She shook her head again.

"After my father chased Matteo out of the house, I was forbidden to see him again. I may still have the poor boy's trousers. A few days later, my father told me he'd solved my marriage problem. I did not know I had a marriage problem, but he'd solved it." Angelina tilted her head.

"He arranged for me to marry Giovanni Fabrizzi, the son of one of his partners. Giovanni was twelve years older than me."

"Like your mother," Benjamin said as he shook his head, and Angelina nodded. "I didn't think arranged marriages existed anymore." His comment was almost a question.

Angelina said, "Not in the big cities, perhaps, but in a society that values the opinions and desires of men more than women, there will always be arrangements. My family called it *un'ambasciata*, the colloquial term for an arranged marriage requested by the groom, but that was untrue. It was a forced marriage, *un costrette combaciare*, at the request of my parents. "Why do you think I connected so well with your article?" Angelina was glad he thought her question rhetorical.

"Aren't forced marriages a crime?"

"Not in Italy," she said.

"Did Giovanni treat you well, at least?"

"No, he was such a *segone.*" Benjamin was unfamiliar with the term, so she clarified. "*Un perdente*, a 'loser' I think you say." Benjamin nodded. She liked the way his eyes smiled.

Angelina continued, "A day did not go by in our marriage when he did not tell me how much I disgusted him—and how fortunate I was that he pitied me enough to marry me. I am sure there were other considerations. My husband's financial affairs were complicated—convoluted would be the better word, I think." Angelina had balled her fists.

"At one point, he made me get colored contacts and dye my hair. The contacts hurt my eyes, and the hair dye made me ill." Her eyes narrowed.

"*Che stronzo*," Benjamin said.

Angelina blinked at his scurrilous reply, staring as she pursed her lips in contemplation and concentration. *While coarsely put, it was accurate.* She raised a balled fist.

Benjamin shifted in his seat. His posture changed; his cheeks reddened. "I am—"

"Yes, an asshole." She interrupted him, unaware of the sharpness of her tone. Her raised arm had extended in front of her, palm open and thumb up, tomahawking to accent her invective. Angelina's other arm was bent at the elbow, the back of her hand against her ribs.

Seeing his crushed expression, she realized what she'd done. *Mannaggia*! She quickly lowered her arms and, without thinking, began rubbing the back of one hand with the other palm.

"No, wait! I did not mean you, Benjamin. I mean, you are correct. He—my husband—*was* an asshole. The asshole." She exhaled, embarrassed by her faux pas, and watched as he exhaled. She smiled an apology as she tilted her head, and the puppy eyes returned.

"Did you ever tell him about the dye? The contacts?" he asked.

"I finally stopped doing it. I did not like pretending to be someone else." Angelina decided not to go into details as memories stirred again.

"You made the right choice," Benjamin told her, again without a hint of irony. "When did your husband die?"

"Last year." The memories were not just being stirred but shaken.

"And your mother?" he asked.

"Both my parents died not long after my marriage." Benjamin shook his head, and Angelina concluded it was sympathy, not pity. She said, "I did not speak much with Matteo after, but I understand he is married and has children. I hope he is happy. So, as you can see, there are only two people in my life today who think I am beautiful." She had raised two fingers, but quickly dropped them. Angelina knew she must be boring Benjamin, if not depressing him.

It is depressing the hell out of me.

"Look, uh…" Benjamin began, shifting in his seat again. "Please don't take this the wrong way. I know we just met and all, but those people who called you ugly, the ones who called you names, were wrong—especially your family. They would've been wrong to say it even if it were true, but it ain't true—sorry, isn't true. You are unique, yes, but beautiful… You are exceptionally beautiful, in my considered opinion. Moreover, your aunt and uncle were correct." Benjamin brought his arms up as if in exaltation. "You have a spirit within you that lights up the room."

Angelina flinched, and he glanced away, but then back, as he lowered his arms. As she mirrored his nervous seat-shifting, he said, "I am sorry if I've said anything improper."

If another man had said it, she would have dismissed it as disingenuous or self-serving. But after their time together today, she did not doubt his sincerity.

Three people in my life? she thought; she hoped.

She glanced up at the name of the restaurant, Loving Hut Vegan Café. A sign? And she dared to believe.

Benjamin interrupted her wish. "So, tell me about your godmother."

INTERMEZZO

The Baptism of Angelina

"For a knight-errant without love was like a tree without leaves or fruit, or a body without a soul."
— Miguel de Cervantes Saavedra —

Several agencies provided national law enforcement in Italy. The Polizia di Stato, or P.S., provided police services to rural areas and supplemented *polizia municipale* units in cities and larger towns. Several specialized units provided services regionally and nationally.

The Carabinieri was an Italian military service with domestic law enforcement responsibilities. It was part of the Army until 2001, when it became a separate branch of the military. Carabinieri units were in cities and larger towns, and they supplemented both P.S. and *polizia municipale* for regular law enforcement. Like the P.S., the Carabinieri had specialized regional and national units that took the lead on organized crime and anti-terror activities. As with the other military branches, it began accepting female officers in 2000.

Valentina's great grandfather, grandfather, and two great uncles had served in the Carabinieri before World War II. When their units refused to swear allegiance to Mussolini after he partnered with Hitler, Nazi officials retaliated and directed the Mussolini government to disband them. With their units no longer recognized, her relatives and their colleagues became active in the anti-fascist resistance. Both of her great uncles died, one in close combat, and the other executed by the German SS after his capture.

After secondary school, Valentina wanted to enlist in the Carabinieri to follow in their footsteps, but the military did not accept women. The P.S. by then accepted women—following a law change in 1981—so she applied. They had approved her application, but she had not yet accepted when she and Isabella met at the Ristorante Embassy. With her unplanned proposal refused, she enlisted in May, before Isabella's wedding, and left for training at the academy in Rome.

Upon graduation, the P.S. assigned her to Pesaro, a forty-kilometer drive south from Rimini. Valentina distinguished herself with her investigative skills and earned several commendations for bravery. Her superiors dealt with occasional accusations of rough handling, more often complaints about her attitude. While she was unrefined and unrepentant, they recognized and appreciated her value. Valentina made no apologies for her approach—no one had ever accused her of having hair on her tongue.

Valentina made the most of a tuition subsidy program and enrolled at the University of Urbino to pursue a *laurea* degree in romance languages. She'd taken French and English in secondary school and learned both British and American English accents while watching comedy movies and television shows, mimicking the dialog, and amusing her classmates and her coworkers with her impressions. Her French accent was only adequate—to her ears if no one else's. She maintained her progress in the program even as her postings changed, and she graduated with a specialization in French while also studying Spanish, Portuguese, and Latin.

***

Two days after giving birth, Isabella had just finished nursing Angelina. They would be discharged tomorrow if all remained well. Her roommate had taken her new son home that morning, so Isabella was alone in the room. She was thankful for the semiprivate room. It was a welcome use of her family's wealth and influence, which she otherwise ignored and resented.

She heard a commotion outside the room. She did not know that Valentina had returned on two weeks' leave, requested upon learning of the impending birth. Out in the hallway, Isabella's father, Giacomo, tried to prevent Valentina from entering. With urging from her mother, Francesca, and influenced no doubt by Valentina's uniform, he instead went outside for a cigar.

After a moment, Francesca opened the door, peeked in, and announced that Isabella had a visitor. She stepped back, and in strode Valentina Marchese, impressive, almost regal, in the uniform of the Polizia di Stato. Isabella could not believe it. Though they wrote often, this was the first time they had seen each other since before her wedding.

Isabella turned to get out of bed, but her soulmate told her to stop. Valentina came over and sat next to her on the hospital bed. They embraced awkwardly, but that did not prevent the embrace from lasting several minutes, the two whispering phrases of apology, affection, and lament.

Valentina repeated to Isabella what she'd written so many times—that she had been wrong to leave Isabella the way she did—and she asked for Isabella's forgiveness.

Isabella repeated what she'd written so often—that no apology was necessary. Isabella insisted it was she who should apologize for not standing up to her father.

Valentina described her career to date. "Bella, this is what I was meant to do. We help people."

"You are not just my protector now—you protect everyone," Isabella said. "What have you been doing?"

"Bella, I enrolled in university, and the P.S. is helping pay for it!"

"Why did you not tell me?" Isabella asked.

"I did not know you would be interested," Valentina replied, adding, "My studies have kept me very busy."

"Cosa stai studiando?"

"Everything—languages, literature, science, philosophy. Why would anyone want to learn just one thing?"

***

Isabella and Tàmmaro agreed on Angelina as the name for their daughter, in honor of both their friend and family attorney, Angelo, and Tàmmaro's mother, Angiolina. Isabella chose the more modern spelling over the traditional "Angiolina" because it reminded her of Valentina—but kept that to herself. Giacomo lobbied for her second name to be Regina, after his mother, and she agreed.

A few days later, back at the house, the family was discussing the upcoming baptism. Her father insisted that Angelo be the baby's godfather.

Isabella smiled in agreement. Maro nodded.

She took a deep breath and said she wanted Valentina to be the godmother.

Her father and her husband simultaneously said, "*Assolutamente no!*"

Isabella stood up to both men for the first time. She said Valentina's service did not give her much time for visits—they would not see her much. She pointed out that it might be a good thing to have a *poliziotta* in the family. She said the words with strength and conviction, not hysteria, before concluding, "If you do not agree, I will leave with Valentina and the baby and never return." Isabella flipped her head back, before lowering it to stare at her father.

Francesca observed her daughter's eyes and her set jaw. She turned and asked to speak with the two men alone.

"No!" Giacomo shook his wife's hand from his arm.

Francesca grabbed his arm again. "*Sì, adesso.*" She eyed Maro, lifted her other hand, fingers down, and wagged them as she said, "*Anche tu!*" She pointed at the kitchen door as she pulled her husband toward it.

Neither Isabella nor her father had ever witnessed such behavior from her mother. The two men followed her mother as Isabella, eyes wide, tried to digest what she had just seen.

She could hear the muffled discussion in the kitchen but could make out few words. After several minutes—it felt longer—the three returned. Isabella's mother announced, "It is decided. Valentina will be the godmother. She will return to the *polizia* and she will call ahead if she plans to visit." Isabella let out a sigh of relief and thanked her.

"Do not thank me, there is more. Your father and husband displayed great wisdom, understanding, and compassion in convincing me of this plan, but now you must listen." Her mother had cupped her hands together before her, almost in prayer, and began shaking them up and down. "Isabella, you are never again to show disrespect to your father or to your husband as you just did. You must agree, or I cannot approve of this arrangement." Her mother lifted her hand, thumb extended, and sliced through the air as she said, "Agree and apologize!"

Her mother's explanation and admonition confused Isabella.

Why is my mother scolding me, saying it was their idea, and telling me to apologize?

Her mother widened her eyes and gave Isabella a slight but forceful nod. A moment later, Isabella's eyes widened, and she nodded once, more slowly.

Isabella collected herself, turning first to her father, then to her husband. She inhaled deeply.

"I am so sorry for my behavior. Women become emotional after childbirth, and I allowed my hormones to cloud my judgment. Thank you so much for your decision. I promise I will never act in such a despicable way again." No actress had ever performed better.

Isabella grasped the maddening logic of her mother's request: it was necessary to protect the two male egos. She was sure her mother had her own apologies to make to her father. She only wished she could've heard what her mother had said to the men in the kitchen.

***

The baptism was a sparkling production. The guest list comprised an impressive cadre of clerical royalty, including the bishop and bishop emeritus of Rimini and the freshly appointed cardinal of Bologna. It included the lay leadership of their parish and her parents' friends.

They were the same people, Isabella thought with disdain.

Everyone fawned over her siblings, Reverendo don Santino Marvelli and Sorella Ilaria Marvelli, as she expected. Not every family could boast both a priest and a nun. She was not envious—she was happy to see them, and happy for them.

There were few friends of Isabella's in attendance. Many had abandoned her once news of her scandal began circulating two years earlier. They were not her friends anyway. Weary sadness replaced the disdain on her face.

None of that mattered to her, as the most important person was there—Angelina Regina Roselli. As was the second most important person, Valentina, resplendent in her dress uniform. Isabella still could not believe Valentina was to be godmother.

She felt blessed and grateful that Angelo was Angelina's godfather. Since she first met him as a teenager, he'd filled the role of a wise older brother. She admired him but was not in the least attracted to him. He was the only true male friend she had ever had. She recognized how fortunate she was. She felt sympathy for her female classmates who had never developed a male friendship. When his fiancée, Antonietta, invited Isabella to be one of her bridesmaids, Isabella had cherished the honor, delighted for them both.

Angelo reciprocated with platonic admiration. He was always so proper and respectful. When she asked him questions—which she had done with increasing frequency over the years—she knew she could trust his advice. When he did not know something, he did not bluff an answer as so many men did. Instead, he told her he would find out and get back to her, and he always did. Advocate was the perfect profession for him.

After the Mass, the family gathered on the church steps before heading to the restaurant rented by her father for the reception. Valentina greeted several people with polite small talk. Francesca approached and held Valentina's hands in hers as they spoke, until Angelo came over and spoke to them. Valentina shook his hand and brushed away a tear. Turning, she approached Maro and Isabella, who held Angelina in her dazzling white baptismal gown.

"Thank you for this great honor. Forgive my tears, but I am so happy for both of you, and for Angelina. If she ever needs anything, I will be there for her."

Maro acknowledged her remarks with a curt "She will not."

Isabella asked Maro to give them a minute. He grunted, turned, and proceeded across the terrace like a guided missile to speak with the bishop who had celebrated the Mass in Angelina's honor. Valentina mouthed *Grazie* to Isabella, who returned a "*Grazie*" aloud.

Valentina apologized for not being able to stay for the reception, as she needed to leave for her new assignment in Ancona. They agreed to write every week. Valentina said she'd send her address to Isabella as soon as she settled into her new apartment. Isabella suggested she might visit Valentina in Ancona if Maro would agree.

Isabella then surprised herself with the thought: *I am visiting if he agrees or not.*

Valentina gave baby Angelina a kiss on the cheek and told her she was the most beautiful angel in the world. The two women hugged, trying not to crush Angelina. Isabella wanted the embrace to last forever—it felt like an instant.

Valentina whispered into Isabella's ear, "I promised I would love you with all of my heart for the rest of my life. I have kept that promise, and I always will."

Isabella suppressed a sob.

"I make you another promise, my princess. If this angelic baby ever needs anything, I will be there for her. I will do everything I can to help her and guide her, as a good godmother should, and I swear to you, I will protect her even though I failed to protect you."

Isabella broke Valentina's hold, stepped back, and locked eyes with her soulmate. "Never say that again!" Angelina stirred at her mother's sharp tone.

"*Cara mia,*" Isabella said, her tone softened. "You *have* protected me—in ways you may never know. You have given me the strength to deal with this life. Knowing that you love me has helped me continue. Because of that, I stand here holding my precious daughter, your goddaughter. That makes her our daughter. I will always think of her that way. You have offered to be her protector, and that brings me such comfort. I will always think of you that way."

Her husband called to her. The new mother said, "*Devo andare.*"

The new godmother nodded and said, "I, too, must go."

***

With a profound sense of déjà vu, Valentina descended the steps of the church.

I just made another promise, and I swear to God, I will keep it. She headed back to her hotel and on to her new assignment in Ancona.

NINE

Angelina

Do you like dogs?

Angelina gave Benjamin a thumbnail description of her godmother, Valentina. Her mother had told her that she and Valentina were friends from school, and because of a romantic entanglement, Valentina had left town and joined the police. Angelina did not share her speculation that her mother and Valentina might have competed for the same boy. She had never asked her mother. As for Valentina, one did not pry, and Valentina never volunteered.

With their coffee finished, Benjamin asked for the check. As Angelina reached for her purse, Benjamin stopped her. "I got this." When she objected, he replied, "I invited you, remember? Besides, it is a business expense. You were helping me with my research."

What research? The only thing we discussed was my life.

She decided it was okay to accept his generosity, and she thanked him. As they left the café, Angelina asked him where he was staying.

"I hope to get a room at the Hotel Polo down on Viale Amerigo Vespucci. I've stayed there before, and I liked it."

"How are you getting there?" She wondered if he'd take a taxi. Unlike other parts of Europe, Italy discouraged ride-sharing services.

"I'm gonna grab the number-eleven bus over by the Chinese supermarket. It will drop me near the hotel."

Her godfather's prediction that her luck would change kept circling in her mind as Angelina considered her options. She lived on the other side of the tracks, literally not figuratively, only a kilometer away, *in linea d'aria. Why did people use that expression to mean a straight line? Had they never watched a crow fly?*

The railroad complex formed a man-made barrier of over a dozen blocks, separating the historic center district from the central marina district and the beachfront. If she walked home through Parchi Callas e Renzi, it would take twenty minutes. The two parks were part of a greenbelt that encircled Rimini from the seafront to the Ponte di Tiberio. She loved the walk.

But I do not want to say goodbye!

The bus stopped only a few blocks from her home.

She made a decision, telling him, "I am headed that way. We could take the bus together if you do not mind my company a little longer."

Please do not mind.

"I would enjoy the company, thanks." His smile agreed with his words.

"Do you need a ticket?" The likelihood of getting stopped by a ticket inspector was minimal, but the fine was not. Angelina had a Rimini bus pass.

"Nah, I'm good. I still have a couple from last time."

She did not completely understand his colloquial response, but from his manner, she concluded he did not need to buy a ticket. They walked around the corner to the bus stop in front of the market. A few minutes later, the bus arrived. They boarded, Benjamin validated his ticket, and they took their seats. *Well, he knows his way around.*

"Shoot!" Before Angelina could ask him to explain, Benjamin did. "I meant to call the hotel on the train to see if they have a room. I'm sure this early in the season they will, but if not, I've got plenty of other options."

The bus turned right to cross under the railroad tracks that split the town. Angelina recalled the afternoon's events—everything she'd seen and experienced—and smiled. Benjamin was unlike any man she'd ever known.

Why has he showed up in my life?

As the bus turned, he slid in his seat, their shoulders meeting for a moment.

"*Scusa.*" Benjamin gave her a shy smile.

"*Va tutto bene.*" She did not realize she had replied to him in Italian. He was so proper and polite. Was he that way with everyone, or did his smile mean something more?

Instead of answering, her conscience scolded her. *Angelina, you are being silly. You are looking for something that is not there.*

Angelina frowned. God knows she had been lonely. But then, thinking of the last few hours, her smile returned. She stretched her arms out in front of her, hands clasped, and inhaled. As she exhaled and lowered her arms, she could not remember feeling more relaxed.

What did my godfather say? "God knows the world could use more romance." Maybe I should do my part. She looked at Benjamin. *Does he have any attraction to me—or is this just my hopeful, hopeless dreaming?*

Before her conscience supplied her with another answer that she preferred not to hear, she decided, *I must find out!*

They bumped again when the bus turned left onto Viale Principe Amedeo near the renown Rimini skyscraper. This time, Angelina smiled in apology. The evening traffic was heavy, so Angelina said, "We could walk faster."

Benjamin's reply both surprised and pleased her. "It's okay. This way we get to talk more."

"*Allora*, okay." She was smiling a little on the outside but a lot on the inside—until her conscience chimed in.

Angelina, he is just being polite.

She relied on her inner voice to keep her centered, but for once she wished it would just *sta' zitta*.

The bus, moving at a crawl, approached Parco Federico Fellini, the crown jewel of the Rimini greenbelt park system. Benjamin pointed off to the left, in the general direction of the Rimini Ferris wheel, La Ruota Panoramica. It was just visible above the roofs of the buildings. The wheel sat where the south beach reached the harbor channel, and the owners dismantled and stored it over the winter months.

"The Republic of Rose Island was out there, past the pier, about ten kilometers offshore."

Though not visible from the bus, Angelina was familiar with the pier. The Molo di Levante Capitan Giulietti was one of her favorite locations, not just in Rimini, but anywhere. She had strolled it countless times—both days and nights. Someone had built a nightclub called Rockisland on a platform where the pier met the jetty. Not wanting to interrupt, she did not mention this as Benjamin described the republic as being nothing more than a large platform, much like an offshore oil rig.

Another coincidence. Both "islands" were man-made platforms constructed over the water.

"An engineer named Rosa built it to be his own private country. He believed that if he built something outside Italian territorial waters, he could live free of taxes and government interference. Italy disagreed. He named the republic after himself and declared himself as its first, and only, president. He issued postage stamps, believe it or not, but never created a currency. Italy dispatched a squad of soldiers and police to take possession of the island. Within the year they destroyed the platform. It is a bit romantic and sad."

Noble and romantic, she remembered, and then, before her conscience could jump in again, she asked, "What happened to Rosa?"

"He claims to be living in 'exile.'" Benjamin put his hands in the air and wiggled the index and middle fingers of each, as if the two hands were waving to each other. When he saw her perplexed expression, he explained, "Sorry, those were 'air quotes,'" and he did it again. "It means I am using a word that wouldn't be my choice. It is a mocking gesture. Rosa said he is in exile but has nothing officially from which to be exiled."

Angelina nodded with a smile. She had seen people do it, but she had never understood why. She enjoyed learning idioms and mannerisms of other cultures.

"That pier is one of my favorite places in the world. There is a nightclub there, which I enjoy, but what I like most is being out away from everyone and hearing the waves dancing on the rocks. I love gazing out to sea and imagining…" She stopped, not wanting to say too much. Benjamin assumed she'd completed her thought and nodded.

Angelina pointed straight ahead to the fountain in the park. "That is another favorite place of mine, the Fontana dei Quattro Cavalli. We call them the *cavallucci marini.*"

"Ah, horses of the sea, not seahorses. Yes, I, too, like the Fountain of the Four Horses." Benjamin described how he found it both energizing and relaxing at the same time.

I thought I was the only one who felt that way.

Realizing her face was giving away her mild amazement, she said it aloud. He rewarded her with a warm smile and a nod of agreement.

As the bus navigated the quarter circle and prepared to turn onto Vespucci, Benjamin activated the stop request to get off at the post office, right before the hotel.

The light changed, and the bus lurched forward, heading toward Benjamin's stop. Again, Angelina struggled with her thoughts.

Am I being silly? I do not want to say goodbye.

"I have a guest room," she announced, with neither preface nor pretext.

What are you doing? her conscience asked.

Shut up, she told it again.

"You were kind enough to buy dinner. Please let me repay the kindness and permit me to provide you with a place to stay tonight. You do not even know if they have a room for you."

Benjamin declined, as she'd expected. "Please, it would be a great honor for me to have a famous American writer stay as my guest. Valentina will be amazed."

Her conscience chimed in, *I am sure she will,* but she ignored the self-mocking thought. She watched his face as a series of expressions appeared in rapid succession.

As the bus pulled up to the stop, he turned to her. "Okay, I would not want to cheat Valentina." He smiled. "Thank you very much for the invitation."

"*Allora*, okay!" Angelina said, then thought, *What did I just do?*

Smiling to mask her rising flood of panic, she asked, "Do you like dogs?"

TEN

Benjamin

I would not want to get on her bad side.

Angelina described her godmother as they sipped their *caffè*. He listened to everything she said, but a part of Ben's mind raced through one disjointed thought after another, unprompted by her description. He had to admit—his companion fascinated him. Remembering how they met just hours before, he found it incredible that they'd reached this point. He recalled the saying "opposites attract," but dismissed it.

We're not opposites, we're just opposite enough, he thought as he gazed out the window. *But she is so different from anyone else I've ever known.*

Uncomfortable with where his musings were going, Ben forced his thoughts in a different direction. He sighed as he sipped his coffee. *This is good espresso.* He developed his appreciation for the Italian approach to coffee the first time he'd visited Italy while in college. He liked his coffee black and preferred a dark roast, so he loved the Italian espresso culture. It took a while to adjust to the smaller serving, but he realized the standard espresso serving was perfect, if one appreciated great-tasting, dark-roast coffee.

In Italy, *caffè* meant espresso. He'd lost count of how many times he'd chuckled quietly—mostly—when an American tourist at the table next to him complained about being "ripped off" by the small serving of "coffee" they had received. He sympathized with the café staff, who told the customer politely—mostly—that they would return with a *caffè Americano.*

He hoped they were smart and just added boiling water to it in a larger cup.

"This was nice." Angelina's comment snapped him back to the moment. He was embarrassed that he'd wandered off daydreaming about coffee, of all things, and hoped she hadn't noticed. *But, yes, very nice,* he thought, as they both took their last sip together.

Ben asked the server for the check, and he waved Angelina off when she reached for her purse. He told her it was his treat to thank her for help with his research. He wasn't sure she bought it, and he didn't know if she'd enjoyed his company as much as he'd enjoyed hers. Anyway, it wasn't a lie. They had spent a few minutes discussing apartment prospects in town. Besides, keeping one's feelings private wasn't lying, was it? But he was unconvinced.

As Angelina tucked in her hair and replaced her hat, Ben realized that between the oversized hat and the platform shoes, she was not as tall as his first impression on the train. Not a model, more like a pit bull. This made him remember the rapper, Pitbull, which triggered his mental jukebox as it dialed up the song "Fireball."

No, not a pit bull, a fireball… yes, fireball, and he smothered his chuckle.

He thanked Angelina for her offer to ride with him. Ben worked hard to keep his smile polite—fighting the urge to break into a broad grin. The bus moved at a snail's pace in the evening traffic. He would normally be impatient to get to his destination. Instead, he relaxed in his seat. He even started to hum before he caught himself.

I am acting like a schoolboy.

But he enjoyed speaking with this woman. Ben enjoyed her company, appreciated her joie de vivre—and boy, did he love the sound of her voice. As they approached Piazzale Fellini, he pointed in the general direction of Rose Island's former location.

Why am I showing off? A flicker of anxiety teased his eyes, but Angelina's eyes were still engaged, and his own relaxed.

When she mentioned how much she liked the fountain in the park, Ben said, "I find it both energizing and relaxing," and realized that was how he thought of her—*energizing and relaxing at the same time.*

He smiled again when she lifted a hand to her chest, eyes wide, and described how she thought she was the only one. He smiled and shook his head. *No, there are two of us.* He decided not to complicate things by sharing that observation.

No sooner had he thought, *Don't complicate things,* when Angelina said she had a guest room and invited him to stay the night. She told him she wanted to reciprocate for dinner.

Talk about complicating things.

This triggered a wrestling match in his head, *I like this woman* squaring off with *You just met her.* The *You just met her* side won, and he said, "Thank you very much, but that isn't necessary."

Angelina dismissed his reply, and he smiled as she played to his vanity.

She probably wants to tell her friends an American writer had been her guest once, he thought. *Fatuous Hemingway stayed here.*

Ben had invented Fatuous—a fictional brother of Ernest—to be his imaginary alter ego. He used it to deflect compliments whenever someone called him a serious writer, triggering his imposter syndrome—the fear that he wasn't a "real" writer, but a fraud. He thought "fatuous" an apt antonym to "earnest."

Fraud or not, Fatuous had a reputation to protect. *He didn't want to be the aloof or ungracious Fatuous.* And he might get to meet her godmother. This Valentina sounded interesting. He was always seeking fresh character ideas for stories. That decided it. He accepted and thanked her for the invitation. Angelina then asked him if he liked dogs.

"I have this dog. He is wonderful, very large. He is a mixture of many breeds. A..." She paused, closed her eyes, wrinkled her nose, then opened her eyes and said, "*Non è di razza.*"

"Not a purebred? A mutt."

"*Sì,* I like this word 'mutt' better than *bastardo.*" She smiled as she nodded. "Two years ago, Valentina gave him to me when he was little more than a puppy, although he was not little even then. She told me he would be my protector, and he is. That is why I named him Raimondo; Raimondo means 'mighty protector.' But I call him Mondo."

Ben nodded at her explanation, then said, "I like dogs, and they like me."

"Mondo does not like anyone at first, so stay away until he gets to know you." As she reached behind him, she added, "And no matter what, do not make him think you mean me any harm."

Upon that ominous announcement, Ben wondered if he'd been wise to accept the invitation.

Angelina pushed the stop request, and they exited at the Piazzalle Kennedy. Angelina pointed them away from the beach, and they walked along a sidewalk that entered Parco Renzi.

Ben commented on the construction behind them. "What do you think of the Sea Park project? It seems rather ambitious."

"Now it is just the first phase, from here back to Parco Fellini. When finished, it will include about fifteen kilometers of seafront." Having turned to look back, Angelina first pointed to the north, her fingers splayed, and then swept her arm to the south, the fingers wiggling—as if they were sea birds flying along the beach.

"Not everyone likes it," she said. "Progressives believe it will reinforce our reputation as a family-oriented beach destination. Others do not like the disruption caused by the construction. Personally, I like it, but I will be glad when it is finished; the short-term economic impact on businesses has been severe." Angelina turned back from the plaza to Benjamin and said, "The future is sometimes painful—but we forget so is the past."

Ben stopped for a moment, then continued, hoping she hadn't noticed. Although Angelina had stated it matter-of-factly, it was one of the most profound things he'd heard in a while. When she described the rift in the feelings of the residents, it reminded him of a comment by Fellini in one of his documentaries.

Fellini was correct, Ben decided. *Rimini really is two different towns divided by the seasons.*

Angelina continued to describe Valentina, finishing with "She is also my protector."

"Like Mondo."

"*Sì*, and do not let her think you mean me any harm either."

Ben smiled, thinking Angelina was making a joke. Her return gaze corrected that assumption. The Hotel Polo was sounding more appealing by the moment.

As they strolled west, they came upon an open stretch of grass between the trees, the side street, and a parking lot. A dozen preteen boys and girls were playing a pickup game of soccer—*football*, Ben corrected himself—the early evening sun providing ample light even among the trees. When the children spotted Angelina, they stopped and ran to her, calling out her name.

In the cacophony of greetings, Ben heard Angelina greet almost every child by name. Several stared at Ben, while others pointed at him and asked, "Who is this man?"

One girl asked, "*È il tuo fidanzato?*"

Ben blushed as Angelina laughed. "No, Teresa, he is not my boyfriend. He is the famous American author, Ben LaRocca, and he will stay with us tonight."

Ben was unsurprised by their bored but polite responses as they greeted him, a few with "*Ciao*" or "*Buongiorno,*" others with a wave of their hands. The girl who asked the boyfriend question nodded, almost a curtsy, as she said, "*Mi fa piacere conoscerla, signore.*"

"I am pleased to meet you also, Teresa." Ben bowed in return and shook her hand. Well, at least one child wasn't bored by Fatuous Hemingway.

The way Angelina had first described her, Ben had believed her godmother was not a live-in housekeeper. But when Angelina said, *He will stay with us tonight*, Benjamin wondered if he'd misunderstood. If Angelina did not live alone, his moral compass now pointed to "proper." He pushed thoughts of Hotel Polo to the background and turned his attention to the children.

"Do you enjoy football?" A few children did not understand his question. Angelina repeated it, yet in a way that did not make Ben self-conscious. They all yelled "*Sì!*" adding specific reasons. Ben smiled as he listened to them yell over each other, lobbying for attention and trying to make themselves heard.

"*Bene, in America, ero un* soccer referee." In response to their puzzled looks, he added, "err... *Un arbitro di calcio.*" The children began jumping up and down and yelling, *"Un arbitro, un arbitro!"* Ben noted they were much more impressed by meeting a referee than an author.

Just like me at their age. Children are the same everywhere. That thought brought a broader smile to his face, and the children noticed.

"Signor LaRocca," a boy with muddied shoes asked, "would you be our *arbitro*? Gilberto is always committing fouls."

"I do not!" Ben assumed that was Gilberto.

"Yes, you do!" several children yelled, as they agreed in their disagreement with him.

Teresa turned to Ben with a solemn expression and said, "*Sì. Lui fa,*" bobbing her head several times as her eyes widened.

The group argued for another minute. Ben appreciated their passion and energy, but wished he had a whistle to get their attention—just as a loud whistle pierced the air and the children froze. He turned to see Angelina remove a whistle from her mouth and put it back in her purse.

"Children, we must go. Perhaps Signor LaRocca can be your *arbitro* another time." The children responded in various ways, but all showing their disappointment.

Ben squatted in front of Gilberto and said, "Gilberto, respect the game, respect the other players, respect yourself. No more fouls, okay?" He spoke slowly, hoping Gilberto could understand his accented Italian. Gilberto nodded.

Ben and Angelina turned to leave as the children returned to their game. A moment later, Ben felt a tug on his arm. He turned to see Gilberto staring up at him. "*Mi dispiace, signor arbitro,*" he apologized. "I will not foul anymore." And then he ran back to the game.

"You seem to be a man of many talents, *signor arbitro.*" Ben wasn't sure at first if Angelina was teasing him, but her smile was warm, her eyes warmer. "What was it like being a football referee in America?"

Ben described how he'd played soccer but was undistinguished. Still, he liked the sport, and when he found out as a teenager that he could be a referee and make money, he took a referee class. *It was better than working at McDonalds,* he thought, but he kept that observation to himself.

"It was a good part-time job. I found I enjoyed it. The responsibility, the connection to the sport, and even when the clueless, angry parents were yelling at me."

"Why did they yell?"

"They believed their ten-year-old kids would not get a college scholarship, half if I called a foul, and the other half if I didn't. As I became more skilled and worked with older children, the parents were less intense and more realistic. With the older kids, it was the coaches who were the problem. Middle-aged men who felt compelled to bully teenagers because they cared more about their coaching ego than their players or the sport. Worse, they felt justified in doing so! A few of my friends quit because of the obnoxious parents and coaches."

"But you did not?" Angelina asked.

"I considered it several times."

Angelina tilted her head and her eyes asked, "Why not?"

"I liked it," Ben answered. I enjoy the sport, I really do. The kids needed an impartial referee for safety and fairness. And... this will sound silly..."

"Tell me," she said, adding, "*Per favore*," with a gentle smile and another tilt of her head.

"Every so often, after a game in which her team had lost by more than a few goals, a player like Teresa would come up to me and ask, 'Who won?' Rather than answer, I would ask her, 'Did you have fun?' and when she'd say yes, I would answer, 'Then *you* did.'"

"Meaning the players enjoyed the game regardless of the score." It was an observation, not a question.

"Many times, not always, but often enough. It was their misguided coaches and parents who focused on winning above character building, skill development, enjoyment, and even—sad to say—the safety of their children."

They turned north out of the park and onto a narrow side street into a residential neighborhood. Ben changed the subject. "The children seem to love you."

As he was preparing to ask if she had any children of her own, Angelina announced, "Here we are! Remember to let me greet Mondo and introduce you."

What about Valentina?

Ben wondered if he was being overcautious. He noted the two-story house was one of the few single-family homes on the street. It sat on a corner, with a small yard on three sides and a driveway separating it from an apartment building.

They entered the gate. Angelina opened the front door, and a large mixed-breed dog ran to her, jumped with its front paws on her shoulders, and began licking her face. *He thought the dog must be part mastiff—it was huge.* He also thought Mondo—which meant "world" in Italian—was the perfect nickname for the dog. Angelina did everything but lick the dog back, telling him how much she loved him and had missed him.

Following right behind the dog was one of the tallest women Ben had ever met. He was just under six feet tall—she was at least three inches taller. He knew she was had been a classmate of Angelina's mother, but she seemed younger. She wore her brunette hair in a short bob pulled behind her ears. Ben noticed her broad shoulders. *Swimmer's shoulders,* he thought, and smiled. *So, this was Valentina. Wow, she's incredibly fit.*

The woman wasted no time as she began questioning Angelina. She did not sound happy.

I would not want to get on her bad side, Ben thought, just as Valentina took notice of his presence.

ELEVEN

Valentina

Your Italian is terrible.

Valentina left her apartment around 1600 hours for the three-block walk to Angelina's home. She hoped Angelina's meeting with her godfather had not been too painful. Last week, Angelo—her fellow godparent—had called to discuss Angelina's upcoming trip. Valentina had offered to make the trip with Angelina; her goddaughter had declined.

"It is something I must do on my own, Godmother," she'd said.

Happy to see Angelina more assertive and independent, Valentina had not disagreed.

Angelina had left her message with her revised itinerary while Valentina was on the phone with a follow-up call from Angelo. He'd shared with Valentina their conversation and his assessment that Angelina had handled it better than he'd hoped. Valentina felt relieved, yet still worried for her goddaughter. The past year had been a series of traumatic events, and Angelina had told Valentina more than once that she felt like a punching bag, both figuratively and literally.

"Angelina will need to generate more income beyond what the vacation house will produce if she wants to maintain her lifestyle," Angelo advised. "Maybe this is the time for us to offer her a financial lifeline."

Valentina had considered it for a moment before deciding against it. "No, we should stick to the plan."

"I understand why, but it does not make me happy," Angelo shared. "In anticipation of your decision, I suggested to Angelina that she consider renting out the ground floor room in Rimini—at least during the tourist season."

Valentina had acquiesced; it was the logical consequence of her plan. Of course, i*t would need to be a woman of exemplary character.* She did not relish having a stranger in their lives.

The relief provided by Angelo's summary lasted until 1730, there being no word from her goddaughter. As the top of the hour approached, Valentina's anxiety for her overdue Angelina escalated. Valentina was anxious any time Angelina walked to the market, let alone traveled overnight through Milano. Well-being aside, she was concerned that Angelina might be too embarrassed to discuss her financial circumstances.

"Am I being silly, Mondo?" The dog neither agreed nor disagreed, content to just listen.

She engaged in a running conversation with Mondo, alternating between "Mondo, I hope she is okay" and "Mondo, it makes my balls spin."

Over the next hour, she called Angelina's cell phone several times, but each time it went straight to voicemail. She left two messages, the first, "*Dove sei?*" the second, "Goddaughter, I am worried. Please call me."

***

Valentina checked with the Trenitalia website and found no reports of train interruptions, just a twenty-minute delay near Parma. As the clock moved all too quickly toward 1900, she wondered if she should call the police, or at least check in with her former colleagues. She sat at the kitchen table to collect herself. Just then, she heard the front door open, and Mondo bolted toward the door. For anyone other than Angelina, he would've been barking. Valentina, relieved, stood and marched out to confront Angelina, not planning to hide her displeasure and worry.

"*Meno male!*" Valentina was forced to compete with Mondo, who was as happy as Valentina was not. She scolded Angelina. "I am buried in worry. What happened to you? Why did you not call? Why did you not answer?" Her barrage did not offer Angelina an opportunity to reply.

As Valentina was speaking, Angelina pulled out her cell phone, checked it, and then slapped her forehead.

"*Colpa mia, Madrina,*" Angelina said in apology. "I forgot to charge my phone. I am such an idiot."

Before Angelina could reply to the other questions, and before Valentina repeated them out of frustration, Valentina saw a strange man come through the door with luggage.

Is he the cab driver? she wondered before she remembered Angelina had only brought a single bag.

"*Chi è questo?*" she asked. She raised an upturned palm toward the stranger.

"*Oh, scusa,*" Angelina replied. She gave Valentina a weak smile as Valentina placed her hands on her hips. "Godmother, may I present the American author, Signor Benjamin LaRocca. Benjamin, this is my godmother, Signora Valentina Marchese."

In clumsy Italian, the man said it was an honor to meet her as he held out his hand. Valentina took no notice of the outstretched hand, and he retrieved it with obvious embarrassment.

"Val, we met on the train today. I yelled at him, and later he gave up his seat for me. It was sweet. We had a great conversation—we could have talked all day. Benjamin is moving to Rimini to write. Then he invited me to dinner. Did you know he is vegan? He took me to this wonderful little restaurant near the train station. We had a wonderful dinner. We took the bus together, and I invited him to stay here tonight. We walked through the park, and the children were playing football. Benjamin was a soccer referee, so we stopped to talk to them."

"*Che cosa?*" Valentina was having trouble following Angelina's enthusiastic explanation and wondered if she'd misunderstood.

"*Un arbitro di calcio.*" Angelina corrected her inadvertent use of the American term.

"I know what a soccer referee is, Angelina. You invited him to do what?" Valentina waved one hand at Angelina, then brought her other hand to her chin.

Angelina inhaled and answered, speaking at a slower pace. "Benjamin needs to find an apartment. He'd planned to stay in a hotel on Vespucci. After he treated me to dinner, I told him I have a guest room and that I would be honored for him to stay the night."

Valentina stood, eyes wide, staring at Angelina. The color drained from her face. She raised her hands to her temples, then crossed her arms against her chest.

"Angelina, this is out of the question. Come with me, please." The "please" was not a request; it was a command. Valentina jerked her head and gestured to the doorway. She escorted Angelina back to the kitchen without even a glance at the intruder. As a result, she missed Mondo approaching Benjamin, as did Angelina.

Once in the kitchen, Valentina said, "*Figlioccia*, we will discuss how worried you made me another time." Valentina called Angelina "goddaughter" when she took on her surrogate mother role. "But this man staying here tonight, it is not proper!"

Angelina protested, "Val, why should he spend the night at a hotel when he now has a friend in Rimini?"

"Una amica? Sei fuori come un balcone!"

"Valentina, I am not out of my mind. Besides, it is my decision, not yours."

"Just because you can do something does not mean you should." This was one of Valentina's most frequently provided pieces of unsolicited and unappreciated advice.

"You know nothing about this man!" Valentina shook a raised palm, accentuating each word.

Angelina stormed back into the great room as Valentina followed. She watched as Angelina stomped to the credenza, searched through several magazines, and found one of the English language magazines Valentina had insisted she read. Angelina opened the magazine and glanced at the table of contents. She turned to an article, then turned and thrust the magazine toward Valentina.

"This is who he is! I told you when I read this story, I felt as if I knew this man. This is that man. Benjamin is the author."

As Valentina renewed her protest, Angelina turned and pointed to the man. He was kneeling next to Mondo, making friends, and being licked for his efforts. "If being a famous author is not enough, look at Mondo—he never likes anyone!"

At the sound of his name, Mondo's tail wagged more vigorously, if that were possible. At the sound of *his* name, the American appeared as if he wished he were anywhere else.

He stood up and began apologizing in English. "I am sorry I upset you."

"*Usa l'italiano, per favore, Signor LaRocca.*"

Benjamin began his apology again in Italian. Valentina struggled to follow everything he said. She was undecided about his accent, which was American, but with a Milanese flavor.

"I've the utmost respect for Signora Fabrizzi and all she has overcome and accomplished," he said.

How much has Angelina shared with this man? At least he is respectful.

"I've found her to be a wonderful travel companion and a wise observer of human nature."

As her goddaughter blushed, Valentina wondered, *È solo un balista?* She had met her share of bullshit artists.

"Angelina has told me all about you," the man continued. He smiled as he raised his palm to her.

Valentina winced at his informality. *So much for respect.*

He said, "She described what you have done for her and what you two mean to each other."

I am sure not all I have done.

He continued, sounding more confident, "Signora Marchese, I would never want to do anything to… uh, jeopardize your relationship, and I—um—I fear I've done that. I will get a hotel room as planned. I hope we can talk again soon." He looked at Angelina, then back to Valentina, and added, "Thank you for protecting Angelina."

"*Bene, è deciso*," Valentina replied.

Now that it was settled, Valentina relaxed. *At least he knows his place. If he is a bullshit artist, he is a good one, but I think not.*

She ignored the sense of déjà vu he'd triggered.

Angelina remained standing, not saying a word as the stranger apologized. She was leaning forward, and several times appeared as if she might interrupt. Valentina was glad she did not.

Finally, Angelina broke her silence and half shouted at Valentina, "*Basta, basta!*" Angelina turned to the man and said in English, "You are *my* guest. You will stay here as *I* intended." Then she turned back to Valentina and glared for several uncomfortable seconds before speaking.

"Excuse me while I make the guest room ready. I suggest you two get to know each other better." Pivoting on her heel, Angelina walked away, leaving no possibility of further debate.

Valentina absorbed everything she'd witnessed during the last five minutes. She arched an eyebrow and stared at the American, who appeared to be ready to crawl into a hole. When she noticed that Mondo appeared to be willing to crawl in after him, she raised the other eyebrow and wondered what had just happened. She remembered another confrontation four decades earlier and pushed it from her mind.

Valentina relaxed both eyebrows and tilted her head. She brought an index finger to her lips and exhaled a "Hmm," just a half breath.

This is the first time my goddaughter has stood up to me.

Instead of making her angry, it made her satisfied—and proud. She circled the index finger in front of her face, pointing to the ceiling.

She did make me a little angry, she thought, waggling her finger. *She had the audacity to yell "Enough!" at me. But my Angelina is growing.* Valentina smiled.

But what had gotten into Mondo? The dog was infatuated with this stranger. Did he keep raw meat in his pockets for such occasions?

The man appeared as if he expected Valentina to say something. When she did not, he attempted to apologize again. Valentina did not hide her frustration. *American men did not appreciate the value of silence—the virtue of contemplation. They must always fill in the gaps with noise.* She interrupted him, knowing her noise to be more important, obviously. She stood up straight and moved toward him, glaring at him from her three-inch height advantage. He took a step back, bumping up against the front wall. To her, he appeared to be considering whether to gnaw off a leg to get out of a trap.

"I will respect my goddaughter's wishes—but understand this, Signor LaRocca. If you make her angry or unhappy, I will beat you so badly you will wish you were dead. And if you hurt her"—Valentina paused and leaned forward—"I will kill you. Do you understand?"

Nodding, he replied, "*Ti, capisco—*"

Valentina cut him off again. "Your Italian is terrible."

INTERMEZZO

The Rimini Method

"The man who fights for his ideals is the man who is alive."
— Miguel de Cervantes Saavedra —

Isabella attended Valentina's graduation ceremony at Urbino. She could not contain her excitement and pride over Valentina's accomplishment. She brought Angelina, now a precocious three—*e mezzo*, she insisted—years old, who couldn't contain her excitement. Maro had wanted nothing to do with it, and when Isabella had asked if she could attend, he'd assented as if addressing a servant. "You have my permission."

Isabella appreciated that Valentina's grandmother, Loredana—her only living family—and her husband were attending. In their late sixties, both appeared to be in good health. Isabella had met Loredana and Enrico—her third husband—at the funeral for Valentina's father seven years earlier. They had not had time for an extended conversation, and she had not seen either of them since.

Throughout the day, Loredana described the circumstances of her first two marriages, one just before the war and one just after, each of which left her a widow. Isabella found her stories fascinating and enlightening, and a little sad, and she appreciated the insight into Valentina's life. Enrico and Loredana took turns offering recollections of Valentina's mother, Mariangela, helping to expand Isabella's understanding of Valentina. Enrico glowed with such paternal pride as he described Mariangela that Isabella was surprised when Valentina mentioned later that he was her mother's stepfather.

The amber-eyed Angelina was a big hit with everyone, polite during the ceremony, yet otherwise uncontainable. She wanted to know everything, pointing at buildings and monuments, as Valentina took her family on a tour of the town. The narrow streets were like canyons, focusing attention on the street level. But when they exited through the Porto Valbona and Angelina saw the Palazzo Ducale di Urbino from the parking area, she proclaimed, "*Voglio vivere là!*"

From time to time over the next few years, her mother would remind Angelina of her wish to live in the castle on the hill.

***

Valentina soon received a promotion to first constable. With the promotion, her superiors told the new *agente scelto* that she was being transferred to Aosta. She had impressed them with her French language skills. The Aosta valley sat between Torino and Geneva, near the tripoint of Italy, Switzerland, and France. Most of the population spoke French as their primary language.

Valentina looked forward to alpine skiing and cycling in the mountains, but that anticipation could not overcome her sadness at the gulf now separating her from Bella and Angelina. Her Ancona assignment had been less than ninety minutes from Rimini by train, and she and her family would meet up for the day at least once a month without drawing Maro's ire. It would now be an all-day endurance run on multiple trains. The visits would have to be overnight, and that would never receive Maro's approval.

Unable to see Bella and Angelina, Valentina instead took overnight trips through much of western Europe. Along with skiing, traveling, and speaking French, the Aosta posting provided one more benefit. She enrolled at the University of Torino and completed a *laurea magistrale* degree in philosophy three years later.

Studying philosophy, Valentina daydreamed of living in the time of the great philosophers, or at least during the Age of Enlightenment.

And I would need to have been born a man, as long as I am dreaming, she thought.

Whenever classmates and colleagues asked her which branch of philosophy was her favorite, she answered, "*Tutti loro, ovviamente!*" She did not understand why it was not obvious to them.

Valentina did not mention this graduation to Bella, knowing her attendance to be out of the question. She also had not mentioned her pursuit of a graduate degree, saying only that she enjoyed studying philosophy. Valentina shared few of her experiences with Bella, preferring to use their limited time together to learn about Isabella and Angelina's lives. She preferred not to alarm them with her more interesting activities, and she knew her less interesting activities to be of little interest, obviously.

Valentina earned another promotion the following year, this time to *assistente*. As before, the P.S. transferred the new senior constable, and Valentina received her first large city assignment, in Milano. Besides the obvious size and population density, there were other differences. Crime was rampant, much greater than she'd experienced even at Ancona with the ferry boat traffic. She expected it around the train station, but it seemed to be everywhere—and it was far and away more violent.

In addition to the professional differences, she had to make other adjustments. The city was noisy! Valentina had enjoyed the tranquility of Aosta and Pesara. Even Ancona was quiet by comparison.

Also, people were rude! She never became accustomed to the lack of civility and decorum in public. They spoke slang and used colloquialisms that abused her ears and her sensibilities. She'd stopped trying to teach strangers better manners when she realized they just became ruder.

Despite these significant challenges, there was much to like. She appreciated access to both the variety and the quantity of cultural events and activities. As she'd expected, she enjoyed the multiculturalism and more progressive civic vibe.

Because crime in the city was both violent and rife, she had to focus her law enforcement efforts on assisting victims of serious crimes. Evil people prowled the city, not just people doing evil things. Valentina liked the feeling of satisfaction it provided—she was not just helping people; she truly was protecting them.

She also appreciated Milano's role as a transportation hub, which helped quench her desire to travel. While Aosta was close to many countries measured by distance, Milano was closer to them, and to many more, measured by time. In a day, she could travel almost anywhere in Europe by train, and just about anywhere in the world from its Aeroporto di Milano-Malpensa.

The most important advantage to working in Milano: she was now less than four hours from Bella and Angelina via direct train, and they from her. Bella would take Angelina into the city for shopping, and the three of them would eat lunch and shop. Valentina would travel to Rimini for an afternoon together at the beach. They would meet in Bologna or Parma for sightseeing or cultural events.

Although Milano was better located than Aosta, she still regretted that the opportunities to visit were not as frequent as when she was on the Adriatic coast. Perhaps that was why the visits felt more precious. When Isabella would ask about her job, Valentina answered truthfully. "It is the same thing every day."

While stationed in Milano, Valentina enrolled in a new international finance doctoral program at the University of Bocconi. Finance and investment had always fascinated her—as she'd told herself when she applied, it sounded like fun. She described it to Bella as taking a few investment courses. She relished the research required, and unlike her fellow ABDs, she enjoyed defending her thesis: "Managing Portfolio Behavior from an Economic Life-Cycle Perspective." She was one of the first candidates at Bocconi to use the PowerPoint software with a video projector, rather than just use it to produce traditional transparencies for an overhead projector.

When she received her *dottorato di ricerca* degree—the Italian equivalent of a PhD—four years later, she was away on an assignment. As she could not attend, she saw no reason to bother Bella with the news.

Valentina impressed her superiors with her capabilities and conscientiousness, and they assigned her to work on an anti-prostitution task force. Her team enjoyed remarkable success, even though—or perhaps because—they did not follow the traditional male-dominated methods pervasive in Italian law enforcement. Rather than treating the women and occasional men as criminals, the team saw them as victims of the people who had ensnared them. Valentina reminded her fellow officers, "We are not anti-prostitution—we are anti–human trafficking."

The following January, the *vice commissario* asked to speak with her. He complimented her, as he often did, on her efforts contributing to the success of the team. He then asked Valentina if a potential assignment might interest her. It was not a transfer, so the choice was hers, but the Rimini *sostituto commissario* wanted Valentina to help him with their human trafficking efforts. He wanted a woman on his team, and he knew she was from the area.

She was familiar with Chief Inspector Morelli. In fact, she'd studied various methods he advocated, and she'd applied them to her work in Milano. After her assistant superintendent described the opportunity and asked if she wanted to move to Rimini, she said, "*Ovviamente.*" She suppressed a chuckle when she saw how her choice had pleased him.

She thought, *He should have known by now that I would say, "But of course."*

Only later did she learn that because of her decision, she was being fast-tracked and promoted to *vice sovrintendente*. She had never thought of herself as a sergeant—once again, it sounded like fun.

***

Valentina appreciated her latest assignment—its location most of all. She visited Bella and Angelina at least once a week. Maro was out of the house most of the time, and had stopped objecting to Valentina's presence, opting instead for disdainful indifference.

Valentina became more comfortable describing her work to Isabella and the ever-curious Angelina. Despite the increased comfort, she did not go into details, and never spoke about the more violent aspects of her work. She did not want to worry them.

It is enough that they know I protect them, without the gory details, she thought.

Valentina did not consider it a rationalization—just the correct approach, obviously.

That fall, her goddaughter entered lower secondary school. Valentina did everything she could to feed Angelina's love for knowledge and learning. She encouraged—Angelina contended that she forced—her goddaughter to pursue both English and French. Valentina's efforts succeeded with English—not so much with French.

It is the MTV, she thought. *I cry for the future.*

Her pride and her joy were both tempered because she was unable to protect her pride and joy. Angelina endured relentless attacks—not physical, but mental and emotional. Her red hair, dark to begin with, had darkened further to a deep auburn color with unusual highlights. Because of poliosis, a streak of ash-blonde hair appeared at the top of her forehead. In the summer, it lightened to silver, almost white.

Valentina considered it distinctive—the children just saw it as different. Between her hair and her amber eyes, Angelina was taunted daily. As awful as that was, the behavior of the man who should've been supporting and protecting her—Tàmmaro, her father—was worse. Not only did he not support her, he directly contributed to her misery. Whenever he was angry with Angelina, he blasted her appearance as some curse from God. Valentina believed in a Supreme Being, but told herself often, *If Angelina was cursed, I want no part of this god.*

Bella and Valentina tried to console Angelina, telling her how precious she was and to ignore the taunting. Her mother would not, could not, bring herself to criticize Angelina's father. Valentina had no such qualms. Bella did not object, but it may not have mattered if she had. Maro was implacable.

Valentina remembered a visit one day when Angelina came home from school in tears. She went to her room, slamming the door without responding to Bella's or Valentina's inquiries. Valentina asked Bella if she could speak with her daughter and took her tilted head and upturned palm as permission.

After knocking and hearing no response, she entered Angelina's room. She sat on the bed next to her weeping goddaughter as Angelina worried at her hands as if wringing a dishcloth. Valentina waited, watching wordlessly. It was a technique she'd perfected working with the human trafficking victims. After several minutes, Angelina calmed herself enough to describe how she tried to make friends, but soon enough the other children pressured her latest companion to have nothing to do with the strange-looking girl.

"I will always be your friend," Valentina told her.

I just wish I could be your father, she thought.

Valentina shielded Angelina from her wish—and from her anger and sadness—unable to do anything else.

***

Valentina and the other officers working on the task force in Rimini developed an approach later known as the Rimini Method. It had a dramatic positive impact on human trafficking in the area, and later in other parts of Europe. The *polizia* had established a partnership with a Catholic foundation. The approach established and built trust with the victims, many of them coerced immigrants. When they found someone who wanted out of the life, the *polizia* would connect the prostitute with the Associazione Comunità Papa Giovanni XXIII.

The *associazione* would provide the victim with support and a place to live. In exchange, the police would arrest the people, mostly men, who had imprisoned the prostitute, who was most often—though not always—a woman, provided the prostitute agreed to testify. Valentina believed—no, she was certain—they were making a difference. Except one time.

Every so often, a woman would say she liked what she did, which never failed to surprise Valentina. One woman from the Balkans—*Just a girl of eighteen,* she remembered—explained, "Each time, I pretend I am in love. It feels good to be loved." Valentina had replied that sex was not love.

After being apprehended several times, the prostitute told the police she wanted out, but was afraid for herself and her family. As soon as the Catholic *associazione* situated her in her new residence, the *polizia* picked up her handlers, who were convicted less than two months later and sentenced to prison. Valentina's team counseled the woman that she should be safe there in Italy, but that she should not try to return home. Unfortunately, the warnings could not overcome how much she missed her mother and family. She crossed the Adriatic to visit them, where associates of her handlers killed both her and her mother.

When a colleague of Valentina's told her about the deaths, she asked, "*Perché mi hai detto una cosa del genere?*" When he did not answer, she yelled it. "Why did you tell me that?"

The colleague said he thought she'd want to know, then left. Valentina sighed.

I want to know, she thought. I just hate being reminded that I am a failed protector.

***

A year later, in the first spring of the new millennium, the police learned that the men responsible for the women's deaths had returned to Rimini. While attempting the arrest, Valentina and several fellow officers shot and killed them after they opened fire and wounded one of her colleagues. She took neither joy nor satisfaction in either her role or the outcome. She told others, they were *malvagi*, and now they were *morti*.

She told herself, *Maybe it will protect the next girl.*

TWELVE

Angelina

And never call me Valentina.

Angelina returned from straightening the first-floor guest room. She showed Benjamin the downstairs bathroom and made sure there were enough towels. It was a relief when Valentina stopped trying to change her mind—she'd prepared for another round of objections.

Angelina opened a bottle of Sangiovese wine and poured a glass for Benjamin and herself. She had to hide her surprise when a silent Valentina retrieved a glass and held it out for Angelina to fill, shaking both the glass and her head once when Angelina did not react quickly enough.

They sat at the dining table in the great room as she and Benjamin provided Valentina with more details of the day's events. Benjamin used his rudimentary Italian, which appeared to grate on Valentina, but she ignored anything he said in English. Before too long, he was speaking in slow motion, pronouncing each word separately and distinctly, yet too often imprecisely. Angelina could not tell if it was the wine, his weariness, or his fear of Valentina, but she felt obligated to put Benjamin out of his misery.

"*Ho avuto una lunga giornata,*" Angelina announced.

It had been a long day, but a surprisingly pleasant one. As she stood, she said, "Benjamin and Valentina, please excuse me, but I need to get some sleep." Then Angelina headed toward the stairs. Turning, she added, "Do not stop talking because of me, but it also has been a long day for Benjamin. We should let him get some rest. Valentina, will you lock up when you leave?"

Valentina replied, "I am sleeping here tonight." She rose to her feet and turned toward Benjamin. "Upstairs." Arching one eyebrow as she looked up to the floor above, she added, "In the room next to Angelina's."

After Benjamin nodded his understanding, Valentina said, "*Buona notte, Signor LaRocca,*" and she climbed the stairs.

Angelina called from the top of the stairs, "*Buona notte, Benjamin.*" She smiled. *I so like that name.*

***

Valentina, already dressed, awakened Angelina in the morning. Angelina asked, "*Benjamin è sveglio?*"

"He was not when I started the coffee. But get dressed, please, before you come downstairs." Angelina appreciated her godmother's sense of propriety—and her housekeeper's recognition of the importance of *caffè*.

Once downstairs, she heard Valentina working on breakfast in the kitchen. She expected to see the guest room door shut, but it was ajar. Thinking Benjamin was awake and dressed, she went to the door and called his name. Too late, she saw he was still in bed. *Well, this is embarrassing.* She glanced away.

Before she could apologize, Benjamin turned onto his back and peered out at her from under the sheet. "*Buongiorno, signorina—err, intendo signora.*" He said it with a goofy grin on his face, which gave her pause.

She asked him in English, "Benjamin, did you sleep well?"

"Both of us did," he replied, and Mondo picked his head up to have his ears scratched. "I am afraid you have caught the two of us together, madame." He lifted his arm with a flourish and dropped his head in an attempted bow—made awkward by his prone position.

Angelina stifled an embarrassed giggle. "I am *so* sorry. Mondo likes to sleep upstairs unless Valentina is here. Then he sleeps on this bed. I had forgotten." Benjamin smiled at her explanation as she considered what she had observed.

I cannot believe Mondo would crawl into bed with Benjamin—or any man. Mondo and Giovanni never got along.

Mondo knew, she thought. *My husband was an asshole.*

As for Benjamin, she'd never seen Mondo so comfortable with anyone, not even Valentina.

"I would sleep down here as well if Valentina was in my regular bed."

After a brief pause, Ben added, "Sorry, that was rude. A bad joke."

Angelina waved away his apology. The joke was bad but not rude. There was truth to it. "I suppose Mondo can sleep wherever he wants," he said, and she laughed, her head bobbing in agreement.

Good, he is not angry or upset. She envied his easygoing manner and ability to adjust. After last night, she'd have been a wreck had she been in his shoes.

"I am glad you slept well, and Mondo too." The dog's head popped up again. "I also slept well. Yesterday was difficult, and I was glad when it was over."

She'd meant yesterday morning. Too late, she realized Benjamin had taken her literally. She watched his smile disappear, to be replaced by a frown. His back stiffened as he propped himself on his elbows and tried to sit up.

"I am deeply sorry for the added stress. You have enough to worry about. I appreciate your hospitality, but I will make sure I find a room this morning so things can get back to normal for you." He did not finish sitting up, and instead leaned back on his elbows, looking at the ceiling.

Merda, cosa ho fatto? she asked herself, but she knew what she had done. *Damn my stupid mouth—how do I fix this?*

"Benjamin, I did not mean you! There were two yesterdays for me. I meant the first one, in Como. That yesterday ended when I met that poor man on the train and yelled at him like a *vecchia pazza*."

He looked so uncomfortable. "You were not a crazy lady," he said.

Good, he understood. She was trying not to mix English and Italian, as she often did with her godmother.

"My second yesterday, after I met you, was a most pleasant and memorable day. One that made it possible for me to relax, forget about the first yesterday, and get the first good night's rest I have had in a long time."

"That's good. I'm glad." His smile returned. Angelina smiled also, when, at first, his posture eased, and then he fell back onto the bed.

Valentina came up behind Angelina and said through the doorway, "*Buongiorno, Signor LaRocca.* We will leave you so you can dress for breakfast. It will be waiting for you when you are ready."

***

Valentina had placed breakfast on the dining table in the great room, instead of on the kitchen table where they often ate. Angelina could not decide if Valentina was showing respect for her guest by eating more formally, or drawing a line to show where too familiar began. It was their standard breakfast: vegan cookies, orange juice, fresh fruit, and *caffè*.

Valentina assumed Benjamin wanted *caffè Americano.*

"*No, caffè espresso, per favore,*" Angelina ordered for him. Valentina arched an eyebrow, but Angelina did not take the bait.

Benjamin came out of his room and sat down at the table. Angelina observed he wore fresh clothes today, but still business casual. It was a good look on him. *But different shoes. Those looked English.*

"*Buongiorno, le signore,*" he greeted them. His pronunciation was better than last night. Angelina and Valentina returned his greeting.

"I understand you had a companion, Signor LaRocca." Valentina made it a statement, not a question, but Benjamin answered anyway.

"Sì, Mondo."

"Mondo has always been an excellent judge of character." Just as Angelina observed a smile forming on Benjamin's face, Valentina added, "I hope he has not lost his touch."

"Valentina!" Angelina glared at her godmother before glancing at Benjamin.

"*Che cosa ho detto?*" Valentina raised both hands in front of her, pinching the thumb and fingers of each together.

Angelina mimicked the same gesture with one hand. "You know very well what you said," Angelina said in English. She turned to Benjamin and apologized.

"No, no," he assured her. "Your godmother was just making a joke. It made me feel more comfortable." He turned to Valentina. "*Grazie, Signora Marchese. Quello era buono.*"

Angelina was skeptical and turned to stare at Valentina. Valentina glanced away, gestured with the cookie in her right hand, and said, "But of course." Then she turned back to Benjamin. "*Prego, Signor LaRocca.*"

Angelina was sure the two had communicated something in the exchange—she was just unsure what.

Benjamin complimented them on the breakfast. When Angelina

assured him the cookies were vegan, he thanked her. "*E anche lei, Signora Marchese, sei vegana?*" He mangled the first part, but they both understood the question.

"No, Signor LaRocca, I am not a vegan." Valentina leaned toward him. "I respect my goddaughter's choices here in her house—all of them. But I like meat too much, especially meat I kill myself."

"Valentina!"

"*Un piccolo scherzo.*" Again, Valentina turned away.

"A bad joke, Godmother."

Was she lying, or just embarrassed? Valentina had never lied to her, at least as far as Angelina knew.

Benjamin turned back to Angelina. "It will only take me a few minutes to pack. Would you mind if I made a few calls first? I might as well make sure I have a room before I leave." Valentina appeared to be ignoring Ben's question in English.

"Yes. No—I mean no, of course not." Angelina could not hide her dismay over Valentina's overt efforts to drive him away. Angelina drew a deep breath as she turned away from her godmother to face Benjamin. "What I mean is, yes, you can make the calls—but no, you do not have to. Please stay here until you find an apartment. Why stay in a hotel?"

As Valentina arched an eyebrow, Benjamin said, "*Apprezzo molto la tua ospitalità.*" He smiled as he shook his head. "But allowing me to stay after today is excessive. I need to get back on plan." Valentina punctuated his comment with a head nod of agreement.

Angelina's mood and her thoughts devolved and fermented into dismay and frustration.

Why does he have to leave? Why should he stay at a hotel when he has a nice room in a nice house with nice company—well, perhaps Valentina has not been so nice, but I am—and a nice dog? Wait—

"Is it Mondo? I can make sure he does not bother you." She'd switched to English, hoping to cut her godmother out of the conversation.

"No, vado mate di cani!"

Her eyes widened. "Benjamin, what do you mean you 'go mate with dogs'?" Benjamin's confession confounded her—Valentina's amusement annoyed her.

"*Scusi, intendo 'matta di cani.'* I am crazy about dogs. Mondo is great. I haven't had a dog sleep next to me for many years. I had a wonderful night's sleep, and I am sure it was because of Mondo." Every time Benjamin mentioned his name, Mondo nuzzled Benjamin's hand to reinvigorate the ear-scratching.

Benjamin reverted to Italian. "Seriously, your godmother is right. You just do not open your home to a perfect stranger and give him a room."

Valentina nodded again, Angelina's annoyance growing with each nod. In retaliation, Angelina used English.

"Benjamin, yesterday I learned I need to rent out this room to balance my budget. If not you, it will be someone else I do not know, an imperfect stranger, if you will. I prefer it be you." Angelina was improvising as she tried to avoid what she was certain was her godmother's steely gaze, likely with both eyebrows arched.

After a few moments, which seemed longer to Angelina, Benjamin conceded. "Well, if you will rent it regardless, then okay." He switched back to Italian. "But it must be a fair agreement. No special treatment for writers." Smiling, he turned toward Valentina.

Is he seeking Valentina's blessing or girding himself for her reaction?

"But of course," Valentina replied, "just until you find an apartment." Valentina reached into her pocket, pulled out a business card, and handed it to Benjamin. "Signor LaRocca, here is the card of Signor Rossi. He is an apartment manager. I am sure he can help you."

As Benjamin thanked Valentina and took the card, Angelina thought it strange that Valentina had the card sitting there in her pocket.

I must ask her about that later.

Angelina began clearing the table, soon joined by the others.

***

They worked out a weekly rent amount that each agreed was fair, even Valentina. Ben asked if he could use the kitchen if he purchased the groceries. Angelina agreed, but Valentina's grimace showed that she resented any intrusion into the kitchen.

Then Benjamin retired to his room to write, stating that he needed to meet a deadline and that he'd begin his apartment search in the morning.

Later, after they cleared the table from the lunch Valentina had insisted on preparing, Benjamin asked Angelina, "Would it be okay if every so often I sat at the dining table to write, as a change of pace from the table in my room? I like to shift my seat from time to time as I work." Benjamin waved his arm from his bedroom door to the dining table. He added, "It gives me a fresh perspective, literally and figuratively." Angelina nodded her approval.

"Thanks, Angie."

"What did you call me?" she asked.

"What do you mean?" he asked.

"Did you just call me 'Angie'?"

Angelina hated that nickname. She could still hear the taunts of her classmates as they had sung it: "*Angie—cupa—Angie occhi da lupa.*" Her husband had used it because he knew she hated it. She glanced at Valentina, who was well aware of how Angelina felt. Her godmother looked as if she was getting ready to watch a boxing match. Valentina even had the nerve to say, "This should be good."

"*Questo dovrebbe essere buono.*" Valentina said, as she held her chin in her left hand, her right hand balled into a fist against her waist.

Benjamin, who again appeared to wish he were somewhere else, was further confused by Valentina's prediction.

I should not be angry with Benjamin. How could he know that name torments me?

Angelina took a breath to calm herself.

"*Benjamin, mi chiamo 'Angelina.' Non chiamarmi 'Angie,' per favore.*" She winced as she said the name out loud.

Ben's eyes widened, but then he exhaled, and Angelina saw his neck and jawline relax.

"Please forgive me. I understand. I hate being called 'Bennie.'" He shook his head.

Why would anyone call him Bennie? She mirrored his head shake.

"I would never call you Bennie. Benjamin is such a wonderful name." When she said his name, his relief was unmistakable. "You need not apologize, Benjamin. I did not mean to worry you."

Valentina must have concluded the boxing match was canceled. "Now that you know what not to call each other, I have business elsewhere."

Angelina had never asked how many other homes Valentina cleaned, but her customers must all be adaptable and accommodating. Valentina had no regular schedule, as far as Angelina could tell.

When Valentina opened the front door to leave, she turned to Benjamin. “And never call me Valentina.”

INTERMEZZO

The Innocence of Death

"Get clear about exactly what it is that you need to learn and exactly what you need to do to learn it. Being clear kills fear."
— Miguel de Cervantes Saavedra —

Valentina had reached a career ceiling in the P.S. While not glass, she thought it was pretty damn transparent. She had contributed to the circumstances, as she possessed little patience for any politics or bureaucracy that interfered with the mission. The higher one went, the more one was expected to embrace the system, not buck it. Her superiors did not object to her attitude toward *i criminali*, just her attitude toward *i suoi superiori*.

The behavior of police and others at the July 2001 G8 summit in Genoa had first offended, then outraged her. Not that she sided with the protesters—she'd despised their behavior and their methods. *They complained of poverty, yet they forced the government to spend millions to maintain order, while they destroyed what little economic opportunity existed.* She saw no problem with their arrests, but she objected to the brutality. Her superiors and colleagues objected to her objections.

The year before, when Italy changed the law to allow women to enlist in Italian military services, she had considered applying to the Carabinieri. Valentina decided the benefits of staying with the P.S. outweighed the negatives. She liked her responsibilities in Rimini and the proximity to her family, and Valentina was confident, based on her record, that she could stay in the province for the rest of her career.

The events of September 11, 2001, changed everything. After the prime minister's speech to the Chamber of Deputies on September 12, Valentina revisited her decision and started calling in favors. In October, the Carabinieri accepted her application.

***

Valentina had asked Isabella to join her for lunch. "Bella, I have something important to tell you." Isabella nodded her head as she finished chewing and swallowed. Valentina said, "I am leaving the Polizia di Stato." Isabella tilted her head, coughed, and took a sip of tea.

"I thought you enjoyed helping and protecting people?" Isabella assumed that Valentina was leaving law enforcement. Valentina was appreciative of her concern.

"I am not leaving law enforcement; I am joining the Carabinieri. After the terrorist attacks in America I fear that the entire world is at risk."

"So, now you are the entire world's protector, yes?" Valentina was surprised; she had expected a protest from Isabella. Instead, Isabella added what would become her standard farewell: "I love you. Please be careful."

***

Angelina was another story. "Why do you want to leave me? I thought you were my friend?"

Valentina sat down with her goddaughter, who avoided Valentina's gaze, instead twirling a lock of her hair. When Valentina began to speak, Angelina stopped and crossed her arms.

"Angelina, last month when we celebrated your seventeenth birthday, the world was different. It felt safe—I knew my place in it. Two days later, that all changed."

Valentina tensed as her goddaughter shook her head and drew in her upper lip between her teeth, still averting her gaze. She watched wordlessly as Angelina stopped shaking her head, released her lip, took a deep breath, and then set her jaw. Valentina relaxed when she saw Angelina meet her gaze.

Good, she sees it too, she thought, before continuing, "I can stay here and protect you and your mother, or I can accept this challenge and try to protect everyone. Do you understand?"

Angelina accepted the explanation with misty eyes before she hugged her godmother, thanking her and telling her to be safe. Valentina held the embrace, saying she was so proud of her grown-up Angelina, before releasing her. Valentina was not trying to play to Angelina's altruism—but it was another trait she loved about her goddaughter.

Valentina told neither Bella nor Angelina that regulations prevented her from being assigned to the Emilia-Romagna region for at least eight years. *No sense in making them feel worse.*

***

When Valentina began her training, she found that while certain procedures and equipment were similar if not identical, there was much to learn, unlearn, and occasionally relearn. She impressed her superiors with the speed by which she absorbed new material. They admired her marksmanship. Most of all, they appreciated her martial arts skills and sheer physicality.

Valentina embraced the Carabinieri, and before long, it embraced her. She felt she was where she belonged. Most of the members were from southern regions, but they accepted her once they saw her commitment. Not long out of training, another *carabiniere* told her that people only became a *carabiniere* for one of two reasons: a sense of justice, or a desire for revenge.

"We know you stand for justice—like us."

Because of her performance, she was fast-tracked into the GIS the following October. The Gruppo di Intervento Speciale was the special intervention group of the Carabinieri, and it partnered with other military agencies. It was ramping up for a greater role in counterterror operations.

Valentina also withheld this information from Bella and Angelina, not wanting to alarm them. Later, a friend of hers died in an attack while stationed in southern Iraq. Bella had only learned that Valentina was in the GIS when, in late November, Valentina came to visit after attending his funeral.

***

Isabella received her diagnosis in September, just before Angelina's twentieth birthday. She'd postponed seeing the doctor for several months, hoping that if she ignored the problem, it would go away. Instead, she learned she had triple negative breast cancer, and it was stage three. Both the prognosis and the treatment recommendations scared her, and she spent much of each day praying for strength and recovery.

Her husband, Maro, was of no comfort, seeming only to care if it would disfigure her. When he learned of the recommendation for surgery, Maro forbade it, saying he would not permit those butchers to disfigure his wife. "God will deliver my Isabella if that is his will."

Isabella longed for Valentina's counsel, but she acquiesced to her husband's advice and began radiation and chemotherapy treatments. Isabella had been praying since the diagnosis. She decided she needed to pray more, and Maro rallied his fellow congregation members to hold prayer vigils at their home.

Each time Isabella spoke with Angelina, Isabella downplayed her condition, not wanting to alarm her daughter. Angelina had two years remaining at university, and Isabella could not bear to be a distraction to her. Plus, her daughter had just announced she was dating a boy she liked, and Isabella preferred not to dampen her high spirits. Isabella wanted—needed—to speak with Valentina in person, but she was on an assignment.

Her family gathered in Ferrara later in the month for the marriage of her niece, Cristiana. Her father, Salvatore—Isabella's oldest brother—had been seriously injured before Cristiana's birth and had died only a few months after her first birthday. Isabella's other brother, Santino, was a priest, and her sister, Ilaria, was a nun. The wedding was the first time that Isabella had seen her siblings since the funeral of their mother in January the year before. It devastated them both when their younger sister described her condition. They urged Isabella to ignore her husband and to have the surgery recommended by her doctor.

Isabella tried to shield Angelina from discussions of her condition, but she could not hide her appearance. Angelina wanted to drop out of school to care for her mother. Isabella assured Angelina she would beat the disease and implored her to finish her university studies.

***

One afternoon, after another discussion, their feelings came to a head.

"Mamma, I cannot keep doing this. I cannot continue going about my life as if nothing is wrong. You need someone to take care of you. I am leaving university." Angelina stood with her arms crossed as she gazed at her mother.

Isabella reached out and took Angelina's hands. She gently uncrossed her daughter's arms. As her arms fell to her sides, Isabella placed her hands on her daughter's cheeks.

"Please do not do this. It will not help me; it will make me feel worse. I want to see you graduate." Isabella inhaled deeply but felt as if she could not breathe.

Angelina pulled away from her mother and lifted an index finger, waggling it and shaking her head, an unspoken rebuttal. She did not notice her mother's labored breath.

Isabella reached out to touch her daughter's shoulder and was dismayed when Angelina shook her off.

"*Fallo per me, Angelina?*" she asked, and brought a palm to her chest as she inhaled again, more deeply than before. Isabella watched as Angelina brought her hands to the sides of her head, as if to keep it from flying away.

Angelina sighed and placed a hand on her mother's cheek before saying, "*Sì, mamma, per te.*"

Isabella felt as if the drapes had been opened in a darkened room, until she saw Angelina drop her shoulders, tear up, and walk away without a word.

One day at a time, Isabella thought, as her world darkened again.

***

In November, Valentina announced she was coming to visit after the funeral of a colleague. Isabella looked forward to sharing her burden with her best friend and soulmate. After she arrived, Valentina mentioned the funeral had been for a friend who was killed in the unfortunate attack in Iraq. Valentina informed Isabella she was in the special forces group, and her unit might also be deployed to Iraq.

With that new and unwelcome knowledge, Isabella withheld her diagnosis from Valentina. She could not bring herself to add to Valentina's worries, and she forbade Angelina from mentioning it. When Valentina left for home, Isabella said what she always said, "*Ti amo. Attenzione per favore.*"

***

In early January, after a somber, almost funereal holiday season at the Roselli home, Maro came back one night before midnight, unusual for him. As on most nights, Isabella had retired early. She'd been sleeping more, yet without improving the fatigue she felt in every cell of her body. She had not heard Maro come into the house, but she soon knew he was home.

There was yelling, followed by Angelina running up the stairs crying. The door downstairs slammed, and Maro plodded up a moment later, yelling at her through her closed bedroom door, wheezing as he climbed the steps. Isabella called to him from her bed. "What happened? Why is Angelina crying? Why are you screaming?"

"She is crying because I am screaming. I am screaming because I finally caught the little disfigured whore." He wheezed before continuing, "She was screwing some boy from school on the sofa. This is why I did not want to send her to university." He followed another labored breath with "Do you see what happens? Like mother, like daughter!" Maro alternated his ranting with labored breaths, saying he'd fix this problem, and then describing how. Isabella rose from her bed to go find her daughter, knowing why but not how she found the effort.

Painful memories returned as Isabella entered the hall, adding to her physical pain as she supported herself with a hand on the wall. Her husband's solution was both familiar and sickening to her, as if she needed something else to make her sick. She did her best to comfort her inconsolable daughter, as regret racked Isabella as much as her illness.

True to his word, Maro followed up on a recent inquiry made by the son of his partner. Before his daughter could damage her—and, more importantly, his—reputation further, Maro negotiated a marriage with the ambitious Giovanni Fabrizzi. The wedding was planned for June. It took all Isabella's strength to gain a promise from both men to allow Angelina to complete her last year of university after the wedding. Isabella lacked energy for anything else.

***

Valentina first learned that Isabella was ill when she returned on leave in late

May, two weeks before the wedding. Valentina had not heard from Isabella more than a few times since Christmas. She'd assumed her letters were not keeping up with her temporary duty assignments, as her team was constantly being redeployed around Italy. Isabella's decision to hide her illness from Valentina disappointed and angered her. At first, she was disappointed in Isabella, but it quickly changed to anger with herself for her self-centered reaction.

Isabella begged for Valentina's forgiveness, saying that God had answered her prayers and brought her protector safely home. Angelina begged for her godmother's intervention, saying God had abandoned them. Maro said whatever happened was God's will.

Maro's behavior and its effect on her godchild disgusted Valentina. After much soul-searching, she chose not to interfere—for fear of being banned from the wedding, but really because she knew it would have no effect.

Short of shooting the asshole, she thought, *I can do nothing except support Angelina and hope this Giovanni is not also an asshole.*

The day of the wedding, Isabella appeared pallid and ghostlike as she struggled without success to conceal her condition. Valentina could not shake the sadness she felt that none of Isabella's friends recognized Isabella's attempts to hide her discomfort and pallor. Nothing about the service or the reception reflected any of Isabella's or even Angelina's touches—Giovanni's mother had arranged everything. Even though it required sitting with Maro, Valentina appreciated being accepted as godmother. It meant that she could chat not only with Isabella but with Angelina's godfather and his wife.

The lowlight of the day came when Maro rose to toast the couple. "I quote the great Florentine historian, Francesco Guicciardini, from whom I am descended: 'There is nothing in our civil life that is more difficult than properly marrying off one's daughters.' Giovanni, I hope you have more luck with her than I did." He concluded with the traditional "For a hundred years!" The room echoed with shouts of "*Per cent'anni.*"

While everyone was laughing, Valentina snickered and thought, *What an asshole.* Unable to restrain herself, she said it. "*Che stronzo.*"

When Maro turned and asked what she'd said, Isabella replied, *"Che strano,"* then added, "She said how strange it was that she did not know you descended from such a great man."

Satisfied, Maro puffed out his chest then sat as the applause subsided. Valentina mouthed *Grazie* to Bella. When Isabella leaned over, Valentina assumed she would tell her to be more careful.

"*Che stronzo,*" she whispered, and giggled. Valentina noticed the three empty wine glasses in front of Isabella, who was holding a fourth. She finished the glass when she stopped giggling. Valentina shushed her.

When Angelina and Giovanni left the reception, Valentina thought she'd never seen an unhappier bride. Angelina was a deflated shell of a person, as if her energy had been used to hide her emotions during the service and reception, and her tank was now empty. Valentina's heart ached. The entire affair resurrected painful memories that Valentina had labored to keep buried.

***

Midweek, Angelina and Giovanni left for Vienna on their honeymoon—Angelina with reluctance, Giovanni with anticipation, looking forward to getting away from *il dramma*. The following weekend, Isabella's condition worsened. After pressing Isabella in the presence of Santino and Ilaria, Valentina learned the severity of her diagnosis, her prognosis, and Maro's treatment plan. Apoplectic, Valentina confronted Maro, threatening him until he agreed to return Isabella to the hospital.

The oncologist reviewed the most recent tests and then met with Maro, Isabella's siblings, and Valentina. Despite Valentina's threats, Maro did not permit her to attend until first Ilaria and then Santino had intervened. The doctor told them the cancer was now at stage four, and there was nothing to do but to make Isabella comfortable. Valentina's intake of air was audible at the other end of the hallway.

Maro said they needed to pray harder.

Valentina told him, "You should pray that I do not kill you."

Valentina notified Angelo in Como, who had asked her to keep him informed. Father Santino summoned Angelina back from Vienna. Giovanni stayed.

"We paid for the room. It is not like I can do anything for your mother."

When Angelina arrived at the hospital in Bologna, she found her mother in a private room, with Valentina, Ilaria, and Santino by her side. "*Dov'è mio padre?*" No one knew for sure, but he was likely at the "club," the euphemism everyone used for the lay society hall.

Isabella died less than a week later, with her siblings, Valentina, Angelo, and Angelina by her side. Angelo had arrived the day before, apologizing for not coming sooner. Santino and Ilaria had contacted their respective orders and received approval to extend their leaves. Maro arrived hours after his wife's death, inebriated.

He kept repeating, "We did all we could. It was God's plan." Angelina pushed Valentina out of the room before Valentina could respond.

"*Per me, Madrina, per favore.*" When Valentina gazed down into her goddaughter's determined amber eyes, a woman stared back.

A strong woman, she thought, thinking about how Angelina had moved her, in more ways than one.

***

Following the funeral, Valentina witnessed little grief from Maro. He spent most of his free time at the *club sociale.* He wanted Valentina to leave, but Angelo, who had remained in town after the funeral, said that as the will named Valentina, she should stay in case there were any questions. The day after Isabella died, Angelo distributed copies of her will to the named parties. Under Italian estate law, if there were no objections and it complied with legal requirements, its instructions were executed the same day.

As soon as he received his copy, Maro began protesting. He understood several items but disagreed. With other items, he misunderstood and invented explanations in his mind. Because of his questions, Angelo scheduled a meeting to discuss the will at the office of the *notaio* who had prepared it. Maro, Angelina, Santino, Ilaria, and Valentina, along with four representatives from the two Catholic charities named in the will, were present in the notary's sizable conference room. Giovanni was still in Vienna and would not return for two more days.

After everyone was seated, Angelo said, "Isabella's will left 35 percent to Tàmmaro Roselli, which is greater than the one-third required by law." Angelo glanced at Tàmmaro, who nodded back. "She left one-third to Angelina Fabrizzi as required by law." This time, Angelo looked at Angelina, who averted his gaze." Angelo turned back to his notes and continued.

"Isabella left several personal items to Valentina Marchese," and he and Valentina nodded to each other.

Finally, Angelo announced, "And the balance has been left to Isabella's charitable trust."

Maro pounded a fist on the table and stood up. "She never said anything to me about a charity!"

"Please sit down, Tàmmaro. She was explicit. The two charity beneficiaries are Catholic organizations to which you belong. I remind you that their representatives are present." Maro glanced around the room and calmed himself with reluctance.

Angelo then said, "Maro, you are receiving the two terrace houses. Please sign this acknowledgment of your acceptance." After Maro signed the release, Angelo continued.

"Even though Angelina received the family vacation house as a wedding gift, estate law counts it toward her share."

Maro responded with a smug smile. He'd worried she would get one-third besides the house. He knew the detached house was worth more than either of the two terrace houses, so it reduced what Angelina would receive from the other investments.

Maro then asked, "But how much do I get besides the terrace houses?"

"Nothing more, just the houses. Their value is greater than one-third, but Isabella was specific that you should have them. She wanted you to have an income stream."

"Okay, but how much is Angelina receiving?" When he was told about three hundred thousand euros, he became enraged. He demanded that he get cash instead of the houses. Angelo told him the will was specific. Besides, he had accepted them—when he signed the release, they became his.

"You can sell them if you need cash," Angelo advised.

"I want cash now!" Angelo held up his hands as if to say there was nothing he could do.

Maro turned to Valentina. "This is because of you! You corrupted my Isabella to create this will."

Both Angelo and the *notaio* told Maro that Isabella drafted the will before Valentina had returned, after Maro announced Angelina's engagement. Unable to control it any longer, Maro's temper took over—

and he unleashed it on Valentina. She rose from her chair, standing four inches taller, and glared as if daggers might erupt from her eyes.

"How dare you yell at me? You who killed Isabella!"

In answer to his protests, she told him, "You decided to ignore the doctor's advice and pray instead. It is your fault she died. You care more about what was in the will than grieving for your wife." Valentina took a step towards Maro and said, "If I might paraphrase Albert Camus"—Valentina pointed a finger at him—"In my society any man who does not weep at his wife's funeral runs the risk of being sentenced to death."

At that, Maro released a snarling yell and lunged at Valentina—she sidestepped him with the grace of a toreador as he fell. He rose to his feet wheezing with the others telling him to stop and calm down.

Instead, he attempted to punch Valentina twice. After ducking the first punch and sidestepping the second, she hit him once in the solar plexus. She warned him, "*Non toccarmi.*"

He bent over coughing, trying to catch his breath. Everyone relaxed, thinking Maro had given up—everyone except Valentina and Maro. He pulled a silver stiletto from his pocket. Maro lunged one more time, attempting to stab Valentina. She deflected his thrust with her left arm, then dropped to one knee and pulled the arm with the knife down, twisting it until the arm snapped with a loud crack and the knife clattered to the floor.

When the knife came out, the other people in the room froze, at first shocked, then stunned by how fast Valentina disarmed him. Afraid to move, they became appalled—a few outraged, a few horrified—when, in the same motion, she spun the screaming Maro over, holding his head as his body flipped and hit the floor, kicking over a side table. With the second loud crack, the screaming stopped.

Valentina glared at the body on the floor. "I told you not to touch me."

***

The death of Tàmmaro Roselli divided the community. His friends and acquaintances accused Valentina of his murder. Those who knew Isabella and the Marvelli family felt vindicated. Angelina did not know what to think. The police received contradictory testimony from the witnesses. It was self-defense. It was provoked. She warned him. He threatened her. She threatened him. He gave her no choice. She did not have to break his neck.

Two Carabinieri inspectors came to Rimini to aid in the investigation. After a brief investigation, the case was closed with the determination that Valentina had acted in self-defense. The official finding documented the testimony of the *notaio*, Avvocato Spallini, Reverendo don Santino, and Sorella Ilaria. They each said Maro had attempted to strike Valentina, and she stopped him twice. She'd had no choice but to defend herself when he attacked with the knife. It was unfortunate that he broke his neck when she wrestled him to the ground.

***

Several days later, Angelina's godfather prepared for his return to Como. As Maro did not have a will, his entire estate passed to Angelina. Angelo told Angelina he'd arrange for the property disposition and place the proceeds into suitable investments for her. She asked him if she could keep the two rental houses, and he said he'd take care of everything. He'd handled the estates of her grandparents, and she had absolute faith in him.

Angelo asked to speak with Valentina alone. After they spoke, there were hugs all around, and he headed for the train station. Angelo's wife, Antonietta, had returned after Isabella's funeral, having no interest in attending Maro's. Afterward, over Angelina's objections, Valentina said she could not stay. There were too many things there that invoked undesired memories.

***

The next day, at the train station, as her train approached, Valentina studied Angelina. She couldn't believe how well she had handled the back-to-back tragedies. Valentina hoped Angelina's marriage would turn out better. She decided to provide some advice to her goddaughter—*my grown-up goddaughter*, she corrected herself.

"You are married now. You and your husband should go have many children." She added, "If you ever need anything, I will be there for you."

"Oh, Godmother, I do not need anything—I need everything."

Valentina hugged her again and boarded her train, trying her best to block the memories of another departure, but without success.

THIRTEEN

Benjamin

What did I just do?

Ben tried to work as he sat in his room after lunch, but his thoughts would not cooperate. He was inundated by memories of the events of the past twenty-four hours. He could not remember ever having such an eventful day. It felt more like twenty-four days, not hours, of experiences.

Every time he recalled any of the events between the time that he'd boarded the train in Milan until he arrived at Angelina's house, he could not help but smile. He wondered if it was giving him a dopamine rush. Worse—no, better, truth be told—each memory triggered others. It was like wiki-walking into an internet rabbit hole.

The memories were a little different—more intense—once they arrived at her home. He met Valentina, and Valentina met him. It had mortified him to be the cause of their argument. He wished he'd declined Angelina's invitation.

What was I thinking? Did I fall for the famous American author bullshit? Is my ego that shallow?

Angelina had said Valentina protected her; Valentina's actions reinforced that statement. He was also sure she'd kick the crap out of him if he ever did anything to Angelina. The death threat was mere hyperbole, or so he hoped. He also remembered other things Valentina had said.

Sure, my French sucks—ask anyone. But he thought his Italian was decent.

Is it my Italian she dislikes, or me? And what about the insults?

He'd tried to build a bridge when she mentioned Mondo's judge of character, if only for Angelina's sake, but both he and Valentina knew she wasn't joking. Yet Valentina appeared to soften when she said, "*Prego.*" But then he remembered breakfast this morning. In particular "meat I kill myself." He was quite sure it was a reminder of last night's warning.

He appreciated her lead of an apartment manager. He'd been compiling a list, starting with a few suggestions from coworkers. He added others because he liked their internet presence. Angelina had suggested one at lunch today and two others last night at dinner. He added Valentina's contact to the end of the growing list.

There were three things he knew with certainty. One, he wanted to get to know this amber-eyed woman better. He didn't believe in love at first sight, but the infatuation he felt was undeniable. Ben wasn't sure it was mutual, but he didn't care. He just wanted to be around her. Two, he'd never call her "Angie" again.

And three, *I am never, ever gonna call Signora Marchese "Valentina."*

***

Ben searched for an apartment each morning and worked on several writing projects in the afternoon. His reluctant concern over Angelina's invitation to rent the room had transformed into grateful relief. The bedroom was not much larger than a hotel room, but he had access to the common areas of the house, and it felt good to stand, move around, and change writing locations. Plus, he had his faithful Mondo as a writing companion. He'd forgotten how much he missed a dog's unconditional affection and companionship. Then there was the apartment search, which was not progressing well. He hadn't planned on spending weeks in a hotel room—he'd have been miserable.

Although he tried to block it from his thoughts, Ben had to admit that what he most appreciated was spending time with Angelina. He and Angelina talked about the world, life, what he was writing—just about anything. He appreciated the intellectual stimulation. Besides admiring her intellect, he admired how grounded she was, and her approach to life. At least that was what he told himself he admired.

One afternoon, out of nowhere, he thought, *She is very fetching.* It surprised him. *Who uses that word?*

But it was true. Each day it became harder for him to ignore how attracted he was to her. He remembered the moment on the train when she took off her hat and he first saw her without her accessories. It made him wonder if there might be something to this love-at-first-sight business. But as Angelina seemed to prefer a platonic relationship, and since he did not want to jeopardize it, and since he especially wanted to avoid antagonizing Valentina, he did his best to conceal his feelings. Or at least restrain them.

It might have been more difficult had Valentina not found every excuse to stop by to clean or cook. He wondered how she managed her other clients, given the time she spent at Angelina's. Whenever she was at the house and Ben and Angelina were in the same room, Valentina would hover not too far away, like a chaperone at a middle school dance. It was of minimal consolation that this made it easier for him to focus on his writing instead of Angelina.

The other benefit to his rental arrangement was access to the kitchen. He could cook his own meals when Valentina permitted—or, to be accurate, when Valentina's absence allowed. She was now cooking two and even three meals a day for them.

Is she trying to send me a message?

Don't be an idiot, he answered himself. *Of course she is. She has been sending you messages since the moment you met.* And they all said the same thing—hands off, go away.

***

On Tuesday, Angelina mentioned she was going to the grocery store. Until now, they'd been using the provisions Angelina had at the house, plus groceries that Valentina brought. Ben wanted to go, both to uphold his promise to buy groceries and to help influence purchasing decisions. Angelina accepted his offer for company—Ben appreciated that Valentina was out and unable to opine.

They headed toward the park where he'd met the children that first evening. No children were present, but it was early. Ben could not remember when the Rimini school year ended, but he thought there still may be a few days remaining in the third term. They crossed through the park, making small talk about the weather, and exited onto Viale Zanzur, a narrow residential street which dead-ended at the park. Like many residential streets in this neighborhood, there were no sidewalks, so Ben and Angelina strolled down the center of the street.

There was also no traffic of any kind, so they were free to gaze, stare, and sometimes gawk at the residences on each side. Ben enjoyed this closer look at Rimini life. Besides the apartment buildings, there were several hotels along the narrow street. Each property had small gardens, flowering shrubs, or both.

"This is a splendid time of year for garden-gazing," Angelina said as she stopped to admire a well-kept example. "I wish my property was larger so I could have a proper garden."

The grocery store was on Viale Tripoli, surrounded by several hotels. The shopkeeper greeted Angelina, happy to see her. He told her to wait a moment while he walked back to a storeroom. When he returned, he gave her a package of *valeriana* he'd been saving for her. Angelina and Ben picked out the rest of their groceries, and Ben paid the clerk. Angelina had brought three grocery bags, but they only needed two. They each carried one after Ben folded and placed the unneeded bag into his bag.

On the way back, Angelina suggested they return down Viale Tobruk to the park. She waved her arm toward the other street. "I like to take a different route. For a change of scenery."

A woman after my own heart, Ben mused, without a thought to romance.

He seldom went the same way twice if there were alternate routes. He was even less likely to return over the same path he'd taken outbound. Why see what you have already seen when you can see something new?

That's what they should put on my tombstone. He chuckled at his joke.

"What is funny, Benjamin?"

He melted again at her pronunciation of his name, but held it together, hoping she hadn't noticed. "I just was thinking how fortunate I am to meet someone else who doesn't like to go the same way twice."

Angelina smiled, and he turned away, ostensibly to study a garden.

When they reached the park, they encountered the same group of children Ben met the first day. Yesterday, as a break from sitting at the desk, he'd spent an hour with them in the late afternoon as their *arbitro.* He'd borrowed Angelina's whistle, the one she carried in her purse, and he'd crafted homemade red and yellow cards from scrap paper at the house.

The children had played with abandon, yet Gilberto only fouled a few times. They'd played on a makeshift pitch, with informal boundaries and various markers for the goals. Ben's most challenging incident was having to decide that a ball kicked between two trash cans was too high to be a goal. The highlight of the match for the children was when Ben had cautioned a boy—not Gilberto—for continuing to argue about the decision. At the showing of the yellow card, the other children had applauded, even those from the miscreant's team.

Today, they were playing another game, a variation of freeze tag. When the children saw them approaching, they ran up to Angelina and begged her to play. They called the game *Strega Ghiaccio.* She handed Ben her grocery bag.

"I can only play for a few minutes, children."

Angelina played the Ice Witch, freezing children, who had to count to one hundred before they could move. Angelina avoided freezing any one child more than twice, as a player frozen three times became the new Ice Witch. It was clear to Ben that the children knew how Angelina played and that was why they had wanted her in the game.

After about fifteen minutes, Angelina tagged a child for the third time. As the children acknowledged it with a mixture of groans and cheers, she told them, "Children, I must take the groceries home."

At first, they balked, a half dozen of the children raising one or both arms in protest. In response, Angelina said, "I need to make sure your *arbitro* has something to eat tonight—otherwise he will not have any energy for tomorrow." The children accepted her explanation, mixing disappointment with enthusiasm in different proportions, yelling "*Ciao*" and "*Vederti presto!*" at them as Angelina and Ben turned to walk home.

This time it was Teresa, the polite girl from the first evening, who ran up to them, and it was Angelina's arm that was tugged. When Angelina turned, Teresa asked, "*Per favore scusami. Allora, è il tuo ragazzo adesso?*"

Angelina laughed and said, "*Teresa, sei una sciocca.*" She patted Teresa's head and said, "No, he is not my boyfriend today either. Now go play, silly."

"Sì, Signora Angelina."

Surprised, Ben chose to ignore the comment and hoped Angelina did not see his fluster. Angelina did not reference it again. As he carried the two bags, balancing one in each hand, he asked Angelina if the game was from the Disney movie *Frozen*.

"Oh, no. This game has been around forever. I played it as a child, and I remember my grandmother telling me she played it when she was a child."

Both fascinated and impressed, Ben admired Angelina's rapport with the children. Wanting to draw her out, he observed, "You are so good with kids."

After she thanked him, he asked, "Why didn't you have any of your own?"

Instead of answering, Angelina stopped. When Ben realized she'd stopped, he stopped also, turning to look back at her. In front of him was a woman fighting to hold back tears. Her lower lip was quivering. She closed her eyes and balled her fists. He could hear her rapid breathing. As she lost the battle, she ran past him toward her house.

Holy shit—what did I just do?

But he knew what he had done. He'd crossed a line, touched a nerve, and shattered the thin veneer of geniality he'd taken to mean something else. Someone like Angelina would have a reason for not having children, but it would be a personal reason—a very personal reason.

He jogged after her, hampered by the groceries. When he realized he would not catch her before she reached the house, he called out several times, "Angelina, I'm sorry!" He wondered if his words sounded as pitiful to her as they did to him.

When he reached the door, it was still open. He stepped inside, put down the two bags, and encountered Valentina.

FOURTEEN

Valentina

I cannot wait to hear this.

Valentina returned to Angelina's house while Angelina and her guest were at the grocery. She wandered around the house, her house-straightening ritual on autopilot. Angelina had become, over time, an acceptable housekeeper. Valentina seldom needed to do more than straighten the magazines, do some laundry, wash the dishes, or cook—she liked to cook. With the American here, she was spending more time at Angelina's and cooking more meals. She did not want him getting too comfortable.

At least Signor LaRocca was low-maintenance. He made his bed, did his own laundry, washed dishes when Valentina let him, and cooked a few meals when Valentina could not stop him. His rent relieved pressure on Angelina's budget, and that relieved pressure on Valentina. She still needed time to arrange her longer-term solution for Angelina.

Valentina gathered several English-language magazines splayed across the table and returned them to the credenza, indifferent as to who had been reading them. She commended herself for insisting Angelina learn proper English, rather than settle for enough-to-get-by English, as so many Italians did. When Angelina was in upper secondary school, Valentina wrote her several times each month, encouraging her to take advanced placement English courses. Angelina had earned several honors.

Now, if she would just improve her French.

Valentina found French to be a most fascinating language—not better than Italian, obviously, but still fascinating. She enjoyed reading the greats, such as Voltaire, Dumas, and Sand, in the original French. After *The Ingenious Gentleman Don Quixote of La Mancha* by her beloved Cervantes, her favorite novel was Albert Camus's *L'Étranger*. She had no affinity for any of the characters, and she despised his views on women, but she enjoyed the detail and complexity presented by Camus.

Each of the first four or five times she read it, she found something she'd missed. French was the perfect language for the farcical story.

If they ever write my absurd story, it should be in French—but if it is an opera, it must be in Italian.

The front door swung open, and Angelina entered, sobbing. She did not close the door, instead heading straight to the kitchen before Valentina could even ask what had happened. Mondo rose and followed her.

She heard the American yelling apologies as he came up the walk carrying two bags of groceries. He put the bags down as soon as he entered, nodded toward Valentina, and headed toward the sobbing. Valentina stepped into his path, and he bounced off her chest, stumbling and having to brace himself on a table to keep from falling.

He repeated "I'm sorry" to the unresponsive kitchen doorway.

Valentina snarled. "Do you remember what I told you I would do if you ever hurt her?" Before he could answer or even nod his head, Valentina placed the fingers of her right hand on his sternum and pressed once, then again and again, increasing the pressure, forcing him to retreat. "Do you?"

He protested, "I didn't do anything to her." He must have remembered he was required to speak Italian, for he repeated it, sounding as if he thought his life depended on it. "*Non le ho fatto niente!*"

Valentina raised her voice over his. "Then why is she crying?" She pinned him to the wall, her hands on his shoulders. She bellowed again, "*Perché lei sta piangendo?*" She added a final "*Perché?*" as an exclamation point to her question.

Mondo returned from the kitchen and began barking, but it was unclear at whom.

As Valentina waited for his answer, Angelina ran back into the room and yelled, "*Fermare!*" Then she yelled it again in English. "Stop!"

Angelina ducked under Valentina's arms and pushed to separate the two of them. Angelina stood with her back to the panting American, her eyes locked onto Valentina's eyes a foot above, and in a soft but firm voice, she said, "*Non di nuovo.*" It was not a lament; it was a command.

Valentina knew what she meant by "Not again." Valentina, now relaxed but still alert, studied her goddaughter. *Angelina stood up to me—again.* Her strength—both physical and emotional—surprised Valentina.

She turned to him, then back to Angelina, and thought, *I cannot wait to hear this.*

INTERMEZZO

The Housecleaning

"Everything I have done, am doing, and shall do follows the dictates of reason and the laws of chivalry."
— Miguel de Cervantes Saavedra —

Valentina did not deploy to Iraq after Isabella's funeral. Instead, the Carabinieri leveraged her finance degree, and she assisted the GIS with counterterror and anti-Mafia investigations. She also did well for herself, investing in stocks, bonds, and real estate. When she returned home for Angelina's wedding, she stayed in the owner's suite of an apartment building she had purchased earlier in the year, one of several she owned.

She later shed all but one of her real estate investments before the crash in 2006. To her, the handwriting had been on the wall. She kept the original apartment building, not as an investment, but because it was three blocks from a house on the south edge of the marina district Angelina's grandparents had purchased for Giovanni and Angelina.

She saw similar handwriting before the banking and general stock meltdown in 2008 and had moved most of her investments into cash and bonds. As the markets were bottoming in early 2009, she moved back into equities and real estate. No one in her circle knew the strength of her financial position, except her lawyer, Angelo Spallini.

Her only vice was her taste in automobiles, and her colleagues thought it was an eccentricity. *Valentina wastes half of her salary on a car payment,* they would say, not that she was swimming in gold. That was okay with Valentina. She believed if others knew she was *nuotare nell'oro*, they would treat her differently.

She found their assumption useful. When she overheard their conversations with their mindless assumptions about her finances, Valentina took comfort in Cervantes: "Three things too much, and three too little are pernicious to man; to speak much, and know little; to spend much, and have little; to presume much, and be worth little."

After Maro's funeral, Angelo spoke to her at the train station. "Valentina, I have a special trust fund for which I want your investment advice. If you will agree to keep your involvement confidential, I believe you will find it rewarding on many levels. Do you have any time to meet with me in Como?"

"I have a long weekend in a few weeks. Can I call you after I double-check my schedule?" Valentina said.

"Of course." Angelo coughed, then reached out for Valentina's elbow, pulling her a few inches closer. "Valentina, listen to me. The Carabinieri supported you but they want you to be more careful—they called you a *cannone incontrollato*. You know they left out a comment reported by Isabella's oncologist, yes?"

"*Eh!*" she said, "*Dovresti pregare che io non ti uccida.*" Angelo nodded. "He did not pray hard enough."

"Valentina!" He had never spoken to her so sharply. "I am your lawyer, but I do not have to be. You must not joke about such things. We have a responsibility to Angelina. She will need both of us, I fear. I was truthful when I said you did not have a choice with Tàmmaro. Do not make me think I was mistaken."

Valentina knew he was correct. "*Angelo, non ti sei sbagliato. Chiedo scusa e chiedo il tuo perdono.*" She expanded on her apology. "Sometimes my sense of humor is a curse." Valentina was relieved to see his smile. She added, "And, most importantly, thank you for your help with Angelina.

***

The Carabinieri leadership thought Valentina was a loose cannon, but not for the reason Angelo believed. They feared what she might do about a brewing sexual harassment scandal.

And after all I have done, she thought.

She put up with the sexual harassment she received and had never filed a complaint. It usually stopped when the perpetrator concluded she was disinterested in men. She decided not to tell them she was also disinterested in women. Their belief system was useful to her. Sometimes she had to beat the crap out of *un briccone* in the locker room. Often it was in defense of another female officer. *They probably fear I will become a supporting witness.*

The following summer, the scandal exploded within the media. Two different investigative reports exposed the widespread sexual harassment that female soldiers faced. Both included the Carabinieri, but one report stated that it was not as bad in the law enforcement agency.

Not as bad? Then I cry for the women in the other services.

The more she read about its treatment of women, the less she cared for her involvement with the military. Still, she endured it for three more years before joining the intelligence agency. One day, having had enough, she decided it was time, and she became a spy. The deciding factor? It had sounded like fun.

Her superiors at her new agency, AISE, respected her close combat skills and her marksmanship. They valued her international finance knowledge. She impressed them with her French, British, and American accents, that she spoke Spanish and Portuguese well enough, and that she could get by with German. What they appreciated most was that she was "bloodied." This disappointed her, as she believed that killing someone should never qualify one for anything but hell. She acknowledged, however, that Cervantes was correct: "There's no taking trout with dry breeches."

***

In 2013, she told herself, *I am getting too old for this shit,* so Valentina transferred from the operations directorate into analysis. In March 2016, she decided being an analyst was no longer fun. Well, it was still fun, just not as much. She did not work for the salary; she worked because she enjoyed the challenges and the opportunity to make a difference. Things had become less challenging to her since she left field work a few years back. Other than an extended assignment in France the year before, and an occasional international conference, she no longer traveled—one of the original draws of the job.

She longed to return to Rimini and to spend more time with her goddaughter. She submitted her papers and began her debriefings with her superiors and internal affairs. In April, after almost thirty-four years of government service, she found herself on a train, returning to her hometown.

The train arrived before noon. Valentina walked to her apartment, pulling a carry-on and carrying her kit bag. She'd kept the apartment, even as she acquired properties with better apartments, and would continue to keep it for as long as Angelina lived only three blocks away. Her longtime manager, Stefano Rossi, had the apartment ready for her, as always.

Once she settled in, she rang up Angelina, who was thrilled to learn her godmother was home. She invited Valentina over for lunch. When she arrived, Valentina was more than a little disappointed. The house was, if not a mess, untidy. Over a less-than-appetizing lunch, she told Angelina that she was looking forward to a change of lifestyle and a change of pace in retirement.

"Where are you staying?" Angelina asked, then added. "You could stay here, if I can get Giovanni's permission."

"Thank you, *Figlioccia*, but I have arranged a long-term stay at the same apartment I have used on my past visits."

"Madrina, how will you make ends meet?" Angelina asked. "*La tua pensione è piccola, no?*"

"I will manage, dear," Valentina replied. She saw no reason to tell Angelina that she was ineligible yet to collect her small service pension, nor tell her that she did not need it. "So how are things with you and Giovanni?"

"Okay, I guess. He is out most nights, but that gives me time to read and walk. Mondo and I like to walk to the beach and the harbor pier."

Valentina knew Angelina could not have children—she had confided in her godmother several years ago, and it had left a bruise on Valentina's heart.

During the visit with her thirty-two-year-old goddaughter, Valentina identified five facts: Angelina did not keep a clean house, Angelina could not cook, Angelina assumed Valentina needed to work, Angelina needed Valentina for company, and Giovanni would never allow it.

"Angelina, could you help me out and let me be your housekeeper, at least until I am standing on my own two feet?"

"*Sì, Madrina!*" Angelina's smile flickered away before it had fully formed. "But first I need to speak with Giovanni."

Valentina said, "*Ovviamente.*"

Valentina then asked what she would've opened with had she not been away from her goddaughter for the past year. "*Angelina, qual è la storia con i tuoi capelli e i tuoi occhi?*"

Angelina's eyes were now brown, and her hair was a brighter red, without her distinctive streak of silver. While the combination was pleasant, it was not Angelina.

"Giovanni told me how he could not stand to look at me. He kept telling me to dye my hair and get contacts. Oh, Godmother, the hair dye burns, and the contacts hurt my eyes."

Valentina asked the obvious question. "*Perché allora li indossi?*"

Angelina looked at her godmother as if it were the dumbest question she had ever heard. She raised her arms to her sides and shook them. "But Giovanni told me!"

"Angelina, that is the dumbest thing I have ever heard. Just take them out!"

"I cannot, Godmother," Angelina said as she averted her gaze, her faux-brown eyes filling with genuine tears. "It is one less thing Giovanni can yell about—it is worth it."

That confirmed for Valentina a problem that until now she had only suspected.

***

After the self-described "sophisticated negotiating" by Giovanni, they reached a housekeeping agreement. From that day on, every time she heard Giovanni reference his negotiating skills, Valentina felt like jabbing pencils into her eyes to keep them from rolling back in contempt. She had felt like jabbing them into his eyes more than once.

The good news was she could spend mornings and evenings at Angelina's, making breakfast and dinner, tidying the house, doing laundry twice a week, and performing a thorough cleaning every week. While the cooking was necessary—*I do not know how they have survived this long*—she could've finished the housework in a few hours a week. She chose those hours because she wanted to be around as much as possible when Giovanni was home. She explained it away by saying it allowed her to pursue her other business during the day.

The bad news was she spent mornings and evenings with them and witnessed how badly Giovanni mistreated his wife. "Badly" was an understatement. He derided her, addressing her as "Angie," knowing his wife hated the nickname. He verbally abused Angelina at every opportunity. Valentina could not understand how Angelina could bear it.

One day, on one of their few lunch dates, Valentina could not hold her tongue any longer. "Angelina, I ask this as your godmother and your friend. Why do you put up with the abuse from your husband?"

"Godmother, look at me, look at my life—look at all that has happened to me. Everything I touch is bad. I deserve nothing good. I put up with Giovanni's abuse because he is my husband. If I did not have him, where would I be?"

In a better place, Valentina thought. She wondered what had happened to that strong, confident woman she saw at the hospital the night her mother died.

***

Over the next two months, Valentina continued her housecleaning services. Giovanni gave her a check every two weeks, with a smug smile she knew he must also use when he bragged about his negotiating skills. She knew about the bragging because she would receive calls from his friends seeking her services. She'd always quote an amount five or six times what Giovanni paid. It drove the callers away and reinforced Giovanni's belief that he'd gotten the best of her.

The emotional abuse he directed at his wife was unrelenting. Several times Valentina spoke up, only to be told by Giovanni to mind her own housekeeping business, followed by Angelina asking—no, begging—her to stop. Angelina even had the audacity once to say, "Godmother, you made me study Cervantes. Did he not write 'Women are born with the obligation to obey their husbands even if they're fools'?"

Valentina told her that her husband was not a fool, but an evil, abusive man.

What she did not say out loud was *What the fuck, Cervantes?*

One night as Valentina was cleaning up after dinner, Giovanni looked at his wife long enough to realize she was not wearing the contacts and her hair streak was resurfacing.

"Angie, you fucking bitch, why do you look like this?" He was on his third glass of wine, and it showed. He rose awkwardly from his chair, and it fell over backward.

Valentina stepped into the kitchen doorway. Mondo, the young but large dog Valentina had given Angelina for her birthday last year, started a low growl.

Angelina said, "I told you the contacts hurt my eyes and the hair dye burned."

"I'll show you what pain is," and Giovanni took a step toward her, raising his arm as if to slap her with the back of his hand.

Mondo and Valentina moved at the same time. The dog was closer, and he growled, barked, and growled again, so Giovanni turned to him, growling and cursing, "*Maledetto cane!*" and kicked the animal in the chest just as Valentina reached him.

Angelina had buried her head behind her arms when Giovanni raised his. This told Valentina as she moved that it was not the first time, just the first time around Mondo—and her.

She grabbed Giovanni and threw him back into the china cabinet. Glass broke. A lot of glass. Giovanni stepped forward, and Valentina punched him in the stomach. Focused on Giovanni, it took a moment for Valentina to realize that Angelina was yelling at her to stop from her place on the floor next to the dog. At first Valentina thought Mondo might be injured, but then she realized Angelina was holding his collar to restrain him from his revenge.

Giovanni recovered his breath and lifted his hands in surrender.

"This little dance was for kicking the dog. If you ever do that again, I will beat the living shit out of you." Valentina nostrils flared. "And if you ever touch Angelina again," she paused and moved closer, her voice now almost a whisper, "I will kill you. Do I make myself clear?" She did not bother to wait for a reply.

"Angelina, get some things. You are staying with me."

When Angelina did not answer, Valentina turned to find her

goddaughter still on the floor, hugging the dog and weeping. She stared up, but not at her godmother. Her eyes were unfocused, looking off in the distance. Valentina recognized it from her military training—the thousand-meter stare. It resulted from post-traumatic stress. "Angelina!"

Angelina refocused her gaze on her godmother. "Godmother, I cannot. He is my husband." Before Valentina could reply, she said it again, with finality, "*Lui è mio marito.*"

Valentina sighed and debated whether to demand to stay the night on the sofa. Instead, she retrieved her bag and coat. Before she left, she turned to Giovanni and reminded him, "*Ricorda cosa ti ho detto,*" punctuating each word of her reminder warning with a finger point.

As she left, she told herself, *God help him if he forgets.*

***

Angelina called Valentina early the next morning. "Thank you for your concern, Godmother, but everything is fine. Giovanni apologized for kicking Mondo. Please take today off—Giovanni and I need some 'us time' to get back on track."

Valentina thought it was a fast turnaround, but she respected her goddaughter's wishes. Valentina called later in the afternoon, then again, each time getting Angelina's voice mail. She called the house phone, but it rang unanswered.

With the hairs on her neck bristling, she headed for their house. She would use the excuse that she was going to the market and wanted to see if Angelina needed anything. When she arrived, there was no answer. After she used her key to unlock the front door, she entered and found the house a mess. They had cleaned nothing from last night—even the two chairs remained upended. Everywhere she looked, Valentina saw broken glass from the china cabinet. She saw Mondo at the top of the stairs, whining.

This cannot be good, she thought.

Valentina called out to her goddaughter as she climbed the stairs. On the hallway floor, she saw blood. She wished she'd brought her Beretta 92 pistol. Mondo followed her into Angelina's bedroom, where she found her goddaughter crying into her pillow.

"*Grazie Dio,*" Valentina prayed, relieved. When Angelina turned to face her, Valentina's prayer became a curse, followed by "*Oh, cara bambina.*"

Angelina's right eyebrow was purple. Her left cheekbone was red, purple, and swollen. She had a swollen lip, which had stopped bleeding. She might have suffered a bloody nose, but Valentina could not tell with all the other blood and damage. She moved to her goddaughter, assessing her for any serious injuries. Besides her battered face, Angelina complained of rib pain on her left side. Seeing no life-threatening injuries, Valentina walked downstairs to the kitchen, telling Angelina she'd return with ice and towels.

***

After she cleaned Angelina's wounds and put ice bags on the swelling, Valentina headed back to the kitchen to make tea. When she returned with the tea, she found Angelina sitting on the bed, her back against the headboard. She thanked Valentina for the tea. They sat for several minutes, neither speaking, until Angelina took a deep breath and turned to Valentina.

"Godmother, thank you for being here, and thank you for not talking just now. With you here yet silent, I could collect my thoughts. If you had started asking all the obvious questions, I never would have gotten that chance."

When her godmother nodded, she continued. "After you left last night, Giovanni chased Mondo into the back room. Giovanni was cursing at him; Mondo was cursing back—barking and growling. I did not know what to do." Angelina sobbed once before continuing.

"He came back into the kitchen and said he needed to speak with me. Then he slapped me, saying that was what I was supposed to get at dinner, and then he gave me a second because you attacked him." She pointed first to her black eye, then to her lip.

"My nose was bleeding. I was crying. Mondo was barking… and I so wished you were here."

"Why did you not call me?"

"I was afraid… afraid and embarrassed. In the m-m-" Angelina stopped, closed her eyes, inhaled, then exhaled slowly before opening her eyes and meeting Valentina's gaze.

"In the morning, he told me you were fired, and that if he saw you anywhere near me, he would have you arrested. That was why I told you to stay away." Angelina whimpered once.

"*Ma che dire di tutto questo?*" Valentina pointed at the other side of Angelina's face and at her ribs.

"I knew you were right last night—I am sorry for being so stupid and afraid. I was packing to leave this afternoon when Giovanni came home early, for once—the bastard… I told him I was leaving." Angelina raised her arms to the heavens as she drew a deep breath. "He screamed at me. He told me I could do nothing without his permission." Angelina sobbed.

She pulled a hand to her chest. "He began beating me, Godmother. I thought he was going to kill me."

"*Perché si è fermato?*"

"I finally could not take it, so I started hitting him back, but it was Mondo that finally stopped him." Angelina described how Mondo came bounding up the stairs and attacked Giovanni, biting his arms and legs until he left.

"That is all Giovanni's blood in the hall."

"Why did you not call me then?" Valentina asked.

"I was too… embarrassed—I was too embarrassed, Godmother." Angelina had stopped crying and was instead staring at her feet.

Valentina had begun crying as Angelina described her beating. Tears at first. Now she was weeping. After a single loud sob, Valentina took a deep breath.

"Goddaughter, please promise me you will never be afraid or embarrassed to speak with me."

When Angelina nodded, Valentina again inhaled deeply and said, "Let us get some things together, and I will take you and Mondo over to my apartment, yes?"

***

Once inside, Valentina showed Angelina the guest room, which she also used as her office. When she saw her goddaughter's hesitation, she asked why.

"You will think I am a silly girl, but could I sleep in your bed tonight?"

"But of course. I will sleep in this room."

Angelina corrected her. "No, I mean with you. Like when I was younger—with my mother. If you would not mind?"

"Of course not. You get settled. I need to go find your husband."

Angelina began to tremble, her eyes wide. Then she started to hyperventilate. Valentina embraced her and patted her shoulder.

"I just need to tell him your marriage is over, to stay away, and that he should worry about you pressing charges against him. I promise, Goddaughter."

After Angelina's rapid breathing subsided, she nodded a hesitant okay. Valentina left the apartment to search for the scumbag. She knew a wife pressing charges against her husband would not get far.

It is like we are living in the fucking dark ages, she thought.

Upon Valentina's return almost three hours later, Angelina asked if she had found him. Valentina nodded, and Angelina asked what happened.

"I told him word for word what I told you I would tell him. I then added that if he were smart, he would leave the province and never return. I think we have seen the last of Giovanni Fabrizzi."

***

The next morning, they were in the kitchen having *caffè* when there was a knock at the door and two Rimini police officers greeted them, accompanied by two Carabinieri officers. A *carabiniere* asked to speak to Signora Valentina Marchese. When he saw Angelina, he asked if she was Signora Fabrizzi. After she said yes, he told her he had unfortunate news for her.

"*Il permesso di entrare?*"

Valentina nodded and escorted the officers into her parlor.

FIFTEEN

Angelina

God and I, we need to have a long talk one day.

After running back to the kitchen, Angelina stood weeping, her hands gripping the edge of the sink. She leaned forward as if she wanted the sink to catch the tears cascading down her cheeks. Mondo stood next to her, whining. She tried to sort out the emotions that overwhelmed her. She was not angry at Benjamin, although she did not know what she felt toward him. He must have thought she was; his "I'm sorry" still echoed in the front room and in her memory.

Angelina banged on the sink with both fists. She scolded herself.

He asked an innocent question, and I panicked.

She felt like a schoolgirl who could not remember the answer to the teacher's question as the other children laughed at her. She stared out the window, glaring at nothing.

Why did God make me love children yet not be able to have any?

She was embarrassed that she was angry with God, for she knew that the real culprit was her husband. She despised her dead, selfish husband for wanting nothing to do with adoption. "Why would I want to raise someone else's bastard?" he'd asked her each time she raised the topic, ending the discussion, such as it was.

Damn him! She kicked the sink cabinet.

She returned to the moment when she heard Valentina's loud voice and Mondo barking in the other room. It took a second, but she realized what was happening.

"Oh my God! What have I done?" Now she was angry at Valentina.

Angelina ran out of the kitchen to see Valentina pinning Benjamin against the wall as she bellowed, "Why?"

Angelina reached them, yelling "*Fermare!*" She ducked under Valentina's right arm, braced her back against Benjamin, and pushed Valentina's armpits with all her strength, this time shouting "Stop!" in English.

Staring up at her godmother, she gathered herself, and said with as much authority as she could gather, "Not again."

Her godmother dropped her arms from Benjamin. Angelina could feel the pulses of his hot panting against the back of her head and realized it was now she who pinned him to the wall.

To Angelina's relief, Valentina relaxed and stepped back, which created space—*breathing room,* she thought, without humor. Angelina knew she must speak before Valentina decided to un-relax.

"Val, Benjamin did nothing wrong. It was me."

"That's not true; I was stupid," Benjamin interrupted from behind her.

"*Benjamin, zitto!*" Valentina blinked at Angelina's abrupt command to shut up.

"All he did was ask an innocent question," Angelina said, with more restraint.

Valentina took another step back. "*Che era?*" She appeared curious, not impatient—at least, not yet.

Angelina stepped sideways, in part to give Benjamin more breathing room, in part to make Valentina turn to her. She inhaled and said, "He asked me why I did not have any children." Then she exhaled with a whimper.

Valentina gave Benjamin a *what-were-you-thinking* look. He half shrugged—a pitiful *I-don't-know* gesture.

"Godmother, all the memories flooded over me, drowning me. It was the memories that made me upset, not Benjamin. I could not answer, I could not breathe—I was panicking. I needed to be somewhere safe, so I ran home." She turned to Benjamin. "Benjamin, I am so sorry."

Before Benjamin could reply, Valentina stared at him, then turned back to Angelina. "I am glad you felt safe coming to me, Goddaughter, but I find it hard to believe this does not involve Signor LaRocca." She turned again to stare at Benjamin, as if to emphasize her skepticism.

"Oh, but it does, Valentina." Before Valentina could overreact, she continued, "If he had not asked, we would not be talking now. And because we are, I feel the weight of the world has been lifted from me. I am not drowning—can you not see?" Angelina had raised her arms as if to help the weight along. Her statement was not a lament; it was an exultation.

The muscles around Valentina's jaw relaxed, and then she pursed her lips. Her eyes widened as she tilted her head to one side. Angelina hoped her godmother could see the transformation she'd just described. Angelina watched as her godmother put on her *I-must-analyze-this* face and turned again to study Benjamin.

After staring at him for a few awkward moments, she said, "Signor LaRocca, help me put these groceries away."

***

Once in the kitchen, Valentina chose instead to make tea, so Angelina helped Benjamin with the groceries. She kept staring at him, trying to apologize with her eyes. He avoided her gaze.

I need to fix this, she decided, as Valentina placed three cups of tea on the kitchen table.

"Benjamin, I am so sorry that Valentina almost killed you."

"I did not almost kill him."

"She didn't almost kill me." Then Benjamin added, "I think."

Angelina waved their objections away with a sweep of her hand. "I am sorry that Valentina almost hurt"—she glared at Valentina—"you. After seeing me with the children in the park, you asked an obvious question."

"It was so obvious he should have known not to ask it." At the interruption, Angelina glared at Valentina again, who elevated both hands above the table and mouthed, *Che cosa?*

"Please allow me to explain to Benjamin."

"Angelina, it is none of his business." Valentina shook a hand with pinched fingers at her.

"Valentina Marchese, I am thinking this is none of your business! Do not interrupt me again." Angelina bit the side of her index finger before flinging her arm at Valentina.

Valentina looked as if her goddaughter had slapped her, but said nothing. She tilted her chin up, turned away in her chair, and stared out the window as Angelina continued. She described how, at first, she and her husband had decided not to have children.

Will I ever escape that man—that asshole? She sighed.

"We took precautions."

"*Contraccezione?*" Benjamin asked.

"*Dio buono, no!*" Angelina blanched at the question. "We timed our lovemaking." *If that is what you want to call it.*

Angelina tried not to let her appended rueful thought distract her.

"*Vuoi dire, il*"—Benjamin switched to English—"rhythm method?"

Angelina regretted that Benjamin felt the need to glance at Valentina when he switched.

"*Sì.*" Angelina nodded. "Later, we tried to have children, but we could not. My husband blamed me for being infertile. He said it was because I looked the way I did. God had cursed me and wanted to make sure no others like me would be born. After a while, he stopped trying, and I stopped caring."

Angelina gazed at Benjamin; his puppy eyes gazed back. She appreciated his silent support. She was relieved he'd not reacted with shock but was concerned that he might instead feel guilty.

Angelina glanced at Valentina, who was no longer staring out the window but looking instead at the hands folded in her lap. Was that a tear? When Valentina turned to glance at her, Angelina gave her a warm smile before continuing.

"Much later, I found out that when we had foregone our lovemaking to keep from having children, it had not stopped my husband." She decided not to say "*stronzo*" in front of Valentina. "He'd found opportunities elsewhere in town, with a variety of women, several who even claimed to be my friend. Later, when he found out I could not have children, he spent most of his time with those other opportunities. At that point, I did not care. In fact, I was happy not to be bothered."

Angelina paused when Valentina muttered, "*Stronza,*" and turned to glare at her godmother. When she saw Valentina's misty eyes, she wondered if she'd misheard.

"So, Benjamin, not only am I disfigured, I am barren. The asshole was right."

She turned to face the disapproving stare of her godmother.

"I am cursed. Godmother, it was not Benjamin's fault. The fault is all mine. And God's."

She promised herself, *God and I, we need to have a long talk one day.*

SIXTEEN

Valentina

But do not forget brothels, Signor LaRocca.

Valentina's opinion that Signor LaRocca was a threat had evolved. One of her guiding principles—courtesy of Albert Camus—was to never ascribe to malice that which could be attributed to ignorance or incompetence. She could not decide whether this American was ignorant, incompetent, or both, but she'd developed a high confidence that he was not malicious. She updated her assessment: he was not so much a threat as an idiot.

What was he thinking to ask such a question?

That was the problem with men—they did not think.

When Angelina began describing her personal life, Valentina was incredulous.

What was she thinking, sharing such information?

And that was the problem with women—they did not think either.

As strange as these events were, they were nothing compared to what had happened when she had intervened.

Angelina is telling me to mind my business? Valentina tried to control her anger. *Me, her godmother!*

She wondered what had gotten into her goddaughter. Valentina turned away to avoid Angelina's reproachful stare, and to hold her tongue while Angelina shared intimate details with this… this… *idiota*!

As Angelina spoke, memories pounded Valentina—waves against a seawall. She understood Angelina's pain—the pain of wanting something you could never have. Angelina's description of Giovanni's behavior was a painful reminder to Valentina that she should've done more to protect Angelina from Giovanni. Valentina hated the feeling of self-pity, so she forced her thoughts back to the Angelina of now.

I must get hold of myself, she scolded herself. *Angelina deserves better.*

Then, to her chagrin, she realized she was nearly crying, but she regained control.

I cannot allow Angelina to see me crying. She needs my strength.

But when Angelina smiled at her, an unfamiliar voice entered Valentina's thoughts and spoke to her.

Look how strong she is, how she has grown. Angelina does not need your strength. She just needs you.

While this inner voice was new, it was also correct. Stepping back from her melancholic mood, Valentina saw a confident, poised woman in front of her, describing personal experiences to people with whom she felt safe.

She took another look at the idiot. He now did not seem like such an idiot.

I am the idiot! Why did I not see this?

Angelina's confidence, poise, and yes, even her strength had been triggered by the American. He'd drawn her out of her shell. The realization flooded Valentina in a tsunami of understanding. He was the one listening to her cathartic monologue, providing nothing more than support and encouragement, while Valentina wallowed in self-indulgent shame.

"Asshole," she cursed herself under her breath.

Angelina concluded her story by telling him that she was disfigured, barren, and cursed. She turned to Valentina. "Today was my fault, and God's, Godmother."

It bothered Valentina to hear Angelina speak that way. Not that Valentina was religious—it was just that believing God had cursed you was nothing but *una scusa* that kept you from taking responsibility to change.

Signor LaRocca shook his head and began speaking, probably to offer unneeded advice. "Angelina, did you ever—"

"Angelina, take off your uniform. You have mourned long enough." Valentina felt compelled to interrupt, to save him from himself. He stared at her with his mouth open, an undelivered question hanging from it.

Angelina turned to Valentina with an inquisitive squint, but then said, "*Va bene.*"

Signor LaRocca closed his mouth, but now appeared puzzled, as if he did not get a joke.

When would men realize that when women describe a problem, they just want someone to say, "I understand," instead of "Let me fix that for you"?

Women were quite capable of fixing problems, she knew.

So, why, then, could they not find supportive men?

That, she did not know.

***

Over the next two weeks, their writer searched for a suitable apartment. He described how the ones he liked were too expensive; the ones he could afford, he did not like. Valentina knew it was unfortunate timing, looking for an apartment in the high season.

Maybe I should talk to Signor Rossi again.

The three of them ate together often. Valentina even trusted the American to cook for her. She recognized that he and Angelina were each unaware that the other appreciated their additional time together. Valentina found their interpersonal dynamic amusing. They obviously enjoyed each other's company. At times, they acted like an old married couple, with fifty years of comfortable compromise behind them. Other times, they were like two preadolescent friends, exploring the companionship each provided with no hormonal overtones.

More amusing, each seemed oblivious to the other's romantic feelings—and each went to great lengths to hide their own. To Valentina, their feelings were obvious, and their attempts to suppress them comical—they were both afraid the other might not reciprocate and would ruin the fantasy. It reminded her of the summer she'd spent with Isabella after they first met.

When not eating, visiting potential apartments, out researching an article, or taking the occasional walk with Angelina, he worked on his writing projects. One afternoon, while Angelina was out, Signor LaRocca described his Republic of Rose Island piece to Valentina.

"So, what do you think?" he asked when he was finished.

"Very interesting. I was unaware of this republic. It never came up at the police academy."

Valentina was sincere. She was curious and driven to learn. She believed herself to be well-educated and well-informed. Unlike many people with similar beliefs, she looked forward to discovering what she did not know. She was comfortable saying, "I did not know; now I do."

"If I could offer an observation?" she asked.

Benjamin grinned. "*Per piacere!*"

Valentina saw the puppy dog Angelina had described to her one evening.

"Well, Signor LaRocca, you speak little of Signor Rosa's motivation."

"You are correct. He has made public statements and posted a video. I hope to speak with people in town who might have known him. I'm also planning a day trip to Bologna. He grew up there."

"I will reach out to a few of my colleagues in the Carabinieri and the Polizia di Stato to see if I can learn anything helpful."

"Thank you, Signora Marchese."

"*Prego.*" She nodded. "But what do you believe was his motivation? He was from Bologna. Why build off Rimini? Why not further up the coast?"

She watched the writer ponder for a moment before he replied. "Well, he included a casino, and Italy restricted gambling. He wanted to leverage the Rimini tourist trade?"

It sounded like a question, but it was his answer. *An appropriate answer. He is not an idiot.* Good. She was glad that was settled.

"But do not forget brothels, Signor LaRocca."

The Rimini sex trade and human trafficking of the last century was something she understood. She never spoke of it, but she was proud of her efforts with the Rimini Method.

"So, Signor LaRocca, how did you become—what does Angelina call you—a famous American writer?"

And he told her, except about the famous part.

INTERMEZZO

The Writer

"The brave man carves out his fortune, and every man is the son of his own works."
— Miguel de Cervantes Saavedra —

Benjamin Dennis LaRocca was born in northern New Jersey in February 1980 to the twenty-five-year-old Joseph LaRocca and his twenty-three-year-old wife, Rose. A second-year schoolteacher, Rose Lombardy LaRocca appreciated that the school where she taught third grade retained her when she took leave for the pregnancy. Joseph LaRocca worked as an actuary for an insurance company.

His father's dad, Beniamino, had immigrated from Sicily in 1938. He was a musician and a singer. He loved his adopted country and insisted his family be in all ways American, including giving his children "American names." To uphold this philosophy, he named his son Joseph—not Giuseppe—to honor his father still in Sicily.

Joseph LaRocca continued the practice and named Ben's older sister Jennifer—not Ginevra—and named him Benjamin, or as his grandmother Maria would say, "Jen and Ben." He loved that about her, along with her cooking. Rose called her children "Jenny and Bennie," which he hated, and was not an accomplished cook by anyone's definition but hers.

Ben played baseball and soccer in high school without distinguishing himself in either. Rather than work at fast-food places or the local soda bottling plant like many of his peers, he became a baseball umpire and soccer referee. Before too long he found he enjoyed the running required of a soccer referee much more than standing behind a catcher who couldn't catch a pitcher who couldn't throw past a hitter who couldn't hit. With the growth of the sport into a year-round activity, by seventeen, he focused solely on officiating soccer.

He excelled at it, which provided him a sense of satisfaction. That satisfaction and his enjoyment of the sport overcame the frustration he felt when being screamed at by parents ignorant of the laws of the game. They acted as if they were at a little league baseball game—where everyone believed it was perfectly acceptable to bully teenaged officials into tears when they "missed the call."

As if he wasn't busy enough, a friend urged him to join the local volunteer fire company his junior year of high school. He was unaware of volunteer fire departments until he overheard his friend Bud talking with another student. Ben had assumed, when he thought of it at all, that being a fireman—"No, Ben, we're called firefighters," Bud corrected—was a job. He learned that he agreed with his fire company's motto, "It's not a job, it's an adventure," which paraphrased a US Navy slogan.

Ben so enjoyed the social aspects of the fire company that he chose a local college rather than go out of state—a decision he later regretted, as he loved to travel. He would've had more travel opportunities had he attended college outside the region. His parents wanted him to pursue a music degree, but he settled on accounting, scheduling as many computer science electives as he could.

As soon as he graduated in 2002, he landed a job with an investment firm in Jersey City. They needed someone with his skill set: an accounting degree, statistics minor, and computer proficiency. They were expanding their data analysis unit to develop automated trading algorithms, and he was the proverbial right person in the right place.

He'd often stare with sorrow across the Hudson at the fractured Manhattan skyline. His parents knew two people who had died in the attack.

Benjamin met his wife at the firm a year later. They dated casually for a year, before beginning a relationship. They married in June 2005, and

Benjamin considered the world, if not perfect, comfortable. He did not realize until much later that what he called comfortable was just him taking his wife for granted. When she walked out in 2012, after determining he could not change, he never saw it coming. When he asked why she hadn't told him her concerns sooner, she threw her hands up in the air.

"I never thought you were completely clueless, *Ben*, until now." The way she snapped out "*Ben*" when angry always felt like a finger flick to his nose.

While married, both Ben and his wife invested, leveraging the resources of their firm. They maxed out their retirement contributions and created a small non-retirement nest egg managed by one of their coworkers. They planned to buy a home in 2008—2009 at the latest.

His mother's parents had died before he got married. In the spring of 2007, his grandmother Maria died from heart disease, devastating his grandfather after their fifty-plus years of marriage. His grandfather died four months later, also from heart disease. His father disagreed, saying Grandpa Beniamino died of a broken heart.

Ben and his sister each received a sizeable bequest from their grandfather's will. Ben considered them both fortunate—in the genuine sense of the word—that the proceeds sat in cash accounts when the market crashed. The convergence of these financial vectors meant Ben invested in stocks at their low point, and he and his wife bought a wonderful home in late 2008 for half of its market value eighteen months earlier.

When his grandparents' heart disease became known, Ben had spoken with their doctor. The doctor warned that he and his father were at risk. The doctor said his grandparents lived into their seventies, but they had eaten a healthy diet for the first half of their lives.

"You and your father are eating crap," he told Ben. "You won't be so fortunate."

With that prognosis, Ben researched the effect of diet on health. The volume and weight of peer-reviewed research that existed to support healthier eating surprised him. The commercials that implied government backing for eating meat and dairy did not mention any of those results. For every study publicized by a meat or dairy industry group touting the health benefits of eating their products, he found twenty studies arguing for reduced animal product consumption, with extensive data to support the recommendations. He learned later that the respective food industries often financed the studies that favored greater consumption of animal products.

Right before Thanksgiving in 2007, Ben went cold turkey, as he described it, and became a vegetarian. It was an unfortunate term to use at the LaRocca Thanksgiving dinner table that year.

His mother kept rotating between "But, Bennie, I worked so hard on the turkey," "But, Bennie, how can a little turkey hurt?" and "But, Bennie, you'll die if you don't eat enough protein."

To the last, he just smiled with love. "Mom, I get plenty of protein."

His brother-in-law David retorted with "Yeah, we know. I can smell it over here." He appreciated his sister's elbow at that moment—David didn't.

Ben later dropped dairy from his diet and ate a vegan diet. It became just another thing his wife disliked.

***

After his separation in 2012, Ben and his soon-to-be ex-wife spent the next eighteen months determining how to handle their finances. His wife declared, "Ben, I care about you, but I need someone who cares about me. I am not trying to take everything. Let's agree to work on an amicable distribution."

Ben suppressed his cynicism as best he could. He believed she wanted a fair and friendly resolution, but he wondered if the motive was her higher salary. They had deferred starting a family, though, and that simplified their discussions.

They sold the house at a significant profit before the divorce became final. They agreed to keep their respective retirement accounts. His wife felt it was only right that he kept the investments purchased with his inheritance. They split everything else fifty-fifty after paying off debts—there was no alimony. When they signed the divorce papers, she kissed him on the cheek.

"Good luck, Ben. And I mean this with affection—don't take your next wife for granted."

While he'd taken the separation hard, the finalization of the divorce in mid-2013 hit him as if the courthouse had collapsed on him. He left his job and returned to his parents' house. He joined a band, began answering fire calls again, and returned to refereeing. Yet despite his myriad activities, he drifted through each day without purpose.

His father told him to get out and date. His mother told him to sit down and eat. And his sister said, "Get your head out of your ass—it isn't a hat." He appreciated the paraphrased reference. She knew he liked *Pitch Perfect.*

Her advice was the most effective. He started writing, picking up an odd assignment from time to time. The following February, an opportunity fell into his lap, literally and literarily. He was sitting in the inner reception area of a magazine publisher in New York, hoping to push an article he'd written.

A woman exited an office, looking behind her while saying, "We must find someone soon." As she turned back around, she had to hop-step to a stop, just missing Ben's legs as he struggled to move them from her path. He remembered his father's advice when walking in the city: "People should watch where they walk and walk where they watch. The world would be a better place."

As she stopped, one of her file folders didn't and fell into Ben's lap. He handed it back to her, apologizing.

She said, "No, that's on me—all good." She studied him for a moment. "You're not by any chance a writer?"

Ben told her he was there to discuss an article he was writing. He left out the part about trying to pitch it. He wasn't lying. He was a writer—just not one who had sold anything of consequence.

"Do you write travel pieces?"

"I love to travel."

"That's not what I asked—never mind, let's talk. Come with me."

And that's how he ended up on a plane to Amsterdam less than a month later, embarking on a new career, he hoped.

SEVENTEEN

Valentina

If someone must be manipulative, it should be me.

Signor LaRocca's description of his evolution as a writer impressed Valentina. She had become more impressed with him, and she realized that her first assessments of this American had been incorrect. Valentina did not often think herself mistaken.

I do not make mistakes. I act on incomplete information that is sometimes wrong.

This was common in the intelligence service. One did not always have time to wait for better information when a decision was needed.

Perhaps I should not be so harsh with him.

"So, that's my story, Signora Marchese."

"Signor LaRocca, your Italian is improving. Please call me Valentina."

By his reaction, Valentina would have thought she'd just knighted him.

"*Certamente, Valentina.*" He added, "And please call me Benjamin, or even Ben."

"*Certamente, Signor LaRocca.*" Some things needed more time.

***

At the end of June, he and Angelina tried to entice Valentina to attend the Molo Street Parade with them. The parade was a street fair held along the south bank of the harbor channel each year. Valentina regretted the growing use of "Euro English." Events such as this and even products were now being labeled and marketed in English, with no attempt to use Italian.

She wasn't a fan of the fascist, but she thought Mussolini got one thing right. Not the trains, despite what everyone thought, but solidifying the Italian language. He banned the use of regional and provincial dialects—most based on Vulgar Latin—and outlawed the introduction of foreign words into her beloved Italian language. Then she remembered that he also outlawed profanity.

He really was a sick piece of shit, she thought.

However, she understood the reason for the linguistical crossbreeding. English was the new world language, replacing French, which itself had replaced Latin.

Well, the new western world language. I am sure the Chinese have their own thoughts.

Angelina had suggested that Benjamin join her at the parade for travel research. It was transparent to Valentina, but not so to him, and he'd accepted her suggestion without question. His response that it sounded like a perfect topic for an article was just as transparent to Valentina, yet opaque to her goddaughter.

But Valentina rebuffed their invitation, seeing no reason to be less than candid. "Why do I want to go down to the harbor and surround myself with a bunch of drunken revelers?"

She noted that Angelina and Signor LaRocca did not share her concern. Perhaps crowds offered a measure of emotional safety.

Valentina had made an exception once to attend the street fair. In June 2013, she timed a visit with Angelina and Giovanni so she could attend the Boy George concert at that year's event. Valentina liked the Culture Club. She'd first followed them the summer she met Angelina's mother. The song "Do You Really Want to Hurt Me" resonated with her for many reasons.

She stopped following Boy George in late 2008, disappointed in the behavior that led to his imprisonment. When she learned that he'd turned to Buddhism after prison, she gave him another chance. Although she did not follow Buddhism—*I like meat too much*—she understood his quote: "I'm Catholic in my complications and Buddhist in my aspirations."

When they learned of her infatuation, colleagues had teased her, saying it was because "Karma Chameleon" must be her personal theme song. Valentina had disagreed. Though she liked the song, she adored Boy George.

"He is just my cup of tea," she'd told them.

They did not get the reference, and she did not care.

***

Perhaps emboldened that her Molo Street Parade research ruse had worked, Angelina soon tried it again. The following week, as Valentina was cleaning up the dinner table, Angelina convinced Benjamin to put his writing and apartment search aside for a couple of evenings to take in the La Notte Rosa with her. "Pink Night" was a multiday celebration along the Romagna coast each July. Locals called it their annual midsummer "New Year's Eve" festival. It had started a dozen years ago and had grown every year since.

As if Italians need another excuse to get drunk at the beaches in the summer. Although Valentina made no attempt to hide it, her smirk was unseen by the others.

Angelina told Benjamin he needed to research it for the travel guides. He again accepted her justification at face value. Valentina had become more amused with each excuse Angelina manufactured to spend time with him, and by his apparent inability to see through them.

"You should come with us, Valentina," Angelina said.

"I am too busy. Enjoy yourselves." Valentina chuckled. *Talk about your thin excuses.*

Angelina refused to accept Valentina's excuse, thin or otherwise. After back-and-forth objections, they compromised, and Valentina agreed to go one night.

Later, watching them interact at a concert on the beach, she could not decide if they were a budding romance or just best friends. They were like siblings sometimes—at other times, like schoolchildren on their first boy-girl date being chaperoned by a parent.

Whichever it was, there were two benefits. First, Angelina appeared relaxed and interested in life, more so than any time since before her marriage. Second, Signor LaRocca was not a threat to Angelina. Valentina appreciated having two fewer concerns in her life.

But I do so hate these crowds.

***

Valentina and Angelina had adjusted to Signor LaRocca's growing frustration over his fruitless apartment search. They were both surprised—Valentina pleasantly and Angelina not so much—when he came back beaming after an appointment with Signor Rossi, the manager Valentina had suggested a month ago.

"At last, I found a decent place at a price I can afford. It isn't perfect, but more than acceptable. It was the person you recommended, Signora—I mean, Valentina."

"Congratulations, Signor LaRocca. Where is it?" Valentina knew precisely where it was. She had not given her suggestion another thought, assuming he'd seen the apartment and passed on it. She wondered now why he had not contacted Signor Rossi sooner.

"It's over in the historic center, a few blocks from the train station. Angelina, it's not too far from where we first ate dinner."

Angelina looked away, expressionless. "That is nice." She studied the back of her hand.

Valentina could see what Signor LaRocca did not, blinded by his relief in finding an apartment—Angelina was unhappy. Now Valentina wondered if she'd made a mistake giving him the card. *No, I had incomplete information.*

Her only goal at the time was to remove the intruder as quickly as possible. Now, her goal was Angelina's happiness.

Why did he not either call the manager sooner or else lose the damn card?

She hoped this did not blow up in her face.

After an awkward minute, Angelina asked, "Why do you have to leave?" It was not just a question—it was a plea.

Before he could answer, she resumed her lament. "What is wrong with here? Is there something you dislike?"

"No, of course not."

"Quindi, cos'è?"

He exhaled. "It's just that I feel like a visitor here. It isn't my space. I need to move forward. I need my space." Turning, he asked, "Don't you agree, Valentina?"

"*Boh!*" But she did know. Valentina sensed that it was not what Signor LaRocca disliked, but what he liked that made it awkward. She gave him points for providing a reasonable explanation. She deducted double for his lack of honesty with himself and Angelina.

Cervantes intruded, and Valentina wondered, *Are we to mark this day with a white or a black stone?*

***

Over the next few days, the mood within the Fabrizzi household was melancholic. Valentina observed that Angelina was morose, making it clear to everyone, including Mondo, that she was unhappy. And Valentina observed a conflicted Signor LaRocca, as he looked forward to the upcoming lease signing but remained disconcerted over Angelina's reaction. Even Mondo sensed the atmosphere.

Valentina felt the weight of her role in all of it. *This might blow over once he settled into his apartment.* She was wrong—it did not blow over, it blew up.

The evening before the lease signing, the three of them were working on dinner in the kitchen, as they often did. Angelina, without prelude, blurted in English, "Are you tired of my company? Is that why you are leaving? Is it Valentina? Mondo? Do you not like the food? Why do you have to leave?"

Valentina stood without commenting as she studied Angelina. Valentina assumed her English was to have a direct path to his brain—as if that were possible. She recognized the rapid speech as a symptom of Angelina's anxiety. He, Valentina concluded, did not. Before she could keep him out of harm's way, he tried to calm Angelina.

Idiota, do not try to fix it!

In retrospect, she realized it might have been better had she said it aloud.

He said, "Angie, now you can rent to someone on a long-term basis."

Merda! *Was he crazy?*

"What did you call me?" Angelina repeated, then in Italian, "*Come mi hai chiamato?*"

Valentina observed Signor LaRocca. The poor man looked like someone who had inadvertently pulled the pin from a hand grenade and did not know what to do next. Valentina thought her observation was more a tactical assessment than a simile.

Angelina began excoriating him, "*Mi. Chiamo. Angelina.*" She snapped the words, one at a time, stabbing at him with her finger as she did. "*Capisci, Signor LaRocca?*"

He nodded as he took a half step backward. Valentina imagined him searching for the pin but unable to locate it.

Switching to English, Angelina told him, "If you are having so much trouble remembering, perhaps you should call me Signora Fabrizzi from now on."

"Angelina!" Valentina scolded her with the single word before Signor LaRocca could open his mouth and make it worse.

Angelina stood up and commanded, "*Vieni, Mondo.*"

When the dog did not move, she balled her fists, closed her eyes, and barked "Argh!" before storming from the kitchen and up the stairs to her room. They must have heard the door slam at the train station.

Angelina's behavior disappointed Valentina—it appeared to devastate the American. She was not sure why she told him, "It will be all right, Signor LaRocca. Something is bothering her, and it is not you." Mondo stared at him as if to agree.

Except it is you—just not what you think.

The three of them ate dinner in silence, the two humans exchanging a faint smile every so often. Angelina refused their invitation to join them. Signor LaRocca cleared the table and went to his room. After considering if she should stay the night, Valentina headed back to her apartment. Along the way, she analyzed everything she'd seen and learned.

She knew Signor LaRocca cared for Angelina, but Angelina acted as if she did not know. He took her passivity as disinterest. The regular close contact with her at the house placed an emotional strain on him. In trying to escape, he'd settled for friendship, or so it appeared.

I was wrong. Angelina does not just have feelings for him; she is in love.

It was obvious he was unaware or else feared to believe it. Angelina took his efforts to keep their friendship at arm's length as romantic disinterest. At least that was what Valentina concluded. Nothing else accounted for her goddaughter's behavior.

Valentina worried about her Angelina's ability to experience love. Valentina knew that insecure people, such as those assholes Tàmmaro and Giovanni, were less likely to develop true intimacy, relying instead on game-playing and manipulation. While she empathized with Angelina's feelings of loneliness the past few years, Valentina was grateful her goddaughter had not sought such false intimacy. Better alone than surrounded by shallowness.

But now, Valentina had discovered a new Angelina—confident and strong. She was no longer an insecure person—if she ever was. She was ready for a genuine relationship, an honest relationship—a mutually supportive relationship.

But what if she feels pressured by his departure? she wondered.

If she tries to manipulate Signor LaRocca, it will blow up in her face. She might never develop a serious relationship with anyone if that happens, let alone with him.

Before Valentina reached her home, the problem statement coalesced for her.

Two people were trying to appear disinterested in each other because they did not want their interest to drive the other away or ruin the relationship.

She found it crazy. Crazy it might be, but it needed a solution.

Now, what do I do?

She remembered Cervantes's admonition: "Too much sanity may be madness, and the maddest of all, to see life as it is and not as it should be."

By the time she reached her apartment, she had decided. She made a phone call.

If someone must be manipulative, it should be me.

EIGHTEEN

Angelina

I wonder if it makes me look silly.

After she scolded Benjamin—deservedly—and Valentina scolded her—unfairly—Angelina stomped upstairs to her room. She slammed her door for emphasis, and to send a message. Then they had the nerve to ask her to come to dinner.

After what they did to me?

She had an unwavering focus: her anger toward Benjamin and Valentina. She wanted nothing to do with either of them, yet they monopolized her thoughts.

Why did Benjamin want to leave? Why did Valentina take his side?

She found no answers. As she wrestled with her thoughts, fatigue wrestled with her. She decided to turn in early. Tomorrow would be difficult, and she needed sleep.

She located her flannel Victorian nightgown. *Tonight, she needed its comfort.* As she dressed for bed, she saw the hat she'd worn that day on the train. Benjamin's comment that the apartment was near the restaurant where they first ate dinner popped into her mind. She smiled. *That had been a wonderful afternoon.*

She frowned. *Wonderful for me, but not for him.*

She finished dressing for bed, trying not to think of him, but failing miserably and feeling miserable.

As she lay in bed, Angelina stared at the ceiling, imagining tomorrow, overwhelmed by conflicting emotions. She cried, her tears trickling at first, then torrents as she wept.

What is wrong with me? Why is this happening?

No answers came to her, and neither did sleep—only her anxieties, waves driven by a storm. Her pulse quickened; her breathing rate accelerated—a panic attack rising within her.

God, I feel like I am drowning!

She forced her breathing to subside; her pulse followed. She did something she had not done since the death of her mother—she prayed.

Angelina made her peace with the God she'd ignored for so long, then asked for help and guidance. She resisted the temptation to ask God to make Benjamin stay. She'd always derided people who prayed for unimportant things.

"Please, God, help my football team win." "Please, God, help me find my car keys." "Please, God, make him like me."

It was as if they thought God was a genie with unlimited wishes. *God should help us become better people, help us make a better world, not give us a winning lottery ticket.*

Whether it was the prayer, her conscience finding an opening, or exhaustion, Angelina realized, *God, I am in love with Benjamin.*

The statement echoed in her mind like a public address announcement at the football stadium.

I am in love with him. That is the problem—I am in love with him. He likes me. Well, I think he does. No, I am sure, yes—no, I am pretty sure.

There was one thing upon which her thoughts agreed.

He is not in love with me. She wondered if Valentina noticed. *No, she would not notice. She is not romantic.*

This profound discovery was a profound relief to Angelina. She now had an explanation for things that had been inexplicable. It reduced the chaos in her mind and gave her an opportunity to plan what to do next—and maybe get some sleep.

She set a new goal: *I must find a way to be with Benjamin, no matter what.*

She smiled, her problem resolved.

No, wait—that was wrong.

I want to be happy, but I want him to be happy more.

Now she had a newer goal: *I must find out what Benjamin wants—what Benjamin needs—to be happy.*

Those were her final thoughts as sleep arrived. Just as sleep took hold, a new thought jolted her awake.

What have I done?

She remembered how she'd treated Benjamin. She became angry again, this time at herself.

Why do I keep mistreating someone who has only ever treated me with kindness and respect? I must fix this.

After considering several approaches, she settled on a course of action for the morning and surrendered to sleep. Her alarm clock displayed 3:08.

***

The next morning Angelina struggled to open her eyes. The sound of doors closing downstairs pierced her deep sleep and awakened her. She was surprised to find herself tangled in her duvet, which had become twisted and now ensnared her. Her body ached.

Did I sleep wrong? And why do I have a hangover? I had nothing to drink.

She told the empty room, "I need coffee before I speak with Benjamin."

With effort she focused her eyes enough to read the clock by her bed.

"9:25. *Merda per merda!*"

Angelina jumped out of bed as if someone had thrown a bowl of water on her. She rushed to dress herself and hurried downstairs, where she saw the door to Benjamin's room wide open. Angelina found Valentina and Mondo in the kitchen.

"*Dov'è Benjamin?*" Angelina asked.

Valentina did not bother to look up as she responded, "He left to sign the papers for his new apartment."

Angelina wailed in despair, and Mondo whined in sympathy. "Why did you not wake me?"

"Did you have somewhere to be?" Valentina asked.

"No, but I wanted to apologize to Benjamin," said Angelina.

"Well, you owe him that. I am sure there will be time for apologies."

"But he is leaving!"

"Once a pope is dead, there will be another one." Her godmother added, "Have some *caffè* and biscotti—you will feel better. I am off to take care of business. I will see you this afternoon."

"I do not want to move on! I need to fix this!"

Angelina could not tell as she left if Valentina could not hear her, or chose not to, but the effect was the same. Angelina's anger toward Valentina returned for a moment, until she realized, *I should have apologized to Valentina first.*

Nodding to herself, she spoke to Mondo. "*A volte, sono così senza un indizio.*"

She could imagine Mondo's answer. "Yes, sometimes you are without a clue."

***

Benjamin returned after lunch. Angelina expected anything but what she observed: he slumped as he walked and the puppy eyes, rather than sparkling, were almost drooping. *My spaniel looks more like a basset hound.* Before Angelina could deliver her planned apology, or even ask what happened, he told her the apartment was no longer available.

"I'm going for a walk."

"Benjamin, wait." She wanted to speak with him and his puppy eyes.

"I'll be back later. We can talk then."

Eyes she'd never seen before glanced at her before leaving through the front door with their owner—not angry, but different.

Angelina empathized with Benjamin's frustration and disappointment, but she sensed an opportunity. In response, she decided on a plan. Angelina began cleaning out her downstairs office so it could become a writing studio for Benjamin. Valentina returned midafternoon and asked her what she was doing.

"Before I answer, Godmother, please let me apologize for my behavior."

After her goddaughter apologized, Valentina said, "Sometimes, Angelina, you are such a finger in my ass." But then she added, "*Ma ti amo sempre. Sempre.*"

Angelina could not remember Valentina ever directing profanity at her but could not disagree. She was unsurprised but still relieved when her godmother said she still loved her—and would always.

Then Angelina described how she planned to help Benjamin stop worrying about a proper place to write.

"Do not try to stop me, Valentina Marchese."

"*Cascasse il mondo?*" Valentina asked.

"No matter what!" Angelina answered with diffidence, uncertain if she was ready for the fall of the world. She crossed her arms, waiting for the inevitable objection.

Valentina asked, "Okay, how can I help?"

Of any of the things Angelina had expected to hear, that was not even on the list. She uncrossed her arms. She had to so she could hug Valentina.

***

Angelina and Valentina spent the afternoon first cleaning out, then cleaning up the office across from Benjamin's room. It had been her husband's office, where he had planned his *schemi e intrighi* and performed his wheeling and dealing.

While they worked, they discussed many important things but nothing of importance. Angelina missed these meaningful conversations of meaningless things. She was thankful her behavior had not damaged the relationship with her godmother. At least, she hoped it was back to normal.

The women transformed the cluttered office into the *stanza di scrittura*, as Angelina now proclaimed it. Anything was better than *l'ufficio di Giovanni,* but she liked the phrase "writing studio." She decided Benjamin was right, remembering his comment that first day at the café.

From now on, my husband will simply be the "asshole." She smiled tight-lipped at the image of him and his *l'ufficio di stronzo.*

"But what if he doesn't like your writing studio?"

"Valentina, he *has* to."

"He does not *have* to do anything. No one ever does. Life is all about choices. Are you prepared to respect his?"

"Ovviamente, Madrina."

"Cascasse il mondo?"

"*Sì*," she said, repeating, "He has to." She tried to make it a statement, but it sounded much more like a prayer. When she saw her godmother's arched eyebrow, it was too much. "But, Valentina, I am in love with him."

As the words left her lips, Angelina froze, overcome with trepidation. She had been ill-prepared to tell her godmother. Valentina would disapprove, of course. Angelina had no difficulty imagining the conversation.

No, you are not, Angelina. You are just lonely and bored. You find this exotic American and his fascinating life intriguing. What do you know of love?

Throughout the day, this conversation had happened multiple times, but only in Angelina's mind. Valentina's response had occurred in none of them.

"Ovviamente, Angelina."

"*Che cazzo cosa hai appena detto?*" Angelina instantly regretted her use of profanity.

But Valentina did not scold her. Instead, in a soft voice, she said, "Angelina, watch your language, please." She followed with "I said, 'But of course.'"

Angelina knew what she had said—she'd just not fucking expected it.

"Angelina, I know you are in love with him. Mondo knows you are in love with him. Shit, I bet even the grocer knows you are in love with him."

Her godmother's revelation surprised Angelina, but she could only think, *And you talk about my language?*

"The only ones who do not seem to realize it are you and Benjamin."

Angelina did not notice it was the first time her godmother had ever said "Benjamin."

"You cannot tell him, Valentina. You must not. Please promise me you will not."

"It is your story to tell" was her godmother's reply.

Angelina did not understand the comment but did not pursue it. Instead, she assisted Valentina with dinner preparations.

***

Benjamin did not return until dinnertime. He found the two women in the kitchen preparing the meal. As he helped set the dining table, Angelina went back into the kitchen to help Valentina bring out dinner.

Valentina told her, "Eat first, then talk, Angelina."

Her godmother's directive made Angelina remember the book *Eat Pray Love*. She adored Elizabeth Gilbert's story, the film version with Julia Roberts not as much. Inspired by this disjointed thought, she decided, *Tonight, it will be Pray Eat Talk. I will worry about Love another time.*

After the three of them sat at the table, Angelina took a deep breath.

"I have something to say."

She watched the frown emerging on her godmother's face. *Too bad. She does not understand.*

Having gained their attention, Angelina said, "I would like to say grace."

She ignored Valentina's puzzled expression. She appreciated Benjamin's slight nod of agreement.

"Like this." She held out her hands to each of them. They joined with her, and then she insisted Valentina and Benjamin reach across the table to complete the circle.

"Heavenly Father, we thank you for all the blessings you have provided us, including this food and the warmth of this company. I thank you also for all the many blessings you have provided me, now and throughout my life. Most of all, I thank you for these friends." Angelina paused, then said, "I know I have not been worthy—yet you have stood by me, even when I did not stand by you. For that, I thank you with all my heart. Amen."

The others answered, "Amen," and everyone released their hands.

"That was very nice, very… heartfelt." Valentina gave her a warm smile.

"Grazie, Madrina."

Benjamin remarked, "That did not sound like a Catholic grace. What denomination was it?"

"The Church of Angelina."

As they ate, Angelina told herself, *But I should stop by the cathedral the next time I visit Como and make peace with the frog.*

***

After they finished dinner and cleared the table, Angelina said she needed to speak with Benjamin.

"Would you like me to leave, Goddaughter?"

"No, please stay," Angelina replied.

Benjamin stood watching her, waiting. He stood at an angle, as if preparing to run, and he shifted his gaze from Angelina to Valentina and then back.

Angelina said in English, "Benjamin, I know losing the apartment has upset you. I also said things last night I truly regret. I hope one day you will forgive me." She could see Benjamin preparing what she knew would be his protest that no apology was necessary, so she preempted it.

"Please allow me to finish. Regardless of how I behaved, this much is true. You need a better place to write, and you do not need the distraction of searching for a place. You should stay here—permanently." She paused, taking a deep breath, giving Benjamin an opening.

He replied in Italian. "Angelina, no apology is necessary. My presence here has been stressful for you."

Angelina shook her head, but Benjamin persisted. "We've discussed this. You and Valentina have been wonderful to me. And Mondo." Mondo nuzzled him, his tail knocking over a glass in appreciation. "But I need a better place to write."

"Yes, you do, Benjamin. And you have one."

She marched to the office and opened the door. "Please allow us to present the Benjamin LaRocca Writing Studio, or Ben LaRocca, if you prefer."

Benjamin gasped and took a half step back when he saw how Angelina and Valentina had cleaned and arranged the room. His jaw dropped, but he did not speak.

"I need to rent this room, no matter what." Angelina pointed at Benjamin's bedroom with a hand, then lifted it toward the ceiling. "I would much rather rent it to someone I know, even if he calls me Angie. I doubt I would find another famous writer to stay here, and I have gotten quite used to our stimulating conversations."

Benjamin shook his head.

Sensing his reluctance was due in part to her behavior last night, and prompted by Valentina's prodding nod, Angelina added, "Please forgive me for being—what is that rude term Americans use?—a bitch, Signor LaRocca."

Before Benjamin could reply, she held out her hand. "My name is Angelina, but you may call me Angie if you must."

Benjamin stared at her hand for a few moments without uttering a sound. Just as Angelina resigned herself to failure, he took her hand and replied in Italian. "Thank you, Angelina. My name is Benjamin. If you will call me Benjamin, I will call you Angelina."

The four of them smiled, but Mondo always smiled.

"So, you will stay?" Angelina asked as her eyebrows rose, trying to cover her forehead.

"Well, I did not say that." The eyebrows tumbled as Angelina frowned, until Benjamin added, "I need to understand the terms of this lease before I agree."

Angelina smiled and hoped her relief was not obvious to her godmother.

Benjamin turned to Valentina. "And what do you think about all of this, Valentina?"

Valentina shrugged. "It is acceptable—but do not forget my promise, Signor LaRocca."

"Valentina!" Angelina's smile was now a scowl, her eyebrows a line of storm clouds as she took a step toward her godmother.

"A joke," Valentina said, smiling, and she tilted her head, her eyes twinkling.

A genuine smile. She *was* joking.

Benjamin must have agreed, as he was still smiling. To Angelina, he was looking a bit silly. She brought him back to earth. "So, about that lease."

But try as she might, she could not hide her own smile.

I wonder if it makes me look silly.

Intermezzo

The Musician

"Where there's music there can be no evil."
— Miguel de Cervantes Saavedra —

Joseph LaRocca's vocation was actuarial science, but thanks to his *papà* Beniamino, his avocation was music. He worked almost every weekend as a part-time musician, playing guitar and saxophone in several local bands. Ben's father appreciated many types of music, but his favorite genres were big band jazz and classic rock, or what he called "real rock 'n' roll."

While Joseph was a significant influence on Ben's love for music, he wasn't the only one. Almost everyone in the extended LaRocca family played musical instruments. They were distant relatives of Nick LaRocca, who had been the first jazz musician to make a commercial recording in the early twentieth century.

Despite his professed and genuine love for all things American, Ben's grandfather most loved Italian music. Music was always playing or being played at his grandparents' house, including opera with Pavarotti and Caruso—*così tanto Caruso*—and popular music by performers such as Louis Prima, Dean Martin, and Caterina Valente.

Louis Prima was an entertainment genius, in Ben's opinion. He did not care much for Dean Martin's persona, but he loved his voice and his *Who gives a shit?* delivery—what his grandfather called "*Me ne frego.*" But Caterina was Ben's favorite. On every visit, Ben asked his grandfather to play one of his dozen Valente albums. He loved her Italian version of "Personality"—"*Personalità*"—it had spurred him to study Italian.

His favorite Valente song, however, was in English: "Stranger in Paradise." His mother played a Valente album called *Classics with a Chaser* often. On the album, contemporary songwriters had written lyrics for several classical pieces to create pop songs, and the album featured an orchestral rendition of the original "Stranger in Paradise," followed by a version where Valente sang the added lyrics.

The song was originally an Alexander Borodin melody from his opera, *Prince Igor*. Ben rarely remembered lyrics to songs, but the quatrain "If I stand starry-eyed, that's a danger in paradise, for mortals who stand beside an angel like her" stayed locked in his memory. It had convinced him he was a romantic.

When he married, he imagined his wife was the angel. It disappointed him to learn, as many people do, that what he'd imagined was not reality.

"Benjamin, romance will only take you so far," his sister said, consoling him after his divorce.

Music was ubiquitous in the LaRocca household during Ben's childhood. His mother played viola and gave private instructions. His father was still active in his rock band, what Ben would later call "classic rock," and filled in as a sax player with several other dance bands. As much as his father enjoyed rock, he loved big band jazz.

His father also worshipped Rosemary Clooney; hardly a day went by when he was not playing one of her records. Ben's mother said his father was in love with Rosemary Clooney. His dad would say, "No, just her voice," but his wife would shake her head in knowing and loving disagreement behind him.

Given his personal affection for Caterina Valente, Ben could understand. He also thought his grandfather might be infatuated with Rosemary. Grandpa Beniamino would sit hypnotized whenever he played her Italian songs, such as "Botch-A-Me," "Come On-a My House," and "Mambo Italiano." He repeated often, "I no care whatta hanybody sayees, thatta girla, she eesa *una paesana*."

One of Ben's fondest memories was when he attended a Clooney concert with his father and grandfather at the Count Basie Theatre in Red

Bank, New Jersey, in December 2001, during his senior year in college. They had purchased tickets before the 9/11 attacks. His father said he was not going to let some terrorists keep him from seeing his Rosemary.

They had great seats in the sixth row of the orchestra. Her voice was enchanting but not as strong as on the records. He assumed it was just age, but he later learned it was lung cancer. Her band was perfect, or at least Ben had thought so. His companions did not pay much attention to the other musicians. He could tell that when the two men watched her perform, they were imagining the *White Christmas* Rosemary on stage, confirming that he and his mother had been correct—it was a crush. Later he learned it had been Miss Clooney's final public performance.

While Ben played several woodwind instruments, he'd settled on piano as his preferred instrument. When he first started playing clubs in a band as a sixteen-year-old, his father would go with him and stay until closing because Ben was underage. By the time he turned seventeen, the clubs had stopped caring and his father only came to listen occasionally.

When he decided not to pursue a music degree in college, his mother did not hide her disappointment. "Why not, Bennie? You are so good at it."

"I listen to musicians such as Brubeck and Hancock, Emerson and Wakeman, Horowitz and Cliburn. I will never be as good as they are on their worst days."

She didn't understand his answer until he added, "I am Salieri in a world full of Mozarts."

At that, she stopped trying to persuade him. He knew likening himself to the composer was egotistical—Salieri was much more talented than as portrayed in the movie *Amadeus*—but it made his point.

He regretted his "butterfuge," a word he'd invented to mean raising reasonable-sounding objections to hide the actual reason—he didn't want to. His stated reason was the truth, just not the whole truth. It kept him from having to admit the real reason.

I couldn't bear to sit in a room all day with grade school musicians showing me how much they didn't practice that week.

NINETEEN

Benjamin

He was having fun with music again.

One Friday night, the three of them had been shopping and sightseeing in the Borgo San Giuliano when Valentina suggested they have dinner at a restaurant she liked on Via Forzieri. While it was one of many seafood restaurants in the district, the *osteria* offered several vegan options. It also featured a wonderful outdoor dining terrace. After dinner, as they left, they could hear live music coming from the park.

Ben asked, "Do you mind if we walk over to listen?" The women interrupted their small talk to smile and nod their agreement.

As they approached, Valentina recognized an acquaintance and wandered over to catch up on local gossip. He and Angelina watched the band playing well to a lively crowd. Ben became wistful, and Angelina asked him if he was okay.

"It's just listening to the band… I miss playing. I enjoyed the music, the other musicians, and connecting with the crowd."

Angelina lifted one arm and extended her upturned palm toward him as she shook her head. "Then you should find a band and play." It was clear to Ben that in her mind, the problem was resolved.

***

The second of the two shipments of Benjamin's belongings arrived five days later. The first, smaller but with most of his clothes, had arrived the week before. Ben was thankful to have more variety in his wardrobe. With the drama and uncertainty around his living arrangements, he'd worried he would need to buy clothing he didn't need.

This second shipment contained his remaining clothing and personal effects, the largest and heaviest of them his Kurzweil electronic keyboard. He played now for his own enjoyment—he hadn't played in public since before he left the States for Europe. Rather than using an amplifier, Ben was content to use his headphones. He wasn't showing off for anyone. He just liked to relax at the keys.

Angelina watched him unpack. When Benjamin opened the case for the keyboard, her eyes widened, her jaw dropped, and she leaned closer. Ben, not seeing her, turned and asked, "Angelina, could I keep this in the writing room? I'll use headphones—I won't bother you, or Mondo."

Or Valentina—especially Valentina, he thought.

The dog had looked up at his name, having become bored with the packages once he had deduced that they did not contain dog treats.

"But of course, Benjamin. Are you going to look for a band?"

"A band? What kind of band?" Valentina had just closed the front door upon her return. Ben thought her question had a suspicious tone for something so basic.

"Valentina, remember last week at the park? Benjamin used to play in a rock band. I told him he should find one here."

Valentina met Angelina's enthusiasm with an expressionless stare. "Oh, a music band." She lost interest in the conversation.

"Not just rock, many types of pop music." Ben sighed. He always regretted volunteering information to Valentina, yet he could not help himself. Valentina turned back.

"Interesting. I see you have an electronic piano."

Ben responded to Valentina's comment, knowing he shouldn't. He clarified that the Kurzweil was much more than a piano, and he offered examples of the songs he'd played. She surprised him with her receptiveness to his comments.

***

That Saturday, at Angelina's urging, Ben walked to a music store in the historic center, not far from where they had their first dinner together, hoping to find musician and band listings. Angelina asked if she could come along to learn about the music business. They entered from the street and navigated through the congested storefront. Ben wandered around the store. When he heard a sharp snap on a snare drum, followed by a roll across several tom-toms, he turned toward the drum kit on display. He recognized the drummer from the concert in the park. He walked over and waited as the drummer spoke with a store employee. Angelina dropped the music magazine she'd been skimming and joined him.

Once the conversation ended, Ben introduced himself.

"*Ciao, mi chiamo Ben LaRocca. Questa è la mia amica, Angelina.*"

The drummer, who appeared to be about the same age as Ben, shook his hand. "*Mi chiamo Luca Tortelli,*" he said, before taking Angelina's hand and bowing his head. "*Signora.*"

"We heard your band last week in the park. When we left, we walked back across the Ponte di Tiberio as you were playing a Motown medley. You sounded great," Ben said.

Luca said, "If you thought we sounded good on the bridge, you should have heard us in Riccione."

Ben laughed at the well-known musicians' joke, that the band sounds better the farther away you are, and some bands sound best when you are so far away you can no longer hear them. He'd never heard it in Italian.

I guess some things are universal, Ben thought.

He laughed to show his understanding. Luca's straight face transformed to join in with his laughter.

"You played in Riccione? Where?" Angelina did not realize it was a joke.

In response, the two men laughed again.

Angelina furrowed her brow. "*Cosa è così divertente?*"

Ben told her, "I'll explain later."

Ben noticed Angelina's little pout after that remark. He relaxed when she rejoined the conversation—but only for a moment.

"Benjamin is a piano player. He is also a famous writer."

Luca raised his eyebrows as he tilted his head, and Ben was unsure which statement prompted his reaction. Ben went with piano player; he was still uncomfortable discussing his writing with others. *Except Angelina and Valentina, of course.*

Ben described his playing experience back in the States. Luca asked if he still played.

"He has his piano at the house. He is searching for a band," Angelina interjected.

Ben nodded and said, "I have a Kurzweil PC3." Luca's eyes flashed again.

"We are looking for a keyboard player. Someone was just filling in the other night to help us out. It sounds as if you know much of the music we play. Are you interested in checking us out?"

Before Ben could answer, Angelina answered for him. "*È interessato!*" Angelina nodded to emphasize Ben's interest. He wondered about her sudden interest.

"Do you sing?" Luca asked, unaware of the new dynamic.

Ben enjoyed singing harmonies and backing. He knew he did not have a lead voice. "*Un po.*"

Angelina cannot answer everything for me. He felt a bit smug, then embarrassed that he did.

"Great. Give me your telephone number. I will check with the guys about a rehearsal and hit you with the telephone."

"Rehearsal? Don't you want a tryout first? To hear me play?"

Ben was not being modest. There was a difference between filling in and joining a band. One was a date, the other a marriage—or at least an engagement.

"No, your agent convinced me." Luca pointed at Angelina with two fingers.

She responded by giving Ben her *I-told-you-so* face.

"Besides, you told me the music you played before you knew we needed someone. You were not trying to impress me." He smiled. "But the actual reason? You brought your Kurzweil across the pond to Italy. That told me you are a serious musician."

"I hope I don't disappoint you."

"Perhaps you will not like us. We will see." Luca pulled out a business card and handed it to Benjamin. "I am a real estate agent to pay the bills. Are you two house-shopping, by any chance?"

Both Ben and Angelina shook their heads.

"Sorry, it is what I do," he said, giving them a sheepish grin.

"I'll hang on to this, just in case." Luca relaxed when he saw Ben's smile.

Luca's phone rang. After a quick "*Pronto*" and "I am on my way," he turned and said, "*Scusa, devo andarmene.*" He pointed at his phone. "My wife is waiting."

Angelina had taken a pen and piece of paper from her purse and scribbled Ben's name and number while Luca was on the phone. She handed it to Luca as he was preparing to leave. He bowed again to Angelina, then said he'd call soon.

"*A dopo.*" As he turned to leave, he added, "Benjamin, you have an excellent agent."

***

Ben and the band got together for their first rehearsal the following week. Luca introduced him to Nic, the guitar player, and Rocco, the bass player. They were a few years older and played like they had been together all their lives. Ben found out later he hadn't been far off. They'd been playing together for over thirty years, since early secondary school. The two shared lead vocal duties.

Ben noted Luca's microphone. "Do you sing, also?"

"If I did, we would not have any engagements," Luca said with a broad smile. "I am the master of ceremonies. I introduce the songs and keep the crowd engaged while Rocco and Nic do all the hard work."

"What is the name of the band?" Ben asked.

Luca replied, "Metodo Ritmo."

"The Rhythm Method?"

"*No, no. Non 'il Metodo Ritmo.' Solo 'Metodo Ritmo.'*" Luca added, "We would be in trouble with the Church if we called ourselves The Rhythm Method."

The experience the first night exceeded Ben's expectations. Their collective talent humbled him. He stumbled a bit at first but soon found a groove—where his playing added to the band.

Luca asked, "So, are you in?"

Ben suppressed the urge to say, *Hell, yeah!* and instead replied, "Sure, if you'll have me."

He wasn't sure whose smile was bigger—his or Luca's.

Metodo Ritmo played an eclectic mix of popular music from the past six decades. There were Italian pop songs Ben needed to learn, but he marveled at how much of their material he knew. Luca did not sing, but the two guitarists possessed wonderful, complementary voices. Ben's modest voice gave them a second harmony part, and they threw an occasional lead vocal at him, something with a simple melody.

Over the next few weeks, Ben rehearsed with the band a couple nights a week. Evenings were best for the others; he was the only one without a true day job. It wasn't too long before they had enough of a repertoire to seek work. He was having fun with music again.

TWENTY

Valentina

They found themselves without even looking.

During the summer months, the population of Rimini soared. Many locals, if not in the tourism industry, took their own holidays to escape the madness. Signor LaRocca mentioned he needed to stay in town to work. Angelina surprised Valentina when said she was staying in town and not escaping to Como as Valentina expected. Valentina then remembered her goddaughter could no longer use her vacation house half the year.

Damn, I had lost track of her financial mess. This must be torture for her.

Valentina chastised herself for being distracted by the *Signor LaRocca situazione*, as she'd labeled it when he first arrived. In the next moment, she reconsidered, realizing it was unlikely that Angelina would've gone on holiday by herself.

Valentina considered how the *situazione* had evolved. She acknowledged his positive influence on Angelina. Her goddaughter's growing self-confidence impressed Valentina, while Angelina's sudden lack of manners distressed her. From the events over the past days and weeks, Valentina was certain Angelina was in love with him—even if he was oblivious.

I do not know what to make of this Signor LaRocca.

That realization itself was a surprise to Valentina. She possessed an ability to judge people quickly and accurately. It had served her well in the P.S., the Carabinieri, and the AISE. Every day, she observed that this American treated Angelina with the utmost respect and admiration, yet

Valentina had never seen Benjamin do anything suggestive toward her goddaughter.

Hmm... I just thought of him as "Benjamin." I should be careful. She remembered how he'd reacted when she told him to call her Valentina. *If I call him Benjamin, he might hug me.* She chuckled.

He liked Angelina, that was obvious, yet he avoided even the hint of romantic interest.

Perhaps his was a platonic love, like during the Medici era, she speculated.

Could he be gay? Valentina thought of *A Special Day*, a movie to which she felt a deep connection. Maybe he is a Marcello to Angelina's Sophia? That would be awkward. Valentina knew the feeling.

She dispensed with thoughts of movies and actors and decided that no matter on which side of the fence he sat, he and Angelina liked each other's company.

I just do not want to see her heart broken if he does not share her romantic feelings.

***

Valentina did not know how exhausting the *situazione* had been until the drama evaporated. She appreciated the respite. Angelina appeared to accept Benjamin's presence in her home with no emotional involvement as a tolerable compromise.

He was writing or practicing ten hours a day, sometimes forgetting to eat or retire at a reasonable hour.

Valentina scolded him to herself. *You need to take care of your health, Signor LaRocca.*

His behavior reminded her of Sancho's description of Don Quixote: "From reading too much, and sleeping too little, his brain dried up on him and he lost his judgment." It was not a concern she would've entertained when they first met. It did not occur to her to tell him—he was a grown man, or as grown as most men got.

Later in August, Benjamin asked Valentina if she had a moment to speak with him.

He certainly is polite and respectful, she thought as she nodded to him.

"Valentina, next weekend, in the Netherlands, they're holding a festival called Redhead Days."

"*Giorni di Capelli Rossi*?" she said, adding, "I am unfamiliar with this."

"*Sì,* Redhead Days. *Perdona il mio inglese.*"

"Yes, I follow you." Valentina noted his accent and language usage had improved.

She thought, *Perhaps it is time to drop this Italian-only rule, maybe even call him Benjamin.*

"The festival this year is the first through the third in Breda, Netherlands. It started small in 2005. Now, thousands of people attend to celebrate having red hair. One of my travel websites asked me to cover it. I would like to take Angelina. She'd have her own room, obviously." He paused, expecting a response.

"Why are you asking me? Should you not ask Angelina?" Valentina noted with a silent chuckle that she had not responded as he expected. She let him off the hook.

"Signor LaRocca, you are showing me proper respect for my role as Angelina's godmother, and I thank you for that. If you need my permission before you ask her, you have it."

At that, he stepped forward and raised both hands to waist level.

Is he going to hug me? She instinctively took a half step back.

He must have thought better of it and instead held out his right hand to Valentina. "*Mille grazie, Valentina.*"

She thought better of him and clasped his hand, shaking it firmly.

***

Angelina returned home just before dinner. Valentina permitted Benjamin to cook that evening. She looked forward to a few of his vegan recipes. After others, she'd stop at one of her many favorite restaurants for a steak or pork chops on the way home. She felt no guilt—just hunger. It was a matter of survival.

He and Angelina spoke at the same time.

"I have something to tell you," said she.

"I've something to ask you," said he.

They both laughed and then said simultaneously, "*Vai tu per primo.*" Then they laughed again.

Valentina did not know whether to feel amusement or sympathy for them. They were like two children sometimes. She cleared the traffic jam.

"Angelina, you go first, please," Valentina insisted. After all, she knew what he had to say.

"I have a job!" Angelina shrieked it, and in English.

"*Che cosa?*" The statement confused Valentina. *Did Angelina just say she has a job?*

"*Mi è stato offerto un lavoro!*" Angelina answered. Turning to Benjamin, she switched to English. "A school has offered me a job."

"Near here?" he asked.

"No, The Borgo School in San Giuliano," Angelina said.

"Like the kids in the park?"

"No, a nursery school. The children are younger, under six years."

It was as if they had forgotten Valentina was there. She interrupted their enthusiastic ping-pong conversation. "*Sei un insegnante?*"

Angelina had never mentioned becoming a teacher to her. Valentina's confusion continued. She did not like feeling confused.

"*No, non un insegnante. Un assistente,*" Angelina said. With a furrowed brow, she asked Benjamin, "A teacher's helper?" She relaxed her brow but then wrinkled her nose.

"Teacher's aide?" he suggested.

"*Sì, un assistente dell'insegnante,*" Angelina said.

Valentina was struggling to absorb her announcement. "*Un lavoro, Angelina, perché?*"

"Why? I have been considering my future, just like you told me. I want a career, something meaningful."

"*Angelina, stai correndo dietro alle farfalle,*" Valentina said as she pulled at her hair.

"Valentina, I am not chasing after butterflies! You know I have a business degree but no experience. Benjamin reminded me how much I like children. After I investigated, I learned I can start as a teacher's assistant with my business degree, and I can take courses to become a full teacher. The dean was impressed with my English skills. He suggested I could also teach evening courses for businesspeople at an LSI nearby." Angelina waved her arm in the general direction of San Giuliano.

Ben scratched his temple. "LSI?"

"*Sì, una scuola di lingua straniera inglese.*" Then, to be sure, she added,

"An English foreign language school."

Valentina processed Angelina's explanation. She concluded that Angelina was still worried about her economic future.

This is my fault. I need to tell her. Valentina said, "*Figlioccia—*"

"Valentina, please do not try to stop me! I have been walking with my head in the clouds all afternoon, and it is because of you."

Angelina then answered the expected question before Valentina asked it.

"You are the one who has been telling me for years I am capable of anything, that I need to take ownership of my life, assert myself—that I need to take charge! So now I am taking charge of my life." Angelina exhaled, crossed her arms, and stared firmly, but not without kindness, at her godmother.

How did she have any breath left after that speech?

Valentina decided her conversation with Angelina needed to wait. She should not cast any shade on what she realized was a momentous announcement.

"Angelina," Valentina said.

"*Sputalo fuori,*" Angelina replied.

"Angelina!" Valentina had never been told "Spit it out" by anyone, let alone her goddaughter.

"*Scusa.*" Angelina dropped her gaze, staring at her feet.

"Angelina." Valentina watched as Angelina's shoulders slumped in resignation. "Signor LaRocca has something to ask you."

Angelina lifted her head, smiled, and turned to him, wide-eyed.

"Oh, Benjamin, I am so sorry. I forgot. I am just so excited, so happy. I have a job! And I also forgot to thank you."

"Thank me?"

"Yes, remember when you asked me about having children?"

Benjamin nodded. Valentina witnessed a man who appeared as if he'd hoped no one would ever raise the conversation again.

"You reminded me how much I enjoy children. You asked me about adoption. It made me think that there are other ways to spend time with children, and then I thought, *I could be a teacher!* Thank you, thank you, thank you!"

Angelina spoke rapidly as her gaze darted around the room. She waved her hands in all directions, as if she were being swarmed by bees. When she finished, her arms were extended in front of her, and she walked to Benjamin and embraced him.

It dismayed Valentina to see him only pat Angelina on her back, rather than embrace her in return.

He would hug me, but not her. She sighed.

Angelina, for her part, did not seem to notice.

"What do you have to ask me?"

Angelina agreed to go before he even finished describing the festival. He appeared surprised when she asked, "Why do we need two rooms? We could get one room with two beds. We are friends, we could make it work."

Valentina wondered if she switched to English because she was excited.

Ben turned away as he rubbed the bridge of his nose. He stared at the floor for a moment then inhaled. "My magazine editor would frown at that. It is better this way. And besides, it isn't costing me anything. The magazine pays for my room; I'll be using hotel points for yours."

Valentina saw Angelina pout—Benjamin did not. She turned away so neither would see her arched eyebrow.

I need to get that under control. It was why she no longer played poker.

***

Valentina enjoyed the quiet weekend, deciding to stay at Angelina's house to take care of Raimondo rather than trek back and forth three times a day. The downtime gave her a chance to get some financial affairs in order. She had much to do, and more to say.

After Angelina and Benjamin returned from the festival, she wished they had stayed away longer. Not so much for their benefit, but for hers. They would not stop talking about it.

"Godmother, there were so many *gingers*. They overwhelmed me!"

That was a word Ben explained to Valentina.

"I always thought it came from an American TV show called 'Gilligan's Island,' but it seems the British have used it to describe redheads for centuries."

Valentina nodded, pretending to care about a television show she'd never heard of nor ever intended to watch.

Angelina was effervescent.

"Valentina, there were even other women there with hair like mine! And everyone else told us our hair was special, the best."

"Now do you believe me? I told you it was beautiful when we first met!"

Benjamin was petulant. Valentina wanted to smack him. Angelina appeared unbothered, perhaps even appreciative.

Valentina was disappointed that nothing romantic developed on their trip, despite their mutual enjoyment. She was glad when Wednesday rolled around, as the two finally shut the hell up about *I Giorni di Capelli Rossi.*

***

That was when Benjamin's agent called from New York. He took the call, apologizing, as they sat in the kitchen after lunch. Valentina watched Benjamin becoming more animated as she listened to half the conversation: "You're kidding?" followed by "That's great. I look forward to it. Thanks. Goodbye." He ended the call and took a deep breath.

"You'll never guess who that was."

"It was Neil, your agent. You told us when you took the call."

Valentina wondered if there was any mental deficiency in Benjamin's antecedents.

"Yes, of course. What I meant was, you'll never guess what that was about."

"Just tell us!" Angelina's raised hand accompanied her remark. She had saved Valentina from just getting up and smacking him.

"I sold my novel. And I received a larger than usual advance!"

"Congratulations! Wow—we need to celebrate!" Angelina said.

"Your birthday is Saturday," Valentina said to Angelina, "If you would not mind sharing the celebration."

"Of course not." Angelina's smile grew to consume the rest of her face.

"Wait, your birthday is this week? When were you going to tell me?"

"Oh, I did not know you cared." Angelina tilted her head and smiled.

Her goddaughter's coy response irked Valentina. Valentina was not sure if Angelina noticed Benjamin's blush, or if she did, whether she derived any satisfaction from it. Valentina studied his reaction.

Was his distress genuine? Hmm... this might be an opportunity, she thought, and she began planning her matchmaking as if she were preparing a counterintelligence briefing.

***

The three of them agreed to go out to dinner on Saturday evening to celebrate. Benjamin said he knew of the perfect place. It had a robust vegan menu, yet it served meat, seafood, and dairy. Valentina appreciated his consideration.

On Friday evening, after dinner, Angelina asked of no one in particular, "What should I wear tomorrow evening?"

Now to put the plan into motion, thought Valentina, without the slightest guilt.

"Oh, I forgot to tell you. I must go out of town tomorrow, and I will not be back in time for dinner."

"Valentina, non essere una tale guastafesta!"

"I am not trying to spoil the party," said Valentina.

"But, Godmother, you need to be there. It is my birthday!"

"I know. Perhaps another time."

"Okay, we will choose a different night." Angelina slumped then looked at the ceiling. Valentina could not hear what she muttered under her breath. Benjamin looked at her, then at Valentina, then away—the puppy eyes did not look happy.

"No, I mean I can go with you another time. The two of you should go tomorrow as you planned." Seeing Angelina's reluctance, she commanded them to go. "*Vai avanti e festeggia!*"

Valentina observed how hard they both worked to show disappointment that she could not join them. She decided not to point out that their efforts were unsuccessful. She found it cute, and she thought nothing was cute.

Pleased with her efforts, Valentina thought, *Ils se sont retrouvés sans regarder.*

She chuckled. *I am such a romantic.* But "they found themselves without even looking" did sound more romantic in French.

TWENTY-ONE

Benjamin

I won't do it again, I swear.

Ben suggested to Angelina that they eat at Osteria L'Angolo Divino, over in the San Giuliano district, near her new employer. He'd eaten dinner there a few weeks back and thought it was a great restaurant with an extensive vegan menu.

They took the bus into the historic center and exited at Via Savaronalo. It was a warm late-summer evening, the sun still more than an hour from setting. It was directly on their faces as they strolled southwest along the south bank of the harbor channel, and Ben regretted not bringing sunglasses, or at least a hat.

He gazed across the channel at the street art murals lining the walls on the far side. The murals reminded him of the Wynwood Walls in Miami. As in Miami, the canal murals were overwritten from time to time. Ben wondered what the protocol was.

Could anyone just decide to paint over someone's work?

He appreciated the Apollo 11 and *Happy Days* murals and hoped they'd survive. Behind them, the late-day sun reddened the roofs of brown and tan tiles in the Borgo San Giuliani neighborhood, the Villa Maria hospital rising behind them. He liked the vibe of the entire *a Mare* district, especially further north and west near the river, and thought he might buy a house there one day.

Rather than continue along the channel to the Ponte di Tiberio, Ben steered Angelina to cross at Viale Matteotti. They passed the steps to the walkway along the north bank and walked another twenty yards before turning left onto Via Marecchia. Ben loved the little street with its well-kept homes—many with frescos celebrating Rimini's nineteenth-century fishing industry.

The neighborhood impressed Angelina—it was her first visit. The street was only three hundred yards long, but it took them fifteen minutes to travel. Angelina stopped and marveled at each decorated home front and garden as they strolled the narrow street.

"Benjamin, take a photo of me here, please." No sooner would he finish one when she would skip to the next house and say, "Now here."

As they neared the end of the street, they encountered a man and woman taking photographs of what Ben presumed was their teenage daughter. The younger woman wore a bright yellow-and-white sundress that covered her knees. She twirled her pleated skirt as the man took photos with a smartphone, the older woman yelling encouragement.

Ben and Angelina hurried to get out of the shot. As they did, the dancer twirled again. With her back to them, her skirt lifted to waist level, and Ben realized she was going commando. He glanced away, hoping neither the family nor Angelina had noticed that he had noticed.

Once past, Angelina asked, "Did you see that?"

"See what?" He tried to conceal his diffidence with indifference.

"Right." A moment later, Angelina added, "That was a nice mole on her left cheek."

"It was on her right."

"Right." They both laughed.

At the end of the street, Ben glanced left at the Ponte di Tiberio. The two millennia–old bridge crossed the harbor channel before terminating at the Parco XXV Aprile, a favorite walking destination of his, and where he had first watched Metodo Ritmo.

They arrived at the restaurant after another block. Ben had made reservations for a table on the veranda, and he was thankful the weather was cooperating.

"Wow. This is wonderful," Angelina told him, as she began to study the menu. "I have lived here all my life, yet you keep finding me all these great places. You certainly make me see my world differently."

Ben nodded and smiled. He noted, as he had expected, that there were more female patrons in the restaurant than men. When his male acquaintances would rib him about being a vegan, he told them that eating at a vegan restaurant was like bringing a cute dog to the park if one wanted to meet women. It was another example of butterfuge—his observation was accurate, but it wasn't his reason.

He couldn't understand why some men—some people—were so insecure about their own choices that they needed to invalidate others to feel better. He shared the observation with Angelina, but regretted his decision, even before he finished speaking.

"How screwed up is the world when guys accept 'I eat vegan to meet chicks' but not 'I eat vegan for my health'?"

"So, you are *un vegano* to meet women?" Angelina's frown was disconcerting, her response more so. She paused for a moment, her lower lip protruding, and as Benjamin wondered what was going on behind those honey-colored eyes, she said, "Me too."

Angelina, expressionless, stared at him for a few moments but then could no longer contain herself. As her laughter escaped, she assured him, "Benjamin, I am joking, kidding. I knew what you meant. I am not, how you say, interested in women."

Ben visibly relaxed. "Oh, no, I didn't think so. I mean, not that there's anything wrong if you were…" He felt as if his tongue had rolled out of his mouth to his feet and he was tripping over it. He saw Angelina's eyes twinkle, and her wide smile become warm.

Is it possible to trip over your tongue and put your foot—check that, both feet—in your mouth at the same time? Whatever it was, he stopped.

Angelina rescued him, describing how she'd seen a meat industry documentary fifteen years ago, and at that moment became a vegan. "*Mi fa cagare!*" she exclaimed in her native tongue.

Ben did not realize it was slang. Did she say, 'It makes me shit'?

He asked, "Shit?"

Angelina laughed. God, he loved her laugh. It was as if wind chimes were ringing in the forest while birds sang to each other.

"No. I meant it disgusts me, what they do to animals. I should have said, '*Che schifo*,' sorry. And you?"

Her eyes continued to sparkle. Was it the setting of the sun in the early evening sky, dropping below the buildings behind him? He tried not to stare, but to make it more difficult, the damn sunlight was conspiring with her hair. As the light breeze rearranged her tresses from moment to moment, the highlights he'd seen before, and others he was discovering for the first time, framed her face. Her strands of silver hair took on a life of their own, wisps of fog across hills of heather. The realization that she had asked him a question snapped him back to the moment.

"It wasn't so dramatic. My four grandparents had died early of heart disease. When the last died in 2007, I expressed my concerns to my doctor, and he agreed. Based on my family history, I was a candidate for heart disease, as were my parents. He urged us to change our diet. After collecting research, I became a vegetarian not long after. It was while I'd been collecting the research that I got the urge to write. When I moved to Europe in 2015, I went full vegan." Ben sipped his wine. *Why am I talking so much about myself?* The thought did not deter him from continuing.

"The Schengen countries have better labeling, and many more options. It made my decision easier." Schengen referred to the cooperation agreement between European countries that predated the European Union. Non-EU countries such as Switzerland and Iceland were signatories of the Schengen Convention. He felt uncomfortable implying he was now vegan.

"Just to be clear, I am not a true vegan. I still wear leather, although I've stopped buying leather products." Tonight, he wore his English walking shoes, and he waved at them to emphasize his point. "At least I am moving in the vegan direction."

He felt relieved when Angelina nodded. He knew her empathy should not have surprised him. She wasn't a militant vegan like some people. To Ben, they were the same as his colleagues who mocked his veganism, just on the other side of the coin.

"Why can't people just enjoy their own skin without needing to diminish others?"

When Angelina agreed, he realized he'd verbalized his last thought.

Oh, how I love that smile. He made sure not to verbalize that thought.

A female server brought the Lambrusco that Ben had requested. Lambrusco was the unofficial almost-sparkling wine of the region. Unlike the sweet, over-carbonated Lambrusco sold in the States, Emilia-Romagna Lambrusco was an outstanding wine for any occasion. They toasted each other.

"Congratulations on your novel, Benjamin!"

"*Buon compleanno, Angelina.*"

Angelina nodded, smiled, and closed her eyes before saying, "The wine is excellent." She opened her eyes and appeared startled when the male server who had just brought their antipasto thanked her.

"Prego," was all she said as she smiled first at the server and then at Ben.

Ben was still feeling nervous, until her comment about the wine—and perhaps the wine itself—eliminated it. When Angelina said how much she liked her starter, he became emboldened and leapt into a rambling observation.

"Before I went vegan, I never paid attention to what they served at social functions. But once I switched, I noticed weird stuff. I would be at an office gathering, and they would serve pizza. Not real pizza like here, but Americanized pizza."

"Ahh, the famous Pizza Hut." Angelina's laugh assured him she understood.

Ben ramped up his intensity. "They'd serve pizza, even though a few folks were vegan and several gluten-free. When confronted, they'd reply with 'Well, we have plain pizza.' Then, realizing the issue, they'd say, 'Right, next time.' After several get-togethers where a handful of people sat not eating, the self-proclaimed social directors started making a big deal about ordering salad for the 'others,' but more often than not, the salad would arrive with cheese and croutons mixed in, sometimes even grilled chicken or bacon!" Ben shook his head, unaware that Angelina was sitting transfixed.

"Someone without dietary concerns had ordered the fancier salad. 'Who wants just a plain-Jane garden salad?' Only the people who couldn't or didn't want to eat the other crap! The worst part was that the pizza lovers couldn't have cared less if no one ordered salad, yet they deigned to decide for the 'others.'" He dropped his hands, embarrassed, as he realized he was using his air quotes gesture. Benjamin took a breath, aware that he'd been on one of his rants.

"Benjamin, I have never seen you quite this *appassionato.*" Before he could decide if that was a criticism, she added, "I like it! But what is a 'plain Jane'?"

He was thankful he'd swallowed before she used his air quotes with her question. He chortled as he described the term.

"*Disadorna?*" Angelina smiled after her question.

He nodded. "Unadorned" was correct.

"*Scondita?*" she asked.

He nodded again. It could mean "unseasoned." He watched, fascinated by her crinkling nose as she scrunched her face, until he became distracted by her sparkling eyes. He wondered what was going on behind those enchanting eyes.

"*Rita-scondita!*" Her enthusiastic—and loud—exclamation drew the bemused attention of other diners.

"What?"

"I just invented that! Like 'plain Jane,' no?" She was so proud he decided not to ask how much wine she'd had.

Angelina complimented him multiple times on the restaurant, its ambiance, the food, the wine. So much so that he feared she might be overcompensating for an average experience, but it felt sincere. It was her birthday, and he wanted it to be special.

For him, the night was anything but average. If not for the fear it would threaten their friendship, he'd have been complimenting not the restaurant or the food, but her laugh, her voice, her smile, her eyes. And those eyes—if only he could stop looking into her eyes, just as aware as the time on the train that he might fall into them and not find his way out. Tonight, he didn't care.

They finished the Lambrusco midway through their entrees. Their female server asked if they wanted another bottle. Ben hesitated, but when he glanced at Angelina, her twinkling eyes said yes.

And then, so did she. "I would love some more."

Ben bowed to the server and extended his hand toward the empty bottle.

Maybe it was her use of the word "love" or the second bottle of wine kicking in—or possibly it was her eyes—but Ben began talking about Love. That is, love with a capital *L*. In retrospect, he realized it was the wine *and* the eyes and her laugh, but the eyes and her laugh had been in on the conspiracy from the beginning.

"In the English language, we use the word 'love' for multiple reasons. We love something if we like it a lot. We love people, of course. We can even be in love. In English, the word 'love' only has four forms: 'love,' 'loves,' 'loved,' and 'loving.'" He raised four fingers. "But in Italian, there are over two dozen distinct words used in conjugations. And being in love, *innamorato*, isn't even one of them." He flipped his hand, now palm up. "Plus, Italians don't say '*Ti amò*' to family; they say, '*Ti voglio bene*.' English should have another word for being in love. It would avoid problems."

Ben remembered conversations he'd endured with both his ex-wife and his sister.

"What problems, Benjamin?"

As he spoke, Angelina never took her gaze off him. That made it at the same time both easier and more difficult for him to continue.

"People don't understand the difference between being in love and loving someone."

"I must be one of those people," Angelina said. I do not understand what you mean." She brought her right index finger to her cheekbone as she cupped her chin with the thumb and middle finger.

"When you fall in love, when you are in love, the experience is all about you, the person in love. You would do anything to *be* with the other person. Being in love is on a continuum that includes fondness, attraction, infatuation, fixation, lust… even obsession. It is not an emotion but a state—a state that advertising agencies all over the world try to convince us to desire."

Angelina had said nothing, nor had she turned her eyes from him. Ben was no longer distracted by them. He was speaking to them. "Love, on the other hand…"

"What about love?" she asked as he paused, and she lifted her left hand so that it too was now cupped in her right hand.

"When you love someone, the experience is not about you, it is about the person you love. You would do anything *for* that person." He inhaled.

"Think about how parents love their children. Mothers talk about falling in love with their child at birth, but a mother would do anything for her child. That is love, so much bigger than infatuation and lust that we should have another way to describe being in love."

Ben saw the birth of a tear in Angelina's right eye, and he realized what he'd done.

I am a fucking moron. Here I am talking about mothers and children to her.

"I am so sorry. I did not mean to upset you. I was stupid to talk about mothers, about children. Please, please, please forgive me."

"Oh, no!" Angelina chuckled. "I am not upset. I was just a little overwhelmed by your speech. You have said things I have also thought and believed. Not about the English word, of course, but the ideas. I never expected to hear a man say them." Angelina lifted a hand to her mouth as her eyes widened with embarrassment.

"Oh, no!" she said again, but this time, Angelina grimaced. "That was rude of me. I did not mean it."

"Yes, you did, and it's okay. I'd be surprised to hear another man say it."

The awkwardness of their respective unnecessary apologies created a natural lull as they finished the meal. When their male server poured the last of the second bottle into their glasses, he asked if they wanted coffee or dessert. The server looked at Angelina, who was still gazing at Benjamin the same way she had throughout his soliloquy.

She appeared startled, then said, "*Un caffè, per favore.*"

Benjamin nodded to their server. "*Anch'io.*"

"*Due caffè,*" the server confirmed, and sauntered away.

The interruption separated Ben from his train of thought. When he reconnected, he wondered why he'd spoken to Angelina about love.

I will scare her away if I am not careful. She doesn't want a romantic relationship. She's not in love with me. We're not a couple.

But from another place in his mind came the memory of an old man's observation. *How do you know you are not?*

Two opposing forces were coming together tonight, and he was unprepared for the conflict he was experiencing. On the one hand, he knew he was in love with Angelina, and was fairly sure he had been since that first day on the train. *Amore a prima vista.*

And to think I never believed in love at first sight. He smiled with the thought.

But it was not only his attraction to Angelina the woman. He knew he loved Angelina the person. It was for that reason—strange as it sounded, even to him—that he'd not yet told her. He wanted to avoid complicating her life, and he could not endure losing her friendship.

The second force had been around far longer. Ben was, at his core, an honest person. Honest even when it was not in his own self-interest. The few times in his life he'd been dishonest, thinking at the time he had a valid reason, he ended up regretting it. By not sharing his feelings with Angelina, he was in a way being dishonest with her. Regardless of his good intentions, he was having trouble reconciling that. The battle was far from over, but Ben had a feeling that honesty would prevail.

For me, it always does, he thought, and sighed.

Ben glanced at the name of the restaurant on the table card, "Osteria L'Angolo Divino." Grasping for anything, he wondered if Angelina could be his "Divine Angel." As a teenager, he'd thought it strange that Italian applied the masculine "*angolo*" to both men and women.

"An angel has no gender, Benjamin," a priest he'd asked once told him.

Where did that come from? Talk about tangential.

Ben paid the check, waving off Angelina's offer. "Today is your birthday, and I am the American author Ben LaRocca." He tried to laugh off his boast even as this time it didn't quite sound like a joke. He followed up with "So what would you like to do now, Lina? I picked the restaurant, now you choose." While he was patting himself on the back for his gallantry, he did not see Angelina's eyes flash.

"What did you call me?" she asked.

"Sorry, what?"

"Did you just call me Lina?"

Ben's life flashed in front of his eyes—at least the last few months.

What the hell did I just do? I truly am a fucking moron.

Those were the closing credits on his life's story—followed by coming attractions.

How do I fix this?

He inhaled, exhaled, and took a deeper breath. "I am so sorry. It kinda sorta popped out. I won't do it again, I swear." He was aware of how pitifully whiny he sounded. He was unaware he was slurring his words.

TWENTY-TWO

Angelina

I am in command for the first time in my life.

Angelina had enjoyed their stroll along the harbor channel. With Benjamin, she was seeing the city differently, as if for the first time. The murals on the walls were no longer background noise. When they crossed the bridge at Matteotti, she thought of Matteo for a moment. She remembered the walks they took—this was different, but she could not describe how.

Angelina had consumed more wine at dinner than at any one meal in years. The Lambrusco generated a warm, fuzzy feeling, like being wrapped in an old chenille blanket. She liked it. She'd enjoyed hearing Benjamin talk about love—but was disappointed when he did not mention her.

Encouraged by her warm-blanket feeling, she decided, *I need to tell him I love him, no matter what. And I know the perfect place.*

She was glad for the *caffè*—it helped to clear her mind, if only a bit. She made a show of offering to pay, but when Benjamin insisted, she smiled and thanked him. It felt much more like a date. She'd not been on a date in…

I have never been on a date. Not like this. Not a boy-girl date at a wonderful restaurant with a gallant gentleman who treats me like a lady. How sad was that?

Benjamin chased the frown from her face when he said he was the American author Ben LaRocca.

I am glad he is comfortable embracing it, and I am glad that I am happy—

or am I happy that I am glad?

When the gallant gentleman had asked what she wanted to do, she became fixated on a new thought: *No man has ever asked my preference about anything.*

It took her a moment to react to what he had called her. When the name "Lina" broke through her warm, fuzzy fog blanket, she felt her eyes widen. *What?*

She'd followed up her mind's question with two of her own. Angelina regretted her questions, especially the accusatory tone of the second. She tried to think of a way to soften it as Benjamin reacted.

She watched with amusement as he stumbled, stammered, and apologized, slurring all the way. Obviously, he, too, was feeling the wine. She rolled the name around in her mind. No one to her knowledge had ever called her Lina.

Lina? I like it. I like the way he says it.

She chuckled at his embarrassment and decided to rescue him.

"No, I like it. Not from anyone else. But from you, I like it." She then answered his original question. "I would like to walk out to Rockisland."

***

Rockisland was a restaurant and club at the end of the Giulietti Pier. It sat on a platform at the intersection of the pier with a perpendicular jetty that protected the marinas and the mouth of the harbor channel. It was the only club Angelina patronized, a coincidental result of its location. On most of her journeys to the end of the pier, she'd not set foot inside the building. There was something about being away from town, out to sea, listening to the waves teasing the rocks, that relaxed her. She loved gazing at the horizon, imagining other places. She had visited the spot dozens of times.

When she first mentioned her fascination with the location to Valentina, her godmother had all but smothered Angelina with her concern. Thinking back, she chuckled.

I can see at the time why she worried I might be suicidal.

Angelina had assured her godmother there was nothing to fear. Valentina told her much later that she realized Angelina was the person least likely to consider suicide of anyone she'd ever known.

Angelina agreed. *I enjoy life—but sometimes its sense of humor sucks.*

Benjamin and Angelina walked by her soon-to-be school, then past the construction at the hospital. As they came to the east end of Via Marecchia, they crossed through the Porta Gervasona, one of the original city gates, and along the Malatesta-era walls next to the Chiesa della Madonna della Scala. The Church of the Madonna of the Staircase sat on the corner with a statue of the Virgin Mary atop its roof. Benjamin and Angelina read the plaque describing the 1608 miracle that prompted the construction of the church in 1611.

According to the legend, stairs in a tower led up from the river to street level. A painting of the Madonna adorned the top of the tower, facing the river. A man and his horse had fallen into the nearby river. The drowning man prayed to the image of the Madonna for help. Fishermen who lived in the neighborhood declared the story of his rescue a miracle and attributed it to the Madonna. The miracle and the painted image inspired construction of the church.

Benjamin pointed out that there was no mention of the fate of the horse.

"Perhaps the horse did not pray hard enough." Angelina tried to make a joke, and Ben chuckled, but she regretted her impiety. "I should not have said that. I am sorry," she said.

The man must have felt as I did the night before our Pray Eat Talk.

Angelina allowed Benjamin to believe it was her love of animals, not her conversations with God, both past and present, that had caused her remark. But it was both.

Their journey took them along the north bank of the channel. As a result, they took the pedestrian ferry by the Rimini lighthouse. The *traghetto di canale di Rimini* was a small on-demand platform boat that shuttled people and bicycles across the canal near the seafront, saving them from the two-kilometer trip up and back to cross at the Ponte della Resistenza.

A teenaged boy with a bicycle and an older couple holding hands crossed with them. Watching them, Angelina remembered the couple at the train station and smiled, then sighed. She remembered the woman's observation. *Hang on to him. There are not so many out there.*

Or was it a command? She sighed again.

Ci sto provando, nonna. But what if she was not trying hard enough?

As they crossed, Benjamin pointed toward the Ferris wheel. "Have you ever been on La Ruota Panoramica?"

"No, but I have often thought about it." Angelina looked at the top of the wheel, seeing it differently, as if for the first time. *I have just never thought about it like this.*

"We should do it before they close up for the season," Benjamin said.

Angelina liked that he'd said, *We should do it.* It felt right. But not tonight—tonight was taken. She had plans for tonight… if only she could figure out what those plans were.

They meandered on toward the Rockisland Club at the end of the pier, weaving their way through couples and small groups of people out on the warm evening. The moon was just starting to rise off to the right, its light shimmering on the rippling waves at the horizon. Angelina felt as if she were being hypnotized and forced herself to turn away.

"Look, Benjamin—see how they built Rockisland like your Rose Island!" The club's platform extended from the stone pier on large pilings.

"You're right. What a coincidence," he replied.

Here again with the coincidences, she thought. *It must mean something.*

Uninvited and unwelcome, her godmother's voice intruded on her thoughts. The imaginary Valentina began lecturing Angelina like *il Grillo Parlante* in *Pinocchio.*

You are being superstitious, Angelina. You are trying to rationalize your optimism because you are too romantic, said Valentina the Talking Cricket.

Dai! What did she know about romance?

Benjamin pointed off to the right. "I like the beaches south of the pier. They remind me of back home." Angelina's head tilt and widened eyes prompted him to explain.

"Because of the long, flat expanse of sand leading to open water. The northside beaches have the visible offshore rock jetties. Most beaches in New Jersey do not have them."

Angelina wanted to ask him to talk more of his home but caught herself. *I want this to be his home. Why should I remind him of somewhere else?*

"Did you know that they have had to extend the pier because the beach to the south continues to widen from sand deposited by currents disrupted by the pier." Benjamin waved his arm from the beach to the water. "The extended pier then causes the beaches to grow further, and the cycle is repeated. I read where the south beach had grown about a kilometer over the last seven hundred years, and that they had extended the south pier at least ten times."

Angelina's whimsical response did not match Benjamin's academic observation.

"If it keeps going, one day the pier and beaches might create a land bridge connecting Rimini to Croatia. We could charge the cruise ships a toll to get through to Venice."

She giggled then stopped, embarrassed. Angelina patted Ben on the arm. "Sorry, it is the wine."

He laughed and agreed with her.

He enjoyed my joke! No one has ever enjoyed my jokes.

Not even Valentina—especially Valentina.

After passing the nightclub, they stopped at the Monumento Alle Mogli Dei Marinai. The Monument to the Sailors' Wives, designed by local Rimini sculptor Umberto Corsucci, was a twelve-foot high sculpture of a sailor's wife pointing out to sea, hoping to see her husband's boat. At her feet, clutching her mother's dress, was her child. Next to the sculpture was a yellow tower with a flashing beacon, warning boats about the end of the pier.

"The woman appears to be pointing toward the former Republic of Rose Island." Benjamin smiled at his rhetorical observation.

Another coincidence?

Stop it, Angelina. Valentina the Cricket had returned.

Angelina laughed and thought, *Sì, Madrina Grillo.*

To chase the cricket from her thoughts, she described the Rimini fishing industry.

"The fishing industry in Rimini goes back centuries." Angelina waved her arm across the channel opening. "They had a formal society that governed the design of the sails on fishing boats—their colors and patterns. They approved each new sail design so it would not duplicate the sail of another boat. That was how the wives recognized their husbands' boats."

"It must have been lonely for them." Benjamin turned to look again at the woman in the statue.

"They were alone often, but they were not lonely. They had their husbands." Angelina wondered why she'd suddenly become so philosophical, so changed the subject to mask the awkward feeling. "Would you like to check out the club?"

They headed back toward the club and sat at a table inside. He ordered a bourbon with ice. Angelina asked for a glass of Lambrusco.

Why change a good thing?

There was no band, only a DJ, which bothered Benjamin. "I know DJs can be entertaining, and one person costs less than a full band, but if there were no musicians, who would make the music that they play?"

Angelina realized it was a rhetorical question, but the wine encouraged her to respond. "They would just stand up there all night with two empty records and go *sckricha-chicka-chicka.*" She moved her hands in opposite circles, simulating a DJ's scratching, as she laughed, then snorted—and then laughed harder because she snorted.

Benjamin gave her a puzzled smile followed by a stronger laugh. "Do that again!"

After repeating her impression, she could not stop laughing, although she tried.

"Sorry, Bem-a-jin." More laughing. "I mean, Benjamin. Did I mention this is good wine?"

"I don't know if it's good, but it sure is happy wine."

Again they laughed, until Angelina regained control. While they were laughing, the DJ dropped what had been an incessant rave beat and started a ballad. Angelina stood, as if rising from a throne; presented her hand palm down, bent at the wrist; and commanded, "Dance with me, Benjamin."

They started tentatively, but soon found the rhythm. Angelina laid her head against the top of his chest. She was glad she'd worn flats—she enjoyed listening to his heartbeat. Benjamin had started with her right hand in his left, but by the end of the first verse, she'd pulled her hand free and placed it on his shoulder. He held her, but not tight enough. Angelina pulled him closer. Soon, there was no separation. She inhaled, unaware that the intoxication she felt was not wine induced.

I like this. It is right. Essere nelle nuvole.

She had never thought she'd one day be in the clouds for a man.

When the song—something about keeping alive—ended, Angelina

decided it was time to tell Benjamin how she felt. He spoke before she could, but as soon as he said, "Lina," the DJ began playing up-tempo music even louder than when they arrived. Angelina shook her head and pointed to her ear, and Benjamin nodded and pointed toward the door. She watched as he found their server and paid the tab.

They left the club, and Angelina told Ben she wanted to see the Faro di Destra del Porto at the end of the jetty. What locals called a lighthouse appeared no different from the yellow tower by the sculpture, only it was red. A predecessor, black-and-white on a shorter pier, appeared at the beginning of Fellini's film, *Amarcord*, and as a result, the lighthouse had a minor cult following. Angelina wondered if the centuries-old, eighty-two-foot Rimini lighthouse by the harbor ferry was jealous of this shorter, younger upstart.

The pier was closed and off-limits after dark, but like a few dozen other adventurous souls, they climbed up the rocks and went around the closed gate. After they both had tried to speak inside the club, once outside in the relative silence, neither said a word.

Angelina took advantage of the quiet and listened to the waves dancing on the rocks. She watched Benjamin as he read the plaques in the uneven light from the club, and from the three-quarter moon, just beginning to rise. The jetty wall facing the sea had a series of plaques mounted, the *biblioteca di pietra*. The Library of Stone consisted of bronze plaques mounted to the large stones, engraved with book titles and quotes from famous authors.

"One day, you will have a plaque here, Benjamin." They were the first words either had spoken since Angelina had said, "Help me climb up, Benjamin."

Like its yellow companion, the red lighthouse was eighteen feet high, with an open maintenance ladder. Angelina gazed at it, lost in thought.

Your companion is yellow, and they ignore him. You are red, like me, and they call you a lighthouse. Maybe I was meant to be a lighthouse.

As they turned to walk back, Angelina reached out to hold Benjamin's arms and commanded again, "Dance with me, Benjamin!"

Before he could finish, "But Lina, there's no music—" she showed him there was, at least for the two of them. Angelina observed other visitors chuckling at them.

"*Dovresti ballare tutti,*" she commanded, accompanied by a royal nod of her head.

Two couples laughed, bowed their heads in reply, and obediently began dancing.

Where did I get this new superpower? she wondered.

After a few minutes, a boat powered past the end of the jetty, inbound for the harbor. It broke the spell, but only for a moment. Angelina stopped and said, "Benjamin, there is something I must tell you."

He appeared as if he wanted to say something first, but then leaned down and kissed her on the lips, just a light pressing of his lips to hers. She stood frozen for a moment, stunned by the unexpected gesture, and by the intense electricity she felt had just arced across their lips.

Misinterpreting her reaction, Benjamin apologized. He must have then realized that not only had she not pushed him away, she was holding him tighter.

"Sorry. No, wait, I am not sorry. I've wanted to do that for a long time." He paused, as if expecting a response.

Angelina wondered if that was what he wanted to tell her. She tried to read his face, but she found puppy eyes instead.

"Benjamin, never do that again." When his puppy eyes closed, she scolded herself for teasing him. "Never again apologize for kissing me." She reached up and kissed him, a proper kiss, and he kissed her back, and her head exploded—or was it her heart?

When they came up for air, she was light-headed, so they leaned against the rocks.

Angelina said, "I have been afraid to tell you how I feel. I am in love with you. I have been for quite a while." She patted her chest. "But I was not sure how you felt, or what would happen if I told you."

Angelina brought her hands together as if praying. "I did not want you to leave when you were searching for an apartment, nor keep you there if it was wrong for you. I could not bear for you to be unhappy or disappointed." Angelina brought her index fingers to her lips before hugging herself with both arms. "And I was so afraid I might learn that you did not care for me. I did not know what to do."

Unlike before, her words were slow and measured—but not because of the wine. Instead of anxiety, Angelina had never felt more comfortable—or confident.

She opened the right arm from her hug and extended it, elbow cupped in her left hand, with the right palm up. "Tonight, at dinner, I realized you at least cared for me, and that I should tell you how I felt, no matter what happened next, so I did." Angelina's left arm now mirrored her right. She took a deep breath. She was light-headed again, or was it still?

So, what happens next? she wondered.

Benjamin smiled and said, "Do you remember when we were talking in the restaurant about love?"

Did she? She had locked herself to her seat with both hands to keep from jumping up and yelling, *Yes, I know love. I am in love with you!* Instead, now as before, she just nodded.

"Remember what I said? When you are in love with someone, it means you want to be with the person all the time. You'll do anything to *be* with that person. When you love someone, you'll do anything *for* the person you love. So, I don't think you are in love with me."

What is he trying to tell me? Is he trying to say I do not understand love, or that he does not love me?

She verbalized her worry and confusion. "What are you saying? Of course I am in love with you. It started on the train from Milano. I was sure when I saw you help that old couple at the Rimini station."

Still smiling, Benjamin said, "Please let me finish. I mean, I don't think you are *just* in love with me. I think you also love me. You have been nothing but supportive of me. I've never had someone like that in my life, except perhaps my sister."

I should like to meet this sister, she thought.

She asked, "But do you love me?"

"I met this amazing woman on the train from Milano. She was stunning. She was intelligent. I connected with her. She bedazzled me, but I wasn't sure I was in love."

He is trying to let me down easy.

Angelina slumped, crestfallen. She decided she could face it, and she tried to stand taller.

"But when I saw you playing tag with those children in the park, I knew. I was in love with you. Smitten *and* bedazzled."

Angelina stood even straighter. In fact, she worried she might float away. "Then why did you not tell me?"

Benjamin replied with "Why didn't *you* tell *me*?" By this point, it was a rhetorical question for each of them, but Benjamin answered her anyway.

"I liked *us*. I didn't want to break us. If I'd told you and you had asked me to leave, it would've been far worse than not telling you—at least so I told myself."

Angelina shook her head. "I felt the same way."

"I can also tell you the moment I knew I loved you. Remember the night you showed me the writing room, after you said grace at dinner?"

"Yes, how could I forget? You knew you loved me when I prayed?" Maybe it really had been Pray Eat Talk Love.

"Not exactly. Your prayer only pushed me to the edge. When you told me that I could call you Angie, I knew."

"You loved me because I let you call me Angie?"

"No, no." Benjamin shook his head and smiled. "I knew because I never wanted to call you Angie again. At that moment I knew I cared more about you than being with you."

"*È tutto così incredibile*," Angelina said, followed by a lengthy sigh. "I also remember the moment I knew I loved you, Benjamin."

"When was that?"

"The morning of your lease signing, when I woke up and realized I needed to apologize and wish you all the best."

"You mean, after 'You can call me Signora Fabrizzi'?"

Instead of saying yes, Angelina reached over and kissed him. Again, a proper kiss.

"I love you, Benjamin."

"I love you, Signora Fabrizzi."

"Do not say that." She pouted. "Say the other name."

"What other name?"

"You know—say it."

"Lina, I love you." She adored his name for her.

Angelina stood up. "Remember this?" She twirled her dress as best she could.

"Yes, but you are wearing underpants." She did not answer him. "Aren't you?"

"How do you know? You cannot see them. Or can you?" And she spun again, trying to tease him.

Angelina turned back toward town and the Ferris wheel. Giggling, she climbed up onto the rock wall and pointed at it. "Take me on the wheel!" she commanded—then she laughed.

I am in command for the first time in my life.

"Be careful on the rocks, Lina."

"I want to spin!" She began twirling, exuberant. Before Benjamin could move to stop or even warn her, Angelina's foot slipped and jammed itself between two rocks. Her spinning motion continued, and with her foot pinned, she lost her balance, her momentum carrying her towards the harbor.

She had time to yell, "Benjamin!" before she met the water.

Intermezzo

The Firefighter

"Faint heart never won fair maiden."
— Miguel de Cervantes Saavedra —

Ben had been home from college a week, having completed his junior year. It was his first Friday night home, but he'd passed on a night out with his buddies. He was still trying to catch up on his sleep, plus he was assigned to referee three soccer games on Saturday. His fire pager went off just after two a.m. He'd checked in at the fire station Monday night so he could start answering calls until he returned to school in the fall.

"Engine 23, Marine 23, Rescue 34, Marine 27, Ambulance 50 first and second rigs, River Road, at the bend, cross street Anderson Lane, an MVA, reported vehicle in the water, water rescue assignment."

He cleared his head and started dressing as the message repeated. Ben had responded to many motor vehicle accidents at the bend over the years, typically one vehicle into the trees or a head-on collision caused by a lane drifter. There were only one or two places someone could access the river there unless they were going fast—really fast.

He didn't bother putting on an outer shirt or socks but donned his sweatpants and pulled on a pair of Wellington ankle boots that he used for a quick response. He started his car, a beat-up white '91 Ford Taurus, put his flashing blue light on the roof, and headed for the station. The accident was along his route to the fire station—he hoped the road wasn't blocked.

As he approached, he was surprised to find only two civilian cars and a lone municipal police car—he'd expected more police by then. The officer must have seen Ben's blue light, and he began jumping and waving at Ben. He recognized Duke—the officer was also a volunteer at his fire station.

"Ben, let's go. They're still out in the water." He watched as Duke locked his sidearm in the patrol car's trunk.

Ben descended the bank, steep in several places, running, slipping, and sliding behind him. When he cleared the bushes, he was shocked to see the back end of either an SUV or a minivan sticking out of the water, fifty feet from shore. The river wasn't wide at this location, more like a large creek. But swollen by the spring rains, the normally lazy surface tossed and swirled as the current raced. They approached the water's edge and waded out, Ben following Duke. Ben watched as the vehicle settled an inch or two—he was sure it had moved with the current.

"How many victims?" Ben shouted.

Duke yelled that he didn't know and started swimming. Ben joined him a moment later. He kept his shoes on to avoid the jagged stones and trash that littered both the riverbank and riverbed.

It took several minutes to reach the vehicle as they struggled with the current. He watched Duke dive under, then surface.

"Ben, I can't see shit."

Ben took out a pocket flashlight, thankful it worked. When he projected it through the back window, it illuminated a seatback, water, debris, and a woman wedged atop a seatback with her head in the air pocket.

"Oh, shit!" they both said. They tried to open the locked tailgate.

"Fuck!" Ben looked back to shore. Four or five civilians stood on the bank gawking, but none offered to help. The engine from his station arrived, and Ben noticed movement in the bushes.

He told Duke, "I'll be right back," and he swam toward shore. Halfway there, he reached the point where he was able to stand. He yelled to Bobby, the first firefighter off the engine, to give him the end of the one-hundred-foot rope coil he held.

"And gimme your Kelly." His baby Kelly tool was a foot-long version of the larger multipurpose tool. Then Ben yelled, "Secure the rope and get more. We have at least one victim."

He swam back, holding the rope and tool. Ben struggled on the return trip. With his hands full, he did not have complete use of his arms. In addition to his exertion, the icy water sapped more of his strength by the moment.

When he returned, Duke pointed to the rising water and said they needed to hurry. Ben gave him the Kelly tool and tied the rope to the bumper. He heard Duke hammer at the rear window. It cracked but did not break.

Duke said, "Shit!"

Bobby swam out to them, having removed his protective fire gear. Tiring from hovering in the icy water, Ben was envious of Bobby's swift water life vest. Bobby took another rope that extended back to the shore and tied it off to the other side of the rear bumper. Duke told them to hang on as he climbed up onto the bumper.

"When I kick this in, you guys are gonna have to get her the fuck outta there fast. Ready?"

He kicked once, then jumped with both feet. The window caved in as he lost his balance and fell back into the water. They heard the air escape as the vehicle sank, and the water gurgled in concert, but the ropes kept the last half foot or so above the surface. Bobby and Ben pushed the glass in and reached for the woman. Duke rejoined them and they pulled the woman by her arm and her hair until they freed her. Ben took her arm, and when her head was out of the water, Duke grabbed her other shoulder as Bobby let go of her head.

After getting her outside the vehicle, Bobby supported her head and said he thought she was breathing. Duke and Ben, each with one arm and using the ropes, swam and pulled their way back to shore, with Bobby holding traction on the victim's neck. As they approached the shore, multiple first responders waded in to aid them, removing the victim first.

At the submerged vehicle, Ben felt as if he'd been working at double speed. He knew it was his adrenaline. When he felt arms grabbing him, everything became slow motion, and realized the adrenaline was wearing off. Floodlights on tripods raised by other firefighters now illuminated the riverbank, and Ben found it difficult to identify people as he gazed into the lights. The shadows of emergency workers created an unusual, almost surreal effect. Ben heard one of the marine units coming upstream from the boat ramp, its outboard motor rising above the excited chatter on the shore. The fading adrenaline and sensory overload made him think of Martin Sheen rising from the water in *Apocalypse Now*.

He thought, *I hope I don't see Marlon Brando on the shore.*

Even though he was only in waist-deep water, Ben was unable to stand. Every muscle in his body ached, and his arms were on strike in protest. He was half dragged, half carried out by other firefighters. He watched as they dragged Duke to shore. Ben wondered if he'd looked as helpless. Bobby came out of the water on his own.

Ben said he was freezing, and someone called for a blanket. He was later told that while the air temperature was about forty degrees, the water temperature was closer to freezing. An ambulance transported Duke, Bobby, and him to the hospital for treatment of hypothermia.

As he climbed into the rig, Ben said, "Shit, I lost a boot."

Ben later found out that besides the woman they rescued, there'd been three other occupants in the vehicle. The woman lived but had suffered several serious injuries; the other passengers had not. Ben and his two fellow rescuers visited the woman in the hospital a week later, and she and her family showered them with gratitude, but it made Ben uncomfortable. For the past week, he hadn't gotten much sleep, haunted by the belief that he should've saved her three companions.

His ghosts—anxiety, remorse, and regret—left the following week when the autopsy reports were released. The medical examiner determined that her three companions had died from a combination of trauma and drowning, and that the deaths had occurred before Ben and Duke reached the water. If she had not been pinned in the air pocket at the rear of the vehicle, the woman would've drowned before they arrived. The ME further stated that if not for the three rescuers, she would have drowned when the vehicle ultimately submerged.

Both the town and the fire department honored Duke, Bobby, and Ben for the rescue. The following year, his fire station received the state award for outstanding rescue of 2001, but by that time, first responders had their minds on things far more serious than one-car motor vehicle crashes.

TWENTY-THREE

Benjamin

Wait, how did I get into my nightgown?

As they leaned against the rock wall, Ben reflected upon the last fifteen minutes. It had been a whirlwind of events and emotions, and he was Dorothy waking up in Munchkinland. Angelina had asked him to dance at the club. The song had been unfamiliar to him, but he remembered a quatrain, "Cause you and your pretty eyes, you keep me alive, keep me alive." He couldn't get it out of his head.

Later, he'd planned to tell Angelina he loved her, regardless of the consequences. They'd danced again outside. And kissed. She'd told him she loved him, no matter what. He'd told her he loved her, no matter what. And kissed, again. It had been amazing. It was still amazing—almost as amazing as finding out they had both been careening along in slow motion the past few months in love with each other but afraid to acknowledge it.

I'm living a friggin' O. Henry story.

He watched Angelina twirl. He knew she was beautiful, but tonight—tonight, she was a Disney princess in his fairy tale.

Maybe it's the wine, but I don't think so. I love seeing her so happy. There's that word again.

The two other couples nearby smiled at them as they danced too. He wondered if they'd have been dancing out here if not for the royal command of Princess Angelina.

When she climbed up on the rocks, he tried to talk her down, literally and figuratively. She was high, intoxicated by the alcohol and the emotion, as was he.

If she's not careful, she could fall, hurt herself—maybe tear her dress.

He agreed to take her to the Ferris wheel and started toward her to take her hand. But for some damn reason, Angelina began twirling. On the rocks. In the dark. Then, before he could do or say anything else, a slip, a cry, a fall, a splash—and his entire world disappeared from right in front of him.

Ben shouted for help. Without seeing if anyone reacted, he scrambled over the wall. The jetty base was constructed at a forty-five-degree angle to the water. He slid and slipped down the wet rock slope toward Angelina. With the moonlight hidden by the club, she was just visible by the distant lights of the marina as she floated in the water, a rag doll bobbing against the jetty. He jumped in alongside her, thankful to see her mouth and nose out of the water, but worried to find her eyes closed and her temple stained with blood.

Treading water, and sometimes finding a subsurface rock to brace against, he carefully lifted her head from the water. Fearing a neck injury, he held her neck between his hands to stabilize it. Two men and a woman climbed over the wall to help. As they reached for her, Ben was unable to recall the Italian for "cervical."

"Be careful with her neck." Then he remembered and added, "*Lesione cervicale.*"

When he turned back to her, a spray of water and the sound of Angelina coughing greeted him as she opened her eyes.

"Benjamin?"

"I'm here, Lina. Are you okay?"

"Non lo so. Quello che è successo?"

"You fell into the water and hit your head. What hurts?"

"Oh."

"Angelina, what hurts?"

"My head. My foot."

"How about your neck, your back?"

"No, I do not think so. Can we get out now? I am all wet," she asked, as if being wet was the problem. He heard sirens in the distance.

Ben and the three Samaritans lifted Angelina out of the water, up the side of the jetty, and onto the top of the same wall from where she'd started. Someone had brought a first aid kit from the club, and Ben cleaned her head wound.

Good. It's a scrape, not a gash. Ben sighed in relief.

Angelina kept complaining about her foot. It was red—it might be swelling. Ben decided to keep it elevated. A police cruiser with two Rimini *polizia municipale* officers pulled up on the pier near the nightclub, followed by a Red Cross ambulance. While the medical technicians assessed Angelina, the officers asked what had happened. Ben did his best to explain. One officer, having heard his accent, started scolding him, and then everyone, that no one should be on the jetty after dark for just this reason.

One of the Samaritan men interceded and told the officers that the American and the woman had just declared they were in love and were celebrating.

"He was on the rocks asking her to marry him when she, so happy, slipped and fell." He looked at Ben and winked. The appeal to *amore* mollified the officer.

A Carabinieri unit pulled up by the restaurant next to the Rimini police vehicle, and a *guardia costiera* launch pulled up alongside the jetty. Ben thought it must be a slow night in town. After a few moments conversing with the Rimini officers, the coast guard launch headed back to its harbor station.

One of the ambulance technicians said Angelina appeared okay, but suggested she go to the hospital to have her foot x-rayed. She'd been answering their questions throughout the evaluation.

Angelina gazed at Ben and said, "*Nessun ospedale. Portami a casa.*" She turned away and pointed in the general direction of her house as if he might not otherwise know its location.

"You're the boss," he said, and wondered how often he'd now be saying that.

Ben thanked the ambulance crew. A *poliziotto* said he'd give them a ride to the parking lot but was not permitted to give rides home. The second officer asked if Ben needed help getting Angelina to the car. Ben decided he did not and carried her.

"I'll call a taxi when we reach the parking lot," he reassured Angelina.

Ben lifted Angelina in a bridal carry and carried her toward the gate, now unlocked. He was relieved they would not have to re-climb the wall to exit. He liked the way she held on to him. Ben watched as the two Rimini *poliziotti* held an animated conversation with the *carabiniere* sitting in his *gazzella* alongside their Alfa Romeo. As Ben approached the Alfa Romeo, one officer opened the back door of the passenger side.

Angelina had closed her eyes while Ben carried her. He thought she was asleep. Then she opened them and said, "You are my heroic prince. Wait until Valentina hears about this."

"I'm not sure I want to tell the good Signora Marchese. I don't need the shit beat out of me today."

The *carabiniere*, having heard first "Valentina," followed by "Signora Marchese," asked, "Valentina Marchese?"

"*Sì, lei è la mia madrina.*"

"She taught a training class when I first enlisted. She is a legend. I remember she said she had a goddaughter. My name is Lorenzo. I will be happy to take you home."

Ben did not know if the *carabiniere* was violating protocol, but he appreciated having one less problem to solve. During the brief ride, Lorenzo spoke glowingly of Valentina. He said he was happy to help a member of her family. When they arrived at the house, Ben thanked him for the ride. Angelina was asleep.

"It was my honor. Please tell Valentina that Lorenzo, the officer who asked all the obvious questions in her investigation class, says hello."

Ben hoped Valentina had not taught many Lorenzos. He imagined that to Valentina everyone in her classes asked questions with obvious answers.

Ben carried Angelina to the front door, unlocking and opening it after some difficulty, just as Angelina awoke, protesting that she could walk. He told her they needed to be careful with her foot and insisted that he carry her. She accepted his butterfuge without further protest, but he immediately felt guilty over his disingenuousness.

Stop acting like her heroic prince, he scolded himself. She doesn't need a prince; she needs a partner.

Ben placed Angelina on the sofa in the great room, trying to avoid Mondo's performance. He was leaping, barking, circling, and whining as if auditioning for a part in *A Chorus Line*. Ben couldn't tell if the dog was showing concern for his mistress or needed to go out—it was both.

"I'll be right back—don't go anywhere." He found no amusement in his attempted joke. When he returned inside with Mondo, Angelina had fallen back into a deeper sleep, and he was unable to rouse her.

Ben considered his options. He could bring her to his room to sleep in her wet clothes.

I don't look forward to explaining that to Valentina.

He could leave her in the wet clothes to sleep on the sofa—no, not that.

He could bring her upstairs to her room and get her into dry clothes—yes, upstairs in dry clothes was best.

"Mondo, stay."

As he navigated the staircase carrying Angelina, he was thankful for the astute and well-behaved Mondo. He had a vision of the dog trying to bound past him while on the staircase, but Mondo sat at the bottom of the stairs as directed. When Ben reached the top, he called the dog.

He gently placed Angelina on one side of her bed and pulled the sheet and blanket back from the other side. Ben found the largest towel in Angelina's bathroom and did his best to dry both her and her dress. He was glad she hadn't lost her shoe. A police officer had held the shoe the med techs removed as they examined and then re-bandaged her foot. Ben had been holding Angelina's purse when she fell, and he'd dropped it. The female Samaritan had picked it up and given it to the officer.

Thank goodness for small kindnesses—and big ones.

After he dried Angelina, Ben probed her closet and dresser until he found a long, substantial flannel nightgown. Ben felt uncomfortable going through Angelina's personal items but decided this was an emergency. With nightgown in hand, he turned to Mondo, who was laying on the floor, and asked, "Now what do I do?"

Ben carefully removed Angelina's dress. Sound asleep, she didn't even murmur.

Wow, she isn't wearing a bra. I wasn't expecting that.

His surprise and embarrassment gave way to admiration, which angered him.

Dammit, I need to focus.

He draped the towel strategically to avoid further distractions.

He placed the nightgown over her head and worked it down her torso. He removed the towel and worked the garment under her butt and along her thighs. Angelina stirred several times, and once opened her eyes briefly and smiled at him before closing them again, but otherwise did not awaken.

Should I remove her panties?

With trepidation, he reached under the gown and removed them.

Ben felt better once Angelina was in dry clothes. He took a breath and glanced again at Mondo. "Piece of cake, huh, boy?" At that, the jukebox started up in his head and began playing the DNCE song "Cake by the Ocean." When he thought of the metaphor, Ben became embarrassed again, then angry.

Now I can remember lyrics?

He did his best to flush the song as he carried Angelina over to the side of the bed with the sheet pulled back. Mondo followed. Ben placed her on her side opposite her injured temple and pulled the sheet and blanket up to her shoulders.

Ben scanned the room. There was what appeared to be, and then proved to be, a comfortable nondescript chair off to the side with an ottoman.

I better sleep here in case she wakes up and needs something.

He set his phone alarm to chime every ninety minutes so he could check on her. Then he sat back and closed his eyes.

Shit! I should've changed out of these wet clothes.

The regret was not enough to prompt him to action before he fell asleep.

***

Ben's alarm chimed four times over the next six hours. Each time, he checked on the sleeping Angelina. Before the fifth alarm, Angelina called to him asleep in the chair.

"Benjamin?" she asked in a whisper, still half asleep. He thought he dreamed it.

After she called to him again, louder, he opened his eyes and glanced at her. She tried to sit up and then said that her head hurt. He asked her where, and she pressed her hand to the top, away from the scrape. He hoped it was a hangover.

I should get her a glass of water. Then, holding his pounding head, he thought, *And one for me.*

"What happened? Did I fall? I think… no, I remember. I fell."

"Yes, into the harbor." Angelina's eyes widened. Ben gave her the condensed version of their final fifteen minutes on the jetty, the ride home, and finally, getting her into bed.

"Did you sleep in that chair all night?"

"Yes. I was afraid you might need something. And I wanted to check on you during the night."

"You did? Oh, my. Thank you. I love you—wait, did I dream that?"

"No, it wasn't a dream. You love me. I love you. We both now know, along with a couple dozen people on the jetty and half of the police force. You were celebrating when you fell."

"I—I remember. I felt like I was floating. I wanted to go to the Ferris wheel."

"So badly that you decided to walk across the water to it." Ben worried if he should've joked. Her soft laugh and softer eyes reassured him.

"You saved me, did you not? I remember! You were my hero, my own personal knight."

"Well, you called me your *eroico principe*. Although I prefer paladin—or better yet, partner," he said.

"And you called me Lina?"

"Yes, I did."

"And we both said we loved each other." Her smile doubled in its intensity when he nodded. "I cannot wait until we tell Valentina."

"I'm not sure that is such a good idea."

"Wait, how did I get into my nightgown?" Angelina asked.

"As I was saying…"

***

Ben asked Angelina for permission to get them both water before continuing. She agreed with obvious reluctance. When he returned with the water, she met him with impatience, just as obvious.

"I decided the best place for you to sleep was here in your own bed, so I carried you up here. Also, I wanted to get you into dry clothes."

"Okay, thank you, but how did I get into my nightgown?"

"I'm getting to that," Ben said, stalling for time, not the least bit interested in getting to it. He exhaled, surprising himself with how loud it sounded.

Just get it over with, he told himself.

"I took off your dress and put on your nightgown."

Angelina inhaled and tilted her head. "So you saw me naked?"

"Yes. No! I mean, yes—but I didn't look!" Ben realized he should have planned how to describe last night.

Man, I am so not prepared for this conversation. It soon got worse.

"So, you saw me naked?"

"Yes, but just a little."

"Benjamin, one either is or is not naked. One cannot be a 'little' naked." He smiled at her air quotes until he realized she wasn't smiling. Angelina's lecturing in that moment reminded him a bit of Valentina—*I am so glad she isn't Valentina.* Angelina cleared her throat, reminding him she expected more explanation.

"I mean I only saw you naked for a little bit, for a moment."

Knowing it needed to be her decision, he prayed, *Oh, please change the subject.* And she did.

"So, after you saw me naked, did you try to have sex with me?"

"W-what? NO! No, of course not." Ben panicked.

Where is this coming from? Did she have a nightmare? Did I approach her in my sleep?

"Why not?"

"What?" This was getting surreal—check that, it was surreal.

"What was wrong with me?"

"Nothing. You were drunk, injured. It would not have been right."

Angelina inhaled, turned to stare across the room, and exhaled, seeming to accept his explanation.

Thank you, God. Now please make her change the subject. And she did—almost.

She turned back to look at him. "Do you want to have sex with me now?"

"What?"

"Benjamin, why do you keep saying 'What?' I like Lina much better."

"Lina, I'm sorry. What do you mean?"

"It is a simple question. Do you want to have sex with me right now?"

Could this get any worse? he wondered.

Ben tried to think about how to respond. He imagined walking through the warehouse of possible answers, his footsteps echoing off its empty shelves.

He gave up and said, "No."

Really? "No" is the best I could do?

"Why not, Benjamin?" Her question interrupted his internal rebuke.

"It wouldn't be right. I don't want you to have sex with me because of, you know, gratitude"—he inhaled—"or obligation."

She switched to Italian. "Is that what you believe this to be—obligation? Is that how you think of me? That I pay men with sex!" Angelina yelled at him as she pointed her finger, jabbing in his direction on each syllable. "*È così?* Do you know what I believe? I believe you are not attracted to me, that you find me repulsive. I think you saw me naked and now cannot stand the sight of me. What man sees an attractive naked woman who asks him to have sex with her and says no?" She extended her arm, palm vertical, thumb up, and made a chopping motion upward.

Suddenly, Ben was back on the train, sitting in her seat. While unprepared for her fury, he tried his best. "You're wrong, Lina. That isn't it at all. I love you. You are beautiful. Please don't say those things."

Angelina didn't respond. Instead, she tried to sit as she moved to the side of the bed then pointed at her doorway. "Get out of my room!"

Ben cringed as she roared. Mondo did not choose a side, instead lying on the floor with his head across his front paws, his gaze alternating between the two of them. None of them had heard the front door open and close a few moments earlier.

As Ben protested, Angelina shouted, "Just stop!" and tried to stand.

She shouldn't stand on that foot, he thought.

He tried to keep her in bed, just as Valentina powered into the room.

TWENTY-FOUR

Valentina

I think you had better explain.

The morning after the dinner celebration, Valentina could not wait to find out how it went. She took pride in her matchmaking. The dinner was just the thing they needed to get the two clueless lovebirds off their respective roosts. Valentina waited until midmorning in case they'd stayed out late, so she left her apartment just after 0930 for a brisk walk to Angelina's. She observed darker clouds approaching from the east, competing with the sun.

Looks like we are in for some stormy weather, she thought.

She arrived at the house and unlocked the door. She never needed to announce herself—her goddaughter considered her family. Angelina had asked Valentina to move in several times. Each time, Valentina had declined, always with a different plausible, but untrue reason. The actual reason—the only reason—was that she wanted Angelina to become more independent.

I want her to be more independent, yes, but I also do not want her out of my sight.

She recognized the contradiction, one of many in her life she acknowledged and owned.

Mondo just as often as not ignored her arrival, so she was unconcerned when he failed to greet her. As soon as she closed the front door, she heard loud voices coming from the floor above.

Is Angelina yelling?

She hustled up the stairs two at a time with quickness that belied her size—if one did not know of her fitness regimen.

As she reached the top of the stairs, she heard Angelina yell, "Get out of my room!"

Valentina heard Ben's voice but could not make out the words.

"*Basta fermarsi!*" her goddaughter shouted as Valentina entered the bedroom. She saw the American forcing himself on Angelina and trying to get into bed with her.

Without breaking stride, Valentina growled as she grabbed him from behind. Valentina swung him away from the bed and threw him into the far wall. The collision with the wall knocked the breath from Benjamin and a painting from the wall, and he slumped to the floor.

Valentina was cursing at the groaning American as she stepped toward him.

"What did I tell you? I said if you ever fucking hurt her, I would kill you!"

She kicked him. He moaned. She grabbed his shirt and began lifting him to his feet.

"*No, smettila. Basta!*" Angelina screamed to her from the bed to stop. "Fuck, Valentina. I said that's enough!"

Valentina blinked. Angelina had never used profanity like that with her. Still pinning him against the wall, Valentina turned to see Angelina getting out of bed. When Angelina stood and put weight on her foot, she let out a gasp and fell to her knees.

"*Ahia!*" Angelina reached for her foot. "That hurts," she said in English.

"Did he hurt you?"

Valentina was still holding Benjamin, who hadn't moved or said a word since Angelina yelled, *That's enough!*

"No, Godmother, he saved me!" she said, still in English.

"Then why was he attacking you?"

"He was not attacking me, he was helping me, and I was being an idiot. *Un idiota.*"

For that she switches back to italiano? Valentina, resenting the intrusion of her rhetorical question, dismissed it.

Angelina said, "*Per favore, abbassa Benjamin con cura. Madrina, per favore, fallo per me.*"

She repeated her plea in English. "Please, put Benjamin down, carefully. Godmother, please, do this for me."

At her goddaughter's plea, Valentina became aware that she had lifted Benjamin so that his heels were several inches off the floor and his weight was on his toes. She lowered him to the floor but kept one hand braced against his shoulder.

"He saved my life last night."

Valentina released Benjamin, who groaned again and appeared as if he might slide down to the floor. Instead, he made his way over to the chair and fell into it, groaning once more.

"I think you had better explain," she told Angelina.

TWENTY-FIVE

Angelina

Why does everyone keep saying 'What?'

Angelina stared up at her godmother's eyes. Her pupils were dilated, black disks that crowded out the blue.

She looks like a great white shark, thought Angelina.

She watched Benjamin collapse onto the chair on which he'd slept, his puppy eyes wide but focused on Valentina.

And he looks like a wounded seal.

As Valentina helped her back into bed, Angelina's foot sent jolts of electricity up her leg.

I wonder if I broke the fucking thing.

The adrenaline coursing within Angelina sharpened her senses, and she was being flooded with vivid memories of not just the past twelve minutes but the past twelve hours.

Valentina sat on the edge of the bed, between Benjamin and Angelina, her attention on Benjamin. Angelina sat up and slid to the edge so she was sitting next to Valentina, not behind her, and so she could see Benjamin. As she gazed at her wounded seal, Angelina realized how foolish she'd been, putting Benjamin in harm's way for no other reason than for being a gentleman. She remembered his last comments before Valentina entered.

Damn it, I know he believes I am beautiful. Of course he loves me. I was stupid to say what I said. Her thoughts returned to the day they met, and she sighed. *Rudely judgmental does not even begin to cover my behavior just now.*

Angelina had to reassure Valentina multiple times that she was fine—

that Benjamin had not harmed her—before she allowed Angelina to describe what had happened.

Before she began, Angelina glanced at Benjamin and asked, "Are you all right?"

He nodded, glancing at Valentina. Valentina stared back without emotion. Angelina relaxed as her godmother's pupils constricted—the shark no longer present.

Valentina turned to Angelina. "*Allora, cos'è successo?*"

"What happened?" Angelina repeated the question to give herself time to collect her thoughts and determine where to begin. She gave up and sighed. "Where to begin?" she wondered out loud.

"At the beginning, Angelina."

"Well, we walked to a great little restaurant over in San Giuliano. We strolled along the harbor channel on the way over, and Benjamin showed me this wonderful little street. Oh, Val, you would love it. It has all these colorful houses with murals and flowers."

"*Sì*, Via Marecchia," Valentina replied as she tapped the back of her wrist with the other hand. "Everyone knows of it."

"*Non me.*"

"Do you never get out and look around?"

Angelina pouted. "You are ruining it, Val. It was special." Angelina decided not to mention the twirling girl. Valentina obviously had no interest in romance. "We ate a lovely dinner, and we discussed important things."

"Such as?"

"Important things." Valentina stared at her until Angelina elaborated.

"Well, I told Benjamin why I became a vegan. He told me about his grandparents' deaths and how that prompted him to become a vegan."

"Eat a vegan diet," Benjamin interjected.

"*Dai!*" Angelina stared at him as she lifted one open hand. "This is my story to tell."

Valentina raised her hands to the ceiling before saying, "For the love of God, then tell it!" And she returned her gaze to Angelina.

No romance, Angelina thought again before continuing.

"We talked about love." As Valentina's eyes widened, Angelina corrected her presumption. "No, not for each other, about, you know, the nature of love. What it is. What it means."

Valentina nodded, but now her right heel was tapping on the floor, so Angelina hurried along her explanation.

"He asked me what I wanted to do, and I told him I wanted to walk out to Rockisland. And do you know what he called me, Val?"

"I do not have any idea." Angelina took no notice that Valentina was wincing each time Angelina said "Val."

"Come on, guess!"

"*Scusa, niente.*"

"At least try, please!"

"Angelina!" Valentina's impatience exploded into the room.

"He called me Lina!"

"*Che cosa?*"

Angelina's impatience now matched Valentina's. "Why does everyone keep saying 'What?'"

TWENTY-SIX

Benjamin

And then she fell into the water.

Benjamin listened as Angelina described the evening to Valentina. He used the time to gather his wits and assess his body for any serious injuries. He could feel his shoulder stiffening, and his side hurt where he'd struck the wall.

Or did the wall strike me?

He'd blocked her kick with his forearm, and he could see the bruise forming, a four-inch red splotch above his wrist.

That's gonna be a good one—I should ice it.

He decided the ice would have to wait. The best thing for him to do right now was to lie low, out of the line of fire.

He heard Angelina's shrill response when Valentina had asked, "What?" Ben thought he should clarify before she got angry again. He remembered all too vividly the Angie incident.

"I'd been thinking of her as Lina but had never said it out loud. I slipped, and it popped out. As soon as I said it, I apologized."

And why has Angelina started calling her Val?

"But I told you I liked it." Angelina turned to Valentina and said, "I liked it."

Benjamin nodded and smiled. "We talked about the complicated relationship between the ever-widening beach and the ever-lengthening pier. Valentina, did you know that each causes the other?"

"*Ovviamente, Signor LaRocca.*" Valentina sighed. "Just like many things in life."

Yup, she's a romantic.

He thought about her frequent use of "*ovviamente.*" He knew it meant "obviously," or "but of course." Everything was obvious to Valentina.

When she dies, her epitaph should read, "Qui dorme Valentina Marchese, ovviamente."

Seeing Valentina rock her head and tap her foot in frustration, he said, "We walked out to the Sailors' Wives monument, and I told Lina—uh, Angelina—that the statue pointed more or less in the direction where they had built Rose Island."

Benjamin described how they'd returned to the club and hung out for a while.

I better not mention love—at least, not yet. Valentina might be a romantic, but she was first a protective godmother—very protective.

Instead, he said, "And then Angelina commanded me to dance with her."

Angelina raised her left hand, almost in salute. "It was not a command!"

"It felt like a command."

She moved the hand away with a backhanded wave. "It was a request."

"A very firm request," he said.

Angelina folded her arms and turned away. "You did not complain at the time."

"*Bambini!*" Valentina had never referred to them as children.

This can't be good. I better keep going, Ben thought, before saying, "We walked out to the lighthouse at the end of the jetty."

"You cannot go there after dark," Valentina pointed out.

"Valentina, have you no romance?" Angelina had unfolded and extended her arms toward Valentina, using them to reinforce the question.

Ben recognized Angelina's comments were not helping, so he reentered the fray.

"We knew. It was just that the night was so special, and the jetty was so…"

"*Romantico.*" Valentina completed his statement.

"*Sì, romantico.*" That confirmed it for Ben. *Valentina is a romantic.*

Angelina's arms were still extended. She snapped her hands at the wrists, stared at the ceiling, and said, "*Appunto, romantico.*"

"Then what happened?"

Valentina might be a romantic, but she was a tenacious bulldog of a romantic.

Ben said, "We danced again. She climbed up on the jetty rocks and began spinning around. She was happy, silly, even."

Both he and Valentina turned to Angelina, who was smiling, wide-eyed, and bobbing her head.

"Angelina, are you an idiot? What were you thinking?"

"I was thinking I wanted to go on the Ferris wheel."

"And then she fell into the water," Ben said, looking at his feet.

Angelina raised her arms toward the ceiling and repeated, giggling, "*Appunto, e poi sono caduto in acqua!*"

Ben had never seen anyone so giddy about almost killing herself.

TWENTY-SEVEN

Angelina

And then you started kicking his ass.

Angelina controlled her giggling. "I was so stupid. I drank too much wine, and I remembered the twirling teenager, and my heart was spinning, so I felt like my entire body should be twirling."

"Wait, what teenager?" Valentina asked.

Angelina forgot that she'd censored that part and explained. "So, you see, Benjamin told me that he loved me, and I had to spin—I needed to spin—on top of the rocks, until I tripped and fell."

"He said what?" Valentina interrupted before Angelina could reveal how Benjamin had saved her.

"He said he loved me. Obviously, I could not believe him at first. I thought he only told me that he loved me after I told him that I loved him, and I thought he was just, you know, placating me. But he was not. He meant it. He described all about being in love not being the same as loving, and about riding the train and being bedazzled by me—he was bedazzled by me, Val! And I believed him!"

The words came spilling out of Angelina faster and faster, as if she were spinning again.

"Angelina, my love, you hit your head last night. Are you sure you are well?"

"Val, please, do not mock me."

"I am not mocking you. I have just never heard you speak like this before, and I am having trouble following you."

"I have never been in love before."

Angelina turned to Benjamin for backup.

"It's true. She told me that she loves me. I told her that I love her. And she started twirling on the rocks like the girl with no panties," he said.

As Valentina arched an eyebrow, Angelina wondered if his comments were helping.

"Exactly, and then I fell into the water! I must have hit my head, because I remember nothing until I was back on the pier. They told me Benjamin jumped into the water and saved my life. Val, not only does he love me, he is my hero! My prince! My protector!"

Angelina did not catch the brief flicker of a memory that appeared on the face of her godmother. She added in English, "My paladin," and she smiled at her paladin. "Val, do you know this word 'paladin'?"

"But of course, Angelina, a knight in the court of Charlemagne."

Angelina rolled her eyes and looked away.

Benjamin clarified that all he did was jump in and help her back out of the water. "I had help. Others came running to help us." He paused and glanced at Angelina. "She said she could not wait until you heard about it."

"Ovviamente," Valentina said.

Angelina nodded. "He examined my foot. He checked my eyes. My God, he was like a doctor. Did you know he was a firefighter in America?"

"Ovviamente."

"Then he carried me to the police car."

"The police responded?"

"*Ovviamente, Valentina.*" Angelina rolled her eyes but immediately regretted mocking Valentina.

Good, she thought, *Val had not noticed.*

"The police were so nice. Even though we were not supposed to be on the jetty. They offered us a ride back to the parking lot, and when Benjamin said he would call a taxi, they gave us a ride home—anything for the family of Valentina Marchese. They called you a legend. Did you know you were a legend?"

Angelina felt her adrenaline wearing off and her body shutting down. She leaned forward with her hands on her knees, as if the world had landed on her back.

Damn, I am tired. I am cooked like a lobster.

Benjamin clarified. "Well, really, it was the Carabinieri, not the police."

Valentina gave an exasperated sigh. "*I Carabinieri?*"

"Yes. An officer named Lorenzo told us to say hello for him. He said he attended a class you taught and asked all the obvious questions."

"*Ovviamente.*" Valentina brought her hand to her temple.

"We brought Angelina home, and I carried her up to her room. She was semiconscious, and we were both soaking wet."

Angelina smiled as Benjamin described carrying her upstairs rather than leaving her to sleep on the sofa. She watched as he kept glancing at Valentina, assuring her he'd only wanted to make sure Angelina was okay.

He is brave and sweet, Angelina thought.

"Because she hit her head, I did not want to leave her alone, so I slept in this chair in case she needed anything."

Benjamin described it as if giving a book report; to Angelina it felt like he was reading her a love sonnet.

He continued, saying that when Angelina awoke, she wasn't clear about what had happened. When he hesitated, Angelina knew why and interceded.

"He told me everything. I felt so silly. I wondered if I had imagined the part where we said we loved each other, but he assured me I had not, and that he loved me." Angelina considered how to describe the next part. "I noticed I was in my nightgown, so I asked him how I ended up in it. Oh, Val, he was so sweet."

Angelina observed Valentina arch an eyebrow again.

"He told me he needed to get me out of my wet clothes, so he undressed me and put me in the nightgown. He was so gallant."

Valentina had not lowered her eyebrow.

Benjamin jumped in again. "She asked me if I saw her nude, and I told her yes, but only for a moment. But that wasn't true—it was more than a moment. It was more than a few moments."

He turned to Angelina and offered his defense, reverting to English. "Dammit, Lina, you are absolutely drop-dead gorgeous, and I stared for a minute. But I only stared, I swear." He took a deep breath, then said, "*Mi dispiace.*"

Angelina's pulse quickened, and her breathing stopped. The giddiness when she described falling into the water had turned into vertigo. No one had ever called her "drop-dead gorgeous," not even Valentina. She tried to imagine what it meant, and it gave her *pelle di pollo*, what Americans called "goose bumps." She watched as Valentina folded her arms, her eyebrow still raised. Angelina paused for a moment to gather herself. She decided she would say bread with bread and wine with wine.

"Val, I asked him if he tried to have sex with me, and he swore on his grandmother's grave that he did not." She saw no shame in inventing the part about his grandmother's grave.

Valentina needs to understand that it was romantic, not tawdry.

"I asked him what was wrong with me and he said there was nothing wrong with me. He said I was drunk, and it would not be right."

Valentina unfolded her arms. Maybe the eyebrow dropped a bit.

"But what was happening when I came in?"

"I asked Benjamin if he wanted to have sex with me now, since I was no longer drunk, but he declined."

"Wait, you tried to seduce him?" Valentina asked, then covered her mouth with a hand.

Ignoring the question, Angelina described how she'd lost her temper when he did. "*Stavo perdendo le staffe*," she said, waving her clenched fists in front of her.

"Val, I had the devil for each hair, I was so angry. I was feeling stupid to begin with, and then I made it worse with my stupid mouth. I told him he thought I was ugly, and that was why he turned me down. But he told me I was the most beautiful woman he had ever known, and that he wanted to make love to me, he just wanted all the excitement to calm down. He did not want to take advantage of the circumstances."

She sighed and took another deep breath. "As you entered, I told him to stop climbing the mirrors, that I was tired of his excuses. I tried to get up to yell at him. He was trying to keep me in bed for my own good when you came in. He was right—you saw what happened when I tried to get out of bed."

Angelina watched Benjamin nodding in sympathy, before adding, "And then you started kicking his ass."

Benjamin echoed her conclusion as he nodded more forcefully. "Exactly. Then you started kicking my ass."

TWENTY-EIGHT

Benjamin

I think we could all use a good cup of coffee.

When he heard Angelina's description of the evening, it sounded so much better than what he remembered. She made him sound gallant—not the tongue-tied, drooling fool that was etched into his memory. She conflated a few details about the police on the pier, but that was understandable. Ben winced as she mentioned his beating.

He interrupted Angelina. "And then you came to my rescue!" he said to her, smiling then wincing again.

"As you came to mine." Angelina smiled as she replied.

As he winced a third time, he wondered if he was more injured than he'd thought. He reflexively glanced at Valentina and was surprised to see her crying.

I don't think I've ever seen her cry. Why is she crying?

Still crying, Valentina moved to Ben. He groaned as he sat up in the chair, his anxiety building as she approached.

He gave himself a pep talk. *I am not going to wimp out. I love Angelina. Valentina cannot change that.* He told himself that he was not afraid of her, knowing full well he was.

"Val?" Angelina called after her, her voice cracking.

When Valentina reached his chair, he tensed and shifted his position—not knowing what to expect. She dropped to one knee next to him, her head still a few inches higher than his. That he had not expected.

"Benjamin, I am so sorry that I, as our Angelina has said, kicked your ass. I am profoundly sorry. You know how much I love my goddaughter, but that is no excuse for my behavior. When I came into this room, I assumed the worst of you. I assumed the worst, even though you have done nothing to justify such suspicions or conclusions."

Valentina extended her arms, and Ben inhaled. With surprising gentleness, she brought them around him and embraced him.

Wow! He winced and exhaled. That he had so not expected.

Ben gripped the arms of his chair and closed his eyes as he tried to absorb everything.

Valentina called me Benjamin. She never called him Benjamin.

She said "our Angelina." It had always been "my Angelina."

She hugged me… And she spoke perfect fucking English, without an accent!

He opened his eyes and said, "Wait, you speak English?"

Valentina released her embrace and said, "But of course. Why would you think I did not?"

"You made me speak Italian all the time!" Ben moved a hand to his chest. "I assumed you did not, or at least not well." The hand moved to his forehead before he lowered it.

Valentina replied, "We have seen what happens when we assume."

"Then why?" Ben asked.

"Because your Italian was terrible. Angelina speaks English well enough. She did not need you to help her. You, on the other hand, needed much help. My plan worked, obviously."

Ben absorbed the news, then realized the implication.

It's not a plan—it's a conspiracy.

Ben turned to Angelina and accused, "You knew?"

Angelina wagged her head, smiled, and then nodded. "Of course, Benjamin, she is my godmother. She helped to teach me English. She asked me to keep the water in my mouth—you know, to keep the secret, to force you to learn—and I agreed. *Era un buon piano.*"

A damn manipulative plan, he thought.

Benjamin realized his thoughts were laced with far more profanity than usual.

"My dear Benjamin," Valentina said. "I promise I will never again think the worst of you. I promise to speak English or Italian or French with you, whatever you prefer. My Spanish is poor, but I so love Cervantes. We could practice together."

Did Valentina just make a joke?

His emotions were being pulled in every direction.

"I also make this promise to you. From now on, I will protect you as I protect my goddaughter. You saved her life last night. You love her, and she loves you. Thank you for being there for her. For being her protector."

Valentina wiped tears from both cheeks as she managed a modest smile.

Ben saw that Angelina was wiping tears from her cheeks as well—but she was beaming.

Valentina said, "But my priority now is to prepare breakfast. I think we could all use a good cup of coffee."

Benjamin was still adjusting to Valentina's perfect English, but he could not have agreed more.

TWENTY-NINE

Valentina

You should stop paying me, yes?

Ten minutes later, Valentina brought a kitchen towel, a pot of coffee, and two cups up to Angelina's room. "Benjamin, if you are not in too much pain, please slide that table over to the bed. And bring another chair from the next room. Thank you."

Valentina poured two cups, handing one to Angelina and the other to Benjamin, then placed the towel on Angelina's dresser and set the coffeepot on it.

"I will be back with breakfast." She left the room and returned to the kitchen.

As she put the breakfast tray together, Valentina congratulated herself again. She was happy for Angelina, and proud of Benjamin. She did not regret having attacked Benjamin, she was only sorry to have injured him. For her, it was the only course of action given the available information.

The fog of war, she remembered from her training.

That prompted a memory from Quixote: "Love and war are the same thing, and stratagems and policy are as allowable in the one as in the other." As she smiled at the thought, another interrupted.

Angelina and Benjamin are like many of the couples in Cervantes's novellas—the beautiful, perfect Angelina; the noble, brave Benjamin. Valentina sighed and shook her head. *I am such a romantic.*

She returned with a tray of plates, utensils, breakfast pastries, fruit, and her coffee cup, and set it on the table Benjamin had moved.

She proclaimed, "*Come il cacio sui maccheroni.*"

Benjamin, taking it literally, said, "Valentina, sorry, but I do not eat cheese."

"Benjamin, you speak Italian, but you do not yet understand Italian. 'The cheese on the macaroni' is a saying, much like your American 'Just what the doctor ordered.' The French might say, '*Exactement ce que le médecin a prescrit.*'"

Benjamin nodded, smiling with understanding, and said, "*Grazie, dottor Marchese.*"

Valentina smiled for a moment and thought, *Doctor? A conversation for another time.*

As the three of them ate breakfast, Angelina and Benjamin shared more details of their eventful evening. The conversation warmed Valentina. She liked this feeling of *la famiglia*. She was not unprepared for Benjamin's question.

"Signora Marchese?"

"Valentina, per favore, Benjamin."

"Valentina, I would like to see Angelina. I mean, I would like to date her. I mean, I would like to see and date her regularly, with your permission."

Benjamin's nervousness engaged Valentina's sense of humor, as it often did, but she appreciated his respectfulness, and was honored by his return to Italian for the question. Valentina enjoyed humor, but she valued respect, honor, and integrity, and so she valued Benjamin.

She replied, "But of course. Why do you think I left the two of you on your own last night? You are good for each other. I have known this since before the writing studio."

This time it was Benjamin who raised a hand and tilted his head, and Angelina whose mouth hung open.

Valentina turned to Angelina. "Would I have ever left you alone with Benjamin had I not known he loved you, and you him?"

As they both stared, Valentina said, with a bow to her muse, "Angelina, close your mouth before you catch a fly."

Angelina composed herself and said, "We are lucky that the apartment fell through and Benjamin ended up renting here. We might never have found each other."

"*Ovviamente*," Valentina said. "Why else would I tell my manager to take it off the market?"

Angelina and Benjamin were no longer surprised. They instead looked like two people who had learned they weren't real—just characters in a Fellini movie.

Valentina decided that today was the right time to have the conversation she'd been planning. She told them the apartment was in a building she owned.

"*Che cavolo!*" Angelina, wide-eyed, cursed in Italian then questioned in English, "You mean you own your apartment?"

"But of course. I own three apartment buildings," Valentina replied.

"Three? But why, then, do you clean houses?"

"Angelina, I clean a house—yours. I never said I clean other homes."

"But you were always leaving for your other customers." Angelina's exasperation was expanding.

"I said I needed to visit my other customers—I did not say what kind of customers. You assumed I cleaned houses. Angelina, how many times have I warned you not to be trapped by logic errors?"

She watched her goddaughter shrug.

"I cleaned yours so your husband would allow me to stay close to you. You assumed I cleaned other houses, *post hoc, ergo propter hoc*. I decided your assumption was useful."

"But I paid you, and you are," Angelina paused, then blurted, "*fottutamente ricca?*"

"Language, please, Angelina. Not rich, but well-off. I invested well when I was in the military. I did not need your money, so I took every euro you ever paid me and invested in your name. When the time was right, I planned on turning it all over to you. Now the time is right."

Angelina was at a loss for words—for a moment—until, reaching maximum exasperation capacity, she all but yelled, "But you knew I was struggling with the asshole's debts!"

"But of course. Please calm down, Angelina. I also knew you needed to learn how to solve those problems, not have a solution magically handed to you without acquiring wisdom for the next time."

Angelina scoffed. "*Davvero?*" Angelina grabbed the sides of her head with her hands. "Really?" she repeated in English.

"Besides, you weren't paying me enough if I were your actual housekeeper. Your husband always bragged about what a shrewd deal he negotiated with his fool of a housekeeper."

Valentina heard Benjamin chuckle quietly. It was clear he understood that Giovanni had been the fool in their arrangement. Until that moment, Benjamin had remained on the sidelines. Valentina appreciated his silence on the issue and interpreted it as respectful agreement. But he was interested, not cowering.

Good. He has a backbone.

"Wait, did you say you invested for me? That I have money? How much?"

Valentina did not consider Angelina's questions rapacious. To Valentina, they were logical.

"The last time I checked, your portfolio was worth about twenty thousand euros." Her goddaughter closed her eyes and shook her head. "As you can see, it was not enough to clear your husband's debts, but it may have distracted you from doing what was needed. And if I may be so romantic, had you not done what was needed, you and Benjamin might never have met."

Angelina nodded and said, "*Capisco. Grazie, Madrina.*"

Benjamin interjected in English, "I need to get out of these damp clothes and take a shower. Plus, I want to check if any of my ribs are sticking out of my sides." He said it with a smile, which only lasted until he winced while getting out of the chair.

"Benjamin, I apologize again. You will be all right. Had I wanted you dead, you would already be dead."

Valentina was not sure why she'd pulled her kick—it wasn't a conscious decision.

Maybe it was a decision of conscience?

Valentina saw him smiling—until he glanced at her and realized she wasn't. She regretted his experience, but she never apologized for anything—well, almost never.

He should be grateful that I apologized.

She watched Benjamin as he eased down the stairs toward his room.

Then Valentina turned her attention to her goddaughter. She could see Angelina was having difficulty processing the events of the past twelve hours. Her goddaughter looked like a deer *after* the headlights struck it.

The deer spoke. "*Madrina*, I love Benjamin. I have for a while."

"I know, *Figlioccia*."

Now that she'd released Benjamin from only speaking Italian, Valentina was looking forward to conversing with Angelina around the house in a mix of English, Italian, and other languages. Valentina believed the ability to shift seamlessly between different language paradigms kept the brain nimble. Angelina said it was because Valentina enjoyed torturing her.

"I am so relieved we did not have sex."

"As am I," Valentina agreed, then switched to Italian. "I am glad he is a gentleman, but why are you relieved?"

"What if he does not like me? I do not know anything. Not really. He loves me, I know that. But what if I am a disappointment?"

"Angelina, you could never be a disappointment to anyone who loves you, and Benjamin does. Do not worry about lust, you have love. If first you find lust, love may never come. If first you find love, though," Valentina paused, remembering another time, "lust will take care of itself."

Angelina seemed oblivious to the melancholy that had descended on Valentina.

"Oh, Valentina, what do you know about love? About romance?"

Setting aside her memories, Valentina considered several responses but ruled out all but one. *Angelina has had too much excitement today. I will tell her of romance another day.* Her mood lightened, and she said, "*Devo filare*," circling an index figure at her side.

"Go where?"

"To clean the other houses, of course." Valentina laughed out loud at her jest. Angelina threw her hands up in the air and turned away, unhappy with being mocked.

"Angelina, get some rest. I will come back later and make dinner for the two of you." She paused at the bedroom door, turned back, and said, "But now that you know, you should stop paying me, yes?" Then she descended the stairs, smiling.

THIRTY

Angelina

I mean, why are you not married?

Benjamin returned to Angelina's room after his shower, barefoot, wearing sweatpants and a T-shirt. He moved without difficulty, albeit carefully.

At least he is not limping, and he is no longer groaning, she thought. The groaning had worried her.

"How are you feeling?"

"Better," he said. His smile disappeared when he coughed and grimaced.

"Liar," she said.

"I did not lie, your honor. I am better than when I was Valentina's cat toy."

"*Che cos'è un* 'cat toy'?"

Angelina laughed after Benjamin described it. "Yes, you were her cat toy. I am so sorry."

"But how do *you* feel, my love?"

My love. She rolled it around in her mind. *I like it.* "Better also, my hero."

Benjamin lifted her leg, removed the bandage, examined her foot, and rewrapped it.

"We probably shoulda iced it, but we were too tired last night. There's no swelling. How 'bout we leave the bandage on, and you stay off it and keep it elevated? If it is still tender tomorrow, we'll get it x-rayed."

"*Sì, dottore.*"

He turned from her foot to her face. Benjamin examined where she scraped her head. He scanned her pupils. She told him she admired his bedside manner. He told her he admired her eyes.

"Benjamin, *coccoliamoci.* Cuddling will help me recover." She patted on the bed beside her. He reclined on the blanket alongside her. "No, not on top. Underneath the sheet, next to me. *Per favore.*"

She hoped her "*per favore*" sounded to Benjamin like an entreaty, neither begging nor commanding.

When Benjamin slid beneath the sheet, she also hoped he hadn't noticed her exhalation—it had sounded like the roar of a jet plane to her. She wondered how he'd not heard her heart beating in her chest. It had become a bass drum kicking twice per second, as if it were keeping time to a dance song from the club last night.

They lay on the bed facing each other, close enough to touch if they dared. Angelina observed Benjamin's discomfort as he moved.

She asked him, "Are you comfortable?"

"Very."

She was ready to dismiss his answer as untrue when she saw the return of the puppy eyes. When he stopped moving, he appeared as relaxed as she could remember. She stared into his eyes, relieved when he maintained his gaze on hers.

"What did you mean by 'drop-dead gorgeous'?" she asked.

"When I saw you without your dress, my heart stopped. If I'd not forced it to beat again, I would've died. And I would've been happy."

"Happy to die?"

"No, happy to have known you."

Angelina considered it the most beautifully morbid thing she'd ever heard.

Or was it the most morbidly beautiful? she wondered. It was by far the nicest compliment she'd ever received.

"What part of me is beautiful?"

"All of you, Lina."

"I do not see myself that way."

He said, "That's because you have to believe it to see it."

"*Sei pazzo!*"

"I am not crazy. You are drop-dead beautiful. Would you like me to drop dead right now to prove it?"

Angelina giggled and shook her head.

I wonder what he would do if I said yes. Instead, she said, "I want specifics, not broad statements from a cheap romance novel."

"Cheap? I'll have you know I paid good money for it."

When he said nothing more, she said, "I am waiting."

Benjamin leaned over and lifted the sheet away from her, tossing it to the foot of the bed. Angelina held her breath.

How can he not hear that bass drum pounding in my chest?

She shivered when he began at her hair and described how it radiated wonderful shades of wine, copper, and gold as the sun and shadows teased it.

He stroked her silver streak and said, "An angel must have kissed you here when you were a baby. When I first saw it on the train, I assumed you colored it. It was the most amazing hair I'd ever seen. It *is* the most amazing hair I've ever seen."

Angelina felt the blood flooding her cheeks.

No one has ever said that to me.

Benjamin locked his gaze on hers, before describing her eyes. "When you took off your sunglasses on the train to apologize and I first looked into your eyes, it felt as if I'd fallen into them and I would never escape. The second time I saw them, it happened again, and I didn't want to escape."

No one has ever said that to me either.

Her eyes were tearing up. Angelina felt her blush intensify along with her pulse, understanding his comment viscerally as his puppy eyes enveloped her.

Benjamin shifted his gaze.

Wait, no, come back, she thought. Then she was glad he didn't.

He took complete inventory, describing first her nose—then her smile, her dimples, her ears, her neck. He proceeded along her body, touching some parts lightly, telling her how everything about her was perfect. When he finished describing her feet, he shifted back up to face her. She fought not to tremble, or at least to hide it from him.

He said, "But the most perfect parts of you are on the inside."

"*Che cosa?*" It was a whisper.

Did he hear me? He had.

He touched her forehead, away from the scrape, and said, "Your mind."

Next, he placed three fingers lightly on the nightgown covering her left breast and said, "Your heart." She inhaled again as the bass drum grew louder, faster—now not just in her chest but in her ears, pounding.

Finally, he swept his hand above her from her head to her knees, and said, "And, most of all, your spirit—your soul. You are a beautiful soul, my Lina."

Angelina fought the light-headedness that threatened to overwhelm her.

Am I dreaming? Am I under a spell?

Inside a dream, under a spell, it mattered not—she had no experience to guide her. From a small, rational corner of her mind, she formed a response.

"You make me sound like a fantasy. No one is so perfect." She exhaled again, the spell broken, the reverie dissipating, the pounding subsiding.

Benjamin studied her wordlessly for a few moments. With tenderness, he reached down to caress her uninjured foot. As he rolled the smallest toe between his fingers, she marveled at how gentle he was.

He whispered in a somber voice, "If you must know, I've tried to ignore it, but this toenail is not even. Now that you've forced me to confront it, my entire opinion of you has changed. Alas, I will need to begin anew my quest for the perfect woman."

The puppy eyes confirmed he was joking.

Two can play this game, she thought.

"Then please, signore, make love to me before you leave so I have something to remember."

Benjamin smiled at her joke. As he gazed at her face, Angelina hoped the subtle widening of his eyes was his realization that it was not only a joke.

"I am waiting."

She also hoped he considered her request a command.

***

"That was wonderful, incredible." Benjamin's warm breath caused a misplaced lock of hair to tickle her nose.

Still breathless, "*Sì*" was all she could manage in reply as she reached up to deal with the recalcitrant hair.

"You are wonderful, Lina," he said.

He had given her something to remember. Angelina gazed up at her lover.

Il mio amante. *I have a lover. I have never had a lover.* She sighed.

She remembered Matteo and corrected herself.

Well, not a great lover, nor even a good lover. Nor one who said I was wonderful.

Her encounters with Matteo, although pleasant, were frenzied, and usually followed by frenetic dressing for fear of discovery.

We might as well have taken our time—we were discovered anyway.

She let out a lengthy sigh, poignant when it began but ending in a smile, as she returned to the moment.

After hearing it, Benjamin, braced on his elbows, must have thought he was crushing her and began pushing away.

Don't leave, she wished.

"Please stay," she implored, as she peered up at him as he supported his weight above her with his arms alongside her breasts.

"I'll never leave you."

She had no doubt, but that was not what she meant.

"No, I mean here, with me," she said.

"I'm not going anywhere."

She believed that too, but it still was not what she meant.

"No, I mean here, with me, within me." That was what she meant.

"I wish I could stay here forever," Ben replied. "But I'm afraid my body will eventually refuse to cooperate." The puppy eyes smiled, and so did he.

After a moment she realized what he meant, and she giggled.

"Then for as long as you can."

She remembered his comments a few minutes earlier.

This last half hour has been wonderful—no, incredible—for me too.

Thanks to what he self-effacingly called his "indefatigable commitment to foreplay," she'd experienced her first orgasm with a partner. When he'd climaxed a few moments ago, she'd followed with her second.

He interrupted her thoughts by kissing her on the forehead, and then lightly on her lips. She felt him straining to keep his weight off her. As he did, she felt what he'd meant by "refuse to cooperate" and giggled again when he apologized. She suggested they roll onto their sides. He nodded, appearing relieved. Angelina laughed again, feeling euphoric with his weight off her diaphragm.

"*Benjamin, grazie. È stato molto speciale.* I hope I pleased you."

"Hope you pleased me? Damn, couldn't you tell, Lina? That was amazing. You were amazing. I hope I pleased *you.*"

Hope he pleased me? No one has ever hoped I was pleased—certainly not the asshole.

"Benjamin, you did not please me."

When the puppy eyes closed, she regretted teasing him. Before he could respond, she added, "You did not *just* please me, you overwhelmed me. It was amazing for me too. That was my first orgasm. And my second."

"You've never had an orgasm?" The puppy eyes grew wide.

She giggled, touched by his concern.

"No, *sciocco,* I have—just never with a partner." She giggled again.

Why can I not stop giggling?

Ben's response surprised her. "Well, then, we gotta lotta catchin' up to do, partner."

Unsure what "gotta lotta catchin' up" meant, she decided it sounded like fun.

As she remembered how she'd described her self-fulfillment to Benjamin a moment ago, her sudden guilt surprised her. But it wasn't caused by Benjamin.

I do not feel guilty about Benjamin—with him I am emancipated!

No, it was because the Catholic Church considered *masturbazione* a sin. She did not support the Church's position forbidding pleasure outside the marital act—she surely had found no pleasure within it.

Angelina had recently started attending Mass. It had nothing to do with Benjamin specifically. She had wanted to reconnect with traditions from her youth. Prompted by this inner conversation, she decided, "I need to go to confession."

"What was that?" Benjamin had closed his eyes, half asleep.

Angelina had not realized she'd confessed her decision out loud.

"Nothing, love, go back to sleep." He smiled and complied.

As she drifted toward sleep, she remembered how he'd worked to keep from crushing her and how much she did not mind, yet how relieved she'd felt when he removed his weight from her chest. She thought about confession again, and then, for no conscious reason, she connected it to the American saying.

Yes, I have much to get off my chest, she thought, and she fell asleep smiling.

***

They dozed for most of the afternoon. When Angelina awoke, it was after four.

We need to get moving. I am not ready for Valentina to find us together in the same bed.

Thinking about her nap resurfaced an unpleasant memory. Her husband would tell her he wanted a *pisolino* whenever he desired lovemaking during the day. The euphemistic nap was a command, not a request.

Wait, it was sex, not lovemaking, she corrected herself.

After Benjamin, she would never again think about her relations with the asshole as anything but sex. She hoped it was the last time she ever thought of him—period. She realized it was the first time she'd ever enjoyed such a nap. An unpleasant word had turned remarkably pleasant.

Angelina gently shook Benjamin and told him they needed to get cleaned up before Valentina returned. She took a quick shower. When she came out, Benjamin was still in bed. She told him to shower in her bathroom, just in case.

While Ben was in the shower and Angelina finished dressing, she heard noises downstairs.

That must be Valentina arriving. "Just in case" has become "just in time," she thought. *We are fortunate we awoke when we did.*

As she struggled with her shoes, Angelina tittered at her nervousness. Her anxiety was well-founded, she believed, as she imagined how Valentina would react to *il loro mettersi insieme.* She then laughed out loud.

The English translation of the Italian euphemism "their coming together"—meaning a relationship—was an even more accurate description of their activities this afternoon.

"Boy, did we ever," she said to Mondo as she headed for the stairs. She wanted to run interference for Benjamin by distracting Valentina in the kitchen.

When Angelina reached the kitchen, Valentina was sitting at the table, reading a book, with another nearby, alongside a plate of fruit. Something was cooking in the oven.

"*Come va, Valentina?*"

"I am not complaining."

Angelina took in the scene. "When did you arrive?"

"Right after lunch." Valentina's nose remained in her book.

"You have been here all afternoon?"

"*Ovviamente,*" she replied, head down, still reading.

Angelina forced a smile as her godmother placed her book on the table and turned to her.

"*Quindi, ti è piaciuto il tuo pisolino, sì?*"

Angelina knew Valentina was not asking if she'd enjoyed an afternoon of sleep. She'd mentioned her husband's *pisolini* to her godmother on multiple occasions, either in complaint or to describe where she'd been.

Damn, she knows! Angelina cursed herself. *Now that Valentina knew, how would she react?*

"Valentina, I hope it does not upset you."

"You mean, your fornication?"

"*Sì, la nostra fornicazione.*"

Angelina sighed with regret, not for her activities, but for Valentina's choice of words. The word did not do her afternoon justice, but she decided not to tickle the dragon.

"Angelina, there is nothing wrong with passion."

Why had Valentina switched to English?

"But I am not married." As she stated the obvious, Angelina wondered what had happened to Valentina's sense of propriety.

"Angelina, you have already had marriage without passion. What is wrong with having a little passion without marriage?"

Angelina appreciated her godmother's philosophy.

But marriage would be nice.

***

That night at dinner, Angelina did not recognize her godmother. It was as if someone else had joined them. The dinner was the most amiable meal the three of them had shared. Thankfully, Valentina avoided any mention of their *pisolino*. Even stranger, she avoided any of the little jabs she often aimed at Benjamin. But the most surprising thing was what she said after she'd cleared the dinner table, having told Angelina and Benjamin to sit and relax.

"Well, I am off for home. I am glad you are feeling better, Angelina, but please stay off your feet. You two should get some sleep. You have had much excitement these past twenty-four hours. Oh, and Benjamin?"

"Sì, Valentina?"

"I trust you to watch over Angelina when I am not here." And with that, Valentina left the house to return to her apartment.

Angelina stared at Benjamin, who was trying to absorb the entire dinner experience.

"Did she just say she trusts me?" he asked.

"Yes. She trusts you." When Benjamin's dropped jaw remained that way, she asked, "Do you know why?" When he closed his mouth and shook his head, she answered her question. "She trusts you because I trust you, and she trusts me."

Angelina did not share with Benjamin that it was the first time Valentina had ever made her feel like she trusted Angelina's judgment.

Today is the first time she has ever treated me as a fellow adult, not her godchild. Rather than upsetting her, the thought comforted her. And provided a sense of satisfaction.

"Do you need help with the stairs?"

"I can manage, my love, but thank you."

"I think Valentina was right. We should go to bed," he said.

"I am flattered, but are you not tired?" She tried to act coy, but he either didn't see it or it didn't work.

"I meant to sleep. Sorry to disappoint you, but I am exhausted. Good exhausted—don't get me wrong—but exhausted."

"I was teasing. I also need to sleep—with you."

Angelina stretched her arms above her head and smiled. *This is wonderful,* she thought, before she wondered, *Wait, where is he going?*

"I need to get a few things from my room—my old room. I will be right there. Do you need anything?"

"*No caro. Grazie.*"

She was glad when he accepted her definition of their new sleeping arrangements without chivalry, feigned or otherwise. When he entered her room—their room—he was wearing his pajamas. He carried his toiletries and a robe and placed them in her bathroom.

Our bathroom, she reminded herself. *This will take some getting used to.*

"I sleep on this side of the bed. Is the other side okay for you?" she asked.

"Perfect—but I would sleep on the floor to be near you."

He smiled, but she could tell he was nervous as he climbed in, facing her.

She smiled, deciding to make him more comfortable if she could. "I am a little nervous, you know. This is my first time," she told him.

"What?" She liked the puppy eyes, even when they were confused.

"Dear, tonight will be the first time in my life—my entire life—that I will sleep with the man I love." She almost said "my entire fucking life," but realized it was implied.

"I must make certain I am gentle, so you remember this sleep tonight for the rest of your life."

I like that he is comfortable enough to tease me.

She thought back about how she'd teased him.

I know I should not, but he is the only person I have ever wanted to tease in my life. Is that weird?

She was conflicted—worried that it meant she was insecure and looking for validation, but also aware that it was because he made her feel safe, an equal.

What was it he said? Yes, she felt like a partner.

Benjamin gazed at her while she pondered the meaning of teasing, but then broke the silence. "What would you like?"

She'd not expected his response. Frankly, she had no experience with anyone, let alone any man, asking her what she'd prefer.

This, too, will take getting used to, she thought.

She wondered how she'd been so fortunate to find him.

Surely someone would have grabbed him by now.

That last unexpected thought prompted her answer to his question.

"Benjamin, I would like to know how someone as… as"—she fumbled, searching for the right word—"*meravigliosissimo* as you ended up with me. I mean, why are you not married?"

I hope he understands my neologism for "absolutely incredibly most wonderful."

She hoped, as well, that he'd not find her question too impertinent. She watched as he sighed and closed his eyes.

When he did not answer, she said, "I am sorry, I do not mean to pry. I meant it as a compliment, but I did not express it very well."

She watched intently, relieved when the puppy eyes opened and gazed back.

"Don't apologize. I understand. It's a fair question." And he answered her.

***

His answer moved Angelina.

No, not his answer, his life story—at least a part of it, she decided.

His decision to share it with her affected her even more. When he finished, she leaned over, kissed him, and said, "Thank you. I understand." And she smiled.

He replied, "You are most welcome. Is there anything else you need, my love?"

"Are you really too tired?"

She was both surprised and appreciative when they both found out he was not.

INTERMEZZO

The Older Sister

"Where one door shuts, another opens."
— Miguel de Cervantes Saavedra —

Benjamin's sister, Jennifer, was three years older than him, which meant that, growing up, she was more like five years older. They did not interact much outside the home, but Ben loved his sister and she loved him. Every so often she'd help bail him out of a problem with his parents, either covering for him when he screwed up or, more often, being his lawyer and mounting a spirited defense.

When she married her husband, David McAndrews, who was four years older than Ben, he felt honored to be an usher in the bridal party. For Ben's wedding, in return, he'd lobbied his wife to add Jennifer as a bridesmaid.

"But she's already married, Ben! It's my wedding."

He'd said, "Then call her a bride's matron, but I want her included."

Later, Jen told him she'd hated being asked, but thinking it was his wife's desire, she'd done it for Ben's sake.

When he told her it was his idea, she scolded him, saying, "Benjamin, if you want a happy relationship, do not tell the women in your life what to do."

That advice took a while to sink in—a dozen years, give or take.

***

After his separation, Jen, sensing his mental state, reached out to him. He soon confirmed her concern. Benjamin was a wreck who wallowed in anger and self-pity. He ping-ponged from angry Ben, "I never want to see that bitch again," to whiny Ben, "If she would just talk to me, we could make it work," and back again. Jen wanted to slap him more than once.

Instead, she just let him vent, told him everything would work out, and kissed him on the forehead. She did her best to keep her husband from teasing Ben when they were together.

"Men are clueless," she often said, with ample evidence to support the assessment.

When the separation became not a trial, but the current step toward an inevitable divorce, Jen changed her approach. Instead of stopping by to see him, she invited Ben to dinner at her home with David and their two children. He was always great with her kids, and she wanted to remind him the world was full of opportunity. Every so often, she'd invite an unmarried girlfriend to join them. He was polite but disinterested—he was not looking for the complication of even a dinner date at that point in his life.

Besides the children and her transparent blind dates, there were two other reasons she wanted to see him. She wanted Ben to witness her husband interacting with her day-to-day, as opposed to special occasion dinners with the whole family. For all his faults, and David had many, none were fatal. She loved her husband, and he loved her, and they had a stable, respectful, loving relationship. She wanted Ben to see that, rather than wrap himself in the twin blankets of solitude and failure knitted by his separation.

The second reason was so she could speak with him and coach him in an informal setting. She knew her brother was principled and kind, despite his ex-wife's opinion. She knew their father's view of the world, as it pertained to women, was not a model for success in the twenty-first century. And don't get her started on their grandfather. She loved him, but despite his "America first" proclamations, he was still deeply rooted to Sicily.

No, Benjamin needed coaching. That was what older sisters were for. His only other option would be to find a fortysomething divorced woman who wanted to rehabilitate him for her amusement. Jen thought her way best.

There were two themes intertwined in her coaching. The first was that he was a wonderful man, but one who needed to be himself, not play a role he imagined others expected. The other was that a woman in a relationship was a partner, not an accessory. He needed to find someone to wrap his entire life around without suffocating her.

When he announced his move to Amsterdam, to the shock of their parents, she recognized her efforts had succeeded. Unlike their parents' protestations that he was running away, she realized he'd seen a new door waiting, unopened. She was proud of his choice to open it. He confirmed her belief to her the day he left. In return, she reminded him of the two most important pieces of advice from her coaching.

"Remember to be yourself, little brother. Why would you want someone who thinks you are somebody else?"

Then she said, "Remember, if you don't treat the woman in a relationship like she is the most important part of your life, then you don't deserve her."

He promised he'd remember and thanked her for her help and understanding.

"Benjamin, I hope you find that woman who loves you for who you are. Call me anytime you need to talk. Agree? Good. Love you, be safe."

And in the grand LaRocca family tradition of inane humor, her last comment was "Don't forget to write!"

THIRTY-ONE

Benjamin

I would be sleeping in the dog's bed.

Angelina started her new teacher's assistant position the next day, or after "our special day," as she referred to it. Ben thought of it as the "Valentina's Date Massacre," but said so only once out loud. And only in front of Angelina. Not in front of Valentina. He wasn't crazy.

Well, I'm crazy, but I'm not that crazy.

That evening, the three of them celebrated with an informal dinner Valentina had prepared. After dinner, Ben cleaned up the dining table and then said he was going into the writing room to practice his band music. He needed to learn synthesized horn parts to several Springsteen songs.

A tavern had hired Metodo Ritmo to play during Rimini's annual Bruce Springsteen Glory Days Festival, and the gig was in less than two weeks. Benjamin wasn't the only person who thought the south Rimini beaches were like the Jersey Shore. Thousands of people from across Italy and around Europe attended.

It had surprised Ben to learn the Boss was as beloved here as back in the States. He'd casually mentioned to his bandmates that he'd often partied at The Stone Pony, the Jersey bar where Bruce got his start.

They'd begged him to describe it, asking for every detail. When he'd mentioned that he'd gigged there one evening filling in with another band, they'd treated him like rock royalty.

Angelina interrupted his thoughts. "We would like to listen to you play."

"Sorry, Lina, but I need an amplifier for you to hear me."

Angelina asked what an *amplicatore* did. Ben described how it projected the sound into larger rooms and enabled the musicians to hear themselves. At band practice, he'd been using a spare amplifier Rocco lent him.

Valentina spoke up. "Angelina, as you know, I still have your grandmother's piano at my apartment. I do not play it much. I think it belongs here. Then Benjamin could serenade us. Yes, I would like that." Valentina did not wait for a reply, walking away as if everything had been decided, which, of course, was true.

Angelina called after her godmother as she headed to the kitchen, "That would be great, *Madrina!*"

Ben merely nodded.

***

Valentina wasted no time arranging the move. The piano arrived on Thursday. The movers placed the baby grand, a Schimmel Classic, in Angelina's great room. Ben was unfamiliar with Schimmel, but learned it was one of the oldest and largest piano makers in Europe. It was a fine piece of furniture, but the years and several moves had taken a toll on the tuning. That evening, Ben mentioned the need for a piano tuner.

"We should visit that music store where we met Luca to see if they can recommend someone. We can go on Saturday." Angelina's statement was more a plan than a suggestion, and Ben just nodded.

I guess I need to get used to these suggestions.

***

On Saturday, Angelina made another plan in the form of a suggestion—that they have lunch first at the vegan café where they'd eaten the day they met.

Ben agreed. "Excellent idea. We'll be returning to the scene of the crime."

"You think our first meal together was a crime?" Angelina pouted.

Ben kicked himself. He'd been aiming for ironic but instead landed squarely on moronic.

He said, "No, that was a figure of speech. A stupid American figure of speech. It was a joke, a poor joke. I am sorry. Sometimes I speak before I think."

Angelina stared at him. He could not tell if her expression was of pain or anger.

My luck, it's both.

As he came to that conclusion, Angelina's eyes started sparkling, a wide smile blossomed, and she said, "Gotcha," pointing at him with her finger like a gun. "I like American figures of speech. I was just messing with you."

When he did not respond at first, Angelina asked, "'Messing with you' is correct, no?"

"Yes—and remind me never to play poker with you."

That expression, he had to explain.

***

The music store was only a few blocks from the café. The store clerk glanced up from his phone as they approached. Ben described Angelina's piano, and that they needed a piano tuner.

"Do you have anyone you could recommend?"

"*Sì, un momento per favore.*" The clerk went into a room behind the sales counter.

He returned after a minute and said, "We have the best piano tuner in the province. He is on the telephone. If you can wait, he will be with you in a few minutes."

Ben and Angelina both nodded, smiling. Ben replied, "*Sì, naturalmente. Grazie.*"

After a few minutes of wandering, Angelina said, "We should shop for an amplifier while we are here."

The store clerk saved Ben from having to respond. He must have gone into the back room while they were browsing, for he returned followed by a much shorter and much older man. Ben and Angelina exchanged surprised smiles of recognition. It was the little man from the train station.

He greeted them, "*Buon pomeriggio. Mi chiamo Umberto.*"

"*Io ricordo! Ciao, Nonno Umberto,*" Ben replied. "Do you remember us? From the train? Back in June?" Benjamin pantomimed bringing the heavy bags to the platform.

Umberto scratched his head, then his eyes widened, and he bobbed his head several times. He smiled at Ben, then at Angelina, then turned back to Ben and said, winking, "How do you know you are not?"

Ben responded, "Now we know." He winked back. "How is your wife?"

"Sophia is still telling me what to do. You'll get used to it."

After Angelina explained why they'd sought out a piano tuner, Ben described the piano and what they needed. Then he asked about the cost.

Umberto closed one eye, stared at the ceiling for a moment with the other, and said, "I will tune your piano for no charge, as a wedding present."

Angelina said, "But, Umberto, we are not getting married."

He turned to her and asked, "How do you know you are not?" And he winked at Angelina.

When Ben protested that they appreciated the gesture, but it wasn't necessary, Umberto dismissed him.

"If my Sophia found out I charged the two of you, I would be sleeping in the dog's bed."

THIRTY-TWO

Angelina

You must keep your mind on the journey in front of you.

Leaving the music shop, Angelina and Ben meandered along Via Vezia toward the park, passing around the Anfiteatro Romano. Benjamin held Angelina's hand from time to time.

I like the way he holds my hand, she thought. *He is gentle—not like the asshole, pulling me along as if I were a wagon.*

At the end of the street, they entered Parco Alcide Cervi near the Monumento alla Resistenza. In 1973, the city dedicated the monument, designed by the Rimini artist Elio Morri, to honor the substantial sacrifices made by the citizens of Rimini Province as members of the Resistance in World War II. The name of the park honored the father of seven brothers, resistance fighters from the Emilia-Romagna region. Fascists had captured and executed the seven in late 1943. While the family was not from Rimini, the family's sacrifice was recognized and remembered throughout Italy.

Angelina had only visited the monument once, many years earlier. As it was a wonderful day, and they were in no hurry, she decided to ask Benjamin if they could visit, knowing he'd agree.

Before she could ask, Benjamin said, "I've never stopped to see the Morri pieces. Do you mind?"

Angelina smiled and swept her arm in front of her, inviting him to the monument.

They stepped past the bronze entrance plaque on a granite stone embedded in the earth, which read, "*ORA E SEMPRE RESISTENZA.*"

Angelina thought, *"NOW AND ALWAYS RESISTANCE." That could be my motto.*

The sculptures sat within a series of overlapping circles, formed by paving stones. Areas enclosed by the circles were at different heights, suggesting steps. Each figure had been placed on a concrete platform that began as a ramp until it leveled off under the sculpture. A bronze plaque was attached to the end of each concrete base, providing the name of the figure. The three figures represented—and evoked—respectively, the concepts of *Il Martirio*, *La Riscossa*, and *La Liberazione.*

As Angelina considered the work, she remembered her first visit years ago. Then, she saw it as a municipal monument, much like the hand sculpture in Como. Unlike the hands, she'd not given it another thought—until today. Today, she read "The Martyrdom, The Recovery, and The Liberation" in a fresh light.

These are monuments to my life! she thought.

The enlightenment she experienced at the sudden awareness buckled her knees.

"Are you okay?" Ben asked as he grabbed her wrist and elbow.

"Yes. I need to watch where I walk on these stones."

Angelina was still trying to process her epiphany. Until the asshole's death, she'd been living the life of a martyr. Until she met Benjamin, she'd been in recovery. Since Benjamin, she certainly felt liberated.

Maybe I was meant to be a monument.

She became uncomfortable with her less than truthful explanation to Benjamin.

"Truthfully, Benjamin, I did not stumble. I was just overwhelmed by the meaning of this monument. It has become very personal for me. I feel liberated, and I know it is because of you."

The puppy eyes smiled at her and assuaged her guilt.

They left the monument and crossed over Via Roma on the pedestrian suspension bridge that took them to Parco Maria Callas. When she saw the football field off to the left, Angelina wondered if Benjamin was serious about becoming an *arbitro di calcio* here.

One thing at a time. I need to give the man a chance. She smiled at the scolding she gave herself. *I am not used to a man who accepts my opinions, requests, and even my directions. I must be careful not to let this power go to my head.*

Angelina liked that they did not speak much, except for small talk. "Look at that car." "Do you like her dress?" "I wonder if it will rain later." She relished the comfort it gave her; it was a new feeling in her life.

We are a couple, like Umberto and Sophia.

As she thought of the piano tuner, she remembered his wedding present. Angelina had noticed how flustered Benjamin became.

He is not ready. I should not rush it, she convinced herself. *But marriage would be nice.*

As they approached the pedestrian tunnel that led under the railroad tracks to Parco Renzi and home, Benjamin described how he'd researched the artist Morri. Angelina knew about his busts at Piazzale Fellini. Benjamin mentioned he'd created the fountain at the Piazza Cavour, near Castel Sismondo.

"I like the peeing boys! I did not know he was the sculptor."

Seeing Benjamin's silly grin, she blushed.

Perhaps I should have said "puer mingens." The Latin sounds more dignified than "peeing boys."

Benjamin appeared blasé, and she relaxed. Then he said, "He also has sculptures up in Covignano at the Santuario di Santa Maria delle Grazie. I believe they're called 'The Way of the Cross.'" When Angelina did not respond, he repeated the Latin name, "*La Via Crucis.*"

The moment Benjamin mentioned Covignano, it had transported Angelina away from the tunnel, to the hills she loved on the other side of the E55 highway south of town. She was off daydreaming about living there. When he said *Via Crucis*, it had pulled her just as quickly back to the dingy tunnel.

Che giustapposizione. She pursed her lips, trying to restrain the smile her thought triggered. Undaunted, the smile bloomed and then beamed as he smiled back.

She then responded to Benjamin's comment. "I think the *colline di Covignano* area is wonderful. We should visit this sanctuary."

Angelina remembered Luca asking if they were looking for a house. As they exited into Parco Renzi, she shared something else with Benjamin she'd never shared with anyone, not even her godmother.

"Benjamin, I have a dream that one day I will live in a wonderful house on a hill outside of town, with a yard big enough for Mondo and a garden—my castle."

In answer to his quizzical expression, she said, "Do not misunderstand. I know you like being in town, as do I." She sighed. "I enjoy being able to walk everywhere, and I appreciate that Valentina is close by. I have told myself I could convince her to move in with me."

She took a deep breath and slowly exhaled. "I have never mentioned this to anyone."

She hoped Benjamin did not find her dream strange, or worse, incompatible with his. She wondered if the thought of Valentina in the same house unnerved him.

"I like to garden. What type of garden?" Benjamin asked, finishing with a smile.

"Any kind."

When she heard Benjamin's response, Angelina's anxiety floated away. She thought of butterflies floating above her garden.

But I am not chasing the butterflies, she assured herself. *They are chasing me.*

As they left the park for the last two blocks of their trip home, Angelina decided their walk was a metaphor for her life. Life was a journey. There were obstacles. Sometimes you had to go around them. Other times you had to bridge over them. You might have to tunnel under them, but you kept going to reach home.

There might be monuments along the way, but you should not spend too long remembering the past. You might dream about the future, but you must keep your mind on the journey in front of you.

Impressed with her deep philosophical musings, she kidded herself, *Maybe I was meant to be a metaphor.*

INTERMEZZO

The Walk in the Park

"I know who I am and who I may be, if I choose."
— Miguel de Cervantes Saavedra —

Isabella Marvelli was angry with Fredo. They'd been dating for a few weeks when he'd convinced her to have sex with him. Her first and only other time had been with a boy who told her he loved her. It had been painful—not lasting long, thank goodness—but not as painful as how he'd treated her afterward. She might as well have had leprosy. She'd told herself, *Never again.*

That was until Fredo started paying attention to her. He was one of those boys all the girls talked about. When he asked her on a date, she had to force herself not to shriek when she accepted. On the first few dates, they kissed, and she liked it. She did not mind too much when it escalated into groping. Unlike Dino, he was not clumsy. When he pressured her for sex, she asked if he loved her.

He said that any boy who told a girl he loved her after a few dates was just trying to have sex with her. She could believe that. He told her she was pretty, that she was hot, and he just wanted to have sex. If it turned into love, great, but he would not insult her by lying about something as important as love. To Isabella it was poetry, the nicest thing she'd ever heard. Feeling more than thinking, she agreed. They met at their special bench in the park, and he guided to her to a secluded spot off a dirt path.

She told him it was only her second time, and she wondered if her experience would insult him or her inexperience disappoint him. He told her it was unimportant, what mattered was that it was their first time. She relaxed and then relaxed more. He was gentle. He did not struggle with the condom as Dino had. She enjoyed it. She wished it had lasted longer. *Not fireworks*, she thought, *but maybe he is the one.*

After that night, she did not hear from him for almost two weeks. In the halls at school, he headed off in a different direction as soon as he saw her. He was "not home" when she stopped by his house.

His mother said, "Perhaps he does not want to see you anymore, dear."

It hurt far worse than anything Dino had done. She caught up to him after school one day and confronted him with her anger and pain.

He apologized profusely, saying he had a paper to write at school and his mother had been sick. Isabella thought the woman had not appeared sick to her, but she said nothing. He told her he still wanted to see her. He asked if she had any plans that evening. When she said she was free, he told her he had to go out with his parents for dinner.

"But meet me in the park at our special bench at nine."

***

Isabella floated home and then floated to the park after her dinner. She arrived fifteen minutes early—she could not be late for her date. Fredo approached on the walk, accompanied by a boy she knew as Vinnie. She ran up to greet Fredo and give him what she hoped was a passionate kiss.

Fredo introduced her to "*Amico mio, Vincenzo.*"

After Isabella said she knew him from school, Vinnie asked, "Do you mind if I walk with you?"

"Well… no. But why?" Isabella said.

Fredo answered. "I feel terrible for how I have treated you. I do not deserve someone as nice as you. You deserve someone better."

She protested. "That is not true. You are perfect—you are perfect for me."

He shook his head and said, "Vinnie likes you very much and asked me to introduce him to you. Vinnie is just the guy for you."

"But I do not like Vinnie; I like you!" Isabella was confused by this unexpected and unwelcome turn of events, even more so by the turn that had taken them off the pavement and onto the dirt path where Fredo had taken her to have sex.

At the same moment, Fredo said, "*Tutto ok. Adesso!*" The two boys grabbed her arms and pulled her behind a thicket. As she screamed, Fredo clamped her mouth with his other hand.

***

Valentina Marchese was heading through the park on the way home from her after-school job at the library. She may have been the only student in her entire school who worked, but her disabled father could not work, and they needed the money. She heard a scream and then sounds of a struggle behind thick bushes off the sidewalk.

When she reached the location of the sounds, she saw what appeared to be a rape in progress. One boy had just knelt between the legs of a struggling girl. She was being held down by a second boy who'd pinned her arms and covered her mouth. Valentina thought she recognized him from school.

She yelled, "What are you doing?" followed by "*Fermare!*"

The boy she recognized now as Fredo said, "This does not concern you. Leave—unless you want to join the party."

Valentina said, "*Certo.*"

Fredo laughed and said, "Okay!" as he did his best to stop the girl's wriggling resistance. He let go of the girl's right arm for a moment to gesture to Valentina. She saw that he recognized her.

"Here, come help me hold her, so you and I can get better acquainted."

As he did, the girl swung her free arm up and punched him in the bottom of his chin, snapping his teeth together as they bit his tongue.

"*Merda, cagna!*" he yelled, enraged by the pain and the taste of blood in his mouth.

He punched her on her right cheekbone. The punch made a sickening sound, and the girl went limp for a moment. As Fredo pulled back to hit her again, Valentina reached him, grabbed his arm, and lifted him to his feet as she kicked at a kneecap. The boy cried out and grabbed his damaged knee with both hands. Valentina punched him twice and finished with a kick that sent him sprawling into a bush.

As this was happening, the girl regained her awareness and kneed the second boy in the groin. She rolled out from under him and flailed at him with a series of punches and slaps, screaming, "Do not dare to touch me again."

The boy was covering his face with his arms, yelling, "I will not. I promise. I am sorry. Fredo said you would like it." Then again, he said, "*Mi dispiace molto.*"

Valentina lifted the boy up by his shirt collar and prepared to give him the same treatment as Fredo. He whimpered at first, then cried and wet himself. She pushed him to the ground, disgusted.

"Get your friend and get out of here before I change my mind and split both your faces," she said.

He pulled up his pants and helped up the groggy Fredo.

As they rose, Valentina towered over the two boys, and yelled, "If either of you ever bothers her again, I will crush you, do you understand?"

The boys bolted back toward the walk without bothering to answer.

Valentina returned to the girl. Her right cheekbone was swelling, but Valentina recognized her as a fellow student, a year behind her in school. "*Sei Isabella, vero?*" She'd seen the petite girl from time to time in the halls and had overheard some of her conversations with her friends.

Isabella nodded.

"I am Valentina, but you can call me Val."

Val carefully pulled Isabella's shoulders off the ground until she was sitting.

"Thank you so much for rescuing me. Please call me Bella." She reassembled her clothes.

"It looks like you were doing okay saving yourself without me. Let me check your face." The swollen face was her only physical injury. "We need to get ice on that. Where do you live?"

"In the Magellano neighborhood on the other side of town. My father cannot see me like this."

Valentina said she lived with her father. "My home is just two blocks away. We can go there and get you cleaned up."

When Bella tried to stand, she faltered and said, "*Tutto gira,*" as she leaned against Valentina to keep the ground from moving.

"*Nessun problema, piccola principessa.*" Then she scooped up Bella and carried her to her home.

"Thank you, my protector."

***

When Valentina graduated a month later, her new best friend, Isabella, sat with Valentina's father. Her father's neuropathy had worsened, and she was grateful that Isabella could assist him. He'd become disabled from toxin exposure after working at a shoe factory in San Mauro Pascoli for twenty years. The three of them went to dinner afterward to celebrate.

Isabella and Valentina spent the summer together, as best friends did. Almost every day when Valentina finished work, Isabella met her, and they explored the town or relaxed at the beach. Isabella introduced Valentina to cultural events she'd only read about. Valentina introduced Isabella to a world not dominated by Isabella's father.

Isabella envied Valentina's relationship with her father; Valentina envied Isabella's relationship with her mother. Their conversations evolved from simple sketches of their lives to include the details you only shared with your closest friends. One day at the beach, after Valentina made an oblique reference to their mothers, Isabella decided they had reached a point where she could ask Valentina what happened.

"We were living in San Mauro Pascoli. I was nine when my mother died in childbirth. She had lost at least one other pregnancy. No one ever talked about it with me, but I had overheard conversations at family gatherings. Anyway, she died this time and the baby—my brother—did not survive either."

Isabella reached over and gave Valentina a hug. "When I was nine, my younger brother was born but only lived in this world for three days. I was devastated. I cannot even imagine how I would have felt if I had lost my mother as well." She watched as Valentina blinked back tears and turned to look out onto the sea.

"It would have been unbearable if not for my Aunt Silvia. She was my father's sister and I had always enjoyed talking with her. She treated me like a person, not a child, "Valentina said. "Her husband died of a heart attack less than six months later. We moved in with her here in Rimini—the same apartment we live in now."

Isabella asked, "What happened to Silvia?"

"She died after being shot in Torino, a bystander at a terrorist attack." Isabella hugged her again.

"I am so sorry, Val. I knew you were alone—I did not realize how much tragedy you have endured."

"Not long after, my dad became ill—we are sure it was from the chemicals at the shoe factory—and he could no longer work. That is why I must work," she told Isabella. Valentina's features had darkened with the approaching weather system.

"I have never known any woman to be the one who brought home the loaf," Isabella replied, shaking her head. She could not conceive of a woman supporting a family. She added, "Val, you know I will always be here for you. We are friends, no?"

"We are friends, yes." Valentina's smile shown bright through the shadows on her face.

***

Not long after Isabella started her last year of upper secondary school, Signor Marchese developed gangrene in his left leg. While in the hospital ward, he caught pneumonia. He died in the first week of October, with Valentina and Isabella at his bedside. Valentina was stoic at the funeral as she received condolences from her friends, her grandmother, and a few distant relatives. She'd been grateful for the support and sympathy Isabella provided.

Over the preceding five months, Valentina had made sure she was Isabella's friend, and only her friend. She did everything she could to distract herself from the deep romantic feelings that had blossomed in her as the two spent more time together. She wanted to avoid anything that might damage the friendship she valued and needed now more than ever.

It did not surprise Valentina when, two weeks after the funeral, Isabella asked to sleep over. Valentina was grateful for the company. During the summer, Bella had spent many nights at the Marchese residence, sleeping in the third bedroom, and occasionally—on what they called girls' nights—in Valentina's room. It did not surprise her when Isabella knocked on her door that night and climbed into bed with her. But it did surprise her—and please and flatter her—when Isabella told Valentina that she was in love with her.

Valentina thought Sancho Panza was correct: "Fair and softly goes far."

THIRTY-THREE

Benjamin

Play well.

Ben and Angelina were greeted at the door by a joyful Mondo. Ben enjoyed walks with Mondo as much as the dog did. Mondo was always disappointed when they left without him; he was always happy when they returned. Ben took the playful dog out to the side yard as he reflected on the afternoon.

This was a wonderful day, he thought.

The only hiccup was Umberto's comment about marriage. It had reactivated a conversation Ben had been having with himself, and with Mondo sometimes when they were alone. *Give the woman a chance,* he scolded himself.

Otherwise, it had been wonderful. He'd spent another enjoyable hour walking and talking with Lina.

I've known no one I have enjoyed talking with more, except perhaps my sister, he thought, and that was only after he'd reached adulthood.

He and Angelina talked about everything and anything. When they agreed, they were happy. When they disagreed, they still valued the other's opinion. In fact, Ben enjoyed their differences of opinion more. Angelina's views helped him to strengthen his position when he believed it to be correct, or to change it when she helped him see something in a new way. Together, they'd solved many of the world's problems.

Now, if only someone would listen.

From time to time, Valentina shared in their conversations about the problems of the world, although Ben had never known her to change her position. He'd never met a person who was always so sure of herself. He'd also met no one else who was—almost—always right. As intimidating as that was, he appreciated her contributions. He always learned something, the most important being not to make her angry.

Ovviamente, Ben thought.

He said something in front of both women that created an interesting moment. It was a nickname for Angelina that slipped out one day when he was feeling silly. She'd mentioned her middle name was Regina, and he responded, without thinking, "I'm gonna call you Lina Gina."

"Fine, as long as I can call you long-distance." Angelina wasn't smiling.

He was preparing another one of his apologies when she interjected.

"What do you think, Val Pal? Am I a Lina Gina?" Now Angelina was smiling.

Ben was off-balance, and the feeling was getting worse. Not only did Lina not appear upset, she'd just called Valentina…

Nah, I didn't hear that right.

"I have told you I tolerate 'Val Pal' only in private."

Benjamin's mouth fell open.

Valentina said, "Benjamin, please close your mouth."

"But, Val, we are family, no?"

"We are family, yes. So, Benjamin can call you Lina Gina here amongst ourselves. And yes, you can call me Val Pal."

"Val Pal?" Benjamin's mouth had opened again. This time words came out.

"Benjamin, dear. If I ever hear *you* say Val Pal again, I will also have a name for you. You will not like it." Valentina wasn't smiling.

"I think I will do some writing."

"Yes, a tactical withdrawal is in order," said Valentina.

"See you later, Bennie." Angelina stuck out her tongue.

Good, she's not angry, he thought, relieved.

Once out of earshot, he said to Mondo, "Val Pal? Remind me never to play poker with Lina Gina."

He had to explain that saying to Mondo also.

***

By mid-October, Ben decided it was time to *prendere la palla al balzo* and ask Angelina to marry him. He liked to catch the ball on the bounce much better than take the bull by the horns.

With Valentina, I will need to make sure the ball does not bounce me. He chuckled. *I'll ask Angelina in December; maybe she will want a June wedding.*

That he'd ask Angelina was essential. That he'd ask Valentina's permission first was obvious. His plan was to secure—he hoped—Valentina's permission, then take Angelina shopping in Milano for a ring, assuming she said yes. He remembered the saying "Man plans, God laughs."

John Lennon rescued his mood when, to Ben's surprise, he recalled his lyrics: "Life is what happens to you while you're busy making other plans." He realized none of the wonderful things that had occurred in the past four months had been part of his plans to move to Rimini.

Another of his plans had been to find a house. He'd revisited it again after they met Luca at the music store. At first, he'd considered San Giuliano a Mare. He liked the older *borgo* but had a special fondness for the newer neighborhoods on north side near the rerouted Fiume Marecchia. He and Lina liked the restaurants in the neighborhood, and her school was in the district. When he began considering marriage, he put that plan on hold.

Then Angelina trashed the plan on the way back from the music store. *Was that God laughing?* he wondered.

Her dream of a house—no, a castle—in the hills with a yard large enough for a dog and a garden was his dream now. He'd miss heading out the front door on a whim and exploring the town, but he wanted nothing more than to make Angelina's dream a reality for them both. Ben changed his plan and asked Luca to keep an eye out for something in *colline di Covignano.*

***

As Ben planned for his conversations, looking forward to the one with Angelina, the one with Valentina not so much, something kept nagging at him. The week after deciding to propose—soon, when the time was right—he decided he needed to ask about something else first.

Valentina was out of town for a few days, visiting several old police friends. The night before she was to return, Ben felt it would be the right time to broach the subject with Lina.

He thought it best to start on a positive note, so he complimented her on the dinner she'd made. Angelina did not get many opportunities to prepare meals. With Ben and Valentina competing in their *Top Chefs of the Fabrizzi Household* reality show, there were few available meal slots.

"*Grazie caro.* I am glad you liked it."

God, how I love the sound of her voice.

"Could I ask you something about Valentina?" When she nodded, he said, "It's a little awkward. Please don't take offense."

"What is it, Benjamin?"

God, how I love the way she says my name.

Ben began to describe the history as he understood it between Giovanni and Valentina.

"The asshole," Angelina corrected him.

"Sorry." He should've remembered. She'd told him several times never to mention that name.

"But what is your question?" she asked. Angelina blinked once but kept her gaze on him.

God, how I love her eyes.

"It's just that..." Ben paused.

God, what an incredibly stupid idea this is.

His mind raced as he searched for ways to extricate himself. He felt like a driver on the highway who kept missing the exit ramp. He watched as Angelina brushed back several locks of hair that had fallen across her cheek.

God, how I love—

"Just what?" Angelina folded her hands atop the table.

"It's just that they never solved Gio—err, the asshole's death. Yet Valentina confronted him earlier in the day. You saw what she did when she only thought I might hurt you. The asshole *did* hurt you. You and I both know she is capable." As he spoke, Benjamin sped up his delivery, as if to get all the words out at once. He took a deep breath when he finished, so deep he was amazed he hadn't inhaled his plate.

Angelina unfolded her hands and placed them flat on the table. Continuing to stare at Benjamin—he could no longer consider it a gaze—she said in a quiet voice, "I understand. Your concern is reasonable, but Valentina did not kill the asshole."

"How do you know?"

"After it happened, I asked her straight-out if she did it. It would not have upset me. I just wanted to know." Angelina maintained her stare as she spoke in a monotone. "She told me, 'I did not kill him,' and I believed her. I believed her then, and I still do."

"But, Lina, how can you just—"

The loud report when Angelina pounded both fists on the table stopped Ben mid-sentence. The flatware rattled, and two of the glasses were wobbling.

Before the glasses stopped wobbling, Angelina began yelling. "You think you know everything, Benjamin! You know *nothing*!" Mondo stood up, just as unaccustomed to Angelina's harsh, booming voice as Benjamin.

Angelina kicked back her chair and stood up just as Valentina walked through the door and stated the obvious: that she had returned early from her trip. The chair fell over backward, prompting Mondo to scamper out of the way. Ben did not think Valentina had heard the earlier conversation, but with her, one never knew.

"What is this about?" Valentina asked.

Angelina yelled something about "know-it-all men" and stormed upstairs.

Ben opened his mouth to call after her but closed it when he saw Valentina raise an eyebrow.

"Benjamin, this will only get worse if you do what you always do and open your mouth."

"Yes, signora. I think I will head off to *prova d'orchestra*."

"Yes, another tactical withdrawal is in order, Benjamin. Play well."

Benjamin considered Valentina's farewell comment. Was it a pleasantry, musical direction, or relationship advice? *Probably all three, he decided.*

THIRTY-FOUR

Angelina

Wait a moment, please?

Angelina heard the front door close as Benjamin left for band rehearsal. She was relieved that he had not slammed the door. She realized she had never seen him lose his temper, and she now regretted losing hers.

If you had been someone's cat toy, you would have questions, the voice of her conscience told her. The voice had not visited her over the last two months. She had not needed it—Benjamin helped her stay grounded.

Okay, I will apologize to him.

He was out later than usual tonight. She hoped he was not reluctant to come home. She liked that Benjamin called her home his now. Unable to stay awake any longer while she waited, she prepared for bed. Once in bed, she found that the eyes that would not stay open earlier could now not stay closed. When she heard Benjamin return from band practice a few minutes later, she did not know whether she was relieved or worried. She decided it was both.

Angelina heard him climb the stairs and enter their room. She listened as he struggled to get undressed in the dark. Angelina reached over and turned on her lamp, turning to stare at him. He nodded his thanks and finished changing.

Because he said nothing, she assumed he was angry with her. He made little noise as he climbed into the other side of the bed. Angelina turned off the light and made a show of going to sleep with her back to Benjamin, to give him space. She was again both relieved and worried when she realized there was a considerable separation between them. Angelina inhaled and turned to face Benjamin, just as he rolled to face her. She was expecting to see his back; she got the sense he was expecting to see hers.

Both said, "I am sorry," at the same time. After a pause, each waiting for the other, they both began again, simultaneously saying, "I am sorry."

Angelina said, "You first."

"No, ladies first."

Angelina thought, *Chauvinistic chivalry? Really? We are not getting into a lifeboat.*

It annoyed her for a moment, until her conscience told her, *Angelina, if you keep this up, your relationship will be in the lifeboat.*

She took another deep breath, and said, "Dear, I realize you are angry with me. I apologize for the way I behaved, for losing my temper. Even if I disagreed with you, I should never have acted that way. Will you please forgive me?" She watched him shake his head.

No one said this would be easy. I need to give him time.

Benjamin then surprised her. "No apology is necessary, *la mia anima gemella*. I must apologize. You told me you asked Valentina, she told you, and you believed her. It is because you love her, and she loves you." Benjamin inhaled, and said, "How can I claim to love you if I ask you a question, you answer me, and I do not believe you? I was wrong. I apologize. I love you—and I believe you. You should never have to worry if I believe you."

Angelina closed her eyes. *Someone who believes me—and in me. And he called me his soulmate.*

"And while I am at it, can we both agree on something else?"

Angelina was still absorbing his apology. She rubbed her nose. "What?"

"We must never go to bed angry. Whatever our disagreement, we must agree that when we enter this bed, there will be no anger. There can always be anger tomorrow, but tonight will never happen again. Promise me, no matter what, that we'll hold our anger until the morning."

Angelina liked that idea. She remembered how many times she and the asshole had gone to bed following shouting matches. It was never pleasant, even if one did not care for the other person, and she loved Benjamin.

Benjamin appeared impatient, waiting for an answer.

"Okay, I will be angry with you in the morning, but now we will go to bed without anger."

Benjamin smiled and he relaxed, but then, as he realized everything she'd said, a slight frown formed, then grew.

Angelina said, "Since we are not angry, *coccoliamoci, per favore.*" When his frown became his silly smile, she said, "But no sex, just cuddling."

"But of course." She was glad his smile diminished, if only a bit; otherwise, she might have taken offense.

As they gazed across the bed, touching each other with one arm, Angelina wondered if the glow she felt inside was visible to Benjamin.

This is true love, she concluded. *I have the most important person in my life with me. I have never felt this way—ever.*

She caressed his shoulder with her hand, then reached up and caressed his face. When he reciprocated, she pushed Benjamin onto his back, fumbled with their clothes, and began making love to him.

"I thought you said no sex?"

Angelina decided her godmother was right—he did not know when to keep his mouth shut.

"This is not sex. It is love." Benjamin accepted the answer with grace, and with unbridled enthusiasm.

Angelina's energy brought the lovemaking to an earlier end than usual, and she collapsed forward onto his chest. She did not mind the lack of an orgasm—there had been plenty of those. As she lay on top of him, bracing herself with her arms, she had two thoughts.

I could lay with him like this forever, followed by, Merda santa, *this is hard.*

She surrendered and rolled off him, having gained new respect for Benjamin's previous efforts not to crush her.

"Thank you, Lina. That was surprising, and wonderful." Benjamin had not opened his eyes.

"I like your plan not to go to bed angry" was all she said before she joined him in sleep.

***

After an uneventful week at school, Angelina woke up Saturday morning with an upset stomach. It passed soon enough. She wondered if she ate something bad at dinner. When Benjamin came out of the bathroom, she asked, "When do you leave for Geneva?"

The organizers of a travel conference in Geneva had invited him to speak. They'd seen him present a session at the Rimini Fiera Conference Center in August and were so impressed that they invited him to fill in for a speaker who'd had to cancel. Angelina would have gone along if she did not have to work.

"I take the train Monday morning," he said, ticking off his itinerary on his fingers. "I speak on Tuesday. Then I am on a panel Wednesday morning, and I will meet Neil for dinner Wednesday night before returning on Thursday morning."

His agent, Neil, was in Geneva on Wednesday to speak with him about several projects. He was in Paris on other business and had planned to fly to Rimini to meet Benjamin before the speaking engagement surfaced. Angelina regretted not taking personal time. She'd enjoyed speaking with Neil, and she had been looking forward to their next meeting.

But I have only been working two months, too soon to ask off.

The following day, she woke up again with nausea and had to hurry to the toilet, where she vomited. She was glad the unpleasant sounds had not disturbed Benjamin. He was still asleep.

Not food poisoning, she thought. *A stomach bug, maybe? Or an early case of flu. Well, I am the one who wanted to be around children.*

Resigned to her state, she glanced at Mondo, standing concerned in the doorway, and said, "I must be careful around others, especially the children." Mondo smiled, but he always smiled.

Later in the day, before dinner, she got sick again. She was glad neither Benjamin nor Valentina were there to see her kneeling before the toilet as if it were a white porcelain deity. She was happy for Mondo's dependable companionship. He whined in sympathy at her distress.

On Monday morning, Angelina was nauseous again. Benjamin was with her, packing, and asked if she was okay.

"*Mi sento solo la nausea,*" she said, before reassuring him, "I am okay. I think I have a stomach bug. Let us hope it is not the flu."

"So that's why you didn't kiss me last night."

She nodded, regretting it as the room started to spin, and then her stomach.

And I thought motion sickness was terrible. I would take sitting backward on a train any day over this.

Once downstairs, Benjamin made breakfast in Valentina's absence. Valentina was spending less time with them, sharing fewer meals.

She is giving us space. Angelina lacked the energy to smile in appreciation.

"You look terrible, Lina," Benjamin said.

"I know. I am not going to school today," she said. "I do not want to give the virus to the children."

"Good idea."

Without a word, Angelina rose from her chair and walked to the first-floor bathroom. She was sure Benjamin heard her distress through the shut door. Mondo was whining, so she knew the dog heard. Benjamin asked if she was sure she was okay.

"Yes, it is just a virus. But I will make an appointment with my doctor."

"Good. Do you want me to stay home? I am sure they will understand."

Angelina had not considered the possibility that Benjamin would change his plans. "What? No, please do not. There is no need. I am fine. I just want to have the doctor tell me, so I am comfortable returning to school."

Benjamin tilted his head and lifted his chin. "Okay, but I would feel much better if Valentina stayed with you while I am gone. Agreed?" He lowered his chin and punctuated his question with raised eyebrows.

"*Sì, dottore.*" She smiled to reassure him.

Angelina drove Benjamin to the station over his protests that he could get a taxi. She gave him an air hug outside the car at the station and then returned home. On the way home, she called her doctor. After describing her symptoms, and that she worked at a school, the receptionist gave her an appointment for the next morning. Once home, Angelina called Valentina.

"Could you stay with me the next few nights, Godmother?"

While she expected nothing less, she appreciated that Valentina said, "*Ovviamente.*"

***

When Angelina returned from the doctor on Tuesday, her godmother was waiting for her.

"So, what did they say, my goddaughter? *Tu vivrai?*"

"Will I live?" Angelina brought her hands together in front of her, fingers laced.

She understood Valentina was just making one of her gallows humor jokes, but the situation was anything but funny, and it left her conflicted. The question required a response; she required more time.

Angelina released her hands and lifted her palms toward her godmother as if to push her away. Instead, she turned them toward the floor and slowly lowered them, willing an imaginary audience to stay calm.

Angelina relaxed her breathing, and said, "He must run some tests. They took blood."

"Tests," not "test," for had she said "test," there would've been more questions, without a doubt.

She could not bring herself to say which test—there was too much uncertainty. She found it too unbelievable. She was unsure she could even convince the words to leave her mouth. Most of all, she did not want to jinx anything.

For someone who mocks the superstitions of others, is this not hypocritical?

Sometimes she wished the voice in her head would shut the fuck up.

You are cursing in your thoughts. You must calm down, the voice counselled her. She sighed.

How the fuck could I be pregnant? was her insubordinate response to the goddamn voice.

***

The rest of Tuesday was nerve-wracking for Angelina. Crushed under the significant weight of an unconfirmed pregnancy, she felt trapped between the need to confide in someone and the inability to do so. Valentina was the obvious choice, but it was too soon. The inability to share her feelings and her condition with her *madrina* added even more to Angelina's burden.

She wished Benjamin were here. Not because she loved him and he was the father, but because he was her best friend in the entire world. Val was an excellent friend, a dear friend, a dependable friend, but she'd always have a role that kept her from being Angelina's best friend.

My best friend would call me Lina.

She wanted Benjamin with her even if he had no other role but as her friend.

That is so weird, she chided herself.

Midafternoon on Wednesday, a nurse from the doctor's office called and spoke with Angelina. The nurse confirmed the preliminary diagnosis. Angelina was pregnant, somewhere between six and eight weeks, but that was only an estimate.

"So, what did they say?" Valentina asked when Angelina hung up the phone. Angelina did not respond, so Valentina prompted her again.

"Godmother, please come sit with me."

Angelina watched as her godmother's demeanor transformed into something unlike anything she could ever remember seeing before. The smile left her face; the twinkle left her eyes. Valentina became something Angelina could best describe as all-business.

Her godmother, rather than come sit, said, "*Un momento,*" and headed into the kitchen. She returned with two glasses of water, handing one to Angelina.

Angelina thanked her and smiled, and then realized how thirsty she was. She drank half the glass, wiped her mouth, and then smiled again.

Valentina smiled back and sat next to her. She said, "Talk to me, my dear goddaughter."

Angelina began weeping. The weeping turned to sobbing and then to hyperventilation.

Valentina wrapped Angelina in her arms. She cooed at her, and said, "There, there. I am here for you. I am here for you."

She alternated between patting Angelina on the back and hugging her so hard it was difficult to breathe. Angelina relaxed and regained control of her breathing. When her sobbing had subsided to sniffling, Valentina pulled back, her hands upon Angelina's shoulders, and said, "Angelina Regina Roselli Fabrizzi, what is it?"

That was the first time Angelina had heard her full name since just after the asshole died.

"*Lo stronzo! Il fottuto stronzo!*"

Angelina saw the stunned expression on her godmother's face and realized she'd said it aloud.

"What are you saying?"

"The fucking asshole made me think I was barren! He told me he had many children running around Rimini and that it was me who could not have any! That fucking asshole. I cannot believe I spent the last twelve years of my life convinced I could not have children!"

Angelina took no mind that her godmother's all-business expression had disappeared, replaced by one that was reacting to the ravings of a madwoman.

"Angelina, please, you are worrying me. What are you saying?"

"Io sono incinta!"

"You are what?"

"I am pregnant!" Angelina had raised her voice—but without anger.

In a heartbeat, she'd gone from being angry to being ecstatic. She described how the doctor had made the preliminary diagnosis yesterday based on an in-office test, but after Angelina insisted then persisted that it must be wrong, he had ordered a blood test.

"They confirmed it. I am pregnant!"

Angelina stared at Valentina, who was beaming. Valentina's expression had shifted from friend to all-business to dealing with a crazy woman, and was now in full godmother mode.

How does she do that?

"Godmother, you are not upset with me?"

"Angelina, I am so happy for you and Benjamin."

At Valentina's mention of his name, Angelina's entire world came to a screeching halt. It did not crash, but it lay frozen in front of her, giving her time to inspect it, to evaluate it, and then to panic.

"*Madonna mia!*" Her raised voice was now a shout. "Oh my God. Benjamin! What am I going to do? Godmother, help me, please!"

A part of Angelina, the tiny part not yet panicking, recognized that her godmother's expression was moving back to the look of someone who was dealing with a crazy woman.

"Angelina, what are you talking about? Benjamin will be as happy as you, or at least as you were a moment ago. What is the matter?"

"Oh, Val, I told him I could not have children. Then I practically attacked him to get him to make love to me. He will think I tricked him to get pregnant."

"Of course not. You are being silly," Valentina said.

"Oh, he will. I know it."

Angelina watched as Valentina studied her for a few moments, as if working out a math problem.

Then Valentina said, "So, you have a poor opinion of Benjamin now. I am glad you have come to your senses about him."

"Yes… What? Wait. No! No, Benjamin is the most wonderful man in the world, in—in the universe! Why would you say such a thing?" Angelina waved the back of her palm at her godmother.

"I did not, you did. I merely agreed with you," Valentina said.

"I said no such thing. You just heard me say how wonderful he is."

"So why would this wonderful man believe the woman he loves must have tricked him?"

"Huh?" Angelina hated these verbal jujitsu bouts with Valentina. They made her head hurt. She said, "Well, if not tricked, then lied to, or at least misled."

"I ask you again," Valentina said, "why would he think such things about the woman he loves?" Hearing no answer, she continued, "Would you believe he'd tried to trick you if your positions were reversed?" Valentina thrust her chin at Angelina.

Angelina shook her head as she closed her eyes and sighed.

"Imagine him wanting children his entire life, convinced he could not have any, then meeting you, the woman of his dreams, with whom he finally gets pregnant." Valentina took a breath. "Imagine him in the bathroom in front of the toilet puking his guts out, only to find that you, the most wonderful woman in the world, have decided that he must have tricked you."

Angelina chuckled to herself at the word image Valentina painted. *Benjamin pregnant with morning sickness?* Angelina smiled at the thought.

Angelina said, "I would never think such a thing. I love him."

Valentina continued to look at Angelina, but her gaze softened as she said, "Neither would he."

"You do not know that."

"I know everything, and I absolutely know that." Valentina smiled.

Angelina noted that the godmother side of her had returned.

Valentina switched to English. "*Figlioccia*, go wash your face. You are acting like it is a tragedy when it is a fucking miracle!"

"*Madrina*, your language!" But it gave Angelina her first real smile of the day.

In Italian, Valentina said, "Come, mother, we have plans to make." She moved to the kitchen table.

When Angelina realized that Valentina had just called her "*madre*," she became light-headed.

I never thought I would ever hear anyone call me "mother."

***

Angelina slept well, which surprised her. Morning sickness still plagued her after she woke, but it relieved her to know what it was, and thrilled her to know why it was. After breakfast, they walked to Valentina's apartment.

Valentina needed to check on Gatto Giorgio, her cat, and she said the fresh air would do Angelina good. They ate lunch at Valentina's, and Angelina helped her with chores. It felt strange to be cleaning the home of her putative housekeeper.

Benjamin was taking a morning train out of Geneva direct to Milano, and then the noon fast train, arriving in Rimini before three. He planned to call once he cleared Bologna and was an hour out. She and Valentina agreed that Valentina would speak to Benjamin when he called, not Angelina.

"Should we go home to wait for Benjamin?" Angelina asked.

Valentina said, "No, it is better if we wait for Benjamin here."

***

Benjamin called at a quarter to two. Before Angelina answered her phone out of habit, Valentina gestured to Angelina to give her the phone. Angelina was both relieved and miffed. Relief won out, and she handed the phone to Valentina, who answered before it went to voicemail.

"Hello, Benjamin, how was your trip?" Valentina spoke in English. She strode to the other side of the room and said, "She is fine. She is just not near her phone right now."

When Valentina glanced back at Angelina, Angelina made sure her godmother saw her scowl. Valentina responded to Angelina with a *What?* shrug of her shoulders.

"Listen, we are at my apartment. You remember the address, yes?" A pause. "Correct. Could you meet us here? Great. Will you have trouble getting a ride from the station?"

Angelina tapped the back of one hand with the other. She bit her upper lip to keep from interfering. Angelina hated hearing only one side of the conversation, and she resented Valentina for keeping her from speaking to Benjamin. She also appreciated it.

I am not ready. I may never be ready.

"Yes, she is fine. We are just taking care of a few things, and it will be easier if you meet us here. Angelina wanted to see you as soon as she could." Valentina smirked at Angelina, as if to say, *See, I told him you wanted to see him.*

"Yes, I will tell her. She loves you too. We all do. See you in an hour."

"We all do"? Angelina wondered what Valentina meant. She should have said, *I love you too.* That was more natural.

Maybe she is not comfortable saying it to him, Angelina thought, but then she remembered that Valentina had said it several times.

Wait—I am a "we" now!

She was glad that Valentina did not see her happy tears. She was unwilling to explain—it would have ruined the moment.

***

As three o'clock approached, Angelina waited with her godmother at the kitchen table, her mind racing. The joy of being pregnant was overwhelming, as was the fear—no, anguish—that she might lose the first man she'd ever loved. No amount of reassurance from Valentina helped.

What a trick God was playing on me to have this happen on La Festa dei Morti, she thought, but with respect. She was no longer angry at God or the saints or the souls—any or all of them.

Angelina's fear had returned, and it grew stronger the later it became. "Godmother, Benjamin will be angry and will think I have tricked him to get pregnant."

"*Non sono d'accordo, figlioccia.*" Valentina disagreed.

A knock at the front door announced Benjamin's arrival. Valentina answered the door and led him and his luggage into her kitchen to find Angelina, red-eyed, sitting on the sofa.

"*Stai bene? Qual è il problema?*" he asked, his words tinged with worry.

Angelina rose while looking at the floor and replied in English, "I am pregnant. I am having a baby." Her tears first trickling, then flowing, chased each other unabated down her cheeks.

Ben's astonishment was palpable, and Angelina braced for what she'd feared. Benjamin turned to Valentina, who stood stoic and stone-faced, then back to a trembling Angelina and said, "No, you're not."

Through her tears, she said, "Yes, I am. I confirmed with the doctor yesterday."

Benjamin is in denial. He does not want this… this complication.

She slumped, averted her eyes, and continued crying.

Benjamin grabbed her hands in his and said, "Lina, *you're* not having a baby, *we* are!"

Angelina could not decide which was bigger, his smile or his eyes. Benjamin's reaction had stunned Angelina—no, it overwhelmed her. He hugged her, leaving her breathless. She returned his hug, smiling through her tears. Angelina watched as Valentina, eyes moist, smiled and gave a nod.

Or was that a bow? Angelina wondered.

When at last they pulled apart, she said, "You are not angry with me?"

"Angry? Lina Gina, I may be the happiest man in the world! No, the universe! Why would I be angry?" Angelina hugged him again and ignored her godmother's *I-told-you-so* expression. If she weren't so happy, Angelina would have stuck out her tongue.

Valentina was correct, she thought. *It is a fucking miracle.*

The room was silent, in notable contrast to the earlier commotion. The three of them stood smiling, but now with different tears—tears of joy—being shed.

Is this what Americans mean by a "pregnant pause"? Angelina wondered, and she smiled at her non sequitur.

After a few more moments of silence, Benjamin cleared his throat to get the women's attention. "Uh, this is… well, uh… it's not quite how I planned it."

Angelina stepped back, wondering why Benjamin was stumbling as he spoke.

"I'd hoped first to… uh, speak with, you know, Valentina, and then… and then to take you shopping in Milano," Benjamin said.

"What are you saying?" Angelina was still on an emotional roller-coaster ride.

Benjamin turned to Valentina. "*Signorina Marchese, con il tuo permesso…*" he began, then he knelt on the kitchen floor in front of Angelina.

Angelina stood frozen, unable to breathe, and Valentina gasped, unable not to, as Benjamin continued in English, "You see, I don't yet have a ring, but…"

"*Smetti!*" Valentina said as she raised both palms. Benjamin stopped as ordered.

Benjamin and Angelina turned. Angelina feared that Valentina meant to object.

"*Aspetta un momento, per favore!*" Valentina ran back to her bedroom.

Angelina wondered, *Wait a moment, please?* To Angelina, it felt like hours before Valentina returned.

THIRTY-FIVE

Valentina

Today was A Special Day for many reasons.

Valentina returned from her bedroom with a small jewelry box. She opened it to display an engagement ring and a wedding band. Both rings were white gold, the wedding ring a simple band. The engagement ring featured a large diamond bracketed by two smaller but not insignificant rubies on each side.

"These were your mother's," she said. "Isabella gave them to me to hold on to until you had children, Angelina. They were her grandmother's. She was afraid your husband would sell them after she died." Valentina could not bring herself to call him "the asshole." The occasion required more dignity than that.

Angelina stood frozen, eyes wide, staring at the rings as she reached across her body to place a hand on Benjamin's arm. Benjamin alternated his gaze between the rings and Angelina's eyes. Valentina wasn't sure if they remembered she was here.

"When I learned you could not have children, I could not decide what to do with these. I should have given them back to you after his death, but they meant so much to me. Please forgive me." She handed the rings to Benjamin.

He asked, just louder than a whisper, "I take it I have your permission?" Valentina nodded with a warm smile.

Angelina stood trembling as tears formed in the corners of her eyes. Benjamin asked them to forgive his English. He knelt before Angelina a second time, but now with the engagement ring that had belonged to her mother and her great-grandmother.

"Angelina, dear, sweet Angelina. I have no idea why you would want to spend any time with a poor hack like me, and yet I have the audacity to ask you to spend the rest of your life with me. You are the most beautiful soul I've ever known, and now that we have shared our love, I cannot imagine what my life would be like without you." He paused and took a deep breath. "As happy as I am at this moment, and as I have been these past four months, I ask you to make me even happier, for the rest of my life, by accepting my proposal. Please marry me."

Valentina had taken out her phone to record the proposal. She watched as Angelina surrendered to her tears while Benjamin spoke, no longer trying to hold them back. She thought Benjamin's proposal was eloquent—particularly under the circumstances—and very romantic.

I love this Benjamin.

Angelina was still standing unresponsive like an idiot, leaving Benjamin waiting on one knee. The moment Valentina saw Benjamin's flicker of worry at the silence, she acted.

"Benjamin, that was a lovely proposal. If Angelina does not say yes in the next five seconds, I will marry you."

Both of her "children" reacted at the same time. Benjamin turned to look at her.

Again with the mouth open, Benjamin? Valentina sighed.

Angelina shouted, "Yes!" and leaped forward to hug Benjamin. Still on one knee, Angelina's momentum knocked him over, and they both fell to the floor, laughing, hugging, and kissing each other.

Valentina still had her phone out. "I want to take a photo of the two of you to mark the occasion, but it would be more dignified if you were both standing and not rolling around on the kitchen floor like two ferrets."

The couple rose to their feet, giggling, and Valentina noted Benjamin was crying too.

A good sign, she believed.

She remembered a Native North American saying from a philosophy course: "Show me a man who does not cry, and I will show you a man who does not have a heart."

Valentina gave them a collective embrace and then gave each a kiss. She noted Benjamin's eyes widening after she kissed him on the forehead. She took several photos but mentioned she'd take more after they had brushed the cat hair from their clothes and brushed their own hair.

Angelina said, "Great. We should go home now."

Valentina said, "Wait. I have something else to tell you."

"Valentina, now you will tell us you are a minister and will marry us, no?" Angelina giggled. "Sorry, Val, but I want our wedding in a church—a Catholic church."

"You should sit down. Next to each other, of course. Let us move into the parlor."

***

Sensing the mood change in the two lovers, she reassured them.

"Please do not worry. I have never spoken of this with anyone. I did not think I would ever tell you, *Figlioccia*, except perhaps in my will."

At the mention of a will, Angelina frowned and said, "*Madrina*, you will never die. You will kick the ass of *l'Angolo della Morte*. You will live forever."

Valentina recognized that Angelina was avoiding the idea of her godmother's inevitable death. *I must tread lightly—I do not want to resurrect memories of her first marriage and its aftermath.*

"Angelina, dear, no one lives forever, except in the hearts of the people they have loved. Relax, please, and let me tell you a story."

Then Valentina revealed the story of how she met Isabella, how they became friends, how they became lovers, and why they could never be together.

"Your mother and I pledged our love to each other forever. Since it could not be with our bodies, we pledged it with our hearts and in our souls. I loved Bella and still do. I never broke that vow, nor will I ever."

She recognized that Benjamin was about to speak, likely something inane about her accepting his proposal. She saved the poor man from his own mouth.

"Benjamin, when I said I would accept your proposal, I meant it, but maybe not in the way you think. Bella, then Angelina, now you. You are the only people outside my family that I have ever loved unconditionally." Valentina patted her chest.

"There are many kinds of love. You told me yourself when you described your conversation on the pier with Angelina before she tried to swim away to escape."

Benjamin and Angelina both laughed.

As much to relieve the building tension as in appreciation of my droll humor, I am sure.

"While I could not bring myself to love you physically, Benjamin, I have never met another man I could tolerate more than you."

"'Tolerate'?" he asked. Benjamin had contorted his face and was trying to reshape it with his hand.

"*Sì, tollerare.*" Valentina nodded, then continued, "Because I could tolerate you, I could get to know you—know this awkward American who intruded on my simple, peaceful life and caused all kinds of commotion for my poor Angelina."

He'd advanced from puzzled to confused. Valentina tried to reassure him. "Please remove that confused expression from your face. There is no reason for it. Because I tolerated you, I could get to know you. Because I got to know you, I permitted you to be around Angelina, and the two of you acknowledged you were in love. And because I learned that you love my goddaughter, and that she loves you, Benjamin, I love you."

"Thank you, Valentina."

"I have never said 'I love you' to a man before, other than my father. I would marry you. It would be a lavender marriage, of course. After all, I once thought you were gay."

"What?" Benjamin appeared dazed.

Angelina also asked, "*Cosa hai detto?*"

"Benjamin, you need to stop going around with your mouth open. It makes you seem foolish." Valentina realized there was more she needed to share.

She recounted how she'd watched the movie *Una Giornata Particolare*, starring Sophia Loren and Marcello Mastroianni, when she was seventeen. It had been a seminal moment in her life, helping her to accept herself and her confused sexuality. Besides relating to the Mastroianni character, she'd known someone like him. More importantly, it made her a feminist with a desire for education and knowledge. Too many men—and even some women—still believed what Mussolini had said forty years earlier.

"Mussolini had the temerity to say, '*Incompatibile con la fisiologia e la psicologia femminile, il Genio è soltanto maschio.*'"

Both Angelina and Benjamin shook their heads in disbelief.

"Yes, he said it. 'Incompatible with female physiology and psychology, genius is only male,'" Valentina repeated in English.

"Che stronzo!"

"*Sì,* Benjamin." Valentina described how she'd learned to accept herself. It had motivated her to go to university and learn everything about everything. As a result, she'd made it her mission to rid the world of fascists—today almost exclusively men—and any other person who preyed on the weak.

"But what I most despise…" Pausing, Valentina brought her hands together as if praying, then said, "What I most despise are men who *assume* that all women, or any women, are weak, just because they are women."

"If they knew you, Valentina, they would never assume that." Benjamin commented dispassionately as Angelina held his arm and nodded. Valentina thought Benjamin's comment was sweet, confirming what she already knew about him, of course.

"Thank you, Benjamin, and if all men were like you, I would have no one to hate."

Valentina wiped a tear from her eye. *And I hate when I cry. I am such a romantic.*

Turning to Angelina, she said, her voice little more than a whisper, "Hold on to him, *Figlioccia*. There are not so many out there."

Angelina smiled, hugged Benjamin, and said, "*Ovviamente, Madrina.*"

"And Benjamin?"

"Sì, Valentina?"

"From now on, I must insist that you pronounce Angelina's mother's name correctly. You know how to pronounce double consonants in Italian, yet you mangle Isabella's name as if there is only one *L*. I fear you watched too much Disney as a child. I am not a fairy godmother, even if you imagine yourself in a fairy tale. Please say 'Isabel-la,' yes?"

"Sì, Valentina. Ti prego, perdonami."

"I forgive you, but the fault is not entirely yours. Your fiancée should have fixed this, long before she was your fiancée."

"You are correct as always, *Madrina*." Angelina agreed without even a hint of sarcasm.

After a moment, Angelina asked, "But, Valentina?"

"Sì?"

"You must have been so lonely, without someone to love after my mother died. I am so sad for you."

"Angelina, my dear, today is your special day. I did not tell you this to turn your joy into sadness. I was never lonely." Valentina clasped her hands in front of her chest. "I never lost my love for my princess Bella, and I never will. As I told you, we shared our hearts, and we shared our souls. But not only that"—she unclasped her hands and brought them to her chest, one over the other—"Isabella gave me you, someone to love as if you were my daughter. And now with Benjamin, I also have a son to love."

As Angelina began crying, Valentina knew they were tears of happiness.

Valentina turned to Benjamin. "*Benjamin, figlio mio, chiudi la bocca, se non ti dispiace.*" When he closed it, she said, "Yes, I am proud to call you my son."

What is it with that man's mouth? she thought.

Angelina sniffled as she gazed at Isabella's wedding band. Valentina watched as Angelina glanced at Benjamin, then back at the ring.

Then Angelina stood, walked over to Valentina, took a deep breath, and said, "Thank you, protector Valentina, for keeping the rings of your princess safe. I will always treasure her engagement ring that Benjamin has used to pledge his love to me. He and I would prefer to exchange more personal wedding bands if you do not mind."

"Certo che no, i bambini."

Valentina watched Angelina glance again at Benjamin, who nodded.

"It would make me…" She turned to Benjamin. "Make us so happy to give you this wedding ring as a symbol of your love for my mother. And for me."

Of everything that had happened during the past twenty-four hours, this was the one thing Valentina had not seen coming. She collapsed back into her chair, smiling through her tears.

She closed her eyes, clutching the ring to her chest, and said, "Thank you with all my heart, my children."

As she thought of the movie title, it occurred to Valentina that today was *A Special Day* for many reasons.

THIRTY-SIX

Benjamin

Then, it is settled.

The last hour had been one emotional high after another. Ben learned he was a father-to-be. He made a proposal he had intended but had not prepared with a ring he didn't know he had at a location he would not have chosen. Ben was thankful beyond measure that Angelina had accepted—yet he was disconcerted by Valentina's counterproposal. He assumed it was Valentina's way of welcoming him into her family.

But still—she thought I was gay?

Angelina squeezed his arm and nodded at the box she was holding with her mother's wedding band. When he looked at her, she tilted her head toward Valentina. Ben nodded back. He felt he knew what Angelina was thinking.

That's pretty cool, he thought. It was fine with him. Better, it was right.

When Angelina stood, announced her—their—decision, and handed her godmother the wedding band, it confirmed his perception.

As unusual as the preceding interactions were, the next was even stranger. As Valentina fell back into her chair, crying and clutching the ring, Ben felt convinced—if only for a moment—that a physical transformation had taken place. The stature of the two women appeared reversed. Angelina was standing tall, confident, decisive—appearing older and wiser. He perceived Valentina smaller in comparison, younger than her goddaughter, if that were possible—more vulnerable, as absurd as that sounded.

Ben shook his head, which cleared the imagined vision, but not the memory. When he looked again, he realized that Angelina was the strong, decisive woman he saw, and Valentina was the tender romantic. It was his understanding that had changed, not their physicality.

He watched Valentina compose herself and try to conceal her crying. He thought she was disingenuous to hide her feelings, but then he remembered how he'd hidden his reason for moving to Rimini from his colleagues in Milano.

The world could use more romance, but it isn't ready for us romantics.

When Valentina stood, he no longer had any illusions or delusions that she was smaller or vulnerable.

"Can we go home now?" Angelina asked. "I am hungry. I am eating for two, you know."

Benjamin imagined that she glowed, but maybe it was only her wide, warm smile.

"Not yet, *Figlioccia,*" Valentina said. "Today is a special day. We must celebrate your *fidanzamento.*"

Ben was adjusting to the mixing of Italian and English, but he did not know what *fidanzamento* meant. It sounded related to "boyfriend," so he asked, "*Cosa significa fidanzamento?*"

"Your engagement, Benjamin," Valentina said while Angelina bobbed her head, smiling.

Shit, I'm engaged! he thought.

"Yes, you are, but I may not have put it so scatologically."

"Shit, did I say that out loud?" he thought he thought.

"Yes, you did, dear." This time Angelina answered.

Both women came over and hugged him in sympathy as he rose, confused. Somehow his brain and mouth had stopped cooperating.

"Can we go to our special restaurant?"

Ben heard Lina's question but did not answer, afraid to open his mouth ever again.

"But of course." Valentina rescued him. Again.

***

Ever since the Valentina's Date Massacre, Angelina had called Osteria

L'Angolo Divino "their restaurant," and now Ben did too. Over dinner, they discussed the next steps.

"I want a church wedding." Angelina repeated her earlier statement. "And soon—because of the baby."

"Of course, Lina."

Ben respected her reconnection with the Catholic church and had even attended Mass with her several times. When he'd mentioned his Catholic upbringing, Valentina had asked him what faith he followed now. He'd said, "I'm not a member of any organized religion—I'm a Methodist." They did not get the old American joke even after he'd explained it.

Valentina said, "How about the second Saturday in December? That gives us five full weeks to plan."

Angelina nodded, but then her eyes widened, and she said, "Oh, no. We cannot."

Valentina asked, "Why not?"

"Advent! It starts on the first Sunday of December this year. One cannot get married during Advent."

"Then, it is settled. Your wedding will be the first Saturday of December. We will need to get moving," Valentina said. Angelina bobbed her head several times as she smiled.

Ben had still not gotten used to Valentina's decisions and their resulting fait accompli. He wasn't sure he ever would.

Epilogue

The Knight-Errant

"There are many who are errant," said Sancho.
"Many," responded Don Quixote, "but few who deserve to be called knights."
— Miguel de Cervantes Saavedra —

Valentina, Angelina, and Benjamin had just finished a home-cooked dinner celebrating the sale of Benjamin's book based on Valentina's adventures. Benjamin had first wanted to write Valentina's biography. She'd declined for several reasons, suggesting instead that he write a fictionalized version.

Angelina asked, "The publisher was okay with the title, *The Rock and the Rose*?"

"They loved it," Ben said. "They asked me how I came up with it. I told them the title happened serendipitously. That I came to Rimini to write about the Republic of Rose Island and then had my life turned upside down—literally—at Rockisland. The coincidence captured the spirit of Isabella and Valentina."

Serendipitously? I need to watch those big words, Benjamin thought.

"I had assumed that Valentina was the Rock and Isabella the Rose, since my mother's married name was Roselli," Angelina said. "What do you think, Val? Does that make a suitable origin story?"

"Well, no." Ben and Angelina turned to stare at her. "The obvious answer is that Benjamin is the Rock and you are the Rose. His name is

LaRocca, and your maiden name, as you said, is Roselli."

"That is right!"

Valentina said, "It may be right, but it is also wrong."

Angelina asked, "It is?"

"But of course, Angelina. You, my true love's daughter, my goddaughter, are the Rock. You are the strongest person I have ever known. Benjamin, my goddaughter's true love, my son, you are the Rose. After Isabella, you are the sweetest individual I have ever known."

Ben, overwhelmed for a moment, managed to say, "Thank you, Valentina." Knowing it to be more important, he kept his author's opinion to himself, deciding to share it another time.

You are wrong, Valentina—possibly for the first time in your life.

You are the Rock and the Rose.

"There is no end. There is no beginning.
There is only the infinite passion of life."
—Federico Fellini—

Dramatis Personae

Rimini Today – June 2017

Angelina Roselli Fabrizzi – a thirty-three-year-old widow of Giovanni, native of Rimini, dealing with financial and emotional pain.

Benjamin LaRocca – a thirty-seven-year-old divorced American attempting to make a new career and a new life in Italy.

Valentina Marchese – a fifty-five-year-old law enforcement veteran and retired spy—Angelina's protective godmother, and Isabella's true love.

Luca Tortelli – a thirty-eight-year-old drummer and Rimini real estate agent.

Sophia & Umberto – a tiny couple in their seventies with wisdom beyond their size.

Rimini of Yesterday

Giovanni Fabrizzi – Angelina's husband, an opportunist who was killed a year ago in an unsolved murder.

Isabella Marvelli Roselli – Angelina's mother, forbidden from being with Valentina, her true love, and forced to marry the much older Tàmmaro, and who died in 2004.

Tàmmaro Roselli – Angelina's father and Isabella's husband, a much older man she was forced to marry, and who died in 2004.

Francesca Marvelli – Angelina's grandmother and Isabella's mother, from a rich family.
Giacomo Marvelli – Angelina's grandfather and Isabella's father, active in the Catholic Church.

Sister Ilaria Marvelli – Angelina's aunt and Isabella's sister who became a nun and was stationed in Africa.

Salvatore Marvelli – Angelina's uncle and Isabella's oldest brother, a teacher who died in 1975, leaving behind his wife and one-year-old daughter Cristiana.

Santino Marvelli – Angelina's uncle and Isabella's brother who became a priest.

Elsewhere in Italy – June 2017

Angelo Spallini – the Marvelli family attorney in Como and Angelina's sixty-year-old godfather.

Antonietta Spallini – Angelo's wife.

Carmelo – the caretaker and manager of the Marvelli real estate in Brunate, on the hills above Como.

Cristiana Marvelli Bacilieri – Angelina's only living relative, daughter of her uncle Salvatore—she is married and living in Ferrara with her husband and children.

New Jersey – June 2017

Jennifer LaRocca McAndrews – Benjamin's thirty-nine-year-old sister, married to David and living with him and their children in New Jersey.

David McAndrews – the forty-one-year-old husband of Jennifer and brother-in-law to Benjamin.

Joseph LaRocca – Benjamin and Jennifer's sixty-three-year-old father and the husband of Rose.

Rose Lombardy LaRocca – Joseph's sixty-one-year-old wife, and mother to Benjamin and Jennifer.

Neil – Benjamin's forty-seven-year-old literary agent working out of New York City and living in the Jersey suburbs.

The Rock & the Rose Series

The Love, Life, and Passion Trilogy

The Infinite Passion of Life

Within Me, an Invincible Summer

What Lies in Thy Heart

The Resilience, Resistance, and Recovery Trilogy

Strong at the Broken Places

Now and Always Resistance

A Time for All Things

Contact the author at D.J.Paolini@Comcast.net

www.theRockandtheRose.com

ABOUT THE AUTHOR

D.J. Paolini is a debut fiction author. *The Infinite Passion of Life* is his first novel. His non-fiction work includes technical editor of three award-winning database programming books. He was the contributing editor with a monthly column for a database industry magazine. He was selected to co-author a database programming book in the popular "Teach Yourself..." series. Paolini was on the team that won an award for best technical documentation for a software program. He has delivered several dozen technical papers in more than one hundred sessions at conferences in North America, Europe, and Asia.

Paolini has had three poems published. He also writes music and has had several pieces performed in the United States and France. He wrote a column for his college newspaper and he received a creative writing award in high school. He has traveled extensively and infuses that experience into his writing. *The Infinite Passion of Life* is the first book in a planned six-book series set in Northern Italy.

In his spare time over the last four decades he has played in weekend rock bands and served as a volunteer firefighter and emergency squad member, including six years as fire chief. He is a licensed soccer referee and serves as the administrator for youth soccer referees in his home state of New Jersey.

He doesn't know what he wants to be if he grows up, other than romantic. In the meantime, he enjoys traveling with his wife Patty and spending time with their children and granddaughter.

Reader Comments

I loved this book! The characters have been tested by life in interesting, and even fascinating, ways. The author skillfully blends the weight that history and culture places on the characters' choices, while also imbuing hope, change, and freshness in the resolution of the age-old issues that surround love and life for all of us. A romantic novel set in a wonderfully romantic place. I look forward to reading more about how these characters evolve as their lives unfold.

— Barbara Bunkle

Two people deeply in love who don't even realize it and an overprotective godmother. What could go wrong? A very entertaining story with great character development. Highly recommended!

— Tina Pastor

Great read...Paolini introduces Rimini, Italy in a way that engages the reader to feel as if they are actually taking a journey along the cobblestone streets in the quaint town. Equally engaging are the main characters and the journey of emotional growth that is portrayed for each. It celebrates self-awareness and self-acceptance and keeps the reader cheering for their happiness and success.

— Jessica C.

The author has filled the story with engaging characters and a beautifully descriptive narrative that makes me want to visit Italy (and learn the language).

— Debbie P.

Lightning Source UK Ltd.
Milton Keynes UK
UKHW011828181220
375492UK00001B/83